Waste Heritage

Waste Heritage

IRENE BAIRD

EDITED & WITH AN
INTRODUCTION BY
Colin Hill

University of Ottawa Press | OTTAWA

LIBRARY AND ARCHIVES CANADA
CATALOGUING IN PUBLICATION

Baird, Irene
    Waste heritage / Irene Baird; edited
and with an introduction by Colin Hill.

Includes bibliographical references.
ISBN 978-0-7766-0649-1

    I. Hill, Colin, 1970– II. Title.
PS8503.A52W3 2007   C813'.52
C2007-903933-2

Published by the University of Ottawa
Press, 2007
542 King Edward Avenue
Ottawa, Ontario K1N 6N5
www.uopress.uottawa.ca

The University of Ottawa Press acknow-
ledges with gratitude the support extend-
ed to its publishing list by Heritage
Canada through its Book Publishing
Industry Development Program, by the
Canada Council for the Arts, by the
Canadian Federation for the Humanities
and Social Sciences through its Aid to
Scholarly Publications Program, by the
Social Sciences and Humanities Research
Council, and by the University of Ottawa.

Cover illustration reproduced from the
Musée des beaux-arts de Montréal;
Solitaire/Recluse by Bertram Brooker.

Contents

Acknowledgements

I am grateful for the assistance, expertise, and support provided by
many people and institutions as I was preparing this critical edition. I
want to express my appreciation to members of Irene Baird's family
for their enthusiastic involvement in this project: Baird's daughter, June
Brander-Smith, and granddaughters, Nora Spence, Cynthia Brander-
Smith, and Gail West, graciously answered my many questions and provided me with unpublished biographical information about Irene Baird
and a wealth of lost book reviews and articles about *Waste Heritage*. This
edition would not exist without the generous financial support of the
University of Toronto, which funded this project with four research
grants. Numerous archivists and librarians helped me locate and obtain
the hard-to-find materials required for this project: thanks especially to
Carl Spadoni, Archives and Research Collections Librarian at McMaster
University; Mary Bond, of the Reference and Genealogy Division of
National Library and Archives Canada; Eric Swanick of Simon Fraser
University Special Collections; Tara C. Craig of Columbia University Rare
Book and Manuscript Library; Anne Dondertman, Assistant Director of
the Thomas Fisher Rare Book Library at University of Toronto; David
McKnight of McGill University; and the reference librarians at the
Vancouver and Victoria Public Libraries. Alan Twigg, editor of BC
Bookworld, provided invaluable information about Baird and answered my
pestering queries with kindness. Mrs. Helen Irvine's research helped me
identify some of Baird's disguised Victoria place names. Jody Mason, a
doctoral candidate at University of Toronto, generously allowed me to
draw upon her research into the 1939 censorship of Baird's novel. Many of
my colleagues at the University of Toronto and at other universities have
offered advice and helped me significantly: I would like to acknowledge

Donna Bennett, Gregory Betts, Russell Brown, Brian Corman, Jeannine DeLombard, Dennis Duffy, Carole Gerson, Alex Gillespie, Marlene Goldman, Linda Hutcheon, Robert Lecker, Mark Levine, Randy McLeod, Nick Mount, Heather Murray, John O'Connor, Maggie Redekop, Mari Ruti, Sam Solecki, Leslie Thomson, Brian Trehearne, Dan White, and Herb Wyile. I cannot say enough to praise my legion of devoted and tireless research assistants; without their work and energy I would have been helpless: Emily Arvay, Jared Bland, Nick Bradley, Punam Dhaliwal, Sam Dineley, Daniela Janes, Katherine McLeod, Salwa Qadar, Kailin Wright, Brandon McFarlane, Jenee Sivaenanam, and Karen Ward. The graduate students in my Modernist Canadian Fiction course at the University of Toronto in 2005 provided a rigorous testing ground for my thoughts on Baird. Eric Nelson, Marie Clausén, and Ruth Bradley-St-Cyr made working with University of Ottawa Press an absolute delight and their hard work and tireless support is much appreciated. The anonymous readers who commented on this manuscript while it was under review at University of Ottawa Press offered excellent suggestions and made my critical apparatus immeasurably stronger. I would not have known where to begin my work on this edition without the guidance of my friend Dean Irvine of Dalhousie University, a skilled, uncompromising, and enthusiastic editor. Most of all, my heartfelt thanks to my family, and especially Olivier, for sustaining me throughout this project in countless ways. I dedicate this edition to my grand-father, Joseph Clifford Hill (1905–1985), whose elusive stories suggest he may have participated in the events that inspired this novel.

Critical Introduction

1. IRENE BAIRD AND WASTE HERITAGE

In many ways, the 1930s are a lost decade in Canadian fiction. The momentum that Canada's new modern realism gathered in the boisterous and nationalistic 1920s was nearly halted when the Great Depression made it difficult for even some of the nation's best-known novelists to publish. There were few opportunities for new Canadian writers in the harsh economic climate of the 1930s, and today the novels and short stories of Morley Callaghan stand almost alone in Canada's memory of the period. Irene Baird's now-obscure second novel, *Waste Heritage*, was first published to laudatory reviews in 1939. Given that many literary histories lament a dearth of Depression-era Canadian fiction, the contemporary disregard of Baird and her *oeuvre* is extraordinary and unfortunate. Few if any early twentieth-century Canadian novelists match Baird's stylistic rigour. *Waste Heritage* is a sustained artistic achievement that incorporates a remarkable economy of style, unity of effect, and psychological depth. Its evocative urban and social realism and frank depiction of modern subject matter rank with some of the best-known international novels of the 1930s and are almost unparalleled in the Canadian novel before the 1960s. It perhaps captures the spirit, mood, and vernacular of the Great Depression better than any other novel of its time. Its creative representation of life in the modern North American city, and of the historic Vancouver and Victoria labour conflicts of 1938, is pointed and uncompromising. It is steeped in the turbulent class and labour politics of its day, yet remarkably it avoids the propagandistic tone of much Depression-era writing. *Waste Heritage* is not a flawless masterpiece, but it nevertheless deserves a place alongside the most important and widely read novels of its period. This critical edition reintroduces Baird's novel to scholars, students, and general readers, and contributes to the recent reawakening of interest in Canadian fiction of the 1930s, which is neither as scant nor homogenous as some literary histories suggest.

Waste Heritage is a work of fiction inspired by the sit-down strikes and labour protests that occurred in British Columbia in the spring and summer of 1938. Its appreciation requires some knowledge of the events of that time, and of the prevailing historical and political climate of the years leading up to World War II. Growing unemployment and economic injustice and disparity in the Great Depression helped to set the stage for the events that Baird fictionalizes. Leftist movements, with their intellectual origins in political theories of the nineteenth century, crystallized in Canada after World War I, and, in the interwar years, labour revolts, including the Winnipeg General Strike of 1919, became almost commonplace. The expanding influence and membership of unions and growing popularity of dozens of leftist parties and formations, including the Communist Party of Canada, the Canadian Labour Party, Canadian Labour Defence League, the Women's Labour Leagues, and the Progressive Farmers' Education League, meant that workers and activists were increasingly organized, often in support of "revolutionary change" (McKay 155). In the spring and summer of 1938, newspapers across Canada gave daily, front-page headlines to the specific labour conflict that Baird's novel re-imagines. Paul A. Phillips's *No Power Greater: A Century of Labour in British Columbia* recounts the events of those turbulent months and their causes and effects, and Michiel Horn's "Transient Men in the Depression" aims to situate Baird's novel, which it calls "the most powerful" Canadian novel of the Depression era, in its social and political context (36). These and other histories are reminders that the economic and social hardships of the 1930s produced a class of unemployed, transient, single men who eventually became "a freightcar army of wanderers" in search of work (36). In a half-hearted attempt to provide for these men, the federal government and several provincial governments, including that in British Columbia, opened special work camps that "were run with varying degrees of efficiency and concern for the public purse" (36). But shortly after Mackenzie King's Liberals defeated Bennett's Conservatives in 1935, the federal camps were shut down. British Columbia, which was "home" to an especially large number of the transient men, closed its camps in 1938 and the desperation of the men was exacerbated. Horn's account describes subsequent developments:

> By May 1938 about 6,000 [unemployed transient men] were in Vancouver. [T]hey supported themselves ... by pan-handling and tag days ... [which were] prohibited by a municipal government determined to get rid of such nuisances, including the men themselves. Meanwhile the provincial government added fuel to the fire by stopping relief to all people who were from outside the province. (37)

Instead of relief payments or work camps, which provided a subsistence living, the government offered free transportation for the transient men back to their home provinces (note that Matt Striker, the protagonist of *Waste Heritage*, has been transient so long that he holds residency in no province) (Phillips 118).

The "sit-down" that reaches a dramatic conclusion just prior to the start of Baird's novel began on 11 May 1938 when twelve-hundred of the transient men occupied three prominent Vancouver buildings: the Civic Art Gallery, the Georgia Hotel, and the central Post Office. Ten days later, the group in the Georgia Hotel agreed to end its sit-down when they were promised a total of five-hundred dollars in government assistance (Phillips 119). The groups in the other two buildings remained entrenched for several more weeks. On 20 June 1938, the RCMP and Vancouver Police received government orders to clear the occupied buildings by force. At the last minute, the men who occupied the art gallery agreed to leave peacefully, and the police launched a raid on the post office (Horn 37). The *Vancouver Province* reported later that the Royal Canadian Mounted Police, armed with riot sticks and tear gas, drove the men from the post office and into the street where they were beaten, in some cases brutally, by police (Phillips 119). A total of thirty-nine people were injured in the melee and thirty-thousand dollars in damage was done by the men as they rioted in the streets of downtown Vancouver, smashing plate-glass windows and looting shops (119). In *Waste Heritage*, Matt Striker "rides the rods" into town shortly after these events have taken place. He befriends Eddy, who has participated in the post-office sit-down and been sickened by tear gas, and rescues him from a beating by a police officer who is ostensibly working to maintain order in the streets after the riot. Baird's story is in a sense anti-climactic; it takes place in the aftermath of the Vancouver (Aschelon) riot and follows Matt and Eddy who accompany the sit-downers as they regroup from their rout and travel to Victoria (Gath) to march on the provincial legislature with their demands of government aid for the unemployed.

★ ★ ★

As a young writer who had recently published a well-received novel, and who knew both Vancouver and Victoria intimately, Baird was ideally situated to write this story. Relatively little is known about the life of the dynamic woman who wrote *Waste Heritage* and her reasons for choosing to fictionalize the events of 1938. There exists no Baird biography, and the few details of her life in the public domain must be gleaned from an assortment of brief articles, journalistic pieces, and obscure archival sources. During her life, Baird strenuously resisted providing biographical material to reporters, reviewers, and scholars (Deacon to Baird, 9 Dec. 1939). Major inaccuracies have appeared in some of the best-known reference works on Baird, and even some of the basic facts of her biography remain unclear and in dispute: as Roger Leslie Hyman writes, "The *Oxford Companion to Canadian Literature* (1967) manages, inventively, to marry her off to John Grierson, the redoubtable architect of the National Film Board, for whom she had worked in the early forties while undeniably wed to Robert Baird, her husband of more than twenty years" (74). Although *Waste Heritage* is not an autobiographical novel, contemporary readers might benefit from an introduction to the life and career of Irene Baird. The brief biographical sketch that follows draws upon both published and unpublished sources on her life and work and incorporates previously undocumented material graciously provided by Baird's descendants. This narrative of Baird's career introduces an *oeuvre* that is surprisingly varied and, apart from *Waste Heritage*, almost entirely unknown.

Irene Violet Elise Todd, known throughout her life to family and friends as "Bonnie," was born in 1901 in Cumberland County, England. Her ancestry was Scottish-English ("The Author"). Her parents, Robert and Eva, owned a woollen mill in Carlisle, in the North of England, and took an active interest in the education of their daughter: "[h]er father ... believed in bringing up children on public affairs and political comment, the *Manchester Guardian* and the *Lancashire Post*. Irene being his only child, he concentrated on her mental and physical development the zeal he would have expended on his sons" (Cox 2). Irene spent her youth in England where her mother chose to have her educated at home by a governess (2). She later attended two expensive boarding schools, which she loathed because of their regimentation, but left school and returned home at the age of sixteen due to a case of whooping cough (2). Her father was an avid fan of fly fishing; after travelling to Vancouver Island on a fishing trip and discovering its glories, he chose to relocate his family there, at Qualicum Beach, in 1919 (2). Not long after her arrival in Canada, Irene Todd met Robert Patrick Hay Baird, and the two were married in 1923 (Spence). The couple settled in Vancouver and had a son, Ronald Hay, in 1924, and a daughter, Moira June Hay, in 1928 (Spence). During this period, the young family kept a maid, as Irene desired a career outside of the home. In 1931, Baird became the first female teacher on staff at St. George's Boys' Private School in Vancouver, where she taught grade one until 1934 (West). Exactly why she stopped teaching is not known, but Baird's experience is perhaps shared by Hughes, the character who writes a book about the sit-down in *Waste Heritage* and becomes a writer only after he loses his job as a teacher and feels his mental faculties diminishing as a result. Baird's daughter recalls a period of the 1930s when Baird lived as a wife and mother while her children attended private school. These were apparently happy years for the family, and Baird's daughter remembers that her parents had a busy social life and a wide circle of friends (Spence). In 1936 or 1937, the Bairds moved to Victoria (Spence). Baird's decision to write professionally occurred around this time when the Depression cost Robert Baird his job as an engineer and the family needed supplemental income ("Novel of Depression" 6). One of the very few glimpses of Baird's daily life in the 1930s is provided by her daughter: she recalls that her mother, an impeccably dressed woman with a powerful presence despite a small stature, climbed the stairs each morning after breakfast to write in her study while the family maid, Margi, followed her with a glass of tomato juice (Spence).

These daily writing sessions led to the publication of Baird's first novel, *John*, by J.B. Lippincott in 1937. It became a Canadian bestseller, and was also published in the United States, England, Australia, and Sweden. Neither the style nor the subject matter of *John* anticipates *Waste Heritage*. The novel is a meditative and philosophical character study of John Dorey, an Englishman who leaves Northern England for British Columbia where he develops a deep attachment to the land and his own ten-acre farm on the coast. The slow-moving narrative is emplotted over the psychological musings of the well-respected, sixty-two-year-old John as he considers both his present environment—the changing seasons, a dispute with a violent neighbour, negotiations with a developer who wants to turn his farm into a vacation resort, a boat he is constructing— and his recollections of formative events in his past—an attempt by his stepbrothers to lure him to England after he is wounded in the Great War, his early years in British Columbia, and a romantic attachment he has been unable to forget. Through everything, John maintains a personal philosophy that emphasizes the importance of a good name, a love of nature, an appreciation of beauty for its own sake, a steadfast trust in God, and an aversion to the encroaching evils of the modern world. Despite the sentimental tone and verbosity of *John*, its reviewers in Canada and abroad were almost universally enthusiastic, and they note Baird's philosophical approach, convincing psychological portraiture, and lucid and emotionally charged prose. Currie Cabot mused, in New York's *Saturday Review of Literature*, that "[f]or this novel, flawless in its way, one would like to find the right words of praise. Restraint is the key-note of its excellence" (11). Claire Keefer, in the *Ottawa Journal*, called *John* "a finely perceptive novel .... Quiet and controlled, it is written with an awareness of hidden currents of feeling that would do justice to the most seasoned novelist" (n.pag.). An unsigned review in the *Sunday Sun* of Sydney, Australia remarked that "[f]irst novels are either the herald of a successful literary career or the epitaph of a writer. *John* ... can be placed in the first category, and all who read it will look forward to further books from the author whose descriptive powers are outstanding" ("First Novel").

In May 1938, the events that would inspire *Waste Heritage* became front-page news. Precisely what motivated Baird, who enjoyed the privileges of an upper-middle class life in very difficult and insecure times, to become directly involved in the labour struggle that the novel recreates is unclear, but in a 1976 article entitled "Sidown Brothers, Sidown" she offers an intimation of her motives: "I found those jobless people irresistible, urgent, challenging. I went to the job as a writer with a tremendously important assignment; how to get it down right, how to make it live, how to make Canadians see it and feel it as I was doing. I lived with the story. I listened to what went to [sic] around me" (82). Although she was not then working as a journalist, Baird found herself caught up in the excitement of the unfolding conflict, and chose to cover the story as a reporter might. Fiction, she concluded, had a pragmatic function in difficult times, and the events she witnessed convinced her that she had responsibility to meet: "it seemed as though journalists and writers both could share a rare opportunity with a story like this, and at the same time do a little something for Canada. From that day on, I 'covered' the story as thoroughly as though some tough news editor had given me the assignment" (84). Baird blurred the boundaries between fact and fiction in her literary project: "I can only say that *Waste Heritage* is as accurate as I could make it. The situation was as it appears in the novel" (83). Baird's sheer determination to follow the story closely, and to root her representation of it in facts and first-hand observation, is evident in her recollection of how she managed to visit the strike locations that were off limits to the public:

> Our family doctor, that unforgettable Scotsman, Dr. D.M. Baillie, was also Victoria's City Medical Officer, and part of his duties was to make a daily inspection of the buildings where the men were lodged. Would the good doctor allow me to go with him on his rounds next day? I promised to look anonymous, sound speechless, and carry a small black bag—the latter to suitably describe me as a nurse! (85)

When the sit-downers left the mainland for Vancouver Island, Baird followed, and she was with them in Victoria during the memorable scene in Beacon Hill Park, reimagined near the end of the novel (84).

Over a six-month period in the late summer, fall, and early winter of 1938, Baird worked from notes and memory and wrote *Waste Heritage* (85). In the spring of 1939, Macmillan of Canada agreed to publish Baird's second novel and successfully urged Random House, in New York, to do the same. A long and difficult process of revision that delayed publication several times followed. Then, as *Waste Heritage* was finally being set for the press, Hitler invaded Poland and nearly prevented the appearance of Baird's novel: while the Blitzkrieg advanced in September 1939, the international focus shifted from the Great Depression to World War II, and *Waste Heritage* instantly lost its claim to topicality. But the novel was too far along to be easily abandoned by its publisher, and Hugh Eayrs, Baird's editor at Macmillan, decided to move ahead with publication despite reservations (H. Eayrs to Baird, 2 Sep. 1939). Baird herself was quick to recognize that the timing of the novel could not have been worse, and on 11 September 1939 she wrote to Bennett Cerf, her New York Random House editor, already billing *Waste Heritage* as a work of historical fiction: "with Canada's entry into the war *Waste Heritage* becomes among the last pieces of documentary evidence of conditions under the old pre-war regime.... Mr. Eayrs has my greatest admiration for going ahead and publishing. He could so easily have done the other thing" (Baird to Cerf, 11 Sep. 1939).

Although many reviewers considered *Waste Heritage* derivative of Steinbeck, its reception was overwhelmingly enthusiastic. Bruce Hutchison of the *Victoria Daily Times* called it "a book for all of America. For Vancouver, and especially for Victoria, it is a social document of first-rate importance, an exploration, a chart, a clinical study, and I think it is one of the best books that has come out of Canada in our time" (4). Margaret Wallace, in the *Saturday Review of Literature* declared that "Irene Baird writes with both fists and an angry will to be heard. She is a vital and interesting novelist" (7). Howe Martyn of the *New York Times* called it "a very unusual book" and considered it a step forward for the national literature: "for a Canadian novel it is phenomenal. Optimism is still official in Canada. Mrs. Baird shows with horrid reality the representatives of a hundred thousand homeless and hopeless youth" (n. pag.). In the *Philadelphia Inquirer*, Frank Brookhouser remarked that Baird "has a photographic eye" and a "receptive ear to the voices of the street" before concluding that the novel is "a powerful preachment ... well worth time and thought" (10). And the *Globe and Mail* found *Waste Heritage* to be a "superb piece of reporting. It is powerful because it will stir its readers profoundly" ("Strong Canadian Novel"). Despite these positive reviews, sales of the novel were very disappointing. In December 1939, Bennett Cerf wrote to inform Baird that "more excellent reviews have come in for *Waste Heritage* .... Unfortunately, they don't seem to sell the book very well" (Cerf to Baird, 27 Dec. 1939). Less than two years later, Macmillan wrote to Baird's agent with the unfortunate news that "sale of *Waste Heritage* by Irene Baird, at the original price, now seems to have ceased entirely, and we propose to transfer this title to our reprint line which sells for $1.00" (H. Eayrs to M. Saunders, 24 Oct. 1941). Another letter from Macmillan to Baird in May 1942 informed her that sales even at the discounted price had stopped; the book was to be remaindered and Baird was free to purchase as many as she liked for 25 cents per copy (H. Eayrs to Baird, 13 May 1942).

If Baird was disheartened by the poor sales of *Waste Heritage* she nevertheless remained a productive and engaged writer for some time to come. Her attention had shifted to the war, and even while she anxiously awaited the arrival of copies of her Depression novel in bookstores on the west coast she had begun a new phase of her career. Five days before Canada entered the war, Baird wrote to Hugh Eayrs about the role of the writer during wartime: "It has occurred to me to ask you if at this time (or in the problematical future) there is any branch of national work in which a writer could be of service?" (Baird to H. Eayrs, 5 Sep. 1939). In the same letter, Baird announced that she had decided to make an application for a Guggenheim award but, "if there was any way in which I could be of use to Canada, the Guggenheim would have to step down." Baird's correspondence with Macmillan and Random House in 1939 about her Guggenheim proposal provides insight into her thinking during this transitional period and reveals that she had plans for novels she never wrote and came close to becoming an expatriate writer. In a 13 September 1939 letter to Cerf from Baird's agent, Marion Saunders, we find a citation of

Baird's proposal for a "grand tour" of the United States to gather material for a new, American novel: she plans lengthy stops in New York, New
England, Southern California, the Southern States, and "as many odd
stops otherwise as there is time for" (Saunders to Cerf, 13 Sep. 1939). But
Baird's ideas and plans were changing quickly, and Baird soon refined her
plans and wrote to Cerf directly with ideas for two more novels:

> The first idea, a novel of heavy industry using Pittsburgh as base, is
> one that powerfully attracts me and one that some day I still hope to
> try. Labor is a strong lover and hard to break away from .... I hope
> that you may approve the California idea. I cannot tell you definite-
> ly what type of novel might come out of it until I have done some
> studying of the geography of the state. (Baird to Cerf, 5 Oct. 1939)

A few days later, Cerf wrote back to Baird with reserved praise for the
"California idea," but cautioned that Steinbeck had already covered this
territory (Cerf to Baird, 9 Oct. 1939). In any case, the point was moot, as
Baird would not win the Guggenheim, and soon embarked on her work
for the Canadian war effort.

The early 1940s were busy years for Baird. She worked as a journalist
and, in 1940–1941, gave a series of radio addresses on the war and lectures
for the Canadian Club. Despite her busy schedule and the attention she
was receiving, she lamented that her work did not have a more pragmatic
function:

> Since travelling for our Canadian Club I have wondered whether
> this club might not have a more practical part in the work of inter-
> pretation between Britain and America than it has had up till now.
> If a way could be opened to extend the range of the organization or
> the scope of its speakers so that they were enabled to make direct
> contact with the American people. (North American Tradition 10)

Her thoughts expressed on radio and at the podium were published in
revised and condensed form by Macmillan in a 1941 booklet called *The
North American Tradition*. This work calls for wartime unity between Canada
and the United States, and encourages the latter country to enter the war.
Baird considers the very foundation of civilization under threat from
Nazism, and argues passionately and patriotically that Canada's destiny is

to act as a bridge between England and the United States during wartime:

> What does it mean to be a Canadian while these forces of danger, of
> policy and of power are reshaping the English speaking world? It
> means to belong to a nation of matchless opportunity; it means that
> no nation of 11,000,000 souls has even been in a position to do so
> much or to leave so much undone. Placed between two great pow-
> ers, not as hostage but as interpreter, respecting both, touched by
> the blood of each, absorbed by neither, it is difficult to see how fate
> could have done more for us. (5)

While Baird was writing (she had begun work on a new novel) and making speeches about the war, her husband, Robert, a World War I veteran,
went to fight in Europe. Baird's separation from her husband would be
permanent; they never divorced, but lived apart until his death in 1952
(Spence).

Baird's war novel, *He Rides the Sky*, was published by Macmillan in 1941.
It is unlike those she proposed for her Guggenheim application. *He Rides
the Sky* is an epistolary novel that purports to be a collection of letters written by a bold, ribald, boisterous, naive, but likeable young Canadian man,
Peter O'Halloran, to his family in British Columbia while he is stationed
as a Royal Air Force trainee and, later, pilot in England. The series of letters, written in a highly colloquial and mannered style, begin in 1938 and
present O'Halloran's thoughts on the war, his bouts of drinking and
cavorting, the intricacies of flying an aircraft, a surprise marriage, his
reports of the deaths of his comrades, and pleas to his younger brother to
avoid enlisting. The letters conclude abruptly with O'Halloran's own
death in combat in April 1940. While the narrative is at times forced and
implausible, the psychological portrait of O'Halloran is convincing and
complex, and *He Rides the Sky* is among the better Canadian novels of
World War II. This novel was far timelier than *Waste Heritage*, and its
reviews were generally positive but reserved: as Eleanor Godfrey wrote in
The Canadian Forum, "It is a familiar story, all the more so because it is told
in letters which, apart from the occasional literary highlighting, are very
much like those we know are being received by many parents here .... The
author of *Waste Heritage* has paused in her pursuit of the powerful themes

which that novel proved she understood ..." (Godfrey 390). The topicality of *He Rides the Sky* did not, however, guarantee its commercial success and sales were again disappointing. Baird would not publish her fourth and final novel for three decades.

Baird's writing career took a new direction when, in 1941, for a short time, she wrote a column for the *Vancouver Sun*. In 1942 she joined the staff of the Vancouver *Daily Province*, but her time there was brief. While working for the *Province*, Baird attended a talk given by John Grierson, the head of the National Film Board (NFB), and approached him afterward expressing enthusiasm for the work the NFB was doing for the war effort. Grierson responded by sending Baird a letter that included a job offer; she accepted the job, moved to Ottawa with her daughter, and began a career as a civil servant that would last more than two decades and dramatically impede her creative output (Spence). She would later remark that "some people can combine creative writing with a responsible career, but I can't" ("Novel of Depression" 6). Her work with the NFB, in publicity and public relations, required her to travel extensively showing and lecturing on documentary films about the war (Spence). In 1943 she served on the Canadian Youth Commission, and published an article in *Saturday Night*, "Will We Fail When Youth Says, 'What Now?'" which argued that Canada urgently needed to begin planning opportunities for youth in the postwar world. During this period she also published articles that explored the role of women in wartime and the opportunities and challenges that would confront them after the war. In "Women and Statesmanship," an article that appeared in *Saturday Night* in 1943, she argued that

> A shattered, seething world, snarling with new dangers, will lie out there in front of us. And it will be a world where women are peculiarly fitted to take responsibility and share leadership for its problems will include the creation of a new social and economic order; new and revolutionary techniques of rehabilitation, child welfare, public health, nutrition, housing—all the common problems of human welfare we know so well .... (16)

In 1944, Baird was appointed the NFB representative in Washington, DC. The next year she toured the United States for the American Association of University Women and spoke on the topic of greater understanding between the United States and Canada. Shortly after, she became the NFB representative in Mexico and moved to Mexico City with her daughter (Spence).

Baird returned to Canada in 1947 and began work for the Department of Mines and Resources (which became the Department of Northern Affairs and Natural Resources, and later the Department of Indian Affairs and Northern Development) where, over time, she took on increasingly important administrative roles. In 1955, the Department of Northern Affairs sent Baird to the Arctic to "get the feel of the North and to write a story about Frobisher Bay's Christmas party for the Eskimos" (Baird, "You Only" 26). Baird was appointed chief of information for the Department of Indian Affairs and Northern Development in 1962 and became the first woman to head a federal information service (Twigg).

A final phase in Baird's creative career was initiated by her travels in the north, and in the 1960s and early 1970s she wrote poetry, short fiction, and articles about the Arctic for several journals, including *North*, *Saturday Night*, *Beaver*, *Canadian Geographical Journal*, and the UNESCO *Courier*. Baird's substantial work on the north has received almost no critical attention. Her poems, including "Arctic Mobile," "Eskimo Church on Christmas Morning," "Ex-Elijah," "Exhibit in Paris," "i don't read you charlie," "Keep Your Own Things," "Land," "Midwinter Flight," "No-destination Jonah," and "Who Will Be I," are usually uncomplicated representations of the everyday lives of Canada's Inuit from a perspective that is sympathetic. Her best short story, "A Learning Situation," represents in Baird's characteristically pared-down and exacting style the experience of a family whose son has gone south. Her articles of the period, including "Diary of a Working Journey," "*Les Africains* Visit the Eskimos," and "Frobisher Bay Talks to the World," grow out of her extensive travels in the Arctic, and deal with the same subjects as her poetry and short fiction.

After her retirement at the age of sixty-five, Baird moved to London, England, where she took a comfortable flat on Onslow Square in South Kensington (West). She travelled on the continent—she spoke fluent French and Spanish—and wrote a regular travel column for the *Ottawa Journal*. She also set to work on her last novel, *Climate of Power*, which drew on her experience as a civil servant and was published by Macmillan in 1971. This novel breaks with her tradition of "plotless" narratives, and offers a story of suspense and intrigue in which the central character, George McKenna, is a high-ranking, workaholic civil servant who is being driven, by an unscrupulous colleague, from his job in a fictional government department that handles northern affairs. Against the backdrop of his unhappy marriage to a younger and adulterous wife, McKenna fights to retain his position and commits a murder in the Arctic that he passes off as an accident. The novel is a well-written and astute study of Canada's north, and an indictment of the government bureaucracy that Baird knew well. Unfortunately, despite its merits, "*Climate of Power* received almost no attention from either critics or the press, was weakly marketed, and died virtually without a trace in spite of its technical excellence, its exciting plot and its important subject" (Hyman 74). The review in *Saturday Night*, which had published some of Baird's most important journalistic pieces, considered the novel "escapist" and insufficiently Canadian and quipped, "[t]he reader of Irene Baird's fourth novel ... soon finds himself lost in what will certainly prove to be the season's literary whiteout" (Muggeridge 29). In 1973, Baird returned to Canada and settled again in Victoria where she lived with her beloved dog, Lady, near her son and daughter and her family (Spence). That same year, after much lobbying by Baird, Macmillan reissued *Waste Heritage* in a paperback edition, as part of its Laurentian Library. Again, reviews were positive—William French wrote, in *The Globe and Mail*, "Why it suffered such obscurity for almost 35 years is hard to explain"—but the novel quickly went out of print a second time and has remained unavailable since (34). Baird began work on a fifth novel in the mid-1970s; it was never published, and all we know is that she called it "completely different" from her previous works ("Novel of Depression" 6). In 1981, Baird died at the age of 80.

2. CRITICAL RECEPTION AND SIGNIFICANCE

Critical interest in Baird and *Waste Heritage* has been sporadic. Only a handful of articles have attended the novel at length, and the first significant pieces to do so did not appear until after it was reissued by Macmillan in 1973. Nearly all of the academic writing on *Waste Heritage* treats it as a work of primarily historical and political significance and offers comparatively little discussion of its literary strengths and weaknesses. A case in point, the first major piece produced on the book, Michiel Horn's review article entitled "Transient Men in the Depression" (1974), argues for the importance of *Waste Heritage* as a social document. Horn summarizes the factual events that inspired the novel and provides a well-documented socio-historical context for it. In the same vein, Robin Mathews's "*Waste Heritage*: The Effect of Class on Literary Structure" (1981) performs a convincing, detailed, and essentially Marxist reading of the novel to illuminate a larger point about Canadian fiction in relation to history, politics, class, and society:

> The protagonist, Matt Striker, in his confrontation with the claims of individualism and communitarian values helps to reveal class structure and the role of class in Canadian society. The novel is instructive because it can provide a basis for rejecting the general sense that there is not class interest in Canadian literature, and it can show why Canadian critics are timid about using an analysis of class as a way of making Canadian literature more accessible and comprehensible to readers. (66)

Roger Leslie Hyman, in "Wasted Heritage and *Waste Heritage*: The Critical Disregard of an Important Canadian Novel" (1982), places more emphasis than most upon the literary aspects of *Waste Heritage* and suggests it has been neglected because critics have incorrectly labelled it "social propaganda"; instead, he argues, it is a "novel of engagement" and "any analysis of *Waste Heritage* must be predicated not only upon its 'utility' as a social document ... but also upon its aesthetic elements" or "those excellences of technique without which its didacticism would be as nourishing as a dry wind" (74, 80). In "Thematic Structure and Vision in *Waste Heritage*"

(1986), Anthony Hopkins, like Hyman, refutes those who would value the novel primarily as a social document and offers a sustained argument in favour of its literary merits: "Her accomplishments—projecting a comprehensive insight through a complex and consistent aesthetic pattern ... places [sic] Irene Baird and *Waste Heritage* in the front rank of Canadian literary achievement" (85).

Other critics have commented on *Waste Heritage* in passing while making larger political, theoretical, thematic, and literary-historical arguments. W.H. Coles's "The Railroad in Canadian Literature" (1978) argues that in the novel "the train becomes a malevolent symbol of the struggle between labour and management as well as a symbol of death and mechanical determinism" (128). Roxanne Rimstead's "Mediated Lives: Oral Histories and Cultural Memory" (1996) points out that Baird "dramatizes the role of the documentary novelist through a character who records bits of conversation and orders events into a marketable product" (153–154). Caren Irr's "Queer Borders: Figures from the 1930s for U.S.–Canadian Relations" suggests that the novel "push[es] beyond the stereotype of the lonely drifter to pair men who support one another in an aggressive, uncomfortable social world" and that the "brief glimpse" the novel provides of "an all-male utopia ... is foreclosed by the contradictions of the culture at large"; the text, Irr argues, has "been written with a national context in mind" and "illustrate[s] much about U.S.–Canadian relations before 1945" (508). Glenn Willmott's *Unreal Country: Modernity in the Canadian Novel in English* (2002) briefly discusses *Waste Heritage* as an "inconclusive bildungsroman" in which, among other things, the boundaries between collective and individual identity are negotiated (33–34). James Doyle's *Progressive Heritage: The Evolution of a Politically Radical Literary Tradition in Canada* (2002) sees Baird's novel as a "lost and forgotten" part of a neglected and Canadian "radical literary heritage" (6).

Doyle's argument is convincing, and other critics have emphasized *Waste Heritage*'s leftist ideology. William French, for example, considers it "a genuine novel of social protest, and we haven't had many of those in Canadian fiction," and most other reviews and articles concede that *Waste Heritage* is offering a social critique that is sympathetic to the plight of the sit-downers (34). But despite its importance as a landmark work in

Canada's leftist heritage, it is difficult to situate Baird's *Waste Heritage* in a singular literary tradition because it resists many labels, draws upon many influences, and breaks much new ground. Baird's novel is perhaps the finest achievement in a body of early twentieth-century Canadian social-realist fiction that includes pieces published in the little magazines of the 1930s—*The Canadian Forum*, *Masses*, and *New Frontier*—scattered works of short fiction later collected in Donna Philips's *Voices of Discord: Canadian Short Stories of the 1930s* (1979), and numerous novels of the period by writers such as J.G. Sime, Frederick Philip Grove, Douglas Durkin, Hubert Evans, Robert J.C. Stead, Philip Child, A.M. Stephen, Nellie McClung, Gwethalyn Graham, Hugh Garner, Len Peterson, and Morley Callaghan. But Baird's novel also resists the "leftist" label that critics often apply to it. While *Waste Heritage* is generally sympathetic to the cause of the unemployed, it is not fundamentally a radical or revolutionary text, and in some ways it is overtly critical of leftist politics of the 1930s. To be sure, Baird admired some of the leading leftist writers of her day, including Steinbeck and agitprop playwright Clifford Odets (Baird to Elliott, 6 Nov. 1939), and her personal sympathies were certainly with the sit-downers and their cause, but she did not consider *Waste Heritage* to be a radical novel. As she later wrote,

> I have never been connected with Communism and I have never thought of myself as a radical if being a radical means wanting to overthrow the system we live in in favour of another political system. I think the reader of the novel will find, however, that I don't praise or condemn some of the most important people in the novel who are obviously connected with radical politics. ("Sidown" 82)

Clearly, Baird did believe her novel had the potential to affect social change. As the BC Legislature in November 1939 debated some of the labour issues raised in *Waste Heritage*, she demanded that Macmillan accelerate its release so it might be read and possibly influence the debate in her home province: "Get it here and get it here quick!" (Baird to H. Eayrs, 5 Nov. 1939). But *Waste Heritage* steers clear of political affiliations and aims to present a balanced reading of 1930s ideological conflicts. It is also worth noting that the novel might never have been published had it been perceived by Macmillan to be radical or even leftist in orientation; Carl Eayrs, who prepared a reader's report on *Waste Heritage* for Macmillan, reassured his brother Hugh that the book could safely be published in Canada as it is "almost anti-red" (C. Eayrs to H. Eayrs, second undated letter).

Regardless of where on the political spectrum one locates *Waste Heritage*, it is certain that Baird was writing, at least partly, in an American tradition. Her critics and reviewers occasionally liken her to Hemingway. Baird, however, has steadfastly denied that Hemingway influenced her. Her journalistic prose and idiomatic dialogue may be vaguely reminiscent of Hemingway's early work, but *Waste Heritage* does not display the same virtuosic style, and she was no admirer: "most of my Hemingway has been confined to *Death in the Afternoon*—a theme that does not encourage imitators!" (Baird to Sutherland, 20 Mar. 1974). The charge that her work resembles, even derives from, Steinbeck is sounder and has been far more persistent. Many critics note this influence and either compare her work unfavourably to Steinbeck's, or celebrate her as Canada's own version of the American writer. Harold Strauss, among her harshest detractors on this point, writes that "like most disciples, Miss Baird has borrowed and magnified all the faults and mistakes of her master ... while largely failing to reflect his virtues" (7). Baird openly and self-deprecatingly acknowledged that Steinbeck influenced her, and she wrote the following to her New York editor about the ubiquitous comparisons in reviews of *Waste Heritage*:

> I am sorry about the Steinbeck angle and from this space of time can only explain it by the feeling that at the beginning the whole job of work seemed so much too big, so much too foreign and incongruous to tackle without some sort of guiding influence, conscious or subconscious. You see it was not a woman's job, I knew nothing about that side of life, and it was when I saw the mess and nobody lifting a hand to do anything about it, it seemed too stinking and too exciting to leave alone. (Baird to Cerf, 9 Dec. 1939)

Reviewers forced Baird to be defensive about some of the obvious similarities they perceived between her work and Steinbeck's: the relationship between Matt and Eddy parallels one between George and Lennie in *Of*

Mice and Men (1937), the strike in *Waste Heritage* dimly recalls the uprising of migratory workers in *In Dubious Battle* (1936), and the tone and subject of Baird's novel are easily compared to *Grapes of Wrath*, although this last work was not published until 1939, and Baird had nearly completed her manuscript by the end of 1938.

By her own admission, as a woman writer treading new ground, she felt in need of an accepted literary model. The fact that she genders this problem is interesting and hardly surprising given the comments many early critics made about her work: Bruce Hutchison wrote, "The first thing you think as you read it is, gosh, how did such a charming little lady learn so many bad words?" (4); Frank Brookhauser mused that "It is hard to believe that this natural dialogue of men ... has been penned by a woman" (10); Hunter Lewis, apparently unaware that Baird had participated in the events her novel fictionalizes, concluded that "the author must be admired for the creative drive which has made it possible for her to describe so sincerely ... events and people which are presumably remote from her personal experience" (4). It is worth noting the double standard implicit in these statements. Many of Baird's critics have denigrated her work by tracing its real and imagined American influences. At the same time, critics have often noted the influence of American authors on the work of Baird's contemporary, Morley Callaghan, and concluded that such influence is proof of his seriousness, significance, internationalism, cosmopolitanism, and modernism.

Baird and her agent Marion Saunders were keenly aware that *Waste Heritage* was not the kind of novel critics would expect from a woman in 1939, and that this obviously generated both possibilities and difficulties. As Saunders pitched *Waste Heritage* to Random House in May 1939, she was careful to distance Baird from her sentimental first novel, *John*:

> With the exception of a few pages, *Waste Heritage* has all the ear-marks of masculine writing. It is a marvel to find a sensitive woman writer able to produce a strong meaty story of this type .... We have been debating whether Irene Baird should change her name for this novel and call herself Robert Hall. (Saunders to Haas, 26 May 1939)

Long after she had decided to put her own name on the cover of *Waste*

Heritage, Baird wrote to Hugh Eayrs and revealed that she still felt significant anxiety and self-doubt about her project:

> How right you are about the work that has to go into any piece of writing that hopes to make the grade. Exasperation, sweat and a stiff behind also together with that beastly sick feeling of wondering whether you couldn't be better employed learning to make a decent cake. (Baird to H. Eayrs, 28 Oct. 1939)

All four of Baird's novels treat traditionally "masculine" topics: the settler experience of a single man, the sit-down strike of unemployed transient men, the war experience of an RAF pilot, Ottawa's federal bureaucracy. That the same author who wrote convincingly on these topics faced nagging self-doubt about the gender-appropriateness of her profession is revealing and indicative of the obstacles that faced so many of Baird's female contemporaries.

Baird was writing at a time when various competing, innovative, and experimental forms of high modernism were flourishing in the United States and Europe. The subject matter of *Waste Heritage* may be irreverent in the best modernist sense but stylistically it is a relatively conservative novel, at least on the surface and in comparison to works by writers such as Joyce, Woolf, and Faulkner. In other words, Baird deals with many of the great themes of modernity—moral relativism, modern technology, the forces of urbanization and industrialization, modern social and political ideals, moral and religious change and decline, human sexuality, evolving gender roles—within a framework that is largely *realist*: *Waste Heritage* provides meticulous detail, evokes the language of everyday life, emphasizes social, political, and historical matters, and is narrated in the omniscient, third-person mode. Baird was aware of the work of some of the most experimental modernists of her day, and her realism was a conscious aesthetic choice that she made partly in response to what she considered the excesses of certain forms of high-modernist expression. In a reply to a letter from Cerf offering her complimentary books from the Random House catalogue, she requested Faulkner's *The Wild Palms*, Dos Passos's *U.S.A.* and Joyce's *Ulysses* (Baird to Cerf, 11 July 1939). After receiving the books, she wrote to Cerf again: "The books arrived today. They are all three so significant, so vital and so exciting that I can't begin to thank you enough for having so generously placed them in my hands" (Baird to Cerf, 26 July 1939). Her praise for these experimental prose modernists, however, would not remain unreserved; four months later, she had changed her evaluation of at least one of the authors: "I wonder whether those critics who most loudly praised him, actually did grasp what James Joyce is driving at. Or whether Joyce knows himself" (Baird to Cerf, 24 Oct. 1939).

Baird has less in common with high modernists such as Joyce than with naturalists such as Zola, Hardy, Crane, Norris, Dreiser, and others who wrote in the United States and Europe from about 1880 to 1910. The influence of these writers has been enduring in Canada, and critics have identified a naturalist strain in the *oeuvres* of some of Baird's most significant contemporaries, including Callaghan and Grove. Naturalism involves an almost scientific approach to literary realism that emphasizes heredity, evolution, societal influences, historical circumstances, and an exploration of many of the traditionally taboo aspects of human experience, including sexuality, psychological disturbance, and unconscious impulses. The most recognizable feature of naturalism is probably its interest in social, environmental, and biological determinism, or its assertion that modern individuals are driven and derided by powerful external and internal forces that are largely beyond their understanding or control. *Waste Heritage* offers central characters, Matt and Eddy, whose fates appear predetermined. Matt's "rage blindness" and Eddy's mental deficiencies are innate faults, arising from hereditary and environmental factors, that cannot be overcome through the exercise of free will. These deterministic forces lead to the tragic and inevitable conclusion of the novel. Hyman has pointed out that "*Waste Heritage* concentrates closely on the relationship between society and the individual in order to demonstrate the workings of social determinism" (80). Indeed, Baird's novel is on one level a catalogue of the various ways that the modern individual lacks the agency to escape larger social forces and factors: class, gender roles, the "organization," economic conditions, ideological paradigms, and Western social values.

In addition to its leftist, American, and naturalist connections, *Waste*

Heritage is a central text in Canada's own pan-national modern-realist movement that comprises works by about three dozen early twentieth-century writers of fiction, including Bertram Brooker, Philip Child, Morley Callaghan, Douglas Durkin, Hugh Garner, Gwethalyn Graham, Frederick Philip Grove, Raymond Knister, Hugh MacLennan, Joyce Marshall, Martha Ostenso, Sinclair Ross, Jessie Georgina Sime, and Robert J.C. Stead, among others. Generally, Canada's modern realists sought a direct, immediate, contemporary, idiomatically correct language, and a narrative objectivism and impersonality. They demonstrated a sustained and experimental interest in psychological writing and the representation of human consciousness. They directed the technical innovations they undertook in these respects toward a mimetic representation of a contemporary world, usually Canadian, and, much as many European and American modernists did, explored the cultural conditions and great themes of modernity. This Canadian modern realism—and its various sub-generic forms (prairie realism, social realism, urban realism, war realism)—is Canada's unique and largely unacknowledged contribution to the collection of disparate international movements that makes up literary modernism. Baird and her modern-realist contemporaries explored the same subjects that fascinated international modernists, but they rejected the brashest forms of modernist innovation—extreme fragmentation, dissonant multivocality, highly subjectivist renderings of human consciousness, overt impressionism, surrealism, and expressionism—in favour of an experimental modern realism that accorded with both their psychological interests and their referential and documentary aims. Baird's novel, with its multi-generic origins and aesthetic, reflects the broader literary period of which it is a part: it comprises elements of various competing and contested modernisms and realisms and demonstrates that these concepts, like *Waste Heritage*, resist easy categorization.

As a pioneering modern realist, Baird was not derivative but an originator, and she played a formative role in the development of the modern Canadian novel. Although several critics have insisted that Baird owes a literary debt to some of the Canadian modern realists, she has angrily denied the influence of several of the major writers who participated in this movement:

> *Waste Heritage* was published in 1939. Hugh MacLennan did not publish his first novel until 1941, and his Depression novel, *The Watch That Ends the Night*, didn't appear until 1958. So he could have been no influence on *Waste Heritage*. To dispose, right off, of other suppositions, I have to admit that I had not read either Garner or Callaghan and have not to this day. Neither had the slightest connection with *Waste Heritage*. ("Sidown" 81)

Despite her affiliation with a loosely coherent school of Canadian authors, Baird's writing was neither nationalistic nor patriotic. In fact, like Callaghan, she considered herself to be working in a North American tradition. She expressed a strong desire to write a novel that would be successful in the United States (Baird to Cerf, 11 July 1939), and did not always draw clear cultural distinctions between Canada its southern neighbour. As she argued in *The North American Tradition*:

> The North American genius has always lain in certain qualities that root back deep into pioneer tradition. It pre-existed our present frontiers and drew no distinction between north and south of 'the line.' ... Nothing of significance that happens to one of our nations can be of complete unconcern to the other. (3)

At the same time, Baird insisted that Canada needed its own fiction and distinct literary tradition: "We shall help nobody by imitating or leaning upon even the most friendly of powers. We have done this in the past and we have done it to our own lack of development" (27).

For Baird, it was not a matter of preferring a North American tradition to a Canadian one (as it was for Callaghan) or vice versa; rather, like many of the modern realists, she did not perceive the existence of an established Canadian tradition that she could engage while she was writing. In fact, she fancied herself, quite rightly, among the founders of the new modern writing in Canada:

> Canadian readers should by this time be old enough to stand a

rather stronger diet than that to which they are mostly accustomed
.... By God I'd love to feel I had some part in building up a literary
tradition in Canada that was equal parts sound technique, vision
and guts. (Baird to H. Eayrs, 28 Oct. 1939)

For Baird, the new tradition was entirely contemporary: as she wrote in
the notes for her Guggenheim proposal, "No form of historical writing
attracts me in the least. There is too much going on today. What I would
like to write would be a novel of some sort of contemporary life ... "
(Saunders to Cerf, 13 Sep. 1939). When she wrote *Waste Heritage*, she drew
perhaps unconsciously upon her American and naturalist influences. But
her decision to write of contemporary Canada in the emerging style of the
modern realists—and *Waste Heritage* is one of the premier modern-realist
novels—established her has an important and vital originator.

The modern realists sought to represent the modern cityscape and
urban experience in a manner that reflected the rapid pace of life and
change in Canada's cities, the threatening and often destructive forces
sometimes associated with urbanization, and the psychological effects of
city dwelling on the individual. Many of the modern realists, including
Baird, offer intense descriptive passages meant to capture the vibrancy of
the growing Canadian city, and convey the impact of technological development on modern life. The first sustained urban portraits in Canadian
fiction appear in the 1920s; these early examples—including the portrait
of Montreal in Sime's *Our Little Life* (1921)—usually present the city in a
positive light and celebrate Canada's urbanization and developing cosmopolitanism. But the 1920s optimism regarding technological advance
and industrialization changed with the onset of the Great Depression
when Canada's urban portraits grow noticeably darker, and the modern
realist becomes most interested in exploring the ominous and foreboding
aspects of the urban world. In *Waste Heritage*, Vancouver (Aschelon) is an
urban waste land where many of the social problems of the novel—pover-
ty, gender inequality, class struggle, failure of domestic ideals, violence,
unemployment—are almost personified. The novel begins with an ominous, threatening, and foreboding image as Matt Striker rides the "clanging" freight train into the city, which is described as a "burnished maze"
of "smokestacks" (1). A fire truck is "screeching" through the streets and

sounds almost "hysterical" (1). Indeed, Aschelon is both an apocalyptic backdrop to the central conflict of the novel, and a symbolic and almost expressionistic projection of the internal states of Baird's conflicted characters.

Accordingly, Baird's symbols of the industrial revolution and modernization are reeking streetcars, screeching fire trucks, towering skyscrapers, menacing crowds, and murderous trains. The pattern of symbolism that runs through the novel is an unmistakeable indictment of urban life in the 1930s, and suggests that larger forces of industrialization and modernization underlie the more explicit social and economic problems at the centre of the story. In the same vein, one of the most remarkable features of the book is its uncompromising treatment of everyday life on the city streets—and in cafés, stores, and other public places—that contrasts markedly with the descriptions of rural life and landscape that are almost ubiquitous in Canadian fiction before 1950. The vivid snapshot of a ride on a Vancouver streetcar in chapter seven—with its visceral images of "Half nude bodies," "sun-baked backs hard with youth," and "chattering monkey-talk" (54)—highlights the everyday experience of working class and unemployed people. While such portraits of the working class are perhaps condescending and unflattering, they are nevertheless sympathetic, and Baird's social critique is directed at the forces that make life miserable, not only for the sit-downers, but for the working class more generally.

As part of this same social critique, *Waste Heritage* strives to affect the reader with a credible portrait of the sordid aspects of life during the Depression. There are numerous little scenes in the novel that approach taboo subjects with frankness matched by few if any of Baird's Canadian contemporaries. The novel frequently depicts the sit-downers as libidinous and uncouth. In chapter sixteen, for example, Hughes and Gaffney read a magazine story about a "half-nude sex-slayer finished in sepia" and make various lewd comments (128). Although such evocative scenes might appear tame to a contemporary reader, they were published at a time when Canadian fiction was infamously reserved about sexual matters. Baird is similarly unrestrained in her handling of the novel's romantic subplot. At first, the inclusion of the romance between Matt and Hazel might seem a superfluous attempt to make the novel conform to popular conventions of the period. But, in the "lovemaking" scene in chapter seven, Baird deals with human sexuality in a manner that is refreshing if unromantic. The fact that Matt and Hazel, who share the dream of employment, home, and family, must consummate their relationship in a public place indicates the degree to which personal agency has been overridden by social forces. The newspaper and historical accounts of the sit-down frequently refer to the fact that the sit-downers are unemployed, transient, and unmarried. The thwarted domestic dream shared by Matt and Hazel is a crucial tenet of Baird's social critique, as it shows how difficult it was for the sit-downers, and for working class single women, to form relationships and start families without the possibility of economic stability.

Waste Heritage is set in a recognizable, historical time and place yet Baird incorporates at least one high-modernist device that leads her away from the straightforward and mimetic treatment of contemporary Canada. Her main cities, Vancouver and Victoria, have been allusively renamed after the Biblical cities, Aschelon and Gath. In thinly disguising these cities, Baird was not trying to obscure the source for the events her narrative fictionalizes: "I had a great advantage. I have lived in Vancouver, Victoria, and up-Island. The story locations I didn't have to invent .... I knew the places, and the real events happened in the places I knew" ("Sidown" 81). Still, she responded to suggestions from her editors and publishers that she use real place names in her novel with an absolute refusal to comply: "In the meantime," wrote Marion Saunders to Hugh Eayrs, "I have received a letter from Irene Baird stating most emphatically that she will not have her place names changed [back] ..." (Saunders to H. Eayrs, 9 June 1939). It is unfortunate that none of the letters Baird wrote defending her reasons for the allusive naming survives, and we cannot be sure why she was so vehemently opposed to naming Vancouver, Victoria, and other smaller cities in the novel. Perhaps she preferred to keep the story as anonymous as possible to "protect her sources" as a reporter might. Perhaps, like Hughes, she was afraid of libel and wanted to protect herself from legal action. Probably she intended the story to have both a geographical particularity and universality. Hopkins argues that "To pre-

vent fact from dominating meaning, she dislocates her narrative geo-
graphically .... Vancouver and Victoria, with deliberate irony, are called
Aschelon and Gath respectively, after Philistine cities conquered by the
Israelites when they occupied the Promised Land" (78). The allusion gives
the events of the novel a heightened significance by likening the sit-downers' quest for dignity to the Biblical conquest. This suggests that leftist
politics and the labour movement have an almost spiritual significance for
the men who are out to "conquer" the "Philistine cities" that have not yet
understood the new religion of socialism. The irony is that Aschelon and
Gath, in *Waste Heritage*, are never conquered; the men leave Aschelon after
their sit-down achieves little, and Gath proves to be no "promised land"
when, at the end of their journey, the men are forced to accept a flawed
and meagre settlement. Baird may also be suggesting more cynically that
expectations of a job, home, family, and dignity have become unrealistic
in 1930s Canada; such a quest for a mythological "promised land" cannot
exist in the modern world, and the aims of the left may be utopian and ide-
alistic.

Waste Heritage is written in a journalistic style, and the simplicity, direct-
ness, omniscience, and objectivist tone of its narrative voice are striking
but deceptive. For the most part, the text has no clearly defined narrative
persona as it attempts to generate the impression of transparency,
extreme impersonality, complete omniscience, and utter objectivity.
Unlike narrators in many overtly ideological fictions of the 1930s, Baird's
narrator does not usually take sides, and the detached narrative throughout offers a classic example of the direct-reportage style common in the
modern-realist novel of the period. Even in situations where didactic comment might easily be provided, Baird strives to maintain the illusion of
objectivity and places her emphasis upon the psychological rather than
the political. Baird's direct reportage focuses on everyday events as it
moves from incident to incident. The novel lacks a gripping or driving
plot. The narrative is episodic and the minor characters that come into the
story do not usually reappear. Details of everyday life are provided
painstakingly and at times almost tediously. All of this is because Baird is
plotting her story over real events that she witnessed first hand and read
about in the paper. Baird's "formless" plot is mirroring the sense of aim-

lessness, monotony, and repetition that was experienced by the sit-down-ers. Hopkins calls the plot "a pattern in which the essential features are indecision, irresolution, and inaction, which lead, when they lead any-where, only to futility or self-destruction" (78). Indeed, the inertia that traps Matt and Eddy is so strong that only the tragic events that close the novel provide some sort of escape: as Doyle writes, "The tragic redundan-cy of the whole experience in *Waste Heritage* is also underscored by the rep-etition of setting in the opening and closing scenes" (121).

At the same time, *Waste Heritage* displays a profound concern with exploring subjective states within its objectivist framework, and with telling a story in a manner that is artful. Like most of her modern-realist contemporaries, Baird is keenly interested in human psychology, and she is especially concerned with exploring the ways that individual conscious-ness is influenced by larger social forces. Hopkins writes that "Never in the course of the novel is Matt able to resolve this inner conflict between personal and collective identity, and his inability to discover a coherent, integrated orientation to himself, to Eddy, to his girl Hazel, to the organ-ization, or to society, leaves him in a state of angry and impotent frustra-tion" (80). Baird's characterization of Matt is in one sense a psychological and naturalistic "case study," as the novel establishes a causal relationship between environmental factors and consciousness: in chapter three we learn that the "blinding flashes of rage" that Matt experiences are linked to his abandonment by his mother (21). Baird also shows Matt negotiat-ing the boundary between personal and communal identity as he recur-rently finds his own sense of self subsumed by the organization he has joined: "Since he stepped inside the hall Matt was experiencing an odd feeling of black-out, as though his identity were being sucked away and absorbed by the powerful currents of an organization. It made him touchy and defensive; at the same time it gave him a sting of excitement" (19).

Baird's interest in psychology is at times more overtly modernist. While she does not employ the stream-of-consciousness device used by some of her most experimental contemporaries, her detached and imper-sonal descriptions often mimic Matt's psychological processes, and she writes using the Jamesian technique of centre of consciousness, or free indirect discourse, in which a third person narrative voice speaks through the perspective of a single character: "The struggle went round and round. It merged with the street noises, the endless rise and fall of men's voices, the snarling of gears, the clatter of a speed cop kicking over his machine. It became one with the still blazing air, the sweaty, fumey smells that no wind relieved, the dusty odour of the ground itself, of hot, rusting iron" (24). This vivid description at first appears omniscient, but is filtered through Matt's consciousness, and the violent atmosphere of the passage reflects not just the scene he witnesses, but also his inner rage. Baird's psychological writing is perhaps most impressive when she depicts the mass movements of crowds, and shows that the line between individual and communal consciousness is blurred. In the crowd scene in chapter four, she describes "Massed bodies, swimming heads, urgent single hurrying ant-like units, formless confusion weaving into pattern, slow tightening into disciplined design. Spat of motorcycles, shrill crowd voices, heavy surging of feet" (27). *Waste Heritage*, then, through subtle modulation of narrative voice, strives at once to present a recognizable, referential portrait of the modern city, and the complex and indeterminate psychological processes of its inhabitants.

Through Kenny Hughes, a sit-downer in *Waste Heritage* who is covering the events of the novel almost as a reporter would, Baird voices strikingly contemporary and self-reflexive comments about her writing and deconstructs her aesthetic and style in a manner that is almost metafictional. On the simplest level, these self-reflexive passages give us insights into the methodology Baird perhaps employed when writing the novel. We learn, for example, that Hughes is quick to record his impressions lest he forget them: "He knew he would not have a place to write later with the meeting scheduled in half an hour and he wanted to record his present impressions as well as the ones he got coming up from the boat while the whole thing was fresh in his mind" (77). The narrator describes Hughes's aesthetic in a manner that is echoed by Baird's comments in "Sidown Brothers, Sidown" discussed earlier, and notes the importance of veracity, detail, local colour, and attention to larger socio-politcal forces. The self-reflexive passages also reflect some of Baird's pragmatic optimism that the book might engender political change; as Hughes tells us, "Some day this book may be important, who knows .... Books have been known to move mountains" (78); "I don't think you quite get what it is I'm trying to do. This book of mine is to be more than just another book, it's to be a ... a kind of a social document, a book that will bring before the nation this whole problem of unemployment that is festering on its body like a bloody sore ..." (128).

There is a sophistication, playfulness, irony, and gentle satire in the self-reflexive passages where Baird comments on how generic and commercial issues influence her project, expresses her own writerly anxieties about the novel, anticipates some of the criticisms others would have of it, and satirizes the conventions of fiction of the period. Baird imagines those who would call her novel too factual and artless when she tells us that Hughes's novel, "never was published ... because it was not a good book. Hughes has all the conviction and the sympathy and he moled around earnestly making notes, the only thing he forgot was to learn how to write" (52). Baird has Hughes acknowledge some discomfort about the taboo subject matter the novel presents: "He would have liked to put him in the book, too, but he was a bit nervous over trying to reproduce some of the things Gabby was in the habit of saying" (7). Further reflecting upon the adventurousness of her novel's subject matter, she has Gaffney "reading out hot bits from a sex-crime monthly, every now and then breaking off to tell Hughes the kinds of things a book ought to have. He said action first, and then plenty of sex ... you gotta have ... lotsa sex ... you gotta be full of sex as an egg" (92, 128). Hughes also feels anxiety about his ability to finish the gargantuan task his book attempts: "He kept at his MS. in a sort of fever so as to try to fool himself that he was not losing out and slowing down and rusting mentally through lack of normal teaching routine" (113). Hughes speaks out on some of the technical problems associated with writing a fiction rooted in historical fact: "This is going to be a hard book to write, far harder than I figgered on," he says. "Quite apart from the actual writing and the entire absence of plot, there are a lot of technical difficulties. One is keeping it clear of anything that might border on libel" (127). And Hughes also shows an awareness of some of the demands of the fiction market: "Naturalistic dialog" is "What a book has to have to sell nowadays" (78).

Waste Heritage obviously explores economic disparity in the 1930s and argues for social justice. Accordingly it reflects the widespread racism of Depression-era Canadian society and a popular and fallacious argument of the period that not only capitalists and governments were the enemy of the sit-downers: so were some of Canada's religious and ethnic minorities. In several passages, Baird's characters voice jarringly racist and anti-Semitic remarks. Harry who runs the greasy spoon is a likeable "everyman" who does his part for the cause; he also says quite comfortably in a compliment to Matt and Eddy, "'Believe me ... you two boys done me the favour. Every once in a while I get to feelin' lonely an' there's nothin' but a bunch of lousy Greeks an' kikes to talk to around here'" (35). Anti-Semitism was rampant in Canada during the Great Depression. Jews and other minorities became scapegoats for economic problems and commentators with various political agendas sometimes accused these groups of taking jobs from "real" Canadians. It is appropriate that Baird, in a text that purports to reflect accurately a contemporary Canada, indicates how deeply ingrained such attitudes were in Canadian society, and even in the ranks of the sit-downers themselves. The anti-Semitism and racism are being "reported" to the reader through a technique of "collective focalization" (Stanzel 172); in other words, the narrative at points reflects communal attitudes and incorporates racist and anti-Semitic beliefs typical of segments of Canadian society of the period: "There was no one around on the block except "Junkie" Adler, the kike, standing in the doorway across the road" (183). This characterization of Adler, filtered through the perspective of the sit-downers, allies Jews with the various forces that oppose the workers. The repetition of the slur "kike" in the passages where he appears, his vampiric accent, and his uncooperative attitude toward the sit-downers suggest that Matt and his companions, who are distanced and disconnected from the larger ideas that inform their movement, feel that their cause has little resonance in minority communities and the anti-Jewish propaganda that fascists, and even some mainstream British Columbians, had been spouting throughout the 1930s, has led the rank and file sit-downers to misdirect their anger and mistrust.

The novel's exploration of racism directed at Asian-Canadians is just as striking. Reflecting the hysteria that surrounded the fear of "yellow peril" in the interwar period, Baird's characters represent Chinatown as a place that is inimical to the aims of the sit-downers. After the trip to the park that starts Matt dreaming of a future that includes a job, home, marriage, and family, Harry drives "back into the city through Chinatown, closed up tight for Sunday and looking like the walking dead, only no one was out walking. He did everything he could to clean the poison out of Matt's system" (35). In a particularly disturbing passage, Baird's narrator presents a racist portrait of Chinese Canadians alongside Matt's violent attack on a woman who has solicited Eddy in the street. As Matt beats the woman, "A shrivelled old Chinaman trotted to the open door and stood there watching. He looked like death watching. Then as the woman fell he made a high gabbling sound and a second Chink came out from behind and they stood together in the doorway watching" (86). Matt and Eddy flee the scene of the attack, and the reader learns that "the two Chinks watched them disappear. They did not go across and pick the woman up. They went back inside the laundry, locked the door and turned off the light" (87). Again, we have the repetition of the racist slur by the narrator, and the refusal, this time of the Chinese onlookers, to get involved in events of importance to the sit-downers. The narrative reflects widespread anti-Asian sentiment of the period and consistently associates Chinatown, and in this passage the "Chinks," with death, suggesting that the demise of Eddy, and of the dream of the sit-downers, has something to do with Asian immigration. More alarmingly, the fact that this indictment of Chinese Canadians is presented side by side with Matt's assault on the woman serves to detract blame from Matt who becomes just another victim in the whole affair. The abandonment of the bloodied woman by the Chinese onlookers demonstrates not only their detachment from mainstream society, but also a complete absence of common decency, and a complicity in the violence. These most unpalatable portions of the text increase its value as a social document. Such scenes remind us of the depth of racist and anti-Semitic feeling in 1930s Canada, and even in the ranks of the sit-downers themselves from whose perspective these scenes are reported. Tellingly, there is no mention of these incidents in any of Baird's correspondence with her publishers. Eayrs and Cerf apparently had no problem publishing these passages and expressed no concern about how the Canadian and American public would receive them.

*   *   *

Why, then, given its aesthetic achievement, documentary significance, rave reviews, a small but significant body of criticism, and appearance during a period of Canadian literature with few representative texts, has *Waste Heritage* failed to find a permanent place in the canon? Why does nearly every critic who writes on the novel bemoan its neglect? Certainly the unfortunate timing of the novel's initial publication during the first days of the World War II played a part. Had the novel appeared in the middle of the Depression alongside Callaghan's *They Shall Inherit the Earth* (1935), it might have gained an immediate cultural currency that it might have drawn on in future years. Yet this does not explain why Hugh Garner's *Cabbagetown*, first published in 1950, has been lauded as a textbook of the Depression while Baird's has not. It also does not explain why a novel like Sinclair Ross's *As For Me and My House* (1941), which was all but ignored upon its release and is now the most written about early twentieth-century Canadian novel, increasingly fascinates critics while *Waste Heritage* receives scant attention. I suspect that *Waste Heritage* has been neglected in large part because it has failed over the years to fit the evolving ideal of Canadian literature sought by many readers. Curiously, the politics of the novel have caused it to be neglected both by a conservative literary establishment and the political left. In the landmark *Literary History of Canada*, Desmond Pacey briefly discusses *Waste Heritage* under the heading "Some Minor Realists" and concludes that it is a "nove[l] of social propaganda ..." (687). At the same time, Baird's novel has never been fully accepted by a radical tradition of Canadian literature for the opposite reasons. As Doyle summarizes,

> [Dorothy] Livesay did not regard *Waste Heritage* as the great Canadian proletarian novel. In a 1978 comment, Livesay compared Baird's fiction briefly with Callaghan's, then went on to express her reservations about both writers .... The problem with both Baird and Callaghan, Livesay suggested, lay in the very feature Baird regarded as her strength, the detachment from political commitment. (119)

In the decades following *Waste Heritage*'s initial publication, the obsession in Canada with the "Great Canadian Novel" meant that critics often sought novels that offered national theses, or spoke about Canadian politics, history, and society on a grand scale. *Waste Heritage* might seem to fit this bill, but such national-thesis novels have usually only satisfied Canadian readers when they presented a positive vision of the country, when they presented an optimistic, celebratory, and patriotic view of a growing nation. For such readers, Hugh MacLennan's *Barometer Rising* (1941) and *Two Solitudes* (1945) were more likely to arouse interest than Baird's almost apocalyptic *Waste Heritage*. In recent decades, a different attitude has prevailed: Canadian readers have perhaps grown weary of novels that focus on big issues and appear didactic and heavy-handed. Hugh MacLennan's reputation has been in serious decline while the enigmatic and ambiguous texts of Sinclair Ross, Elizabeth Smart, and Sheila Watson continue to fascinate. To many contemporary readers, *Waste Heritage* might seem too political, too earnest, too focused on the social world. It may not present readers with the kind of Canada that they want to recognize or remember. Such readers might be urged to see this novel as product of a unique and important time, to note the relative balance that Baird usually maintains, to understand its innovative and experimental devices and deceptively complex narrative technique, and to appreciate the psychological complexity of its central characters.

3. A TEXTUAL HISTORY OF *WASTE HERITAGE*

It is possible, through a consideration of various published and unpublished sources, including those housed in archival collections at Columbia and McMaster Universities, to reconstruct a textual history of *Waste Heritage*. This archival material—comprising letters between Baird and her Toronto and New York publishers and other significant people, internal memos, hard-to-find reviews, sales figures, telegrams, and other documents collected in Macmillan and Random House files pertaining to the publication of *Waste Heritage*—provides a detailed and nearly complete record of the processes the novel went through at Macmillan and Random House from submission to publication, and after. It also offers some insight into how and why Baird wrote *Waste Heritage*. The editing of the novel involved collaborative work between Baird and Carl Eayrs, the brother of Macmillan editor Hugh Eayrs. The novel also faced numerous material hurdles that Baird and her agent had to negotiate with Macmillan, which produced the text, and Random House, which purchased U.S. rights for publication under its own imprint.

Little is known about where Baird may first have sent her manuscript, and whether or not it was rejected by other publishers, before Macmillan agreed to take it. The first extant letter on the subject comes from the Macmillan archives, and is dated 26 May 1939. In this letter, Marion Saunders, Baird's literary agent, writes to Hugh Eayrs and spells out the details of the contract between Macmillan and Baird for the novel's publication (Saunders to H. Eayrs, 26 May 1939). On the same day, Saunders wrote to Robert K. Haas of Random House and revealed that Macmillan had agreed to publish *Waste Heritage*, that it was possible that Baird would agree to change her allusive place names back to real ones, and that Hugh Eayrs wanted to do "a little editing and some cutting between the first and second quarter of the book" (Saunders to Haas, 26 May 1939). Hugh Eayrs's decision to publish was partly based on a reader's report provided by his brother, Carl:

> the characters are wonderfully drawn .... The plot is good and the interest is held the whole way through, although it drags at times. It does need to be knit closer together ... by cutting out about 10,000 words .... [I]f this is published before the election it can become a powerful weapon in the hands of Manion and the Conservative party .... The novel is dynamite, because it's so powerful and because it portrays conditions so truthfully. (C. Eayrs to H. Eayrs, first undated letter)

Carl Eayrs ends his report by promising, "I can put more color into the mob scenes .... I've made extensive notes on corrections and where they should be made, but I haven't put them in yet. I shall when I do the re-weaving. I propose to rewrite on separate paper the portions I am changing, so that if you think the original is better you will still have it."

Since Baird's original manuscript does not survive—Macmillan destroyed it with her permission in 1940 (Baird to Elliott, 10 Sep. 1940)—it is impossible to ascertain exactly how much editing of the text was done by Eayrs, how much by Baird, and whether or not Eayrs actually rewrote significant portions of the novel himself. But extant documents do provide substantial details on the editorial process. Saunders wrote to Hugh Eayrs on 2 June 1939 asking him to edit the manuscript, even though Baird had asked for it back in order to "polish it up": "I do not believe Irene Baird can cut her manuscript as well as you could, and I think it will still need editing by you" (Saunders to H. Eayrs, 2 June 1939). Over the summer of 1939, Carl Eayrs set to work on *Waste Heritage*. He did not write to Baird until 24 July 1939 to inform her of his work, although much of the work had already been done at that time (C. Eayrs to Baird, 24 July 1939). Only two days after writing to Baird, he wrote to his brother Hugh, outlining in detail the work he had undertaken:

> My time so far has been taken up in cutting unnecessary words out, or substituting shorter phrases, and in this way, in the first seventeen chapters I have cut out 2500 words without actually reweaving .... I am hoping to cut out some 7,500 words in the next eight chapters by re-weaving—by shortening and combining some of the chapters just prior to the settlement between the government and the sit-downers at Garth [sic] (Victoria). Those chapters are rather wearisome and can be easily cut without hurting the characterization or general scene at all .... I have carefully thought over every sentence I have cut out to make sure that I am not harming the style or continuity or characterization in any way .... In the first seventeen chapters I have just scored through, with a ruled line in green, the words or sentences I have cut out, so that in any case where the author thinks I am wrong she can place a tick over the line to indicate she wants the original left in .... In the eight chapters to be re-woven, I shall type my version out on separate paper, leaving the original as it is, and using the author's phrases as often as possible so that the style will not be patchy at all. (C. Eayrs to H. Eayrs, 26 July 1939)

Clearly, then, the manuscript was rather heavily edited, and substantial sections of the finished product have been "re-woven" by Carl Eayrs. This process apparently involved some significant re-writing on the part of Eayrs, but how much is unclear, and Baird certainly had final authority to approve or reject any changes.

In a letter Baird wrote to Hugh Eayrs on 2 August 1939, she expressed some concern about the editing of her manuscript and the possibility that portions will be changed without her approval. She also revealed that she had been carrying out some editing on her own:

> I hope that his [Carl Eayrs's] recommendations may be in such a form that I can adapt them to the MS. myself as it is hardly possible for even the most skilled of editors to work easily or intimately in another writer's material. I have also been doing some tightening and smoothing on the rough draft so that certain structural improvements may be ready to incorporate in the original. (Baird to H. Eayrs, 2 Aug. 1939)

Hugh Eayrs responded to Baird immediately to reassure her that Carl Eayrs "has worked in such a way that all his suggestions leave your original intact if you wish it but are there for you to incorporate as you desire .... [T]he point is you are now free to accept and reject as you will and you are to return the MS. to me ready for the press" (H. Eayrs to Baird, 7 Aug. 1939). On 23 August, a satisfied Baird wrote back to Hugh Eayrs. She was now in possession of the edited manuscript, and she described in detail her responses to the Macmillan emendations:

> Please tell Mr Carl Eayrs how much I appreciate all he has done .... While I have re-typed much of the script for the sake of clearness, I have been careful to use most of Mr Eayrs recommendations and where I have not used them specifically a very similar phrasing has been substituted. Actually, before the MS. arrived I had cut considerably more than he had done, particularly in the middle chapters. Where he had pruned I had slashed .... As for the last chapter, I should prefer that this remain standing by itself .... [W]e have cut 25 chapters to 23 .... There seems to be no doubt that this subject will be the ace election issue. I hope this may redound to the benefit of all of us. (Baird to H. Eayrs, 23 Aug. 1939)

The process of editing *Waste Heritage*, then, was a collaborative one in which substantial emendations by the editor were given final approval by the author. That Baird was satisfied with this process and happy with the finished product is apparent in her laudatory comments above and complete detachment when Macmillan wrote to her in July 1940 to ask if she wanted the manuscript destroyed. Apparently she saw no point in preserving what she considered an insignificant and inferior original manuscript, and she ignored this query; when Macmillan wrote again in August, she replied without her usual haste: "Certainly, go ahead and destroy it if this is your usual custom with published MSS" (Baird to Elliott, 10 Sep. 1940).

While *Waste Heritage* was being edited by Baird and Carl Eayrs, other important developments affecting the production of the novel had taken place. Several other titles for the novel had been suggested and rejected by one or more of the interested parties: *The Sowing Wind*; *Sidown, Brother! Sidown!*; *Strike!*; *Wrath to Come*; and *Plow These Men Under!* (Saunders to H. Eayrs, 2 June 1939; Saunders to H. Eayrs, 9 June 1939; Baird to H. Eayrs, 11 July 1939). Bennett Cerf, editor at Random House, had agreed to publish the Macmillan edition under his own imprint despite serious reservations about the commercial viability of the novel in the United States:

> I must emphasize three points that are decidedly against the book in the United States. One, the Canadian locale and the certain confusion in geographical detail due to the disguising of the actual names of the cities involved. Two, the strong possibility that the book would be labeled as warmed-over Steinbeck, with a situation so similar to *Of Mice and Men* as to almost cry for unfavorable comment by critics. Three, the fact that books of this nature never have sold here and probably never will, especially when they are about sit-down strikes—a labor device that is now illegal in the United States. (Cerf to H. Eayrs, 30 June 1939)

Cerf continued that he reluctantly agreed to publish the novel in part because "it would be worthwhile nailing an option on the author's next book." Despite the geographical confusion mentioned by Cerf and other readers of the novel, Baird steadfastly refused to change the names back to real ones, although her specific reasons for preferring the allusive ones do not survive (Baird to C. Eayrs, 26 July 1939). Saunders had renegotiated some minor clauses in Baird's contract (Saunders to Haas, 6 July 1939), MGM Studios had requested a copy of the novel for possible movie rights (Saunders to Haas, 6 July 1939), Random House agreed to sell jackets for the novel to Macmillan (Cerf to Rogers, 17 July 1939), Angus and Robertson, an Australian publisher, turned down the book (Saunders to

Haas, 7 Aug. 1939), and The Toronto Star Weekly expressed interest in possible serialization of the novel, which came to naught (Newman to Saunders, 18 July 1939).

As Macmillan was typesetting Waste Heritage in September 1939, World War II began. Apart from the crisis of relevance this provoked for the novel in the eyes of Baird and her publishers, discussed previously, the development had a significant impact on the material production of the novel, and affected the form of the published text. A delayed shipment of paper slowed the production schedule, and as a result Macmillan, in an effort to make up for lost time, elected not to send Baird the proofs for correction: this may explain the large number of errors and inconsistent spellings that made their way into the Macmillan and Random House editions, and have been corrected in this edition (H. Eayrs to Baird, 11 Sep. 1939). Random House had agreed to buy printed sheets of the novel from Macmillan, but on 25 September Macmillan had to write and apologize for a paper shortage: "Due to the outbreak of the war the mills have received orders from customers placing anywhere from one to two years' supply. This has caused a situation where orders are not filled until a period of seven to nine weeks, and perhaps longer in some cases, has elapsed" (Rogers to Miller, 25 Sep. 1939). Despite the pessimistic forecast, Macmillan was able to ship sewn sheets to Random House on 12 October (H. Eayrs to Cerf, 12 Oct. 1939).

On 6 November, Hugh Eayrs wrote to Baird with more bad news. This time, it seemed the novel was going to require censorship owing to the Defense of Canada Regulations, which were law now that the country was at war. Eayrs's letter quoted a passage from the regulations:

No person shall print, circulate or distribute any book, newspaper, periodical, pamphlet, picture, paper, circular, card, letter, writing, print, publication, or document of any kind, containing any material, report or statement, false or otherwise ... intended or likely to prejudice the recruiting, training, discipline, or administration of any of His Majesty's forces. (H. Eayrs to Baird, 6 Nov. 1939)

Accordingly, Eayrs suggested the need to alter several passages of the novel to meet the requirements of the regulations, and subsequently Baird carried out the revisions (Cerf to H. Eayrs, 17 Nov. 1939). The sewn sheets

that had already been sent to Random House would not require emenda-
tion as the Defense of Canada Regulations had no legal power south of the
border, and they were therefore published in the original form Baird had
intended. As a result, the Random House edition became distinct from the
Macmillan, and was published a few weeks sooner. The Macmillan edition, which censored three significant passages and caught a few of the
typos that appear in the Random House edition, became the second published edition of the novel, although Macmillan had handled the project
from start to finish.

In 1946, a French translation of the novel by René Ouvrieu was published in France by Maréchal under the title *Héritage Gaspillé*. Copies of this
edition are almost impossible to obtain today. In 1951, Baird wrote to
Macmillan suggesting that they issue her novel in an affordable reprint
(Baird to Gray, 24 Dec. 1951). Macmillan wrote back and said it would
consider her request, but nothing came of it (Gray to Baird, 28 Dec. 1951).
Two decades later, in April 1973, Baird wrote again to Macmillan. This
time interest in Canadian literature was peaking and she revealed that she
had recently met the "distinguished Canadian poet," Dorothy Livesay,
who had reportedly complained to her that, while she teaches *Waste
Heritage* in university classes, it is very difficult to obtain. Baird enclosed a
summary of the excellent reviews the novel received upon its 1939 publication, and suggested that the novel be reissued (Baird to Clark, 16 Apr.
1973). Donald Sutherland wrote back promising to "undertake some market research, particularly in the college marketing area" (Sutherland to
Baird, 19 Apr. 1973). A flurry of internal memos followed at Macmillan,
and reader's reports recommended republication, although one of them,
by Michiel Horn of York University, suggested that the one-armed driver
of the novel was implausible (Horn to Derry, 24 July 1973). In the meantime, McClelland & Stewart had written to Macmillan indicating that they
wanted to publish *Waste Heritage* in the New Canadian Library, and offered
a 6% royalty on the first 10,000 copies, and 8% thereafter (McKnight to
Pomer, 21 June 1973). Macmillan replied that "This offer doesn't appear to
us to be attractive enough to warrant our releasing the rights, and we have
decided to re-issue *Waste Heritage* ourselves" (Pomer to McKnight, 28 June
1973). Macmillan carefully calculated the costs of a reprint, and in August

1973, Finn Bay wrote to Baird: "The costs of reprinting a paperback edition are unfortunately higher than we had anticipated and the only way possible, with an acceptable list price in mind, would appear to be to photograph the existing copy" (Bay to Baird, 15 Aug. 1973). On 18 August 1973, Baird wrote back, indicating that she had sent two copies of the novel to them to dismantle and photograph. She also enclosed a rewritten version of chapter four in which not Harry, but his son Russ who is not an amputee, drives the escape truck. She also expressed her hope that the new edition would be published with a critical introduction (Baird to Bay, 18 Aug. 1973). Finn Bay wrote back a letter on 23 August that indicated just how desperate Macmillan was to save as much money as possible on the reprint: the one-armed driver section will stand, as it will be too expensive to change the text in any way, and an introduction would add unacceptable costs to the edition (Bay to Baird, 23 Aug. 1973).

Baird became dissatisfied with the work Macmillan was doing on her novel, probably because she now knew that McClelland & Stewart was interested, and a New Canadian Library edition at least offered a critical afterword. Less than a month later, on 23 September, Baird wrote a terse note to Macmillan requesting a copy of the 1939 contract (Baird to Bay, 23 Sep. 1973). Baird was now rethinking her decision to reissue the novel with Macmillan, as an internal memo from Sutherland to Ramsay Derry dated 10 October reveals:

> This author is curiously tricky to deal with. You will know that M&S have claimed to us that she hadn't heard from us for months about this book. This is of course false—she has had extensive correspondence with us and has been given [the] estimated finished book date .... I had a telephone call from a Vancouver lawyer representing her asking questions about the 1939 contract, asking where we are with the book, and indicating that two other publishers have been making offers .... I have told him that ... we would be both angry and uncooperative about any withdrawal at this stage. (Sutherland to Derry, 10 Oct. 1973)

On 10 October, Baird wrote to Macmillan and told them what they already knew: she had hired a lawyer as no new contract had been drawn up (Baird to Bay, 10 Oct. 1973). A worried Sutherland replied the next day, stating that "[w]e have proceeded with production of *Waste Heritage*, as a quality paperback, without waiting for a contract, because we have been anxious to get the book into the hands of English faculties and students .... [I]t would be useful to know if you are anxious to have an advance against royalty" (Sutherland to Baird, 11 Oct. 1973). A contract was drawn up on 15 October. On 22 October Baird sent a letter deriding the press for not drawing up the contract earlier and she demanded the return of the books she had given them to dismantle and photograph (Baird to Sutherland, 22 Oct. 1973). Over the next months irritated letters from Baird met ingratiating ones from Macmillan as the parties discussed how the books had been destroyed in the photographic process (Baird to Bay, 29 Oct. 1973), her $500 advance (Baird to Sutherland, 30 Oct. 1973), her dissatisfaction with the cover (Baird to Sutherland, 11 Feb. 1974), and the slow process of books reaching bookstores on the west coast (Baird to Sutherland, 19 Feb. 1974). Although early sales figure for the Laurentian Library edition were promising—Bay wrote to Baird on 25 July 1974 with an estimate of 2000 copies sold—the book went out of print a second time soon after, and *Waste Heritage* was unavailable for over thirty years (Bay to Baird, 25 July 1973).

This current edition of *Waste Heritage* is the inaugural title in University of Ottawa Press's *Canadian Literature Collection / La collection de la littérature canadienne*. It uses the 1939, uncensored, New York Random House edition as copy text, and provides explanatory notes for problematic terms and references, and textual notes that detail alternate readings, corrections, and editorial emendations. Baird's novel reappears at a time when the development of modern Canadian writing is being re-evaluated by critics, and when early twentieth-century literary forms are being vigorously reconsidered both in Canadian and other literary traditions. The multi-generic form of *Waste Heritage* invites its consideration within the ever-expanding debates about the assumptions and boundaries of various realisms and modernisms. Recent scholarship by critics such as James Doyle, Ian McKay, Cary Nelson, Barbara Foley, and Paula Rabinowitz has helped to reinvigorate interest in a rich and still scandalously underexamined leftist literary heritage in Canada and beyond. The class and labour politics that inform this heritage are rapidly evolving in tandem with twenty-first century national and global realities. In this context, *Waste Heritage* remains an important social document. It is a text that is uncommonly inviting to critics, students, and general readers interested in some of the most relevant and lively literary, social, and political debates of the modern and contemporary periods. *Waste Heritage* focuses attention on an historical period and social class that are under-represented in North American fiction. Its scrupulous treatment of Depression-era socio-historical realities, and the narrative sophistication and self-reflexivity with which it constructs memorable characters and events, demand a rigorous re-evaluation of its significance.

WORKS CITED

The following abbreviations for archival sources are used in the citations below:

MFMU—Macmillan Company of Canada Fonds, The William Ready Division of Archives and Research Collections, McMaster University, Hamilton, Ontario

RHCU—Random House Records, Bennett Cerf Papers, Rare Book and Manuscript Library, Columbia University, New York.

"The Author." Unpublished biographical note. MFMU, Box 65, folder labelled "Waste Heritage."

Baird, Irene. "Article Mobile." North/Nord 9.6 (1962): 44–45.

———. "Blow Spirit." North/Nord 13.1 (1966): 18–19.

———. *The Climate of Power.* Toronto: Macmillan, 1971.

———. "A Delicate Balance." North/Nord 20.3 (1973): 13–15.

———. "Diary of a Working Journey." North/Nord 12.1 (1965): 15–24.

———. "Eskimo Church on Christmas Morning." North/Nord 17.6 (1970): 14–15.

———. "The Eskimos Look Over Us." Northern Affairs Bulletin 6.5 (1959): 31–34.

———. "Ex-Elijah." North/Nord 16.1 (1969): 20–21.

———. "Exhibit in Paris: Mask 1: Summertime and Mask 2: Wintertime" North/Nord 16.6 (1969): 25–28.

———. *He Rides the Sky.* Toronto: Macmillan, 1941.

———. "I Don't Read You Charlie: A Twisted Tale." North/Nord 19.2 (1972): 10–11.

——. John. Philadelphia: Lippincott, 1937.

——. "Keep Your Own Things." North/Nord 11.1 (1964): 10–11.

——. "Land." North/Nord 11.6 (1964): 16–17.

——. "A Learning Situation." North/Nord 14.6 (1967): 10–16.

——. "*Les Africains* Visit the Eskimos." North/Nord 8.4 (1961): 20–24.

——. Letter to Finn Bay. 18 Aug. 1973. MFMU, Box 65, folder labelled "Waste Heritage."

——. Letter to Finn Bay. 23 Sep. 1973. MFMU, Box 65, folder labelled "Waste Heritage."

——. Letter to Finn Bay. 10 Oct. 1973. MFMU, Box 65, folder labelled "Waste Heritage."

——. Letter to Finn Bay. 29 Oct. 1973. MFMU, Box 65, folder labelled "Waste Heritage."

——. Letter to Bennett Cerf. 11 July 1939. RHCU, Box 65, folder labelled "Irene Baird."

——. Letter to Bennett Cerf. 26 July 1939. RHCU, Box 65, folder labelled "Irene Baird."

——. Letter to Bennett Cerf. 11 Sep. 1939. RHCU, Box 65, folder labelled "Irene Baird."

——. Letter to Bennett Cerf. 5 Oct. 1939. RHCU, Box 65, folder labelled "Irene Baird."

——. Letter to Bennett Cerf. 24 Oct. 1939. RHCU, Box 65, folder labelled "Irene Baird."

——. Letter to Bennett Cerf. 9 Dec. 1939. RHCU, Box 65, folder labelled "Irene Baird."

——. Letter to Nora Clark. 16 Apr. 1973. MFMU, Box 65, folder labelled "Waste Heritage."

——. Letter to Carl Eayrs. 26 July 1939. MFMU, Box 65, folder labelled "Waste Heritage."

——. Letter to Hugh Eayrs. 11 July 1939. MFMU, Box 65, folder labelled "Waste Heritage."

——. Letter to Hugh Eayrs. 2 Aug. 1939. MFMU, Box 65, folder labelled "Waste Heritage."

——. Letter to Hugh Eayrs. 23 Aug. 1939. MFMU, Box 65, folder labelled "Waste Heritage."

——. Letter to Hugh Eayrs. 5 Sep. 1939. MFMU, Box 65, folder labelled "Waste Heritage."

——. Letter to Hugh Eayrs. 28 Oct. 1939. MFMU, Box 65, folder labelled "Waste Heritage."

——. Letter to Hugh Eayrs. 5 Nov. 1939. MFMU, Box 65, folder labelled "Waste Heritage."

———. Letter to Ellen Elliott. 10 Sep. 1939. MFMU, Box 65, folder labelled "Waste Heritage."

———. Letter to Ellen Elliott. 6 Nov. 1939. MFMU, Box 65, folder labelled "Waste Heritage."

———. Letter to Ellen Elliott. 10 Sep. 1940. MFMU, Box 65, folder labelled "Waste Heritage."

———. Letter to J.M. Gray. 24 Dec. 1951. MFMU, Box 65, folder labelled "Waste Heritage."

———. Letter to Donald Sutherland. 22 Oct. 1973. MFMU, Box 65, folder labelled "Waste Heritage."

———. Letter to Donald Sutherland. 30 Oct. 1973. MFMU, Box 65, folder labelled "Waste Heritage."

———. Letter to Donald Sutherland. 11 Feb. 1974. MFMU, Box 65, folder labelled "Waste Heritage."

———. Letter to Donald Sutherland. 19 Feb. 1974. MFMU, Box 65, folder labelled "Waste Heritage."

———. Letter to Donald Sutherland. 20 Mar. 1974. MFMU, Box 65, folder labelled "Waste Heritage."

———. "The Lonely Shore." *North/Nord* 11.1 (1963): 34–35.

———. "Mary No-More." *North/Nord* 18.6 (1971): 17.

———. "Midwinter Flight." *North/Nord* 9.4 (1962): 27.

———. "No-destination Jonah." *North/Nord* 15.6 (1968): 22–23.

———. *The North American Tradition.* Toronto: Macmillan, 1941.

———. "Presences." *North/Nord* 10.6 (1963): 26–27.

———. "Sidown, Brothers, Sidown." *Laurentian University Review* 9 (1976): 81–86.

———. *Waste Heritage.* Toronto: Macmillan, 1939.

———. *Waste Heritage.* 1939. Laurentian Library. Toronto: Macmillan, 1973.

———. *Waste Heritage.* New York: Random House, 1939.

———. "Who Will Be I." *North/Nord* 13.5 (1966): 16–17.

———. "Will We Fail When Youth Says, 'What Now?'" *Saturday Night* 7 August 1943: 6–7.

———. "Women and Statesmanship." *Saturday Night* 58 (2 Jan. 1943): 16.

———. "You Only Take the First Trip Once." *North/Nord* 13.6 (1966): 26–30.

Bay, Finn. Letter to Irene Baird. 25 July 1973. MFMU, Box 65, folder labelled "Waste Heritage."

———. Letter to Irene Baird. 15 Aug. 1973. MFMU, Box 65, folder labelled "Waste Heritage."

———. Letter to Irene Baird. 23 Aug. 1973. MFMU, Box 65, folder labelled "Waste Heritage."

Brookhouser, Frank. "'Steinbeck' in Canada." Rev. of *Waste Heritage*, by Irene Baird. [Philadelphia] *Inquirer* [Public Ledger] 27 Dec. 1939. 10.

Cabot, Currie. "A Man to Know." Rev. of *John*, by Irene Baird. *Saturday Review of Literature* 9 Dec. 1937: 11.

Callaghan, Morley. *They Shall Inherit the Earth*. 1935. New Canadian Library. Toronto: McClelland & Stewart, 1969.

Cerf, Bennett. Letter to Irene Baird. 9 Oct. 1939. RHCU, Box 65, folder labelled "Irene Baird."

———. Letter to Irene Baird. 27 Dec. 1939. RHCU, Box 65, folder labelled "Irene Baird."

———. Letter to Hugh Eayrs. 30 June 1939. MFMU, Box 65, folder labelled "Waste Heritage."

———. Letter to Hugh Eayrs. 17 Nov. 1939. MFMU, Box 65, folder labelled "Waste Heritage."

———. Letter to G.E. Rogers 17 July 1939. MFMU, Box 65, folder labelled "Waste Heritage."

Cole, W.H. "The Railroad in Canadian Literature." *Canadian Literature* 77 (1978): 124–130.

Cox, Carolyn. "Novelist Goes to the Films." *Saturday Night* 9 Jan. 1943: 2.

Deacon, W.A. Letter to Irene Baird. 9 Dec. 1939. Private collection of June Brander-Smith.

Defense of Canada Regulations. Ottawa: Patenaude, 1939.

Doyle, James. *Progressive Heritage: The Evolution of a Politically Radical Literary Tradition in Canada*. Waterloo: Wilfrid Laurier UP, 2002.

Eayrs, Carl. Letter to Irene Baird. 24 July 1939. MFMU, Box 65, folder labelled "Waste Heritage."

———. Letter to Hugh Eayrs. First undated letter from C. Eayrs to H. Eayrs. MFMU, Box 65, folder labelled "Waste Heritage."

———. Letter to Hugh Eayrs. Second undated letter from C. Eayrs to H. Eayrs. MFMU, Box 65, folder labelled "Waste Heritage."

———. Letter to Hugh Eayrs. 26 July 1939. MFMU, Box 65, folder labelled "Waste Heritage."

Eayrs, Hugh. Letter to Irene Baird. 7 Aug. 1939. MFMU, Box 65, folder labelled "Waste Heritage."

———. Letter to Irene Baird. 2 Sep. 1939. MFMU, Box 65, folder labelled "Waste Heritage."

———. Letter to Irene Baird. 11 Sep. 1939. MFMU, Box 65, folder labelled "Waste Heritage."

———. Letter to Irene Baird. 6 Nov. 1939. MFMU, Box 65, folder labelled "Waste Heritage."

———. Letter to Irene Baird. 13 May 1942. MFMU, Box 65, folder labelled "Waste Heritage."

———. Letter to Bennett Cerf. 2 Sep. 1939. RHCU, Box 65, folder labelled "Irene Baird."

———. Letter to Bennett Cerf. 12 Oct. 1939. RHCU, Box 65, folder labelled "Irene Baird."

"First Novel Has Big Appeal." Rev. of John, by Irene Baird. Sunday Sun [Sydney, Australia] 10 Apr. 1938. n. pag.

French, William. "The Mood of Protest—In C Minor." The Globe & Mail 2 Mar. 1974: 34.

Garner, Hugh. Cabbagetown. 1950. Toronto: McGraw-Hill, 1968.

Gerson, Carole. "Waste Heritage." The Oxford Companion to Canadian History. Ed. Gerald Hallowell. Don Mills, ON: Oxford UP, 2004. 652.

Godfrey, Eleanor. Rev. of He Rides the Sky, by Irene Baird. The Canadian Forum 20 (Mar. 1941): 390.

Gray, J.M. Letter to Irene Baird. 28 Dec. 1951. MFMU, Box 65, folder labelled "Waste Heritage."

Hopkins, Anthony. "Thematic Structure and Vision in Waste Heritage." Studies in Canadian Literature 11 (1986): 77–85.

Horn, Michiel. Letter to Ramsay Derry. 24 July 1973. MFMU, Box 65, folder labelled "Waste Heritage."

———. "Transient Men in the Depression." Canadian Forum Oct. 1974: 36–38.

Hutchison, Bruce. "Loose Ends." Rev. of Waste Heritage, by Irene Baird. Victoria Daily Times 30 Dec. 1939: 4.

Hyman, Roger Leslie. "Wasted Heritage and Waste Heritage: The Critical Disregard of an Important Canadian Novel." Journal of Canadian Studies 17.4 (1982): 74–87.

Irr, Caren. "Queer Borders: Figures from the 1930s for U.S.–Canadian Relations." American Quarterly 49 (1997): 504–530.

Keefer, Claire. "One New Novel Picked From Many." Rev. of John, by Irene Baird, Ottawa Journal 4 Dec. 1937. n. pag.

Lewis, Hunter. "Irene Baird Adds to Her Literary Stature With Novel About Vancouver Strikers." Rev. of Waste Heritage, by Irene Baird. The Vancouver. [n.d.]: 4.

MacLennan, Hugh. Barometer Rising. 1941. New Canadian Library. Toronto: McClelland & Stewart, 1991.

———. Two Solitudes. 1945. New Press Canadian Classics. Toronto: Stoddart, 1993.

Martyn, Howe. "The Literary Scene in Canada." Rev. of Waste Heritage, by Irene Baird. [New York] Times 7 January 1940, n. pag.

Mason, Jody. "State Censorship and Irene Baird's *Waste Heritage*." *Canadian Literature* 191 (2006): 192–195.

Mathews, Robin. "*Waste Heritage*: The Effect of Class on Literary Structure." *Studies in Canadian Literature* 6 (1981): 65–81.

McKay, Ian. *Rebels, Reds, Radicals: Rethinking Canada's Left History.* Toronto: Between the Lines, 2005.

McKnight, Linda. Letter to Bella Pomer. 21 June 1973. MFMU, Box 65, folder labelled "Waste Heritage."

Muggeridge, John. "Corridors of Power." Rev. of *Climate of Power*, by Irene Baird. *Saturday Night* 86 (May 1971): 29.

Newman, A.H. Letter to Marion Saunders, 18 July 1939. MFMU, Box 65, folder labelled "Waste Heritage."

"Novel of Depression Years Reissued." *Quill and Quire* June 1974: 6.

Pacey, Desmond. "Fiction 1920–1940." *Literary History of Canada: Canadian Literature in English.* Vol. 2. Ed. Carl F. Klinck. Toronto: U of Toronto P, 1965. 658–693.

Philips. Donna, ed. *Voices of Discord: Canadian Short Stories of the 1930s.* Toronto: New Hogtown, 1979.

Phillips, Paul A. *No Power Greater: A Century of Labour in British Columbia.* Vancouver: BC Federation of Labour, 1967.

Pomer, Bella. Letter to Linda McKnight. 28 June 1973. MFMU, Box 65, folder labelled "Waste Heritage."

Rimstead, Roxanne. "Mediated Lives: Oral Histories and Cultural Memory." *Essays on Canadian Writing* 60 (Winter 1996): 139–165.

Rogers, G.E. Letter to Lewis Miller. 25 Sep. 1939. RHCU, Box 65, folder labelled "Irene Baird."

Ross, Sinclair. *As for Me and My House.* 1941. New Canadian Library. Toronto: McClelland & Stewart, 1989.

Saunders, Marion. Letter to Bennett Cerf. 13 Sep. 1939. RHCU, Box 65, folder labelled "Irene Baird."

———. Letter to Hugh Eayrs. 26 May 1939. MFMU, Box 65, folder labelled "Waste Heritage."

———. Letter to Hugh Eayrs. 2 June 1939. MFMU, Box 65, folder labelled "Waste Heritage."

———. Letter to Hugh Eayrs. 9 June 1939. MFMU, Box 65, folder labelled "Waste Heritage."

———. Letter to Robert K. Haas. 26 May 1939. RHCU, Box 65, folder labelled "Irene Baird."

———. Letter to Robert K. Haas. 6 July 1939. RHCU, Box 65, folder labelled "Irene Baird."

————. Letter to Robert K. Haas. 7 Aug. 1939. RHCU, Box 65, folder labelled "Irene Baird."

Sime, J.G. *Our Little Life: A Novel of To-Day.* 1921. Early Canadian Woman Writers Series. Ottawa: Tecumseh, 1994.

Spence, Norah. Letter to Colin Hill. 1 Nov. 2005. Author's personal collection.

Stanzel, Franz K. *A Theory of Narrative.* Trans. Charlotte Goedsche. Cambridge: Cambridge UP, 1984.

Strauss, Harold. "'Waste Heritage' and Other New Works of Fiction: Irene Baird's Story of Industrial Conflict in Canada—Peter Mendelssohn's Novel of Nazi Germany." Rev. of *Waste Heritage* by Irene Baird. *New York Times Book Review* 10 Dec. 1939: 7.

"Strong Canadian Novel." Rev. of *Waste Heritage* by Irene Baird. *Globe & Mail* 25 Nov. 1939. n. pag.

Sutherland, Donald. Letter to Irene Baird. 19 Apr. 1973. MFMU, Box 65, folder labelled "Waste Heritage."

————. Letter to Irene Baird. 11 Oct. 1973. MFMU, Box 65, folder labelled "Waste Heritage."

————. Letter to Ramsay Derry. 10 Oct. 1973. MFMU, Box 65, folder labelled "Waste Heritage."

Twigg, Alan. "Irene Baird." *BC Bookworld.* 1 Feb. 2006. www.abcbookworld.com.

Wallace, Margaret. "Labour on the March." Rev. of *Waste Heritage* by Irene Baird. *Saturday Review of Literature* [New York] 21.8 (16 Dec. 1939): 7.

West, Gail. Letter to Colin Hill. 1 Mar. 2006. Author's personal collection.

Willmott, Glenn. *Unreal Country: Modernity in the Canadian Novel in English.* Montreal: McGill-Queen's UP, 2002.

Waste Heritage
by IRENE BAIRD

TO MATT & TO EDDY

AND TO THE

OTHER HUNDRED THOUSAND

PART I

·

Aschelon

CHAPTER ONE

The freight steamed clanging into the yards. The engine bell swung backwards and forwards, the heavy tolling kept up even after the long line of cars had clashed to a shuddering standstill. The sun glared down onto the burnished maze of storage tracks, and off in the distance the grain elevators and the awkward span of the old bridge stood out against a hard blue sky. Closer in, on the far side of the tracks, the pier roofs, splashed white with dried gull droppings, cut between the smokestacks and masts of the waterfront. From uptown came the screeching of a fire truck. It sounded hysterical, as though it had picked up the feel of what was going on around it.

Matt Striker rolled the door of the box car open a crack, waited for his eyes to grow used to the strong light, then slid the door wider and dropped down onto the hot, sharp flints of the roadbed. For an instant his narrowed eyes combed the long lines of standing cars for yard police, then he reached back for his pack, slung it up onto his shoulder and moved quickly up the tracks towards town. He walked the length of the empty nine-thirty Trans-Canada and when he came out from the shelter of the last cars he headed up towards the Capper Street grade crossing. Two things were noticeable about the way he moved; he moved with experience yet like a stranger to the Aschelon yards. Any city bum could have told him the things he did wrong and given him a shorter route into town. He thought it funny that he did not see any bums around. He did not see anyone except the crew of his own train. Just the glare on the tracks, the high rear walls of waterfront buildings, the tiered uptown skyline.

His skin and his wiry blond hair were dull with track dirt and his black shirt and jeans were grey with blown grit. The frayed cuffs of his jeans bellied down over his dusty shoes but higher up they fitted tight across his narrow hips and neat bottom. He walked back down on his heels with his pack slung over his shoulder and his hands hooked into the two front pockets of his jeans. He moved mechanically as though he had got so used to moving around that he could go on and do it in his sleep. His face wore a curiously dead look, giving the impression that he was either doped or not properly awake. His eyes were grey and narrowed by sun and between them a crude scar dug deep into his freckled nose bridge, extending towards the left eye. Beneath the air of superficial immobility there was wary, half-animal watchfulness.

On the first street corner he stopped and fished up a crumpled scrap of paper from the back pocket of his jeans, spreading it open so that the pencilled words came clear. Then he glanced up at the street name lettered in black on a yellow sign half-way up the light standard. He frowned at the sign, looked down at the paper again, then shoved it back in his jeans and moved on. He did the same on the next corner and the next. He did not seem to know the names of any of the streets except the one written on the paper.

Half-way up Capper Street there was a small lunchroom with the door standing open, called Harry's Place. That is, the inner door was open. The screen door was closed and had holes in it, where the wire had rusted and gone into little jagged tears. Harry's name was lettered in white across the window. A grease-marked card with Saturday supper specials, a cup of synthetic coffee and a cut of the same kind of pie, shared window space with a handful of dusty paper flowers and a well diluted bottle of ketchup. Harry, himself, was leaning out among them swatting bluebottles with a rolled newspaper. A sprinkling of dried-up corpses lay among the flowers.

When Matt saw Harry there he stopped and went inside and pulled out the piece of paper. He asked, "Can you tell me how I get to 1111 East Third?" He pushed the paper across the counter.

Harry did not look at the paper at first, he stared at Matt. Matt never forgot that first look Harry gave him, measuring him, sizing him up. He felt there was something between himself and Harry right from that first day. Harry's face was fleshy and calm. Small bright eyes peered out from the rolling flesh and sweat glistened among his broken features and along the line of his shiny black hair. When Harry fried hamburger, all the grease seemed to rise to his head. He looked around fifty and the build that would feel the heat a lot. His right arm was off about three inches below the shoulder. A certain quickness of movement not usually associated with so heavy a man, as well as the thickened shoulders and folded nose, showed where he had once been good in the ring (locally) but that since his accident he had not been able to keep the weight away.

Matt repeated the address. "Yeah," Harry said, ruminating, "I heard you good the first time." He pulled a toothpick out of the jug on the counter, pushed it in one corner of his mouth. His jaws began to grind up and down. He eyed Matt steadily. Then, "Better wait," he remarked at last, "better wait till things quiet down around there. You don't want to go bustin' into a hot spot like that. They got enough boys like you there awready and plenty of 'em has their heads broke."

Matt's body stiffened. "What d'ya mean? What's all the mystery?"

"You mean you ain't heard?" Harry's voice was incredulous.

"Heard what? I just got in town fifteen minutes ago."

"You didn't hear yet about the big sit-down in the Dominion Building an' the public library being broke up?"

Matt's eyes lost their cold deadpan look. He dropped his pack and swung up onto a counter stool. "What d'ya mean, 'broke up'?"

Harry said, "I mean the single unemployed boys staged a sit-down in them two places and sat there for nineteen days an' nights because they couldn't think of no other way to force the authorities to provide 'em with a program of work an' wages, an' this morning early the cops chase 'em out with tear gas an' riot sticks. Don't tell me you didn't hear nothing about all that yet?"

Matt's face grew taut with interest. He leaned forward. "I never had the chance to hear anything yet, I tell you I just got in town."

Harry gave a low rumbling laugh. He said, "You didn't come riding the cushions, I seen too many not to know the signs." He turned and spat out the pick. His little eyes surveyed Matt shrewdly. "Are you one of them transients the authorities is raisin' such a stink about?"

Matt nodded. "Sure, I'm a transient," he said quietly, "I was born back in the province of Saskatchewan but that province don't own me no more. Six years now I bummed around trying to rustle up some kind of a steady job. I bummed around so long even the country don't own me no more."

Harry's voice broke in softly, "You an' who else?"

Matt smiled coldly. "Sure ... me an' who else? A hundred thousand other boys. Every place we go the authorities as good as tell us, 'You boys get th' hell out of here, see? There's no work an' no prospect of any. Now you boys get the hell out before we citizens has to call out the police to protect ourselves.'"

Harry's heavy head swung up and down, his chins concertinaed into one another. His voice grew satirical. "Tell me somethin' new, somethin' I ain't been listenin' to for the past eight years, then maybe you'd stand a chance of makin' a hit with me." He scratched his stump and his face grew serious. "Seems like the country's waitin' for Hitler to give you boys a job so you can all be heroes overnight."

"Sure, an' get blown to hell an' damnation in the morning! That's one job I don't take. If we was a bunch of beef cattle at least we'd get gov'ment grading."

"Pretty bitter, ain't you?"

"No. I just see things the way they are, that's all."

Harry considered Matt in silence. He studied the drawn, dirt-grained features, the powerful shoulders, the hard mouth, the narrow eyes. He shook his head. "Jesus," he muttered, "you can't be more than eighteen ... nineteen?"

Matt laughed. He showed strong even teeth stained and badly dis-coloured. He said, "Don't get me wrong, I was born in nineteen sixteen, August twenty-first. I'm not so young."

"Touchy, huh?" Harry said. He began to grind on a fresh toothpick. "Stick out my fingers and you snap like a turtle."

Matt passed his hand across his face. "I'm tired, I guess. I didn't sleep much last night."

"Where'd you pick up a car?"

"At Bisbee, around 3 a.m. I had one helluva time picking up a through train. I thought all the time I'd get waked up an' thrown off at some one-horse dump."

Harry turned and reached for a thick mug, twisted the spiggot on the urn and flushed a cup of coffee. He had a neat trick of doing a half-dozen things at once with his left hand. He pushed the cup over. "Here," he said,

"I guess the dining car rates was kind of high on the train you come on."

Matt stared uncertainly at the steam rising from the mug, then he looked at Harry. "I got no money to pay for this."

Harry scratched his stump. "Sure, I know that."

"O.K., then, thanks." Matt doused milk into the cup, dropped in three lumps of sugar, then stirred it quickly and drank, steadying the spoon between his fingers.

Harry watched him in silence, then pushed over a cut of apple pie. "Why did you say that just now about havin' no money? You could just as easy have drank the coffee an' told me afterwards."

Matt smiled faintly, beginning to feel the effects of the hot coffee. "I guess you had that trick played on you plenty times," he said. "Bums eatin' up a fifteen cent meal then sittin' back an' telling you to go ahead an' call the cops."

Harry grinned and went at his stump again. He said dryly, "Go ahead, eat the pie. I wouldn't have offered it to you if I seen you was an ordinary bum."

Matt finished the meal and slung up his pack. More than ever he felt there was this thing between himself and Harry. "Thanks, Harry," he said. "My name's Striker, Matt Striker, in case we ever meet again. I'll go on up to headquarters anyway. I wish to God they didn't bust that sit-down before I got here though. Maybe now it's too late to do me any good."

Harry walked with him to the door. He stood leaning his stump against the jamb, squinting up-street into the sun. The rumbling laugh came again. "You won't think that once you get further uptown. Ever since daylight this town has been buzzin' like a hive of goddammed bees. Everyone playin' cops an' robbers."

Matt paused, adjusting his pack. "How's the public feel about it?"

"From what come over the radio this morning I think the public is still in sympathy with the boys, whatever they bust up when they was evicted."

Matt's face sharpened. "Bust up?"

Harry jerked his big head sideways and spat out a mouthful of chewed splinters. He took a moment to answer and when he spoke he spoke carefully. "I guess the gas made the boys kinda mad. When they was drove out they ran amok an' smashed up a lot of store fronts before anyone could stop them." He leant closer, his face grew wise, the little puckered eyes snapped. "You heard how a swan can bust a guy's arm?"

"Sure, anyone knows that."

"Maybe you didn't hear of another kind of bird can bust a plate glass window." He touched Matt's arm, grinned and stood away.

Matt stared at him a moment, then his lower lip rose in disgust. "Sure, I get you," he said. He spat. As he began to move away, Harry called after him, "Mind you, I'm not sayin' ..."

Matt grinned back over his shoulder. "I know it, Harry, I'm not sayin' you said it either. Thanks again for the handout. Be seein' you! Oh, say, where is that street, by the way?"

"The street? Oh, sure! Bear straight on till you come to Alcazar. You won't have no trouble pickin' out Alcazar today, around ten thousand other guys has picked it out ahead of you. Cross over Alcazar and keep right on for four blocks then turn into Snider and East Third is right off Snider, around that corner where the big drugstore is. Think you got all that?"

Harry went over it once more and Matt repeated it and Harry laughed and said if he forgot it, Christ, there'd be plenty cops to tell him!

"Don't worry," Matt said, "I won't forget."

Harry laughed again. "That's what I'm afraid of," he said, "drop by again some time."

Matt moved off smartly. The dead look had passed right out of his face. The animal air was marked now, quick, and wary and defensive. He went up wholesale row, past the narrow store fronts crowded in close together, the second-hand stores, the cut-rate pants pressers, the barber shops and poolrooms and cheap, time-pay jewellers and the shoddy office blocks filled with advertising dentists and palmists and beauty parlors. Every two or three doors down was a place to eat. Everywhere knots of people stood talking. They stood about on the street corners and hung around the radios in any place that was open for business. All the way uptown Matt caught snatches of the busy raucous voice of a news announcer. He picked up a word here and there. He did not stop to pick up connected sentences. He let himself be caught by the drift of the crowd that milled up Alcazar, centering round the five blocks where the big department stores were, and the heaviest damage had been done.

A cordon of police was drawn up in front of the smashed-in store fronts keeping the crowds back. Here and there a moronic souvenir hunter dived for a scrap of broken glass or any relic that had been missed by the early morning clean-up job. The people milled solid for five blocks. There was a line of seven street cars where the service had got dislocated. They snailed along striking their gongs. The shrill of the gongs, the honking of horns and the jamming-in of gears kept up all the time as the traffic crawled along in first. It was one of those freak turn-outs. A woman leant from a car yelling and waving a red flag. No one paid any attention to her. That was the kind of thing that was in the air all over town. Hysteria. Mob hysteria. All on account of a few hundred jobless evicted from a three-weeks-old sit-down.

The kind of things people did that day were the kind they do in a market panic or just after war has been declared. Strangers talked to one another with the same uneasy intimacy. It seemed like that whole town had been expecting trouble now for a long time, and it was glad to have it break on a fine Sunday, so everyone could get something out of it. The police were handling two forces at once, the traffic that choked the downtown streets, and the exasperated state of public opinion. Suburban and uptown beats were stripped right down, every man available was concentrated in downtown areas.

Matt shoved through the crowds on Alcazar to take a look at the mess. He said to a man standing alongside of him, "Where'd they get all the cops? I never knew there was that many cops in the world."

The man turned excitedly, "I heard a rumour they're rushing them into town from all over, preparing for another sit-down. What do they expect, that's what I want to know. What do they expect?"

Matt shrugged, "Looks like they expected a riot!"

The man turned and looked at him then. He was a little skinny chap in a neat dark suit and eyeglasses and he seemed like some kind of a low-priced, white-collar man, only now his collar was limp with the heat. The strong light glinted on his lenses. He flashed them over Matt, over his black shirt and jeans and the roll slung on his shoulder by a piece of coarse twine. He asked uneasily, "Are you one of the boys ... I mean one of the boys that were evicted from the sit-down?"

Matt eyed him without any emotion at all. "I just got in town a half hour ago," he said, and began to move away.

The man called after him, "Are you going to join up with the rest of the boys?"

"Sure, why not? I got nothing to lose."

"I suppose that's the way most of them feel." The man's face grew troubled. He turned and hooked his arm through that of a stout woman beside him. "Well," he said, trying to sound easy, "I hope you have luck." The woman turned her head once and stared back at Matt, then said something to the man and the man turned too. They acted queerly, as though they had an uneasy conscience.

Matt stopped sight-seeing after that, and half-way down Alcazar he took a short cut and turned into an alley that cut through the end of the sixteen hundred block and up into Snider, that way. A man told him that if he wanted to get to Snider quickly there was no sense in trailing the whole length of Alcazar. Matt said, "o.k., I'm glad you told me," because details of Harry's directions had been crowded out of his mind.

He turned into the alley. It was a long narrow brick-bound canyon, topped by a maze of high tension wires. At the far end a big man in plain clothes with a grey soft hat was cracking down on something that looked like a bundle of waste with a head on it. Matt heard the club crack down and he saw the other man slump to his knees with his hands up, protecting his face. The club cracked again. The man slid down heavily and lay still.

Matt headed in, cursing in his throat. His feet slap-slapped on the concrete as he ran. He took a wild, running sock at the plain-clothes man and he felt the club side-swipe. He shouted, choking, "*Lay off, you dirty bastard, you!*"

The man shouted back, "*Mind your own business or I'll knock your goddammed head off!*"

Matt's eyes went pale with fury, besides, he could not see or hear anything properly now. He took a vicious poke at the man's broad face, then the club caught him again and he went down. He did not have a chance to use the boots or any of the old riot technique. His body slid heavily against the wall and his feet pushed out in front like a comedian in the Mack

Sennett days. What he took was not so much a hard crack as a strictly accurate one. The blow did not re-open his scar, it was nothing like the beating he took in Clever back in '35. All it left him was stupid, and slugged, and sick with rage.

When the brick wall opposite anchored again he began to be conscious of a voice speaking. It spoke gently and monotonously. There was no anger, no expression in the voice, simply a repetition of words over and over. He put his hand to his head to feel for blood and brought it back clean. Then he pushed up onto his feet and stood steadying himself against the wall. He shook his head sharply to clear it and looked along the alley to where the voice was coming from.

The man that had been down was back on his feet. He was standing there talking to himself. His cotton jeans were short and tight and his shirt tails yanked out in back. His hands, disproportionately large, hung from his heavy shoulders with a curious air of helplessness. He was no taller than Matt but his breadth of shoulder, large hands and feet and clumsy movements gave an exaggerated impression of size and weight. Blood wormed down the side of his face, spreading below the ear, coming from above the hair line. There was a cut over his right eye but that was not the place he was bleeding from down the jaw line. That was higher up, above the hair somewhere.

Matt walked up to him and shook him. He demanded, roughly, "Who in hell d'you think you're talking to?"

The figure turned slowly. The face was young and quite empty, the eyes were expressionless with fear.

Matt felt a tickling in his armpits. He cried out sharply, "Hey, snap out of it. What happened to you?" He did not like the look in the eyes or the smell that hung about the boy's clothes. They jerked his mind back to '35 and Clever.

The boy stared at him silently, then he raised his arm and thrust it under Matt's nose. "Smell," he muttered, "that's what happened to me. Gas. Smell on that shirt."

Matt stepped back quickly, pushing the arm away. "Look," he said, "lemme get this straight. First wipe your face off, I don't like it so close to me." He pulled a sheet of newspaper from his pack. The boy wiped his cheek, then stood there helplessly with the bloody paper in his hand.

"For Chrissake!" Matt cried, exasperated, "set fire to it, shove it down a drain. Don't go on standin' there with it in your hand!"

The pale eyes groped confusedly around, then the boy went over and pushed the paper between the slats of a drain. "O.K.," Matt said, observing him closely, "now what's your name and how did you come here?"

The heavy dazed features contracted with the effort of thought. Finally the boy spoke haltingly, "I knew a guy once ... his name was Eddy ..." he paused. His eyes came up to Matt's face, his tongue came out and moistened his cracked lips.

Matt prodded him briskly, "Okay, his name was Eddy. What's a guy named Eddy got to do with it?"

The boy hesitated, "I think maybe I was that guy named Eddy."

Suddenly he began to sway. Matt caught his arm and steadied him. "Look," he said less sharply, "you got to take it easy, Eddy, you got yourself all busted up. Sidown."

Eddy shrank back, he dragged his arm away. "Don't you tell me to sidown. Don't anyone never tell me to do that again."

Matt stared curiously, "Listen, Eddy," he said, "I know you must have come from that sit-down this morning but where before that?"

Eddy frowned, his big hands picked at one another. "I don't remember nothin' except that sit-down now," he said. "I think once I worked out in the country at a job spreadin' manure," he broke off and smiled, "that was nice manure, smoky." Then the brief light died and his eyes clouded again with disappointment. "Maybe I did that or maybe I just thought I did from listenin' to other guys talk. I don't remember nothin' but that sit-down now. Look!" he cried, raising one foot as his mind drifted off abruptly, "that's all the shoes I got in the world! Some day I'm goin' to get me a good pair. I never had a good pair in my life before an' by Jesus, some day I'm goin' to get 'em!" He spoke with a deep brooding anger as though the words touched on an old sore.

Matt eyed him closely and nervously. He grasped him by the arm. "Sure, Eddy, why not? Come on! let's get goin'. Didn't you have nothin' in your hand, no blanket, nothin'?"

Eddy glanced about him vaguely. He shook his head, "I guess I lost it when we come out," he said. He put his hand up, wiped off a fresh trickle of blood and cleaned his hand on the seat of his jeans. They went out the end of the lane and were swept into the crowds that milled along Snider and up East Third and Fourth. The hard August sunshine blazed down on the sidewalks and gas fumes hung in the heavy air. The heat rose off the concrete and was caught and held by the close, straining bodies of the crowds. The same heat shone on the faces of the people, hard, eager, excited. There was no direction in that crowd yet. It seethed loosely and dangerously, hungry for a fixed objective.

Matt felt a crushing grip on his arm. He spun round, his manner edged and nervous.

"I only wanted to give you something," Eddy explained timidly.

"Sure, you did. You wanted to give me a scare an' you done it." Matt rubbed his arm irritably. He stared at Eddy askance, "They could use a boy like you around a circus herdin' elephants."

Eddy dived down into his pocket and dredged up two crushed-looking candy bars. He held one out. As Matt took it he glanced at Eddy with sudden suspicion. "Where'd you get these bars, Eddy?"

"I got them when we come out of the sit-down."

"How come there was a candy store open at five-thirty in the morning?"

Eddy's jaws worked the caramel and nut mixture up and down like a cow chewing its cud. He explained simply, "All the stores was open when we come out. All you had to do was put your hand in through the busted windows an' take what you wanted. There was women's clothes layin' around an' garden tools ..."

"But there wasn't no candy bars layin' round them big, smashed-in store fronts. I asked you how you got the candy bars, nothin' else ... just how you got these bars."

Eddy frowned, his memory labouring. Half a block further on he caught sight of an empty gas bomb lying in the gutter. He pointed to it excitedly. "That's how I got 'em!"

Matt glanced from Eddy to the bomb. "Nuts," he said, "I don't believe it."

"That's how I got 'em," Eddy repeated stubbornly, "there was this dead gas bomb layin' around so I picked it up an' threw it through the candy store window."

For a moment Matt was silent, then his eyes narrowed. He said softly, "So you smashed in a whole store front just so you could get a coupla candy bars, eh?" Suddenly he shook himself. His eyes moved nervously to Eddy's face then jerked away. He cried out sharply, "Goddammit, Eddy, I never met up with a guy like you before. Maybe I should of left you to that cop after all!"

CHAPTER TWO

Half-way up Snider Matt stopped a man to ask if they were going right. He pulled the paper out and let him read. The man was young and keen-faced, he looked like a bus driver in mufti.

"I don't know this town yet," Matt explained, "I've been trying to get to this place now for pretty near an hour."

The man looked from Matt to Eddy then rested on Matt's dangling pack. "If you want to join up with the rest of the boys," he said, "then headquarters won't do you any good. They all went on down to the Luther Hall after they were evicted. I think they have some kind of a temporary camp down there," he turned and pointed, "three blocks over."

"Thanks," Matt said, "I can remember that far."

"I guess they didn't have any place to go so they had this hall kind of loaned to them."

Matt frowned, "Where'd the authorities think they'd go? You mean they turned 'em loose onto the streets?"

"That's what I heard." The man reached into his pocket and pulled out a half-smoked pack of Sweet Caps. "Here," he said, "take them, I wish it was a whole pack. Hope you have luck!" He smiled, touched Matt briefly on the arm and went on.

Matt shook out two cigarettes. "Seems like he handed us the keys to the city. Maybe it's a good omen."

Eddy stared at the cigarette. He rolled it helplessly between his fingers.

"What's th' matter now?" Matt demanded, "don't anything ever make you happy?"

"We got no matches."

Matt removed the cigarette from between his lips. "That's right, too, neither we have." He stopped a man passing by and asked him had he a spare light. He was an elderly, grey-faced man shrunken into neat, shabby clothes. He looked like everything he had ever done had been attempted against too long odds.

He stared at Matt for a moment then his eyes moved to Eddy, then back to Matt again. A faint flush stole into his sallow cheeks, his lips drew back. "If I had my pockets full of matches," he said, "I wouldn't give you bums one of them."

Matt smiled coldly. "Is that so, mister?"

"I know your kind. The most of you wouldn't take a job if it was offered to you."

Matt stepped up close. "You got no right to say a thing like that."

The man laughed harshly, "If anyone has, I have."

"What right have you got? Who are you, anyway?"

The man's voice shook a little. His words rushed out hungrily, angrily. "Shuster's my name. I own a grocery store on Alcazar next block to Lincoln's, one of the last that hasn't been eaten up by the damn chain system. Everything I have is tied up in that store. These past fifteen years I've turned every cent I own back into it ... got no pleasure out of any of it." He stopped and his tongue came out and darted along his thin lips.

"So what? That still don't give you the right to call us bums."

The man's eyes burned suddenly. "So this morning what happens? You hoodlums threw rocks and gutted my store front, smashed every inch of plate glass I had in the place! You!" he choked, "and you!" His voice rose, his hand came out and pushed at Matt's chest. "I never carried a cent's worth of insurance. I'm not a big department store that can afford to carry riot insurance, I tell you I never carried a cent's worth of insurance!"

Drawn by the raised voices a crowd drifted up, began to ring round hungrily. Eddy stared at the swimming mass of eyes. He tugged at Matt's arm. "We got to get out of this. I can't stand no more people starin' at me ... not after that sit-down."

Matt shook him off. He cried angrily, "You got no right to pick on us, mister, we was never near your window!"

A policeman came shouldering through the crowd. The people fell open but they closed in again instantly, silently, like water. An excited murmur ran round, eyes lighted, jaws dropped a shade. A fat woman in a birdsnest hat and white canvas shoes run over at the heels and clutching a white imitation leather handbag, strained forward behind the officer. She stared, pop-eyed, at Eddy's bloody head.

The policeman asked what all the trouble was about. He was an experienced cop and he knew what today meant and what the people were saying and what the papers would be printing tomorrow. Short of breaking up a riot he had to give everything he did today a certain dignity and an unmistakeable restraint.

Matt said quickly, "There's no trouble. We was walking along and we stopped ..."

Shuster broke in excitedly, "One of these men stopped me and asked for a light."

"Which man?"

"That one. Oh, my God," Shuster exclaimed with a sort of tired ferocity, "when I think what I've been through today because of men like him ..."

Matt headed right back into the argument. He swallowed his anger and held his voice down. "Sure, I asked him did he have a light. Then he says he knows who we are, that we're boys from the sit-down an' starts calling us a lot of names."

The woman back of the policeman called out shrilly, "You just try and arrest those boys and see what you get!" There was an angry mutter from the crowd. A man's voice jeered, "Sure, go ahead an' try it!"

The cop's face did not change at all. He was experienced and he knew what was going on on every side of him. He asked Shuster if he wished to prefer a charge.

"Charge!" the man muttered bitterly. He shook his head, his eyes dulled. "No good," he said hopelessly, "not now. I never carried riot insurance. All the big places could afford to carry it but I never could. Every cent I made I put back into the business, never got any pleasure out of any of it ... " Suddenly his voice stopped. He looked round at the faces pressing in hungrily and something inside of him seemed to collapse. Without another word he turned and rabbitted off into the crowd.

For an instant the tension hung, then the cop began to break the people and get them moving. Matt never saw a cop break a crowd so fast before. Inside of half a minute all that was left of it was the fat woman in white feeling around among the loose change in her handbag.

She pulled out a quarter and pushed it at Matt. "Here," she panted, "go buy your own matches. Never mind those police, they don't dare do a thing to you boys." She eyed Matt in a way that showed she wanted to do more for the cause of unemployment than a quarter's worth.

He slipped the money in his jeans. "Thanks," he said and moved away fast. He did not look around to see if Eddy was coming up behind, he just kept on moving fast. Not because he was scared, but because during the last few minutes he had begun to get touched with the mass hysteria of the streets and to understand what Harry meant when he said the whole town was crazy. The only thing he wanted now was to locate the Luther Hall, find someone there that wasn't crazy and get himself in.

The woman stood looking after him, then she saw Eddy. She caught him by the arm and pointed at his head. "Tell me what happened," she gushed, "tell me what happened to your head?"

Eddy tried to back away. The woman kept after him. He tugged at his arm and his face grew scared. "Leggo my arm," he muttered hoarsely.

"Tell me," she persisted, "what did you boys do all those weeks sitting there so bravely holding the fort?"

Eddy ceased to struggle and a change came over his face. He smacked at the woman's fingers, shouting, "God damn you, why did you have to talk about that sit-down?"

She let out an angry yelp and backed away. Eddy kept after her, shouting, "I cleaned toilets, that's what I done on the sit-down. Every day I cleaned toilets. I cleaned 'em with disinfectant an' when there wasn't no disinfectant ..." he made a lumbering dive and smacked her hard across the tail. She screamed and Eddy dived for her again, shouting, "Why did you have to talk about that sit-down?" He made a grab from behind and his fingers fouled in the belt of her dress, and as she struggled in wild, clumsy, overweight terror the belt ripped off, and Eddy was left with it dangling in his hand. He stood staring at it and his face grew wild with fear. He let it drop and it fell, coiling heavily like a thick red snake. He heard Matt's voice behind. "Run!" Matt hissed, and he felt a yank at his arm and he began to run with Matt beside him.

They hared off down the block, teetered an instant on the sidewalk, then dived through an opening in the traffic and plunged into an alley on the other side. Behind them the traffic line closed solid again. There was a movie house on the corner of the block with double doors opening onto the alley. Matt darted into the doorway, dragging Eddy after him and they flattened themselves, sweating and heaving. From two blocks over came the excited squall of a squad car.

Matt waited till the racket in the distance had died down. "O.K.," he said, "you can come out now." His eyes were slitted with fury. He muttered between his teeth. "You crazy bastard, you! I ought to crown you for this!"

Eddy avoided his eyes. "I didn't do nothing, it was that woman grabbed me an' wouldn't let go. I was scared."

"*You* was scared!"

"Sure, I was scared. She started asking questions about the sit-down. She didn't have no right," Eddy cried, his voice rising, "she didn't have no right to ask me questions about that sit-down!"

Matt glanced at him uneasily. He saw Eddy's eyes darkening, the frightened stubborn anger closing his face. He made an effort and swallowed down his own anger.

"O.K.," he said sharply, "you can skip the rest." He bent down and tightened the twine on his blanket roll. The big knots had worked loose during the stampede. Then he straightened up, pulled in his hard stomach, pushing his shirt down front and back. He pulled out a soiled length of cotton cloth and wiped his face and neck, the nape and the sweat cup below the Adam's apple. He dabbed cautiously around his left temple but the rag came away dry. All there was to see was a dark place coming up.

He cleaned himself in silence, his mind working like a bees' nest. Finally he said, "Now, you listen to me, Eddy, and try to get this good."

Eddy's mind strove to swing into focus. His mouth dropped open a shade.

"Now I come in town with a definite reason. I never had such a definite reason for doing anything in my life before an' I'm not going to get in any kind of trouble an' mess up my chances because of you or anyone else, understand?"

Eddy eyed him anxiously, "I never meant to get you in trouble."

"You never meant to but you damn near done it jus' the same."

"I never mean to get anyone in trouble."

"Yeah? An' I'll bet in spite of it you can get more guys in dutch in a week than a blond confined to barracks."

Eddy justified himself obstinately, "I ain't crazy," he insisted, "only when I'm scared or when anyone talks sit-down." A look half childish, half cunning spread over his face. "Before I got beat over the head I wasn't crazy at all, I jus' made mistakes."

Matt was unimpressed. Suddenly he caught Eddy by the shoulders and shook him. He cried sharply, "I done that shaking with a reason, see, because I got something to say to you, an' that shaking'll help fix it in your mind before we go out on that street again an' you start headin' us into more trouble." His hands dropped. He stood away. "Now when we get down to the hall we're through, see? I don't want nothin' more to do with you, I don't even know your name."

Eddy's head moved up and down, he did not say anything. A fresh thread of blood oozed from his hairline and trickled down his cheek. Matt dragged out the cloth once more and wiped it carefully clean. His eyes were cold, his voice hammered without pity.

Eddy's eyes did not leave Matt's face. He repeated haltingly, "You didn't do it because you meant a damn thing ..." He stopped, hesitated, stared at Matt helplessly, "I don't remember no more."

Matt laughed. The laugh had a touch of hysteria. "All right, all right, skip that, too. Only don't come near me, that's all— just *don't come near me!*" He slung up his pack and stepped out onto the street. He moved differently now to when he came off the freight, smartly and fast, and with a defined objective.

Eddy followed, keeping a few paces behind. He did not attempt to draw level. At the top of Luther Street Matt waited for him to come up. He said, "Now remember what I told you."

"Oh, sure," Eddy agreed earnestly and without preliminary thought, "I remember."

Matt looked into his face, his own tightened with exasperation. "Like hell you do!" He turned and began to walk on quickly. Behind him came the heavy slap-slap of Eddy's feet. It ceased for a moment when they turned a corner and got separated by the crowd, then the sound came back again. Suddenly Matt was scared by it. He wanted to turn round and shout to Eddy to quit trailing him. The sound made him jittery.

CHAPTER THREE

The Luther Hall on the corner of Luther and East Third stood next to a vacant lot on one side and beyond the lot was the smoke-discoloured brick wall of the Golden Heart Mission, Undenominational, All Faiths Welcome. Along from the mission a Greek lunchroom and a two-for-one pants presser and a Jap drygoods and dressmaking and it went on that way all down the block. Back of the lot rose the rear elevations of white and oriental rookeries where in case of fire it was advisable to dive out the upper windows and get killed the quick way.

A gang of men were at work cleaning up the lot, staggering under junked hardware and the rusted entrails of automobiles and stacking them close up by the fence. A lot worked only in pants and undervest, skins oily in the hot sun. From time to time a man stopped off to wipe the sweat out of his eyes or squat down to drag on a cigarette. There was no shade anywhere in that part of town, the heat writhed up off the sidewalks and seemed to hang visible in the air. The heat stank; of sweat and dust and gas fumes.

As the clean-up squad worked the cleared space was filled with men dumping their packs and blanket rolls. Others sat hunched along the sidewalk. Red-eyed, slack-shouldered, they muttered among themselves, mouths tightened by a grim, brooding anger. The feeling of anger was everywhere, raw and seething. From time to time a man sitting off by himself kept getting up and going away and vomiting.

On the opposite sidewalk the crowds kept up their slow, solid drifting. Stopping and goofing, getting moved on and stopping to goof again. They stared at the men excitedly as though they were an isolated group, something apart from the main herd. The way the same crowd will mill around and watch prisoners being herded into the patrol wagon.

As Matt and Eddy came by a man got up from the sidewalk and went off, hacking in his throat, coughing up gobs of bloody mucus. A second man, hurrying by, called out to Eddy and asked him where had he been all morning. Then he looked again and stopped and came on over, and he parted Eddy's matted hair carefully with his fingers and peered down at the clot of half-dried blood. "So that's why you didn't come over!" he said. He had a soft way of speaking that made it seem as though the voice of some other sort of man had been installed inside him by error. Therefore most people that met Hep the first time looked at him twice.

He was spare, clean-shaven and harsh-featured with heavy black hair, and eyes that came from a long way back in his head. He could have been anywhere between twenty-eight and forty and the more you knew him, the harder man he became to judge the age of. His features were drawn by years of nervous tension and perpetual conflict, yet he gave off a curious air of inner immobility. He was dressed in a blue shirt and dark trousers and he wore an old pair of brown canvas sneakers.

Eddy's hand came up and touched his cut temple gingerly. He explained with a touch of apology, "I got beat over the head, Hep." He pulled at Matt's arm, "This is my friend."

Hep's eyes swung over, observing Matt narrowly and with the utmost attention. Then, "Glad to know you," the soft voice said, "Have you been a friend of Eddy's for long? I don't seem to remember your face."

Matt shifted his feet, fidgeting with his pack. His instinct was to move away, to break away from Eddy before it was too late. He answered ungraciously, "Eddy and me only met today. I jus' got in town this morning."

Eddy pulled at his arm again. "Tell him what you did."

Matt flushed with annoyance. "I didn't do anything."

"He stopped me from gettin' my head beat off," Eddy announced proudly.

Hep asked, "Did you come here to join up with the rest of the boys?"

Matt said quickly, "Sure, I did. I never got any place on my own." Once more Matt's feet stirred impatiently. He shifted his pack down off his shoulder and let the weight rest on the ground.

Hep seemed to conclude some kind of keen, internal survey. "Okay," he said, "get along inside and maybe you can get yourself assigned to a squad in time for the big meeting this afternoon. I don't know, though, they're very busy inside there right now." He called to a boy sitting along the sidewalk and told him to take Matt inside and see if he could find a committee to pass on him. "Maybe you can get in my squad," he said to Matt, "there's been some vacancies since morning. Eddy, you stay here with me, I got work for you to do."

Eddy's face sagged with disappointment. "Can't I go along, too?"

"Hell, no! I said I had work for you to do. First, though, we got to find one of the red cross boys to clean up your head."

Matt and the boy went off together. The boy had blond hair and a pale face. His face was a different cut to Matt's, weaker and more sensitive. His movements were loose-jointed and without definite co-ordination, and his hands and feet were long. He had a nervous habit of jerking his head back and slapping at his blond pompadour. He said his name was Charlie but from this habit of his he got called Slappy. He said there were eighteen other Charlies in the division so they had to give them some kind of a tab. From the way he spoke Matt judged he must have been with the boys since the first of the sit-down in June. He did not have a chance to get anything more out of Slappy then, he just rabbitted behind him through the crowd, trying not to lose sight of the back of his head.

Stepping inside the hall from the bright sunlight, at first Matt could not make out anything distinctly. The smoke made it hard to see, too. As his eyes got used to the light he took in a few rough, general details. There was a platform at one end on which men were working and trestle tables running the way of the room. Men were hurriedly clearing dinner away, sweeping up cutlery and clashing it into tin pails, stacking dirty dishes and carrying them to the basement below. In one corner a doctor and the first aid boys were working on a line-up. The air smelt of sweat and smoke, of carbolic and coffee grounds and the heavy, stale odour of stewing meat and onions. The gas-saturated clothes of the men gave off a sickly stench.

Charlie pointed to a man writing on a cleared space at one of the tables. "Okay," he said, "there's your committee."

"Just him alone?"

"Sure. You're lucky to find anyone to look at you today. What'd you expect? A full meeting of the executive?" Charlie started to go away then he came back again, "Don't try to tell him any fairy tales, Link don't stand for anything like that."

Matt retorted touchily, "Why th'hell should I?"

Charlie looked nonplussed. "I dunno," he said, "some of the boys try it when they first come in, that's all." He went over and spoke to Link at the table.

Since he stepped inside the hall Matt was experiencing an odd feeling of black-out, as though his identity were being sucked away and absorbed by the powerful currents of an organization. It made him touchy and defensive; at the same time it gave him a sting of excitement. He tried to pick up the atmosphere quickly, the feel of a mass of men, of hurry, of action, of numbers, of detail, of the dangerous anger boiling in the air. He heard Charlie call to him, saw Link leave off writing and look up. Then Charlie faded.

"Well?" Link said.

Matt dug down and fetched up the scrap of paper. "A guy named Pete that has an all-night lunch wagon gave me this when I changed cars at Bisbee this morning early," he explained, "I told him I was beating it down to Aschelon to join up with the sit-down and he gave it to me so I would know where to go."

Link's eyes grazed the paper then he folded it neatly and laid it on one side. He had flat black eyes and a colourless face, high in the cheekbone, almost Mongolian-looking. He wore a grey Fedora, dark pants and a white shirt. His clothes looked good and well cared for. His hands were soft and clean and the nails unbroken. He put Matt through the routine questions and asked him was there anyone there could identify him as coming from Saskatchewan, anyone that might have known him in the old days. Matt said he never had time yet to find out.

Link eyed him with a faint smile. "There's a sprinkling of boys from pretty near every one of the nine provinces here," he said, "but you have to remember that every province in this country is so goddammed exclusive that it won't stand for being contaminated by trash from the province next door."

Matt grinned coldly. "Jus' one big happy family. There's one thing you don't have to tell me. I found it out for myself long ago." He leant over the table. "Listen," he said, "I'm not up on the politics of this thing, I don't know what's goin' on behind it. I don't give a goddam about politics, all I want is work!"

"Where did you try last?"

"Where did I try? Say, I spent three months this spring trampin' the country around Colynos, jungling up nights and snitching food where I could, tryin' to land a job on a farm or at one of the mills. I'd hear of some job twenty, thirty miles away an' hitchhike after it, an' when I got there the first question would be, what experience did I have? Some places they didn't even wait to ask that, they said they had a dozen tramps around every day after the same job. I tell you after a time that sort of thing does something to you!"

"Okay, okay," Link said, calmly, "don't get so hot."

Matt cried violently, "I get hot because I don't know where I'm at! I had this thing thrown at my head so long."

"You had what thing?"

"This kind of thing. One farmer says to me, 'You jobless boys is all alike, you don't know anything about anything. I'll bet you don't know a damn thing about milkin' a cow or workin' around stock.' An' I ses to him, 'No, sir, but I'd like to learn,' an' the son-of-a-bitch comes back very sarcastic, 'Maybe you would too, but what happens to my stock in the meantime? I got no time to run a goddamn school of agriculture.' That kind of thing," Matt cried. "I tell you, I heard that steady for the past seven years—in the country, in the city, every damn place I went to."

Link referred back to the paper under his hand. He asked evenly, "Were you ever in any kind of trouble back in Saskatchewan? Ever do a stretch for anything?"

Matt's eyes flared suddenly, "I did two stretches. First time I got fifteen days on a vag. charge, that was in Medera. Second time I got thirty days for incite to riot. That was in '35 when they had that big trouble in Clever."

Link's pencil travelled again. He asked without looking up, "You like to fight?"

The light died in Matt's eyes, leaving them coldly defensive. "I don't go round pickin' fights."

"But some things just make you mad."

"Some things make me so mad I jus' can't see ..." he broke off abruptly, his face narrowed. "Say, what are you tryin' to find out?"

Link tapped delicately with his pencil. For an instant the flat black eyes looked off into space. Then, "I'm trying to find out whether you're a trouble-maker," he said deliberately, "that's one of the things we have to know." He raised his head, looked straight at Matt, "What happened that time back in Clever?"

Matt frowned, picking at the roughened edge of the table. He knew sooner or later the question had to come. "Look," he began, hesitating, "there's something ..." he put his hand up, touched the scar.

Link nodded. "I thought that."

"How'd you know?"

"Never mind that. What is it? Shoot. There's a line-up waiting behind you."

Matt glanced back over his shoulder and a boy's face stared back at him without interest. He leant forward to speak, then drew back. "Some other time," he said.

Link glanced at him then glanced away. "Okay," he said, "if that's the way you feel. All I asked you was what happened in Clever?"

Matt hesitated a moment then he began to speak rapidly. "There was this big jobless demonstration going on in front of the city hall and some-one threw a rock an' they called out the riot squad. I got smacked on the head by a riot stick. That was the first time I ever got blind-mad in my life. After that I didn't care what happened. Later on I found they had me booked on an incite charge."

"What d'you mean, 'blind-mad'?"

Matt saw it coming. "Do I have to mean something?"

Link's head went down, writing. He took a card off a pile, and filled it in, stamped it and handed it up. "That's all for now. You'll be assigned to a squad. Go and mix around among the boys." He slid Matt's sheet aside, pulled up a fresh one and the boy behind stepped up. As he moved off Matt heard Link beginning the same routine again. He touched his nose, frowning. There were times when he was so scared of these blinding flashes of rage that his whole body went stiff and his mouth dry. They brought to mind the last time he ever saw his mother. A big blonde woman, standing in the doorway of the two-room flat, her face a frozen mask of anger. She stood there, tight-lipped, cursing his father while from doorways up and down the passage heads craned out, watching and listening with a wistful lustful excitement.

After that she finally went out and disappeared. She never came back or sent any word. That happened in 1930, the second bad year. She went away on January 10th, 1930, when the cold snap was at its height. Matt never saw her after that though his father later identified her. He was fourteen at the time.

He moved around uncertainly now, talking to men here and there. He went to the head of the stairs and peered down. There were more tables in the basement and women toiling over hurriedly improvised cook stoves. Big cans and lard pails steamed on the tops and men were packing water for dishwashing between the stoves and the dishpans. The thick, wet crockery slid as it was piled and every now and then a dish crashed down and the pieces got kicked aside. Most of the women were elderly and wore cotton aprons stretched over their street clothes. They toiled in a kind of grim dishevelment, like an emergency unit pressed into service, and with no proper facilities.

A boy hurrying by headed into him, turned back and swore and a man clattering down the steps bunted him aside with a muttered word of apology. After that he went and sat on a bench by the wall. He felt suddenly tired, pooped out. The stale air made him heavy and slugged, that and lack of sleep. He felt a curious sense of anti-climax. It seemed as though every one of these men was cemented into a whole by the events of the past three weeks, the past twenty-four hours in particular, and as though he was the only one on the outside.

He looked around, studying the grim, brooding faces. They wore the same look as the faces along the sidewalk, heavy, red-eyed, keyed to the same exasperation. Here and there a boy had his head swathed in fresh bandages. The anger seething among them was not sudden, hot passion but an old, ignored disease and the fact that it was cumulative gave it power and made it unpredictable.

That was the feeling Matt picked up during the confusion of those first hours and it stirred and clarified the forces working in himself, concentrating them into a unit even as the men round him were concentrated into a unit so that he drew power from more than himself, purpose and direction from a source outside of and greater than himself. For the first time in his life he began to feel part of a whole though as yet he did not feel actually taken into that whole and accepted by it.

A man came in the side door, looked round, then strolled over and sat down on the bench beside him. He said in a friendly voice, "Hello, brother, aren't you a new one around here?" He wore a pink shirt, and tweed vest and trousers, and his dark hair was neatly parted and slicked down. His mild brown eyes did not seem to match the way in which his nose had at one time been broken. Matt did not know how to classify him, there were a lot of things about him hard to reconcile with one another. He pulled out a pack of cigarettes and a trick lighter, one of those little gadgets Woolworth's is always bringing out.

He noticed Matt looking at it, so he flicked it again to show how it worked. He slipped Matt a cigarette and let him try the lighter. He laughed and said, "Maybe they didn't have one like this where you came from."

"If they did," Matt said, "I never got hold of one." He took a deep drag. It felt like he hadn't tasted real smoke in years.

The man slipped the lighter back in his vest pocket. "My name's Benson," he said, "Lafe Benson. Just call me Lafe, all the boys around here call me Lafe."

"Thanks, Lafe," Matt said. He dragged hungrily on the smoke. He felt his face muscles begin to relax and the sense of anti-climax to ease up. Lafe let him smoke half the cigarette in silence then he said casually, "I suppose you heard there was quite a fight in the streets early this morning."

"I heard something," Matt said, "Did any of the boys end up in the jug?"

"Around twenty-seven, they tell me. Fifty got taken off to hospital an' a half dozen cops."

Matt nodded, "Seven to one, that's about the usual rate."

Lafe's brown eyes twinkled. He smiled and his voice held a shade of deference. "Sounds like you had experience."

Matt's mouth tightened. "I was all through that trouble they had in Clever in '35," he said quietly, "they smeared those riots over every front page in the country but in the end nothing come of it. The only ones to get anything out of that stink was the newspapers."

Lafe took a long drag on his cigarette and crushed out the stub. When he spoke his meaning was unmistakeable. "The only ones that get anything out of organized trouble is the newspapers," he said, "all boys like you an' me stand to get is busted heads." He glanced at Matt's scar and allowed his eyes to stay there fractionally.

Some instinct in Matt leapt on the defensive. He knew now Lafe was getting at something. He did not give him any lead. Lafe pulled the pack out again. "Another smoke?"

"Thanks," Matt said, "I could smoke a dozen of these an' still not feel I'd had anything."

"Take the rest of the pack then." Lafe worked the trick lighter again. Matt pushed his face down and caught the tiny flickering tongue of flame.

"Thanks," he said, slipping the pack into his pocket. "This is the second pack I had given me since I got into town, seems like it's great to belong to an organization."

Lafe stood up. For an instant the eyes of the two men locked, then Lafe said softly, "Sure, it's great—just so long as you know where the organization is taking you!" He moved away.

Matt's eyes followed him uncertainly, "Yeah," he murmured, "yeah, I guess that's right, too." He felt like someone had kicked the only solid ground he ever knew out from under him. He watched Lafe go over and sit down on the other side of the hall, pull out a second pack of cigarettes and offer them around. He showed off the trick lighter, too.

Hep had come in the door. He stood there all the time Matt was getting picked up. Now he came over. "Well, I hear they put you in my squad after all."

Matt was uncertain how to take that, he was not sure that he liked Hep. He asked noncommittally. "How many's in a squad?"

Hep felt the hostility in his manner but he did not show anything. Hep must have felt it because he picked up these things by instinct. He got that way from working around trouble so long.

"There's ten boys to a squad," he explained. "If I told you the names they wouldn't mean anything to you. It takes a little time to get broken into any kind of an organization so take all the time you want."

Matt looked at him quickly, trying to sense what he was really getting at. Hep was watching Lafe on the other side of the room. After a moment he went on, "Take time to pick who you go around with, Matt. Who you start going around with you usually end up with in an outfit like this." His eyes took in the surrounding confusion calmly. The soft voice had a peculiar quality of penetration. Matt found himself resisting some powerful fascination about his presence.

"You got to remember," he went on with a half smile, "that this dump isn't any kind of a club room, it's more like a military headquarters, and the only rule that stands up in a fight is, dog eat dog." He nodded towards Lafe, "There plenty good boys an there's also a few sonsovbitches."

Matt's chin came up slowly, he opened his mouth to speak then changed his mind. "I didn't know this was a closed corporation."

Hep commented dryly, "All corporations is closed corporations."

A boy ran in the side door and handed him a slip of paper. He read it frowning. "I have to go now, Matt. See you later. We fall in outside at one-forty-five." He left with the boy trotting at his side. The boy had to trot to keep up.

After that Matt went back outside. He felt restless and the noise and the heat indoors gave him a penned-up, dopey sensation. The clean-up squad was resting now, squatting with their knees up, arms hanging loosely. Some lay flat out with their hats tipped over their eyes, others lay on their elbows talking and smoking. The line still sat along the sidewalk. The cleaned-off space was staked out with bundles of ragged bedding. Every man that could pre-empt a space dumped his belongings. The lot was dotted with blanket rolls and cartons tied with string and a few battered grips. It looked like a refugee encampment without the goats and women and children. The lot was patched with rank, oil-stained grass and the best sites went first, that is the sites with a small growth of grass to soften the uneven ground. If it had not been for the presence of police and the drifting crowds, the piled-up junk and the backs of the rookeries, the heavy anger seething in the air, the scene might have been comic. As it was it was merely stark and crazy and dangerous.

Matt shopped around till he found a spot to dump his roll. The reason the space had not been already staked was because it lay close up by the piled junk with barely enough room to stretch out. He lay down to test the length and the man ahead moved a foot or two farther away. Matt thanked him and lay down with his hands clasped behind his head, and let the sun come at him.

The man glanced round sourly. "Don't thank me," he said, "I didn't do it for you, I did it so I could lay more comfortable myself." He spoke with the accusing whine of the chronically destitute. Through half-closed eyes Matt could see his slack shoulders and unclipped neck hairs. When he turned, his face was scored with deep, querulous lines. He had a habit of glancing up from under his eyebrows as though expecting a blow.

Matt flexed his muscles and felt the sun burn into his skin. He said, "I haven't had a good stretch-out like this in days."

The man's head twisted round again. "I had too much damn stretch-out, I slept on the ground for pretty near a month, marble floors an' noospapers, that's the way I slept. I had too damn much of this whole business, I don't see where it's gettin' us anyway." He pushed his head out and spat. He cried shrilly, "Gas! That's what they give us!" He hacked in his throat and coughed up a second gob of mucus. The mucus was mixed with blood.

Matt turned on his elbow. "Why d'you stick with the outfit then?"

"Why? I gotta eat, didn't I?"

"From what I seen so far it looks like you boys has been eatin' pretty good."

The man's voice worried on angrily, "There was flies on that meat we had for dinner."

Matt lay back in disgust. "So what? You didn't have to get out an' rustle for that meat. What's a few worms when you get 'em brought to you on a plate?"

The man scratched at his armpits. He was silent for a few moments. Then, "Listen you," he began, insulted, "just because you're new around here don't think you know it all."

Matt closed his eyes. "I know enough not to go around beefin'."

"How long have you bin here, anyway?"

"Since morning."

"Then you don't know nuthin', not anythin' at all."

Matt did not answer. Through his closed eyelids he knew the man was still there. Then he heard him rise and once more the beaten, persistant whine, "I tell you, we don't get nothin' permanent out of all these fancy trimmin's—women an' meetin's an' parades. Wait a month, we'll be back on the rods. I seen things like this before."

The man seemed to stand there waiting for an answer. Matt did not say anything. After a few moments he heard the shambling footsteps turn and move away.

But the echo of the words remained in the air like hornets. Matt thrust them from his mind but they came back, settling and stinging. He dealt with them savagely, with a loathing made sharp by a hundred old latent fears and memories. The struggle went round and round. It merged with the street noises, the endless rise and fall of men's voices, the snarling of gears, the clatter of a speed cop kicking over his machine. It became one with the still blazing air, the sweaty, fumey smells that no wind relieved, the dusty odour of the ground itself, of hot, rusting iron. After a time it ceased to possess sharpness or continuity or form. It changed to a dense darkened wave, swallowing all form.

He eased his head till it rested on the crook of his right arm. His mouth twitched, his brows contracted uneasily, the small side muscles of his face grew tight. Presently the conflict slackened and the tortured muscles eased. A man stepped over him carefully to avoid treading on his fingers. He did not hear the man go by. He slept a heavy, slugged sleep like dropping down a well. Down, down, his mind groped sightlessly after the pool at the bottom, the deep still pool that was always more darkness ....

He was awakened by Eddy's hand slapping a wasp off his cheekbone. Eddy's hand came down flat and the wasp zoomed out from under it. Matt sat up and stared round stupidly. Then he saw Eddy. His head was criss-crossed with clean bandages, and he wore a white shirt and a pair of good corduroys, which came down over his shoes almost hiding them.

Matt rubbed the side of his face angrily. "What in hell did you want to do that for?" he demanded.

"I was scared that wasp would sting you."

"Hell, that wasp wouldn't have done anything."

Eddy shook his head. "I was stung by a wasp once, a long time ago ...." he broke off, his mind groping uncertainly.

He began fumbling with a bulge in the front of his shirt. He produced a crushed package and held it out shyly and eagerly. "I thought maybe you might be hungry, then I thought they wouldn't give you nothin' down in the basement because they didn't know you yet." The package fell open, disclosing a mess of wilted lettuce soaked in mayonnaise, two slices of tomato and a broken cut of apple pie.

Matt did not look at the package, he looked at Eddy and some part of his mind close to the surface snapped nervously awake. He asked, "Where'd you get this, Eddy? I didn't see nothin' like this downstairs."

Eddy's eyes slid away and he did not answer.

"C'mon, Eddy. Where'd you get it?"

Eddy's fingers picked at one another. After a moment he confessed sullenly, "I guess one of those women down in the basement brought her dinner along with her."

Matt choked. "Oh, fer Chrissake!" He stared at Eddy helplessly. Eddy was watching him now, his face a mixture of triumph, cunning and fear.

"Eat it," Eddy begged, "you got to eat it now I got it for you. I would of got you anything you wanted out of one of them big department stores like I was tellin' you about as we come along only those places ain't open no more."

Matt eyed the wilting mess in his hand. He muttered, "Jese, Eddy, I don't know whether I ought to apologize to you or turn you over to the cops."

There was a sudden welling-up of the men around the door. Hep broke through and came striding quickly towards them. Matt's face hardened suddenly into decision. He caught Eddy by the front of the shirt and spoke rapidly. "Listen, Eddy. If you want to stick with me you got to do everything I say an' do it right. Every damn thing. Get that?"

Eddy looked startled then he nodded. "Everything," he murmured.

Matt's voice was brittle with exasperation. "You don't just *say* it, you *do* it, see? Before you do more than just eat an' sleep an' take Hep's orders an' go to the can you got to come an' ask me, understand? Not just a few little things you got to come an' ask me about, but everything ..." He broke off abruptly as Hep came up.

He eyed Eddy's bandaged head with approval. "Maybe they can use you up on the platform this afternoon. They got to have something to show the public."

Matt took him aside. He said, "I wouldn't do that if I was you."

"Do what?"

"Use Eddy for a guinea pig."

"What's the matter with that? He's one of the steadiest boys in this whole outfit. He's simple but he's steady."

"Not since he got smacked."

"You mean he's still rum-dum? I didn't get time to talk to him much."

Matt shrugged. "I guess he's okay, only for a day or so someone's got to watch him pretty close."

Hep pulled at his long upper lip. "Maybe we better get him transferred."

"Where to?"

"Just transferred."

"You mean kick him out of the organization an' land him in the nut house?"

Hep flashed round irritably, "I mean we got enough loose dynamite laying around as things are now! Hotheads an' trouble-makers an' pigeons an' plain, old-fashioned belly-achers. We can't afford to go around looking for trouble. Hell, we got a thousand men to think for!"

For a moment they glared at one another. Matt felt himself growing red and angry.

Hep said impatiently, "If you got any ideas about Eddy, shoot. I can't afford to stand around here all day."

Matt looked across at Eddy. He was watching them. His face wore the expression of a dying man lying in the next room to a consultation of his physicians. For the second time Matt plunged to a decision. "See here, Hep," he began, "can I take over Eddy? Be responsible for him for a couple of days, watch he don't get in any kind of a jam."

Hep's sunken eyes probed Matt narrowly and deeply. He would not commit himself at once. He stood pulling his lip. At last he said, "If you do this, you have to remember something an' never forget it any part of the time."

"Remember what?"

"That you don't do this just for you or for Eddy. If anything goes wrong you're responsible to every other man in this organization."

Matt's face was still. He waited a moment. Then, "Okay," he said, "I'll take that chance."

CHAPTER FOUR

Out front of the Luther Hall the squads were falling into line. Men running, jostling, pausing to stand confused until their places were assigned, rising stiffly from the sidewalk, hurrying over from the lot. Squad leaders strode quickly up and down the lines checking on their men. At the head of the column two boys strove with a broad white cotton banner that fought against them in the hot wind. The banner bore the jobless slogan, JOBS NOT JAIL.

The back windows of the tenements crawled with craning heads. A part of the crowd had swarmed up onto a billboard and they and the tenement people screamed advice and encouragement to the men below. A cameraman, hatless, coatless, sweaty shirt tight against his chest, had shinnied up onto the billboard, too. He hung there squinting down getting action shots. Massed bodies, swimming heads, urgent single hurrying ant-like units, formless confusion weaving into pattern, slow tightening into disciplined design. Spat of motorcycles, shrill crowd voices, heavy surging of feet.

Matt dived for the washroom, bucking a tide of running men. A boy still in there lent him a comb and Matt sloshed water over his face and combed it through his hair. The more water he put on the more it fought back against the water. As he came out he stood aside to let a girl pass by. She was coming up from the basement. She was a synthetic blonde with small, pale features. Her make-up had run with the heat of the basement so that, being tired, she showed it. She wore blue slacks and a blue cotton candy-stripe sweater and her hair was tied with blue ribbon. Her face was the deadest thing Matt had ever seen. When she spoke her voice was that way too, flattened out. Behind her sweated a stout woman with frizzed, light brown hair, a girlish straw hat and a flowered rayon dress that was too tight all over. She had on a Woolworth-matched set of choker and earrings and was going through plenty of trouble with her feet. When she spoke she had a loud friendly manner and when her mouth was quiet, not talking, it set like a steel trap. Whenever she saw Matt she cried, "Did you get any dinner? I don't seem to remember you down there?" and she glanced at the girl and laughed. "We should know the most of the boys' faces by this time, shouldn't we, Hazel?"

Hazel said, "I guess so, Aunty," and went on out into the sun. She did not seem to take any interest in anything beyond getting outside in the air again. As he went by Matt asked casually, "Comin' to the big meetin'?"

She shook her head. "In this heat? What do you think? I'm going for a swim."

"Why not come to the meeting? The sea's there any day."

She tossed him a smile, casual, fed-up, half mocking. "Maybe it is, but I don't get the chance to go in it." He swung on past her, calling back, "Have it your way then, the sea wins."

She waited for the aunt to come up. "Which one is he?"

The aunt pushed at the sides of her frizzed brown hair. "Which one is who?"

"The boy that just went ahead," Hazel said, "the one you asked did he have any dinner?"

The aunt's black eyes picked up Matt's back. She said, "I never saw him before, that's why I said did I know his face." They went on down steps.

"Did he tell you his name?"

The aunt flounced impatiently. "My heavens! Why should he? He seemed in a great hurry to get by."

Hazel smiled her slight significant smile. "He seemed in a great hurry to get by me, too," she said.

Matt ran on down the line. He found Hep checking on his boys; Charlie was there, too. Hep exclaimed sharply, "You were a long time. What happened to you?"

"Nothing except there was a line-up at the can." Charlie looked after Hep as he went off haring down the line, lean and concentrated. He said, "There goes one guy that don't like to be kept waitin'."

Matt snorted touchily, "Yeah? Well, what's the idea of his sayin' it like I did it on purpose? Those old cans back there has a line-up like Greta Garbo."

Charlie grinned, slapping absently at his blond pompadour. "Hep don't mean it like that," he said, "but if he told you to be here in five minutes then he don't mean six. He told us all the same."

"And you didn't care?"

"Hell, no! That's the way things has got to be around here."

The first of the columns began to move. The cotton banners bobbed and swayed, bellying in the fists of the bearers. A pair of speed cops cruised ahead opening a lane. As the long line of rhythmic shuffling hardened to a measured tramp the tenement watchers shrilled a cheer; then as they caught sight of the cops' red machines the cheers soured to catcalls and the boys on the billboard joined in and between them they razzed the police badly. The men had a lot of public sympathy, not just sentimental mob sympathy but a hair-trigger, highly emotional reaction that made the handling of the crowd a dangerous, thankless job. Almost anything the police did that day could have been wrong. There was not much talking among the men and their silence was grim and it was significant. It spread to the people themselves so that they watched silent and amazed and ashamed. The faces of the men silenced them. The sight of hundreds of them marching in this shoddy crusade and the knowledge of what lay back of it quieted the people and at the same time made them one in a common ignored evil and an old shame. But the people were not important, just as the borne slogans were not important nor the veiled hysteria nor the police peppered thickly along the route. The only thing that was important was the youth of the men marching.

Matt felt the mood of the hour settling on him. He gazed up at the big office buildings, the handsome new hotel block, the Aschelon Trust with the chased copper doors, the Stock Exchange building, where within a few downtown blocks the eyes, ears, nerves, whole sensory mechanism of the city was concentrated. He looked up the seething length of Alcazar where the people waited thickly along the sidewalk and, "Look," he said to Charlie suddenly, "what's the idea of this big meetin' this afternoon anyway?"

Charlie slapped at his hair and his hand came away sweat-oily. "They figger to ship the whole bunch of us over to Gath to sit right down on Big-Hearted Gus' doorstep until we get action."

"Who is this Gus I heard the boys yappin' about?"

"Gus? He's the headman around here, the one that wears the brass buttons in this province."

Matt frowned, mulling over the fresh angle. "Gath," he said, "I heard that name a lot, too. What is Gath anyway?" A man in front twisted his head round to grin. He said, "It's easy to see you havn't been around this province long, sonny. Gath's the capital."

"What's that supposed to do to us?" Matt was beginning when he broke off exclaiming, "Holy Jesus! Look at those people!"

The head of the column had slowed, entering the ball grounds. The slowing down passed all along the line, the shortened, half-shuffling steps. On one side the bleachers were solid with people. They poured up Troy abreast of the parade; like a rising tide they surged in from the side streets. Men, women and children, they perched like flies along the fenced-off square, shouted down from the low flat roofs of corner service stations, down from the roofs of houses. They ran and jostled and tripped and ran again. They broke in waves. It looked as though the people would never stop coming.

At one end there was a platform with flags and a mike and next to it a sound-truck with loudspeakers. A half-dozen men were standing on the platform and two boys with bandaged heads. One of the men was standing up by the mike waiting to open the meeting over the air when the excitement of the men's arrival had died down. Matt tried to edge close enough to see his face clearly because the features looked half familiar but from that far back in the crowd the distance was too great and the light too bright. He asked a man next to him who that was and the man looked at him in a funny way and said, "That's Laban. Didn't you know?" Matt thought if the man followed by asking whether he was a stranger around here he would have hauled right off on him because the next one who asked that again Matt was all set to haul off on.

Laban was a short dark man, bitter, shrewd and dynamic and he worked that crowd with the skill of a high-priced animal trainer. When his voice blared out, harsh and metallic, complete stillness fell. Matt did not catch the first part of his speech, he picked it up just as soon as his ear grew accustomed to the canned delivery. Then suddenly he heard and the words struck him and seared him like splinters of hot steel.

".... They can hound these homeless boys back and forth across the country," Laban shouted, "but they cannot break their spirit nor alter their demands. And what is it that they do demand? The right to work! Only the right to work! And what do they get?"

A voice yelled hysterically, *"Tear gas an' riot sticks!"*

A roar rose from the crowd, as though these were the words it had been waiting for. Menacing, sullen, it surged and hung. It did not want to die away.

Laban stepped back, brought forward the boys with the bandaged heads. "I want you all to meet some of these boys for yourselves. To see that they are not cattle with some ugly disease but human beings with the wants of human beings and the rights of citizens ..."

Matt's skin began to prick with excitement, the hard bright light dazzled his eyes. They burned with staring and he could not rest them nor tear them away. All about him men and women stood there, bodies oily with heat, chins raised and tense. The voice of Laban thundered on, harsh, embittered, flaying all counter-argument with savage contempt. Suddenly the voice stopped and when, out of the snapped rhythm, it went on again it was not loud with contempt but slow and soft with menace so that the shoulders of the people seemed to advance and the jaws to point and the faces to stiffen. "... Now these boys intend to do more than starve without protest, they intend to take their case the whole way. To Gath itself. To camp there in their hundreds until their demands are met, if it takes all winter!"

Laban stopped again and this time the crowd surged back to life. It let out a second mighty roar. Matt felt the massed power grip him, catch him up, make him a part of it. He saw the faces of men and women, mouths hard with shouting, the expression in their eyes hard and blind, their bodies beginning to awake and sway. A man ahead of him yelled, "We're gonna hold the fort!" Massed voices seized on the words. They broke into singing, shouting the chorus, "Hold the Fort For We Are Coming!" thundering triumphantly the ancient hymn, strong and measured like the feet of men marching.

When Laban finished a man with eyeglasses and thick white hair stepped up to the mike and started to head into the fight from the social-conscience angle and the crowd was tired of him before he said anything.

The way Laban had left them the people were steamed up and hungry to play. They let the second speaker get delivered of his opening remarks, then a man in front shoved through and monkeyed up onto the sound truck, yelling, "Let's go get the boys out of jail! Come on! Let's go get 'em now!"

From where Matt was standing the man was only a figure up there waving its hands, making cracked noises in its throat, but the people in front caught the words and took them up and made them into a mob chant. "Let's go get the boys out of jail ... go get the boys out of jail!" They surged forward, chanting, and a policeman riding in from the side to try to break the charge was swept from his horse and trampled.

Matt shouted, "By God, it's a riot!" He caught hold of a man running. "What happened in front there?"

"They're going to bust in the jug!" The words were picked up by a hungry network, "They're going to bust in the jug!"

"They are like hell!" Matt cried. He grinned back into the man's face, his eyes shone. He looked around for a rock to slip in his pocket and shouted to Eddy, then he began to run. The old mob blood-lust gripped him. He had not been in anything like this since '35. He caught glimpses of police trying to ride in through the crowd to break it and he heard the wail of the riot squad coming up. Ahead the mob moved on with heavy, shuffling feet. The shouting had died down now; it moved mechanically and its mood changed from sport to hunting; the animal quality was there and the prey was there and they were being drawn the one to the other.

Suddenly the mass movement ahead seemed to falter and lose momentum. Matt strained upwards but he could not see anything. He climbed up on top of an empty automobile parked by the curb and a part of the crowd broke away and came back and milled around the car asking what happened.

Matt shouted down, "Looks like they got someone up there talking to them."

"Someone up where?"

"A man up there hangin' onto a light standard or something."

A coatless man danced on the sidewalk, yelling, "A what?" He tried to climb on the roof, and Matt shoved his foot in his face to keep him from coming up in case the weight was too much.

A woman called out to know what was happening. Matt did not hear her, he was staring at what was going on over the heads of the crowd. He stared, fascinated, because he had never watched one man break a mob before.

The man was half-way up a light standard, hanging on with one hand, waving with the other. He looked like a black doll tied to a stick. Below him milled the heads of the crowd.

The woman yelled, "Who is it up there talking to them?"

Matt cried, "Shut up, will you? I can't see from here." He was trying to pick up what the man was saying but it was too far away.

The little black figure hung there pleading and gradually the crowd's form began to change. It changed from the tight, infuriated mob formation and began to open out and drift and lose direction. Gradually the numbers fanned out and began to scatter and remained milling uncertainly about the streets. They could not re-form again, even after the man dropped back onto the ground.

Matt climbed down off the car and wiped his face. "God," he said, "what a break the police got that time!"

The coatless man was angry because he did not get up there to watch any of it, so he began to make trouble in an oblique sort of way. He saw Eddy with his head bandaged. He started staring at him and when he saw it made Eddy nervous he stared some more. He said, "What happened to you? Did you get your head caught in a pair of nutcrackers?" He broke into a laugh and pointed at Eddy, because he was that sort of a man. The crowd stuck around and a lot of fresh people stopped and joined it, hungry for a new focus of sensation.

Matt glanced around quickly and he saw how they were cut off on all sides. He went over and took the man a little aside and said, "Lay off him, will you? Eddy don't like crowds."

The man resented Matt's attitude. "Maybe Eddy don't like crowds but maybe crowds like Eddy!"

Matt nodded, "That's just the trouble, mister."

The man looked startled, "What d'you mean by that?"

"Nothin'," Matt said, "just lay off Eddy, will you, please?"

The woman who had shut up after Matt spoke to her, climbed up now from her ringside seat and stepped back into the argument as one of the contenders. She was tall and angle-faced with skin like a plucked fowl. She could not resist the sight of Eddy. She cried, "Oh, you poor, poor boy! Does your head hurt very much?" and she came right over and stared at him as though he were something digestible.

Eddy's pale eyes blinked frightenedly. He stammered, distressed, "No, lady, not much now." The woman stepped up closer. She was the type that would vote against lynching but take home the burnt-up pants buttons of a negro as souvenirs.

Matt saw he had to work on her too. He said, trying to make it private, "I'd leave him alone if I was you, lady. Eddy's taken a bad smack on the head today an' it's liable to make him act queer."

The hen reared back and gave Matt a mean, virginal look and the coatless man interposed angrily, "The way you're wet-nursing Eddy, anyone would think he wasn't safe to have around."

Oh my God, Matt thought, pull one more like that and see what it does to you. His eyes darted over the crowd and it was ringed solid. He said, nervously, "Oh sure, mister, Eddy's okay."

"Then let him do his own talking."

"Sure, sure," Matt said quietly, keeping close to Eddy's other side, "what was it you wanted to know?"

Eddy saw the woman's face come closer and it merged confusedly with the face of the first woman that had come at him. He grew suddenly angry. He shouted, "Now you go away! You come at me this mornin' an' you come at me again now!"

There was a sharp breath-intake from the crowd. The woman's mouth dropped open. "Now you get away from me quick!" Eddy shouted threateningly. "You get away an' leave me alone."

The woman gasped, "What does he mean? I never saw him before."

"Oh, yes, you did. You followed me ... you followed me right through town. Didn't one smack be enough?" His arm came up and Matt caught at it. He dragged Eddy after him and headed into the crowd, shouting, "This man is sick! This is a sick man! We got to get to a doctor! Open up quick!" He shoved right in among the people pulling Eddy behind, and the crowd fell open grudgingly because this was the second bit of red meat they had been cheated of in an hour.

An old Chevy was rattling towards them down the street, coughing up her guts. Matt dashed out in the middle of the road and held up his hand. The driver jammed on his brakes to drag the relic to a standstill. Matt wrenched at the door, shouting, "Sick man! Get us to a doctor quick!" He shoved Eddy in ahead and climbed in behind. The driver gave one startled look around then he shoved in his clutch, his foot came down on the gas button and the car jerked ahead.

Matt looked back out the rear window. The crowd was slowly coming to life, the coatless man was out in the road yelling angrily. Then the Chevy slewed around the corner of the block and the picture was blotted out. He climbed over into the empty front seat. The driver's head came around. "Well, Sweet Jesus! Who'd of thought of seein' you again so soon!"

"*Harry!* Of all the breaks! Step on it quick! We got to get clear in case that bunch turns a cop onto our tails."

Harry opened up the old crate so that his arm shook as he gripped the wheel. Proudly he shouted above the roar, "She's got a sweet engine. Picked her up for fifty bucks cash. They don't build cars like that any more."

Matt looked around at Eddy. He was sitting rigid, his eyes staring ahead. Matt shouted to break up his mood, "You all right back there?"

Eddy's eyes came slowly round, his face relaxed. He nodded. Matt did not hear what he said because of the chattering of the car.

Harry slowed her down. "Where to?"

Matt said, "I never got the length of that yet."

"What say we take a little drive around the park as you're new to the city? It won't take above a half hour."

"Thanks, Harry, that would be swell. Say, were you down at the meetin'?"

"Was I? For about fifteen minutes there I thought that mob was goin' to cut loose and tear up the town. When it started to move I hared off an' picked out my car an' beat it like a bat out of hell."

Matt half turned in his seat. "I quite forgot," he said, "this is Eddy. I met up with him after I left you this morning."

Harry screwed his head around and beamed. "Glad to know you, Eddy." He eyed Eddy's bandages, "Looks like you met up with someone else before Matt met up with you."

Matt leaned towards him quickly, whispering, "Don't ask him nothin' about that, Harry. He took a terrible beatin' an' it's left him kind of rum-dum for the time. Eddy's okay, only don't talk sit-down, an' don't talk cops."

"I get you," Harry said, pleased to have the information privately like that. "What say we go on down to my place after an' have a cuppercoffy?"

"Sure, that would be dandy. I guess there's no special hurry about our gettin' back. They're all busy as hell around there now an' they're not goin' to miss us."

They drove out to the park and round the concrete driveway that skirted the sea. Planes were passing overhead, flying against the hot blue sky, glinting in the sun. The sound of the motors came on, zoomed heavily, then swept out to sea. Always there was the feeling that they might swing round and the sound come in strong again. The bay glittered with hard metallic light, and the mountains were striped with snow. There were not many cars in the park today. Most of them were haring around town, helping to build bigger and better traffic jams.

Harry held the old crate down to easy cruising speed. Presently he leant across to Matt. His fleshy face puckered with secrecy. Harry had all the makings of a swell conspirator only without the power to deceive. "Listen, Matt," he hissed, bringing his lips closer to Matt's ear, "what happened back there? You didn't need no doctor."

Matt shook out the three last cigarettes from the pack Lafe gave him, lit Harry's and stuck it between his lips. He explained, "Some loud-mouth tries to bother Eddy with a lot of fool questions, then this woman horns in ..."

"You don't tell me?" Harry chuckled obscenely.

"That may sound funny to you, but you don't know what Eddy pulls this mornin' an' then this on top of it!"

"This mornin'?"

Matt told him about the morning. "If you hadn't of come along when you did," he said, "most likely Eddy would have ended up by being jugged for assault. Seems like every old woman in town wants to get her hands on him like he was a prize baboon or something."

"Maybe he arouses their motherly instinct. There are some guys like that an' there's nothin' they can do about it. Oh say, Matt, did you hear that one about the sailor?"

"I heard plenty ones about sailors."

"Yeah, but I'll bet you didn't hear this one. This one's about a sailor and an Indian chief."

"No, I never heard that one," Matt said. Harry went ahead and told it. "Ain't that a honey?"

It was a minute before Matt got through laughing. "I heard one like that before but I never heard it told so well. The time I heard it, it was about a logger."

"Aw, what's the diff? Sailor? Logger? Both is the kind of guys that has to stay out of town a long time!" Harry's rumbling laugh came again. He was pleased with the way Matt made the telling of it seem original and important.

Half-way round the park there was a bridge linking up the two sides of town. Harry pulled up so Matt could look back down the bay. Seen from there the skyline looked like something out of the Arabian Nights only more modern, taller and with a lot more class. The thing that gave it the Arabian Nights touch was the unreality of the buildings at that distance. They tapered up with more perfection and beauty, with more smoothness and greater power than belonged to them. They looked very beautiful, and if they had been old they could not have looked that way because the beauty of the old does not compare with the line of the new. Matt never looked at a city that way before. He never sat above that much water and looked down a bay on the one side and out to the open sea on the other.

Harry asked him would he like to get out and Matt said sure he would. He began to feel the place getting hold of him. Harry watched him lean down over the guardrail and the minute he said that about getting out he was sorry because he knew that he had committed an error that he could never undo. He sat there smoking, scratching his stump and worrying, knowing that he had done this thing he could never undo.

Matt was watching a tug come up, bucking the tide. It swayed and wallowed, heading in against the rip. The rips showed by the white, rough-edged water. There was a little fish boat passing the tug with a shower of grey and white gulls planing over it and a few brown speckled gulls. Matt watched them fascinated. He could not drag his eyes away from the gulls at all. They swept above the boat's stern, fighting the currents in the upper air, poised, hardly seeming to make a yard, then wheeling suddenly and swooping for a dive.

Harry's foot touched the gas button delicately. Matt climbed back in. "Lovely, ain't it?" Harry said when they were going again, "kinda like those travelogues they show you at the movies."

"Yeah," Matt said, "it's lovely all right." He did not say anything for a long time. Harry sat there worrying about the error he had committed. He got right out of that neighbourhood as quickly as he knew how, and he dived into a maze of run-down shacks and swarming streets and out of reach of the dangerous, poisonous beauty. He went back into the city through Chinatown, closed up tight for Sunday and looking like the walking dead, only no one was out walking. He did everything he could to clean the poison out of Matt's system.

"You know something," Matt began when Harry was pretty sure he had done a job on him.

"Maybe," Harry said gloomily and his heart went right down because he knew at once he had just been burning up so much gas.

"Know what I'd like to do?" Matt said.

"I dunno," Harry said. He knew too damn well.

"I'd like to live here all the time. I'd like to get me a job an' be some use to myself an' some use to someone else for a change. That's what I'd like to do, Harry. God," Matt said, staring straight at the closed-up fronts of the Wong On fish market, "I never saw such a lovely place as this is!"

Harry did not say anything until he had to. Then he answered, heavily, "But you ain't never goin' to do any such thing."

"What d'you mean? They don't want me back where I come from! When they get this big works program going that the boys is staging the sit-down for, why shouldn't I? Hell, Harry, why shouldn't I get me a job here an' settle down?"

Harry slewed the car round a corner and dragged her up in front of the lunchroom. "If I knew the answer to that one," he said morosely, "maybe they'd make me prime minister!"

He opened up the lunchroom, lit the gas, and gave them coffee, pie and a corned beef sandwich. When they were through Matt pulled the quarter out of his pocket and slid it across. Harry stubbed his big finger on it and slid it right back. "Skip it," he said, "it's been a pleasure. I'll bet everyone in town feels they want to do all they can for the boys."

Matt looked at Harry and for a moment he could not speak. Then, "By Jesus!" he exclaimed, "you are the best guy I ever ran into, Harry. I tell you I ran into plenty guys in my time but you are the ace!"

Harry swatted viciously at a bluebottle to hide his pleasure. He said, "Believe me, Matt, but you two boys done me the favour. Every once in a while I get to feelin' lonely an' there's nothin' but a bunch of lousy Greeks an' kikes to talk to around here. Every time I want to talk I have to go out someplace."

He walked with them to the door. The evening air was close and heavy and the street lights and the Neons had begun to come on. The sky signs were impressive, too. They and the Neons together made the night sky really look like something. They did a lot for the stars as well. They made the stars appear as though they did not have enough watts or else were hung too high to be practical. Matt sniffed the air. "I'll bet that bunch has a nice sail over tonight," he said.

Harry nodded. "I'll bet they collected a nice little wad towards expenses, too," he remarked. "Before the trouble started they was harin' around, rattlin' their cans, borin' into that crowd like termites."

"If anything big breaks in the way of news, Harry, we'll try to get it to you."

"Thanks, Matt, I'd appreciate it. S'long. S'long, Eddy."

Matt walked quickly away. He muttered, glancing up at the big Neon clock in the Brand block, "I guess we shouldn't have stayed so long, I didn't realize how late it was."

Eddy, half-running, answered, "But the food was nice, Matt. I was hungry when we got to Harry's place."

Matt turned on him furiously. "You! You!" He stopped, choking, "Why, you sonovabitch! *Don't you even remind me you're alive!*"

They ran foul of Hep a block away from the hall. When he saw them he burst out, "Where have you two been since afternoon?" He said the words as though he had been waiting to get them said for a long time. Matt resented his tone. He answered at once to prevent Eddy's floundering around with the truth, "We didn't get in any kind of trouble."

"That don't answer my question. I asked where you'd been."

Matt looked steadily back at him. "We ran into a guy named Harry. He took us for a drive around the park."

Hep's eyes darkened with suspicion. The soft voice inquired, "How'd you get to know a guy named Harry so well in this time?"

Matt felt his first animosity coming back two-fold. He answered coldly, "I could tell you that but it would take time."

Hep started to speak, then he changed his mind as to what he wanted to say. "Time's something we haven't got around here," he said. "You two boys hightail in an' get a bite to eat if the food isn't all gone."

"We had ours."

"Well, go on down to the basement anyway. Those women are doing a swell job and they need all the help they can get."

Matt called after him, "Is it true they're shippin' a bunch of the boys over to Gath by the night boat?"

"Sure it's true. Weren't you at the meeting?"

"You mean the one that nearly bust up in a riot?"

"Hell no, the one the boys held after."

"How many's goin'?"

"A million!" Hep shouted, "maybe two million. Now get th' hell on downstairs."

CHAPTER FIVE

They found the last sitting of supper finished and the women at one of the tables having a meal of their own. They sat with their hats on, eating cold meat and salad and drinking tea out of thick china mugs. Their faces were tired and oily with the heat. Some of these women had been there since six in the morning, preparing three big meals for upwards of a thousand men. The pots and lard pails still steamed on the stove tops and the tables were re-set for breakfast with a plate, a mug and a handful of cutlery laid cornerwise at each plate.

The girl, Hazel, was down there, too, and another girl that had come with her mother. Hazel was going around with a big enamelled jug filling the women's cups. Matt said, "Maybe I can do that for you. That jug looks kind of heavy."

She glanced around, then saw who it was and let him take the jug. "Thanks," she said, "it is heavy."

"Did you have a good swim?"

"Yes, I had a dandy swim." They stood there looking at one another and smiling. Eddy had slid in to the table at the other end and sat there watching them. One of the women sloshed him full a cup of tea and pushed it across. He took it and thanked her, then drew away. He did not want the women speaking to him, he did not want to get drawn into the conversation or noticed at all. Not after the way Matt had gone after him while they were walking up to the hall.

"Sit down, why don't you?" Hazel's aunt called out to Matt from the end of the table. "Did you have any supper yet?" she giggled. "Seems like I'm always asking you did you have a meal."

"If there's anything left," Matt said, "we'd like some. We had a piece of apple pie an' a corned beef sandwich around six o'clock but the effect's wearing off by now."

Hazel went over to the table where the big joints of meat were, carved down red to the bone. Matt followed her. "Look," he said, "you sit down an' let me handle this."

She shrugged. "All week I handle it only mine isn't cooked, it's the raw kind."

He stared at her, not understanding. "I wrap it," she said, "I wrap meat in Lincoln's basement."

He glanced down at her pale, small-boned hands with the carmine-rose cracking off the nails. "You sure don't look like your job."

"I'm lucky to have it."

"Yeah, I know," Matt said, "but just the same that seems more like a man's job." He stood there holding his plate and Eddy's while she scooped out gobs of potato salad and laid it beside the meat. She answered in her quiet realistic manner, "If they hired men then they'd have to pay more. It's not the hours that get me, it's the smell ... that and the bloodstains."

Matt made a sharp sound in his throat. "God," he muttered, shocked. Something about the way she said it came at him between the eyes. Nothing had ever had quite the same effect before. Not even approximately the same effect.

She held up one of her hands. "Wouldn't that make you tired? There ought to be some kind of a guarantee."

"Huh?"

She fluttered her fingers critically. "Looks like that polish has been on a week, I guess it's the salt water. I put it on Sunday mornings and take it off Sunday night. Store regulations. Nail polish isn't sanitary in the meat department." She went back to the table and sat down, and Matt slid the plate over to Eddy and went back beside her.

He asked, "Do Lincoln's step on your tail for every little thing? I mean," he reddened, "do they get after you a lot?"

She lit a cigarette and sat there quietly watching him while he ate. "I tell you," she said, "some things are a joke. Those regulations are a joke. They won't let us girls wear anything on our nails, but I wish you could see the women picking up the chops and steaks and smelling them and dropping them back again. I wish you could see that for a day," she said.

He picked up her mood. He felt this about her from the first, that she was a realist. He asked, "Why does the store stand for it?"

"Because the customer is always right. They're not supposed to do it but they do do it."

"Yeah, I know," he said frowning, "it's the same way with a lot of things." He got the feeling that he was included in this problem in her mind, and it gave him a sense of intimacy and the feeling that he had known her a long time.

"I tell you," she went on, "it's the same way with the exchange racket upstairs. The store puts up big notices in a lot of the departments about no goods exchanged, but the women try and pull the trick just the same."

"Do they get away with it?"

"The ones with the fat charge accounts do. You wouldn't believe it about some of those women, they're nothing but a bunch of lousy bandits, but you know how money is."

"No," Matt said, "I never did."

"Never did what?"

"Knew what money was."

She laughed. "Oh, God," she said, "you're funny!" She sat there smoking while he finished his meal. He enjoyed the feel of her there, companionable, not making any demands, not trying to make any kind of an impression. He noticed she seemed to know a lot of the boys, and he found out later that she used to come and help out with her aunt at weekends while the three weeks sit-down was on and the women sent in meals cooked in their own downtown kitchen.

At the other end of the table the women sat with their elbows up, talking in tired, quiet voices. Overhead the hollow drumming of feet kept up, the creak of men hurrying across old floorboards. A harmonica was playing somewhere. Every now and then during a brief pause in the upstairs racket the soft, jogging notes came clear.

Finally the aunt heaved to her feet, waved a bare, droopy-muscled arm and called down the table, "Time to go now, dear. Remember, tomorrow's Monday!"

Hazel crushed out her cigarette and rose. She said to Matt out of the side of her mouth, "That woman!" she said, "that woman and the things she's always wanting. All right, aunty, I'm coming." They let the aunt go on ahead. "I don't suppose you ever met a vampire, did you?"

Matt shook his head. "I never heard the word before."

"That woman's a vampire," Hazel said, "every nickel that comes in the house she snitches for pills or God. Sometimes I feel I could wring Christ's neck!"

Matt went with her as far as the door. All the way he tried to think of something to say so he would be sure of meeting her again. When they got to the door he asked, "Going for another swim tomorrow after you get through work?"

She looked at him a moment. Colour spread slowly up her cheeks. "Perhaps," she said coolly, "Why?" Then she smiled.

Matt spoke fast. "Maybe I could meet you somewhere an' we could go together."

"Don't you boys have nothing to do but sit around here and wait for a settlement?"

"Sure we do, but I could get an hour off in the day sometime."

The aunt called from the bottom of the steps, "Hurry, honey. If we run we can pick up a bus on the corner."

"That woman," Hazel muttered. "You wouldn't believe. Always wanting something. Coming, aunty! Listen," she said, "I didn't even ask your name."

"Matt. Matt Striker. I just got in town this morning. Rode in on a box car."

Her face hardened. "The Boy Rod-Rider!"

"So what? If I hadn't had the get-up to jump that car I could have been sittin' around Saskatchewan yet, rotting!"

She stopped kidding him. "I didn't mean it like that," she said, "I was looking at it another way."

"What way?"

"I meant where's a date with you going to get me? I got nothing, you got less. Besides I've only known you a half hour."

The voice of the aunt came again. Matt said, "You've known me more than a half hour. Remember this morning?"

She looked at him and smiled. The voice of the aunt came again angrily. "Okay then," Hazel breathed. "Make your date quick."

"Attagirl! Where do we meet and when?"

She stared off into the darkening street. Then, "Six-thirty on the corner of Alcazar and Shroeder outside the tobacco store. If I'm not there you'll know I couldn't make it."

"I'll wait!" Matt called after her. He saw the big red bus come lumbering round the corner and the aunt heave into it and Hazel make it at a flying run. Then the bus grunted, pulled out from the curb and slid heavily off down the block.

He strolled over to the lot after that and stopped to watch a half-dozen of the boys playing blackjack. Banker was dealing from a pack of greasy cards. He glanced up over his shoulder. "Want to sit-in on a little game?"

"What you playin' for? Matches?"

"What d'you think we're playin' for? The national debt?"

Matt grinned and moved away. "I don't carry matches around in the hot weather," he said.

A man got up. "If you want my place," he said, "you're welcome. I just broke even but I sure worked up a sweat."

"Thanks," Matt said, "but I couldn't keep my eyes open. I've felt kind of slugged all day." He eased down and lit a cigarette. The voices of the players came to him:

"Hit me one but make it soft." The light slap of the card falling. The voice again in disgust. "Don't you never have nothin' smaller than a lousy queen?"

"Stand!"

"I'm standin'."

"Me, too."

"Sock me hard." Slap. "That's fine, that's dandy. I'm standin'."

"Let's see what you got there." The slight craning of heads. Banker lays out his cards. A voice, "Sixteen! Watch this one bust him." The snap of a turned card. "*Five!*" The chorus in disgust:

"If I had his luck I'd do it for a livin'."

"Wanted a five an' got a five. By Jesus!"

"What were you standin' on? Eighteen? Me, I never had luck with no eighteens. Musta been born the wrong day of the month or somethin'." Soft scratch of the gathered-in matches and the slapping of the cut pack. The fresh deal, the quiet chorus, the slight shifting of feet or bottoms on the dusty ground. After a time the sounds ceased to register. Matt's head drooped forward. For the second time that day he fell asleep.

He was wakened by Hep's shaking him and Hep's voice in his ear. "Chroust! I didn't think anyone could sleep at a time like this!" Matt got up stiffly, knuckling sweat out of his eyes. The darkness was filled with the shapes of hurrying men. Along the sidewalks the crowds milled once more, curious, excited. The tenement windows were blacked with heads. The familiar exhibitionalistic trappings of the afternoon only staged beneath flickering, shabby lights and the glare of the billboard.

Matt hurried inside, slapped cold water onto his face, joined the long line-up at the can and ran on outside. The men that were sailing by the night boat were massed at the head of the line carrying their packs and behind them surged the balance of the jobless army. Bare heads, fedora'd heads, faces young, aging, slack, taut; eyes hungry for excitement, dull with experience. Hard glare on hard mouths, angry shadows, empty grins, sweat smells, hysteria, maintained discipline. The figures of men running as they snapped into line, shouted orders, the shoving, tight-massed bodies of the crowd, raw flickering of lights, the dark solidity of police uniforms, action shots and the low, continuous seething of talk.

The columns ahead began to move. Matt felt the same sharp, danger-ous thrill of the afternoon. His face was stiff and fresh after the cold water and his body jerked back to energy by the shot of sleep. All that he saw and heard now was intensified by repetition. The hysterical cheering of the people, the hard tramp of feet, the rhythm of swinging arms white in the half dark, the spattering of cops' machines.

Suddenly the men began to sing. They marched, singing, through the Neon-brilliant downtown streets. They sang old army songs and "Hold the Fort" and beside them ran the people, seizing on each familiar chorus with a frenzied mob hunger. They surged into the depot ahead of the marchers, shoving, fighting, monkeying up onto the roof of the pier, massing wherever there was a ledge or an open space. They burst through the locked doors, flooding out onto the long, narrow neck of the pier. They jammed the depot so that again and again a lane had to be opened for the men to pass through.

As the boat pulled out the wild singing turned to cheers. The black mass mushroomed suddenly with bobbing points of white. From the bow of the boat the little body of men waved back, singing and cheering. Bareheaded they sang the anthem. The people joined in, thundering, shouting, swelling it till it became a battle cry. The feeling of the people was so intense that they lost all sense of proportion both towards them-selves and towards the occasion. When the boat swung out and was hid-den by the sheds they were left shaken and dazed without direction. There had never been anything like this in the city before; never anything to com-pare with it.

Matt's face was rigid. Tears of excitement choked him. His hands were clenched so that the nails tore into the palms. Beside him a woman was sobbing hysterically. She kept repeating, "I can't see them. I can't see what it is they're doing." He could not see anything beyond a heaving mass of shoulders, blurred profiles, striving heads. He could not speak nor think coherently and afterwards, trying to recall details, he found whole sequences blacked out.

He caught sight of Hep turning, fighting his way back. He gasped, "The mob's broke up the whole formation. Each squad has to look out for itself going home. Chroust! I never saw people act this way before!" His black hair hung lank, his lean, sweating face wore a dazed, triumphant look.

Matt fought his way behind Hep, shoving Eddy ahead, using his body as a battering ram. Back of him he felt the massed mob movement as the tide began to turn and flood back over the streets. He felt himself swept up and carried towards the downtown blocks as the head of Hep swam on before him. On the corner of Alcazar and Troy below the Aschelon Trust Building the rhythm broke suddenly. The mob surge slowed and the people began to mill around in a mood of dangerous drunken play.

Hep's head jerked back shouting, "Keep right behind me, this mob's liable to do anything. Keep a hold of Eddy, too!"

Matt yelled, "I'm on your tail all the way!" He felt an elbow drive into his side. A man next to him was reaching down into his pocket. He had a rock in his hand. His arm swung back. Matt seized the arm and twisted it savagely and the rock dropped. Matt yelled, "You crazy bastard, you! D'you want to start a riot!"

The man swung on him, letting fly with a vicious poke that went wild. Matt saw him then. He yelled, "*Lafe!*" The man swung again, catching him on the side of the jaw. Matt felt the old rage-blindness, the brain-splitting fury. The supreme insult of personal assault. He was crying with rage. He choked, "*Pigeon! Goddam pigeon!*" He smashed out and his fist contacted the already-broken nose, and blood spurted from the man's face like from a jerked faucet. The head rocked back and the body slumped against the tight-wedged bodies of the people.

Hep was turning back. His face was livid. He yanked at Matt, dragging him off, diving him into the crowd. When they came out in the clear his nostrils were pinched with rage and he took a moment getting himself back under control. He panted, "You dam little pipsqueak, you! What d'you want to do? Bust this whole town up in a riot?"

Matt gaped at him, then he started to laugh. "Oh God," he said and laughed and laughed. He could not get himself under.

"What's so funny?" Hep asked, wiping his streaming face. He was white like paper and there was a rigidity about his whole face. "For Chrissake what's so funny? Did you *want* to start a riot?"

"I just stopped one," Matt gasped. He was shaking and he had a stitch from laughing and it hurt. His face hurt, too—his jaw where Lafe hit him.

Eddy tugged at Hep's arm. "There was this guy with a rock," Eddy said. He raised his arm, imitating Lafe. "He was all set to throw it through one of those big windows. I seen it, Hep, I seen it aimed in his hand."

Hep slewed round. "What's that? What in hell are you talking about?"

Matt made an effort and got himself back in hand. "That's right," he said, "that was Lafe Benson that gave me the first smoke I ever had around here." He put his hand up and felt along his jaw line tenderly.

Hep pulled out a handkerchief and wiped his hot face and round the back of his neck. When he spoke his voice was filled with disgust. "I'm sorry, Matt, I'm the one should get kicked around. I didn't see his face. All I saw was you socking him. I guess I was jittery anyway."

"That's okay," Matt said stiffly, "anyone's liable to go crazy in a mob like that." Through his first resentment shot a hot thrill of triumph that Hep should stand there apologizing to him.

Hep said, "Remember how I warned you this morning to be careful who you picked to go around with?"

"Sure, I remember."

"Well, here's another thing. That Lafe'll just disappear, drop out, an' before you can turn around there'll be another Lafe. That's how it goes with that brand of bird; wing one and another flies right in an' takes his place."

The high whine of a police siren broke in. A speed cop shot by the end of the block sledding to a riot call.

"Sounds like that mob decided to turn playful."

"You goin' back there now, Hep?"

"Sure I am. I got to try to collect up the rest of my boys. You two go on back to the hall so there's two less to account for."

"Can't I come along? I don't want to miss anything."

"I said to go along."

"Yeah? Well, suppose I don't go."

Hep glared at him. He hissed like an angry snake, "What th' hell do you think you are anyway? One little squib or the whole damn revolution?"

Matt's chin shot out resentfully. He got set to blow off then caught Hep's eye. "Okay," he muttered sulkily, "I'll go along."

"You bet you'll go along. An' check right in as soon as you get there."

"You don't take any chances, do you?"

"Damn right I don't take chances ... not with the way things've been today." He turned to Eddy, "You go right along an' check in same as Matt does. You got that?"

Eddy nodded respectfully. "If they all snapped into it like you do, Eddy," Hep added, his deep eyes warming for an instant, "we'd have a damn sight less trouble around here."

Matt looked after him resentfully. He said, "I didn't like that guy first time I met him an' I don't like him any better now."

Eddy stared at him shocked. "Him?" he said, "Hep?"

"Yeah, sure, Hep. Who d'you think I meant? The king of Spain?"

"I don't know nothin' about no king of Spain," Eddy said gravely, "all I know is Hep ain't like other guys, he's a prince. I heard him called a prince often."

Matt laughed, feeling small and angry. He began to walk on fast. "I guess I'm just too democratic to appreciate him, then," he said.

A clock bonged one. Along the bare, bright-lit vista of Alcazar the first cars began to stream as the crowd slowly broke and scattered. The hysteria was played out now, leaving the air flat and heavy and uncharged. The people were no longer a loud and conquering mob but an unled herd stampeding for home. As the two men walked through the emptying streets and the lights grew fewer Eddy kept closer to Matt, almost touching him. Eddy's face was white and tired and his bandages were dirty. That night gave Matt the first real insight into the things that scared Eddy, not just the ones that scared him recently but those that bored back deep into the past and were grown down into his mind. Matt did not stop to wonder about them with any real insight then; nothing was stable, all thought was flux. Anger, excitement, shock, climax, anti-climax, they seethed in his raw, aching mind as the pain throbbed in his jaw. His mind did not try to deal with them, nevertheless they penetrated and grew, forming some secret substance of which in tomorrow and in the days to come his mind was to be made.

Outside the hall they ran into pickets who told them where to check in and later they went back outside to find someplace to lie down. As they stumbled cautiously among the dark humped figures on the lot a man raised his head, blinked at them and saw Eddy's bandages pale in the bleak light. He dragged an old straw pillow out from under his head. "Take it," he mumbled, "it ain't so good layin' a hurt head on the ground." He stayed awake a little time to talk. He asked in a soft, hoarse voice, "How'd she go?"

"Fine," Matt said, "I'll bet this town never saw anything like it before."

"Yeah? I wisht I could of been there."

"Why didn't you?"

The man pushed one foot free of his blanket and wiggled his toes. "Feet," he whispered, "all shot to blazes. They never was much good an' they softened up a lot on the sit-down." He fumbled in his clothes, passed Matt a cigarette and a light and went back to sleep. He must have noticed Matt was a kid and badly strung up.

Matt sat there a long time hunched against the piled junk. He watched the broken squads drift back, the side door open and shut, the thin shaft of yellow light that struck the steps each time a man went in or out. Those that came outside to bed down looked like grave-robbers, stepping, stumbling among the sleepers. Those that lay beneath the billboard drew their blankets up or used their arms to shield their faces from the light.

All this Matt saw with the hard burning eyes of the sleepless. Now that he wanted to sleep he could not sleep. A bomb ticked ceaselessly over in his brain, his bruised jaw ached dully. He listened to the far-off howl of a train, began to count the number of times the police patrol went around the block.

Once a boy reared up cursing in his sleep. The lips drew back, the blind eyes glared at Matt so that he felt his skin itch and the palms of his hands grow damp. He leant over and laid the boy back gently with the flat of his hand.

A man pushed open the side door, peered round then came over, easing down on the ground beside Matt. He said softly, "You didn't get to sleep yet?" His hand felt down into his side pocket and pulled out a sack of tobacco.

Matt heard the tiny scuffle of the shaken tobacco. He said in a low voice, "I couldn't seem to settle down." He saw Hep's face as the match flared. The two cigarettes made little solitary beads of light. Presently Hep spoke again. His voice was not his voice at all. It had no authority.

"Look," the voice of Hep said gently, "don't try to take in too much territory."

Matt's head jerked round, suspicious and touchy. He could not make out anything beyond sharp black planes and a burning tip that moved up, glowed for an instant then moved down again. He asked uncertainly, "What d'ya mean by that?"

"I mean it's been a long day, you had quite an initiation. Don't try to get what it all means at once. There's a lot of angles to this thing," Hep said, "a lot of angles."

Matt pushed his hand over his face dazedly, fighting off anti-climax. "God," he muttered, "today feels like a million years."

"Yeah, I know. That's the way it goes sometimes, but don't let it bother you."

They smoked in silence, islanded among the sleeping men. Snores, groans, rustle of newspapers, muttering of sleep-talkers, thudding of bodies heaving uneasily on the broken ground. Matt felt his nerves beginning to let up, the drowsiness creep over him. His eyes ceased to burn and he stopped counting when the patrol went by.

"Hep!"

"What is it?"

"I never saw anything like that mob down at the boat tonight. I never saw anything like that in my life before."

"There's never been anything like it."

"They acted like mad people."

The position of Hep's shoulders did not alter, only the shifting tip of his cigarette. "Sometimes," he said softly, "it seems like the authorities was out to act against their own interests, like they never took the trouble to find out little things about human nature."

"How come?"

"This time yesterday the public had gone stale on sit-down, all fed up with trouble; then along come these busted heads this morning an' see what happens. If they'd of handled this thing different an' let those boys come out quiet, this whole situation would have petered out like a wet squib so far as the public was concerned. See what I mean?"

Matt's mind jerked suddenly awake. He said, "You're tryin' to teach me something, aren't you?"

"Maybe." Hep's voice had grown cautious.

"Why are you?"

"I wouldn't know about that yet."

"Because you think I might be worth something?"

"I tell you I wouldn't know about that yet," Hep said quietly. He got up and stood looking down. His hand came out and touched Matt's shoulder. "Jaw still sore where Lafe hit you?"

Matt felt along the bone gingerly. "My jaw's okay, I'd forgot all about it."

"Well, so long. Try to get some sleep."

Matt watched him picking his way across the lot and disappear in at the side door. The tiredness was on Matt now, soothing as a drug. He rooted down, stretched his blanket up over himself and went to sleep. He slept like a dog and towards morning he had the same dream again ... the dream about the well and darkness and his mind groping and falling towards a bottom that was not there.

CHAPTER SIX

As Matt climbed the basement stairs next morning a boy dove into him head on. He stepped across, blocking the boy deliberately. "Hey, you," he drawled, "what's all the hurry?"

The boy's black eyes flared with excitement. "Didn't you hear?"

"Hear what?"

"That we planned a march on one of the big stores, Lincoln's, I think."

Matt's shoulders dropped. He pushed his hands down in his jeans. "Look," he said, "just what is it you're talking about?"

"I heard we're goin' to march right after dinner an' stage a sit-down in Lincoln's an' then when the cops come we're goin' to say t' hell with 'em an' have a real scrap. Not just a mess like Sunday but a real fight right there in the middle of town."

Matt's mouth curled with contempt. "What are we goin' to fight with?"

The look on the boy's face altered and grew vague. "I dunno ... rocks an' clubs, I guess."

Matt moved slowly aside. "Someone's been feedin' you meat when you don't know the difference yet between horse meat an' hamburger."

The boy flashed round. "Oh, I don't, huh? Who taught you to be so smart?"

"I'm not smart, I just use my head."

The boy flushed and his voice rose angrily. "Who d'you think you are around here?"

"Never mind who I am," Matt said, "I got your number anyway."

A man paused to listen, then another. A crowd grew swiftly. Hep came through the door, took in the scene and broke the men apart. He drew Matt quickly outside. "What happened back there?" he asked.

Matt shrugged. "Just a kid with the jitters said there was goin' to be some kind of a bust-up. This camp's lousy with rumours, that's what started all the trouble. Why don't they give out more information around here?"

Hep bored sharply into the seat of his discontent. "The executive gives out all the information that's healthy and the boys hold their meeting same time every morning. Weren't you at the meeting?"

"Sure I was but there's still a lot of things I'd like to know."

"There's a lot of things we'd all like to know." Hep paused. For a moment he eyed Matt steadily. "An' just one thing you have to remember an' keep on remembering."

Matt felt himself smarting beneath the calm, probing gaze. He stubbed his toe in the dirt, muttering with a puzzled discontent, "I never remembered so much in a short time before. Ever since I come in here I've been rememberin' rules. What else do I have to remember?"

Hep walked ahead. He pointed back across the lot. "Commere, Matt," he said. "What do you see?"

Matt slitted his eyes against the strong light. A line-up of boys sat along the sidewalk. Loose-shouldered, droop-mouthed, slack-eyed; eyes emptied by years of staring at nothing. They lounged about the doors gassing, smoking, their gaze following the passers-by with a dull, mechanical interest while from the inside of the hall a steady stream of men boiled in and out. The air was sticky and close and reeked of gas fumes. A group of Jap children were playing on the sidewalk outside the

Jap store down the street. The backs of the rookeries dripped with grey wash.

Matt frowned at the line-up of hunched backs. "All I see is a big bunch of men, mostly," he said, wondering what Hep was getting at.

Hep said quickly, "An' that's pretty well all there is to see around here—that an' trouble. We started out with five hundred an' we got close to fifteen hundred, everything from school teachers an' truck drivers an' last years' high school kids down to plain, ordinary, stinkin' bums. We got a cross-section of pretty near every trade an' profession in the country." Hep paused. His eyes moved farther into the distance. After a moment he went on, "The most of those boys is decent but all of 'em aren't. You get that with any organization. Now suppose the executive was to turn loose a lot of valuable information, what good d'you suppose it'ud be by the time they came to use it?"

Matt was silent. Then, "I guess that's right," he admitted grudgingly. He fingered his bruised chin and grinned. "You talk to me like I talk to Eddy."

"I talk to you like I talk to the rest of the boys," Hep said, calmly. "I don't play no favourites an' I don't waste my time for nothing. There's just two kinds you have to reckon on in a bunch like this—not counting pigeons an' trouble-makers, which are two kinds you can't reckon on anyway—an' those are the boys that want work an' figger they can get it by mass protest backed up by a strong public opinion, an' the ones that use it as a good way to eat."

Matt said quickly, "We got the public opinion all right. Look at last night!"

Hep dropped his butt and stamped it carefully cold. He answered dryly, "I can't, it's gone." He began to walk back towards the hall. "I started in to tell you something, Matt, an' got sidetracked. You came to me beefing like a kid that can't cut up an' do as he likes in school. You were saying to yourself, 'T'hell with the rules!' You got hot for a moment back there, didn't you?"

Matt nodded soberly. "Yeah, I guess I did."

"An' I took time out to tell you why we got to have those rules. The only thing that's going to get us any action is by educating the public that these boys here are not just a bunch of irresponsible bums an' hoodlums but men with a strong case." He stopped at the foot of the steps. The soft voice grew menacing, "That's why we have to have discipline around here—*an' by Christ it has to be discipline!*"

Matt's head came up, his face tightened. For the first time in his life he felt the steel edge of personal responsibility. He said quietly, "You don't ever need to tell me that again."

Hep's angular features relaxed in a brief smile. "If I didn't believe that," he said, "I wouldn't have told you the first time." He looked around, "Where's Eddy?"

"I left him cleanin' spuds in the basement. I was on my way up when that kid butted into me. Can I go an' take a look-see around town for an hour?"

"Sure you can, but take Eddy along with you. Watch out you don't get in any kind of trouble. The way the city is this morning, drop a match an' you're liable to get your head blown off. I heard they picked up around twenty-five of the boys for tin-canning already."

"Okay," Matt said, "I'll be careful." He went back inside to find Eddy.

As they walked up the street together he noticed Eddy wearing his frayed denims. "What happened to that swell outfit you had on yesterday, Eddy?"

Eddy looked down at his bare ankles and split Romeos and his face grew ashamed. He explained, "The guy that owned them wanted to get up an' move around." He sighed. "I never got those shoes yet."

Matt laughed. "Don't worry, Eddy, you will."

"When will I?"

"Remember all those people down at the boat last night?"

The light went out of Eddy's eyes. "I remember."

"Well, all those people down there meant you're goin' to get those shoes very soon now."

"Really, Matt? I didn't see no shoes down at that boat, only people yellin' an' gettin' shoved around." His eyes fell on a second-hand store across the street. The windows were crammed with junk, everything from bed-pans and bridge-work down to sheet music and ukeleles. Above the doorway there were slickers and racked suits and bunches of boots hanging, logging boots and rubber thigh boots and one big pair of light tan oxfords. Eddy pointed to them excitedly. He cried, "Look Matt! There's a dandy pair! Let's go over an' talk to the man an' maybe he'll hold them."

Matt dragged him back. He said quickly, "We'll go pick out those shoes another day, Eddy. Tomorrow or maybe when we get to Gath. I'll bet they have swell second-hand stores over in Gath."

Eddy's face altered slowly. He looked at Matt with the expression of an undeceived child. He muttered sullenly and hopelessly, "I'll bet they don't have no second-hand stores in Gath at all—not ones with bunches of boots hangin'."

They walked on up wholesale row where the powerful green produce trucks were backed into the curb. The big plate glass store fronts along Alcazar had been replaced and police stood guard at the main entrances of Lincoln's and Haywards. Most of the large downtown buildings had their main doors policed and all but a single entrance closed off. Seeing the police posted there made Matt wonder if there was anything to the kid's wild rumour of another sit-down.

On the corner of Troy and Alcazar they came on the first tin-canner, a stocky, Jewish-looking boy in glasses. He wore, like all the rest, a bright blue chest band lettered in white with the jobless slogan: JOBS NOT JAIL. Matt stopped. "How come they didn't pick you up yet?"

The boy's head came up suspiciously, then his mouth dragged with contempt. "Don't make me laugh," he said, "the faster they pick us up the thicker we come. Some of these cops is so green they don't even know how to make an arrest."

"Maybe it'll be your turn next."

"So what? I'm not worrying. They can't jug the whole fifteen hundred of us." The boy rattled his can. A man came by and dropped in a quarter. The boy sniggered. "I tell you it's a joke. These cops they have out on the streets today is a joke. The boys is just makin' fools of 'em."

Matt's face narrowed. "Were you ever in th' jug?"

The boy eyed him with hostility. "Who are you anyway? A pigeon?"

"If I was," Matt said, "d'you think I'd waste my time on a nickel bunch of firecrackers like you?" He grinned in the boy's insulted face and went on.

They stopped below the windows of the Bulletin offices to find out what the crowd was about. On the inside a boy was pasting up late flashes. News of yesterday's rioting, estimated damage, number of injured, the first contingent's arrival at Gath and information as to the men's future plans. Below the window the crowd milled, curious, excited, confused. A woman's voice exclaimed, "Those boys certainly show courage in taking their case to Gath after what happened yesterday."

A man's voice, "That's not courage, that's just a piece of cheap publicity."

"The authorities came right out and warned them they needn't expect any more in Gath than they got here."

"And what did they get here?" An angered boiling-up of voices now and the man again, loud with outrage. "They should get right after these trouble-makers with machine guns ... and I wouldn't mind being on the end of one myself."

Matt glimpsed the man ahead, rolling brick-coloured neck, shaved sleek, full tailored shoulders, the sun turning his Panama to dazzling white.

Matt spoke up coldly. "Were you ever on the end of a machine gun, mister?" There was a dead pause, then a burst of half nervous laughter, a twisting of heads. A little sweating man in shirt sleeves called out, "That's tellin' 'im, son!" The laughter again, less nervous, more curious and assured.

Matt felt Eddy pluck at his arm. Eddy's face was scared and he whispered frantically, "Let's get out of here, Matt, there's too many people around." Eddy was breathing hard. The old panic dilated his eyes. Matt turned quickly and headed out of the crowd.

"Easy, Eddy, I shouldn't have spoken out of turn there. Here, I'll fix you a cigarette so you'll have something to hold on to."

Sweat beads clung to Eddy's temples. One temple had a big blue-black bruise. His face was filled with distress. He whimpered, "I told you how it would be if we went into a crowd. Seems like every place we go we step right into a crowd. I'm a trouble to you," Eddy panted, rushing the words so he could not recall them, "I don't think you an' me ought to go around together any more."

Matt paused with an unlit cigarette half-way to his lips. He stared at Eddy in amazement. "Just what do you mean by that, Eddy?"

Eddy did not look at him. He hurried on in anguish, "I heard what Hep said before the meetin' an' what you said about the guinea pig. I heard Hep say, 'He's simple but he's steady,' an' you say, 'Not since he got smacked, he's not.' I heard all that," Eddy cried miserably. "You got to get away from me, Matt. You told me that yesterday an' I still hung around but you got to get away from me. You're only goin' to get in trouble if you don't."

"Nuts!" Matt started to say in that edgy way he had when anything baffled him. He was deeply moved. Far more moved than when his mother went away. For a moment he stared at Eddy uncertain and perplexed, then his manner changed. He said shortly, "Look, Eddy, I never did anything in my life t'oblige anyone an' I'm not startin' in now. I go around with you because I like to, not because I have to." He started on, his feet driving at the sidewalk in hard, quick strides. "If I didn't have you I wouldn't have anyone."

Eddy trotted a half pace behind. "D'you mean that, Matt?"

"Sure I mean it." Matt broke off. He laughed harshly. "Only I never thought of it till now."

They stopped to buy a paper at a newstand on the corner of Vickers and Troy, a block away from Pier F where the boys had sailed from last night. Matt said he wanted to see the pictures. The newsman refused to break his quarter, he gave him a copy of the Bulletin with the back sheet partly ripped. He said he could not sell that one anyway. He was a short, middle-aged man in a tweed cap, soiled white shirt, and grey suspenders. When he talked he had a habit of snapping the suspenders for emphasis.

He asked Matt if they were two of the sit-down boys and said he was not surprised the blow-up had come when it did; what surprised him was that it had not come a lot sooner. He told Matt to call around tomorrow and maybe he would have another paper. He presented Eddy with an old copy of Crime-Thrills.

The boys thanked him. "You seem to take a lot of interest in this thing," Matt said.

The man's voice altered. His hands tightened suddenly on his suspenders. "I got three boys," he said "the oldest has been living at home now for two years an' the others is about ready to quit school. There's only room for me in the news business, why wouldn't I take an interest?" He leant forward, beating a tattoo on Matt's chest. "Look," he cried out angrily, "I got three boys starin' ahead at nothing. Why wouldn't I take an interest?"

They walked uptown as far as the war memorial to find a cool spot to open up the paper. The memorial stood in a small park with a miniature fountain and shrubs and clipped turf and a few shade trees. Charlie and a half-dozen of the boys were sitting with their legs over the stone parapet.

"Hi!" Charlie called out, "come on over an' join the committee!"

"Did any of you boys see a paper yet?" Matt asked. He swung up and a boy moved over and made a space for Eddy. Matt opened up the paper and Charlie craned over his shoulder. They studied the pictures in silence. Then, "Chroust! Was that how it was?" Matt asked.

Charlie laughed. "If that was what they printed," he said, "you can figger out for yourself what they cut. See that kid down there layin' in the gutter?"

"I see him. Where is he now?"

"Where is he now?" Charlie echoed excitedly, "where d'you think he is now? He's in hospital with a busted eye, that's where he is now." His hair flopped forward and he took a quick slap at it. "That kid's name is Chandler, he's a Gath boy. He used to be in our squad, I guess you must of took his place. He was a nice kid but he spoke out of turn."

"So I see," Matt said. He looked at the picture of the boy in the gutter with his sweater torn half off. The cut next to him was of an elderly man getting swatted about the head.

"Come on," Charlie said, "let's take a look at the rest of the paper. Read it out so we can all hear."

Matt read aloud:

"Yesterday's rioting brought to a head the case of the unemployed sit-downers who for the past month have been in occupation of two of our most prominent public buildings. That the grim farce has at last climaxed in bloodshed can be no surprise to anyone.

"This paper strongly condemns all forms of lawlessness. It refuses, however, to subscribe to the current policy or lack of policy of long-distance stalemate and smug indifference. This issue is not new. It was not new five years ago. Nor is it a purely local responsibility. It is a national responsibility demanding action by national authority and on a nation-wide scale.

"There is a fantastic and bitter anomaly in the sight of youth, homeless, workless, unskilled, unwanted, shuttled back and forth across a country that is potentially among the richest in the world. Evade, excuse, temporize or explain, the issue remains the same. The right of these men is to work."

"If I could write like that," Matt said, "I could write a book about this thing."

A boy next to Charlie leant out from the line. He had a round, coarse face, merry pig's eyes, an impudent nose and a mouthful of bad teeth. His behind had a way of bouncing when he walked. He wore a soiled yellow sweatshirt and a monkey cap set far back on his head. Gabby was nineteen but he settled right down to the profession of unemployment like a veteran. It gave him the first spotlight he ever enjoyed. There were a variety of jobs that he might have done well only he never learned any of them. Gabby could take it and he could dish it out and practically everybody liked him. He talked fast and tough, soaking his dialect up from the movies like a happy sponge.

He said to Matt, "Brother, you took the words right outa my mouth! Meet the guy that's goin' to do that very thing. Mister Kenny Hughes, the genelman on my right. Don't be shy, Kenny, come forward an' take a bow."

Poor Hughes blushed right up his face. He leaned forward and nodded at Matt shyly. He was a spare, studious-looking bird in glasses, a young ex-schoolmaster from up-country, beginning to tarnish from two years of doing nothing. He used to be bright and inclined towards idealism, now he was introverted and occasionally bitter, knowing himself to be slowing down mentally with every added day of idleness. The only thing that kept him going nowadays and roused him out of himself was the idea of this book. He got it while the sit-down was on, all those hours of doing nothing. He meant the book to carry real weight and he kept a diary and went over his notes every third day to keep them up to date. He sweated after technical detail and local colour, trying to get at what was really going on behind this whole situation and all that naturally made him sensitive

[handwritten margin note: Band is talking about her own life]

about the book in case it should not be published in the end. It never was published, not, as Hughes went around saying after, because it would have ripped the administration to pieces and forced a change of government, but simply because it was not a good book. Hughes had all the conviction and the sympathy and he moled around earnestly making notes, the only thing he forgot was to learn how to write.

"Are you really going to write a book?" Matt asked, staring at Hughes as though he were some kind of a strange bird. He wondered what part of a man it was that did the writing, not anything that showed up on the surface.

Hughes was embarrassed but he was pleased, too. Any spark of attention, however brief, temporarily eased his sense of inferiority, his terror of dry-rot. "I'm going to try to write it," he said, grinning shyly.

"No kiddin'," Gabby broke in, winking at Matt, "Kenny's goin' to give us little Eliza an' the bloodhounds ... goin' to write about the poor, sufferin' unemployed."

[handwritten margin note: Uncle Tom's Cabin referrence]

"Seriously, though," Hughes said, "I believe there's a story here. That sit-down caught the imagination of the public; they're going to remember what happened for a long time."

"Do you know something?" Charlie said, picking at a pimple on his neck. "The public's got one hell of a long memory, from today to tomorrow an' that don't include yesterday!"

A man at the end of the line leaned forward, a heavy man with strong black hair and broad-planed, Slavic features. Where his shirt fell open at the neck a thick web of sweaty dark hairs showed. He had an air of dignity about him in the same sense as Hep had dignity, that is, a sort of undisputed privacy of mind. The two men had nothing else in common, only this feeling of dignity.

He handed a paper to Hughes. "Read that," he said in his faintly gutteral voice, "maybe you can use it in your book."

"Read it out," Charlie said, "the guy that writes the leads for the *Record* could be a friend of mine if he didn't stink. That guy's about as sweet as a whore's breath."

"What do you care," laughed Gabby, "what's halitosis when you got hot pants?"

"When didn't you have 'em?"

Gabby pulled his cap off and fanned himself elaborately. "I was born hot. When I was a baby I had hot diapers. Ask my mother!"

Hughes broke through the laugh. He said seriously, "I think you ought to hear this," and he began to read aloud slowly and taking trouble to make it clear, just as though he were taking a class of forty children, breeds and whites.

"The events of Sunday should sharply awaken the citizens of Aschelon to the truth of a situation that has caused many of them to lose their sense of proportion and indulge in much sickly sentiment and misplaced emotionalism. We refer of course to current unemployment disorders.

"It has become a public scandal as well as a menace to the safety of citizens that a handful of malcontents and transient panhandlers should defy the laws of this province and thereby hold it up to nation-wide ridicule."

"Transient panhandlers! That's me." Matt muttered, "nice agreeable guy this is. I'd like to smash his face in!"

"Listen," Hughes insisted, "you ought to hear the rest of this."

"A large proportion of these men do not belong in this province. They are habitual trouble-makers unwanted in their own communities because they refuse to accept steady employment. They should be shipped home without delay.

"The well-known technique of street fighting is only one of the tactics employed to create publicity, feed emotionalism and confuse the public mind. Those familiar with the facts behind these riots are not so easily misled. They recognize when they meet them the hallmarks of organized disorder. The good name of this city is being held up to ridicule by the work of a few paid agitators who care nothing for the men they are inciting except as a means of income and cheap notoriety."

Gabby made a rude noise. He said, "They oughta turn that guy over to the street cleanin' department. Wheel him around in the wagon where he'd feel at home."

Hughes leant over and handed the paper back to Saul. "But keep it for me," he said, "I may need it to refer to."

Saul eyed him with pity. He liked shy, introverted Hughes even while recognizing that he was crazy. He said in his slow, deep, gutteral voice, "Draw it, don' write it."

"I don't understand what you mean."

Saul struck the palm of one hand sharply with the fingers of the other. "Look, Kenny, what you are trying to do is crazy from the start-off. You are splitting your head to write about such things ... don't do it. Draw a squirrel cage ... in one end, round an' round, out the same end. Jus' draw that," Saul said, "there you have the same thing in a few lines instead of in a hundred t'ousand words."

There was a silence. "Gosh," Charlie muttered, "how'd you ever get to think of a thing like that?" Hughes was smiling uncertainly.

Saul heaved to his feet and spat on the sidewalk. "I don't have to think. It comes in my head without thinking." He glanced at Matt. "Hey, you," he called out in an altered voice, "What's the matter with you over there?" He struck Matt sharply across the knee, "Snap out of it! I don't like to see a boy look the way you do. There is something not healthy going on in his mind."

Matt turned his head deliberately, stared at Saul between the eyes. The scar place showed up raw in the bright sun. He asked, "Were you ever booked on an incite charge?"

Charlie and Gabby laughed but Saul did not take it that way. "I never was yet. Why?"

Matt slid down off the wall. He answered quietly, "I was once back in '35. Maybe I will be again."

Saul touched the paper sticking out of his pocket. "You don' like it?"

Matt eyed him coldly. "I don't like it. I never did like being called dirty names."

CHAPTER SEVEN

Matt had some trouble getting out that night to keep his date with Hazel. He did not have the same trouble though as he would have had if Hep had not known Hazel and the aunt beforehand. He said they were going out to one of the beaches for a swim.

"Swim?" Hep said, "where's your trunks?"

"I didn't have any," Matt said, "I never thought of it."

Hep said, "You young squirts never think of anything unless it's pinned right on your ear."

"I guess that cans it then," Matt said, "unless I can get the loan of a pair."

Hep scratched his ear testily. "Go ask Charlie, he's a native son. Maybe he'd lend you a clean shirt, too, or you might get one off Kenny. He's dressier than most of us."

"Sure, go ahead," Charlie said when Matt asked him. "I got nothing to get me into a clean shirt for tonight."

Hazel was late. She said she just missed a street car and that where her aunt lived they only ran every ten minutes. She was wearing the blue slacks and candy stripe sweater and a little monkey jacket that did not quite reach her behind. Her blond hair was rolled into smooth curls and the outdoor light showed up where the hair was growing in dark at the scalp. Her makeup was fresh, not much colour and lots of lipstick. She had the feeling of what went with her type and made the most of it. She looked very small and trim and carried her bathing kit rolled under one arm.

"I had one hell of a day," she said smiling when she saw him. "I hope you had the same." They walked down past the Palace on Shroeder where the new Bette Davis picture was showing. She stopped to look at the stills. She said, "A boy I once went around with said I looked a bit like Bette Davis, kind of blond and washed-out." She pushed at her curls. "I bet Bette'll grow quite sharp-looking when she gets on."

Matt felt a million miles away from her, tonight, not intimate and close the way it had been yesterday. "These movie stars don't last long," he said. He hated the way Bette's leading man looked, all slicked-up and Hollywood.

"I'll bet they have a good time while they do last."

"They say a lot of them end up lookin' for extra parts."

"That was in the old days," Hazel said. "They make them save their money nowadays whether they want to or not."

"I thought that was just the kids."

"Maybe it is," Hazel said. "I thought it was all of them."

They caught a street car, the fare coming out of Matt's quarter. That left him with the return fare and one cent over.

The street car had its windows shoved right up to the top and the people next the windows sat with their bodies pressed up close to the bars as though that way they could get a little extra air. Half nude bodies, bare, sun-baked backs hard with youth; children, restless and skinny, chattering monkey-talk; stout, tired women, faces drooping into sweat folds, sweating hands clutching cotton bags shapeless with food; clean, lean-faced men in shirtsleeves kneeing children that squirmed and cried, women in swimsuits and sweaters showing flabby mottled calves that spread soft and pale as lard when they sat. Air charged with hamburgers, hot dogs, peanuts and gasoline. A long white beach swarming and shrieking and the dragging steps of the first families turning for home.

The sea was flat-still and the colour of pewter where the sun was beginning to leave it. Where the sun still struck it was orange and purple and green and shot with silver lights. The bay was flecked with yachts and a freighter was going by far down in the water heavy with lumber. As it passed through the area of sun the lumber turned bright orange. The mountains behind broad and snow-bearded were blue in the evening light.

They swam out to the emptying raft and lay face down talking. Hazel said she was too tired to dive or do tricks. Matt liked her best that way anyway. With nothing on but a pair of blue trunks and a bra she had a cigarette-ad body. Slim flanks with everything concentrated up above and most of it made public. She swam better than he did, faster, easier. He told her this was the first time he had ever touched salt water. She found it hard to believe till he told her more about himself and the place he was born in and the way he had lived. They stayed out on the raft till the sun went down and the air turned chilly.

"You'll be going over to Gath soon, I suppose," she said after they dressed and began to walk up the dusty, emptying beach. "Some day this week. Some day this week you'll be going," she repeated, buttoning the monkey jacket and shivering suddenly.

He answered at once, "Just as soon as we get marchin' orders. Another two hundred of the boys left at noon today. I guess they'll ship the old hands first, the ones that's been in this thing longest."

"You'll be glad won't you?"

"Glad! Say, listen, Hazel. I'll be gladder of that than of anything that ever happened to me. Maybe you think that's nuts but it's true."

She stared down at the pale, trampled sand. For a moment she did not answer then she said slowly, "No, I don't think you're nuts but I think you're all tied up in this thing body and soul. Take it away and what have you got left?"

He smiled. "Before this it was always lone-wolfin', fightin' up against something you couldn't see an' not gettin' any place. But it's different now, I got an organization behind me to back me up. Did you ever get that feeling, Hazel, of havin' an organization behind you?"

She laughed, "I work for one. I have that feeling all the time."

He turned and looked at her sharply, "No kiddin'," he said, "this means something to me. It's the first time I ever saw any real hope or plan in anything."

She thought, he's all tied up in this thing now. It's the only one means anything to him.

He turned on her suddenly, his eyes cold and bright. "How'd you like it if ever since the time you was sixteen you'd bummed around, if every job you went after there was a hundred other guys there ahead of you, if every place you went there was cops on your tail movin' you on so you couldn't start trouble—if you'd lived that life for the past six years, how'd you like it?"

She was watching him now, her face still. "Go on," she murmured, "go on and get it said."

His face relaxed and he laughed with a touch of shame. "Nuts," he said, "what kind of a lousy way is this to be talkin'!"

"Funny," Hazel said, "I like it. I must be nuts, too."

They waited on the corner for a street car. Across the bay the lights of the suburbs gleamed in bright, flickering rows. The illusion of movement among the lights was very strong. Back of the tiered downtown blocks the sky was a hot orange stain. A few burdened figures still toiled along the beach. The sea was fierce blue. Not mild and sunbright but dark and passionate with night. The sea and the beach and the darkness stank with the old day smells.

In the half-empty street car Hazel asked suddenly, "Do all the boys feel the way you do?"

"I guess so. The young ones do anyway. Why?"

She stole a look at his quiet set face and changed what she was going to say. Oh God, she thought hopelessly, what does he know about all this? He's like a baby. Why don't men know things the way women do?

When the car stopped they stood on the corner of Alcazar and Shroeder. Hazel said, "I wish I had someplace to ask you, Matt. A lot of the boys have gone to private homes. I wish I could take you home but I can't."

"That's okay," he said, suddenly angry and embarrassed at having no money. It never came at him and hit him between the eyes before the way it did now.

"That woman, that aunt of mine," she said, "she's funny alright. She doesn't mind me going out with boys but she doesn't like them around the house."

Matt said stiffly, "I guess I can walk home with you anyway." Across the street the travelling lights outside the Palace were going round and round and couples drifting up to the box office. Hazel began to fumble in her bag. He felt her pull at his arm. "Come on," she said.

"On where?"

"Come on into Cal's up the street there. I found a dollar bill I didn't know I had."

His face set stubbornly. "Not on your life. I never ate off a woman yet an' I'm not startin' now." He was boorish about it because of the way he felt. She still hung on to his arm. He thought, I'll bet that Bette Davis there hasn't got half of what this kid's got, not anywhere. "I don't eat off a woman," he said, surly.

She pulled at his arm almost crying. "You great big lummox, you!" she said, "what do you think you are anyway? Can't you see I'm almost dead on my feet, I've got an eight hour day back of me. Can't you see that?" she said. "I've got to eat somewhere," she went on, choking, "I'm cold, I tell you, and I can't go home because that woman, that aunt of mine, holds a prayer meeting in the house Monday nights. Oh come on. Come on do! I've got to go in somewhere warm and sit down!"

"Okay," he said stiffly, "if that's the way you feel. I guess we shouldn't have stayed so long down by the water."

They went into Cal's Coffee Counter and had soup, liver and bacon, pie and coffee all for twenty cents a piece. Cal was a stout Greek with wavy grey hair and a nose straight out of the top drawer, Grecian as the Parthenon. Hazel said how he got away with his prices was something only a Greek would know, that he must have some drag in the city and skip out under the pure food regulations. She said whatever he had kept him busy all year round, day and night. Like the beer racket, she said, there's someone getting their cut out of all these things.

A curly-haired, ruddy-faced boy came in and slid up onto the stool next to Matt. He had an educated look, like he worked in a bank or very junior in a bond house, anyway someplace where these things counted. He must have eaten there regularly because Cal did not need to ask what his was, he just started in preparing it.

"Hi, Cal," Ruddy-face said pleasantly, "what's new in town tonight?"

Cal grinned fatly all over his face. His white-coated shoulders moved up. "No more sit-downs, that's all I know, Mister Riddle," he said, and slid a bowl of clam chowder across, laughing. He did not need to make jokes in order to laugh, laughing was just a habit he had. This rich laughter about nothing brought him lots of customers.

Ruddy-face broke up crackers into the soup and stirred it to cool it off. "Honestly," he said, "I watched a bunch of those boys go off by the boat at midday and I thought, suppose they do go over to Gath where the heck's that going to get them?"

"It gets 'em to Gath, I suppose," Cal laughed. "I don' know no other answer to that one, Mister Riddle." He moved on down to wait on a new customer.

"That may be so," Ruddy-face persisted, still talking to Cal as he moved to the urns in that fat, stately way he had, "but suppose they do get there, what's that going to do for them? A little bunch of men like that aren't going to crawl up the pants of the government, no matter how badly they want work."

"I tell you something, Mister Riddle," Cal said, stopping with a mug of coffee in one hand, "they're not goin' to crawl up pants that's t'ree t'ousand miles away. At this distance they are not bombing planes, they are just a little bunch of mosquitoes. Jus' the same," he added, eyeing his window, "I'm glad I am not in their line of march yesterday morning, I'm glad about that."

Matt began to fidget. Hazel touched his knee. "Don't mind them," she said, "they don't know what they're talking about." She pushed away her plate and opened up her bag and began to do up her face, watching herself in the long chromium mirror back of the urns, watching Matt, too. She worked on her face quickly as though she wanted to be ready to leave in a hurry.

A man with a long thin nose and eyeglasses, who looked like a ratepayer, spoke up from the other end of the room. "If you ask me," he said, "the most of these men don't want work. If they'd wanted work they'd have gone out and rustled for it, not waited around to be spoon-fed by the government." He got up, came along and flipped down his quarter.

Matt stood up as he passed. "Did you ever try it?"

"Try what?"

"Lookin' for work."

Ruddy-face swung round on his stool. "Are you one of the sit-downers?" he asked with interest.

"Never mind that," Matt said, "I asked this man a question."

Cal's foreign eyes slid around his lunchroom all ways at once. He burst into a loud laugh, a very genial laugh and all the time his eyes were hard and cautious. He made that loud noise to cover up, to distract attention and to gain time. The man Matt spoke to flashed him an angry glance and slid out. Cal boomed, "Jokes, jokes, we all got to have our little jokes!"

"That was no joke," Matt said, breathing hard. "I asked him a question he couldn't answer. I don't stand for cracks like that."

"Come on," Hazel said, standing up, "I have to be getting back." Her hand came below the level of the counter, pressing money into his hand. "I have to be getting home now," she said, smiling brightly, "or that aunt of mine will be giving me heck." Guts, Matt thought, this kid has guts, guts and everything. There never was a girl had it in as many ways as she has. He paid, feeling cheap and shamed, and they went out into the street.

They found it difficult to talk at first, walking down Shroeder. There was a long queue stretching round the corner for the late show of Bette's picture. Hazel said she guessed they would have to hold the picture another three days. The queue made it easier to snap back into talking. It was something common and impersonal to get hold of.

As they passed by Matt nodded at the big, brightly-lit stills. "I guess that's what the most of you girls want—Hollywood."

She laughed. A harsh, nervous laugh. "'Hollywood! The town where one in a million gets a break!' I read that somewhere."

"I'll bet it's true," Matt said. "Why is it all girls think about is getting in pictures?"

"They don't,—all. I don't want to get in pictures but I go around with a lot of girls that do."

"What do you want?"

"You wouldn't believe me if I told you."

"No kidding," he said seriously, looking down at her. "What is it you do want?" She was silent. They walked on another half block and stood waiting for the lights to change. When they got over the other side of the street he asked her again if she knew what it was she wanted.

She nodded soberly. "I want a home of my own, a place where you don't get chased around and spied on, where you don't have to punch a time clock every morning to prove to yourself it's another day. I could do with a slew of kids, too."

"Kids!" he echoed. "You!" He stared down at her puzzled, obscurely angry.

Her face altered at once. "Oh, sure, I like kids. Crazy, isn't it? I told you you wouldn't believe me."

He laughed uneasily, "I don't know that it's crazy," he said, "but you've got expensive tastes. Those things cost money."

"Sure, I know it. That's what all the boys say nowadays. It's cheaper to be a Glamour Girl, more fun, too."

They came to the last block on Shroeder just before the bridge where that dance hall they call the Swing Bar had just been reopened. It had black double doors with chromium fittings and brilliant green Neon lettering overhead. Jake Gimbel's Hot Shots played there.

There was a caged-up platinum blonde in the box selling admissions. She was an old woman, around forty, and the effect of the strong overhead light showed up the bleach and the effect was terrible. She looked as though she should have been taking regular treatments for what ailed her. Half-a-dozen boys in dark suits and two in white pants lounged around the doors watching for girls to show up or just watching for girls.

One of them with rich, black, *stacombed* hair and a sallow face and a little black toothbrush on his upper lip, called out to Hazel, "Hello Beautiful! Coming in later?"

She waved at him and smiled, "Not tonight, Art!"

He pushed his shoulders up from the door jamb, came out into the street, slipped his arm through hers and stood with his fingers feeling up her wrist. "Come on in for half an hour."

She did not pull away, she tried to ease out, joking him, "Can't you see I have a date already?"

He turned and made a play of looking up and down the street, gave a comic imitation of a sailor sighting out to sea. Finally he said, "I looked everywhere and still I can't see it." When he smiled his teeth were not so good as his clothes and his shoes and his general appearance led you to expect. Suddenly he appeared to see Matt for the first time. "Oh, pardon me, sir," he said, his foolish little pinch-pointed face staring Matt up and down coolly, "but are you one of the 'boys'?"

Matt's eyes narrowed and his shoulders dropped. "Sure," he said, "I'm one of the 'boys'."

"Doing your bit for the unemployed, eh, Hazel? I didn't know you were interested in sweet charity."

She freed her arm neatly, then flashed him a bright smile. "Maybe you didn't know it, Art. I'm funny that way, I do my charity on the side."

The pimp stepped back, grinned familiarly and called after her. "That's the first time I ever heard of it from that position!" The boys round the door laughed.

They went on over the bridge. Matt said coldly, "That was a beauty. How did you ever come to pick up one like that?"

She shrugged. "I like to dance."

"With *him*?"

"Why not?"

"Have a good time?"

"Not very, the parties get rough towards the end."

"What happens?"

"Nothing, just the usual. You'd think a girl could go to a dance once in a while and not have to pay the cheque."

"What d'ya mean? Don't these slick fellers that ride around in cars have any money?"

"Oh, sure, they have money but they don't spend it for nothing."

His head slewed round sharply in the darkness. "God," he breathed, in quick disgust, "you're the coolest one I ever met. Cold-blooded." Shaken, he began to walk on. After a long time he asked, "Don't your aunt ever say anything?"

"That woman," Hazel said, choking a little, "she believes what I tell her. I think maybe if I didn't turn in my paycheque at the end of every week she'd stiffen up morally. But she's O.K. She's always been kind to me."

"She must have been, to let you run around that way."

"Why not? I have to have fun sometimes. It's not her fault that a girl has to have fun."

She stopped, leaned over the guardrail. He stood beside her, smelling the saltiness of her hair. The soggy roll of swimsuits wrapped in the towels smelt strong, too. Down below the water was black and oily and ringed with moonlight. On one side the backs of the houses came right down to the beach, on the other side the driftwood sloped off into a jungle of alder. Beyond the alder the houses began again, their upper windows vaguely pricked with lights, the lower part falling away into the main heavy mass of shadow.

Behind them the sky signs danced drunkenly and the night traffic roared up over the ramp, cutting the air with hard blades of speed. Their figures were invisible both to the sweeping lines of light and to the secret life moving up and down the bay. They stood there beneath the superstructure and it blotted them out. They did not even cast shadows. They were not significant nor necessary in any way.

"I know what you're thinking," Hazel said, "but it isn't so. I get by the best way I can. I never had anything given me and I never asked for anything."

His arms came out, went round her shoulders. Her shoulders were shaking. "Like me," he said, "I've always been the same way."

"Maybe that's how we got together," she said. "I saw something about you from the first. Among all that crowd of boys I saw something about you. That's the way it always goes."

He glanced at her suspicious, suddenly jealous. "You had lots of experience, I guess. How many of the other boys down at Luther Street did you go with?"

Her face flashed round, very white and small in the dark. "Not any, I swear not any! It was you from the moment I saw you. That's the way it always goes. I don't fool myself and I wouldn't fool you."

His arm tightened. She heard the change in his breathing. His arm grew tight and hard. He pulled her round, her head went back, her lips and her whole body accepted his fiercely. She whispered, "I wouldn't cheat on you, get you all hot for nothing. Not like a lot of girls would ..."

His face hung over her. She could make out the narrow gleam of his eyes, the dark scarred place up between the eyes. He asked roughly, "Where's this gettin' us? Where's all this gettin' us?"

She answered him, her voice shaking with passion and with a kind of scorn.

"What do you care if you want a thing badly enough?"

"Do you want this badly?"

"I don't know, I want something badly. I guess it's this."

"I didn't think you were that sort."

"Every woman's that sort."

"Where?"

She half-freed herself, pointing, "Down there, down there in the trees where it's dry!"

★ ★ ★

He checked in with Hep at eleven-thirty-two because he took note of the time as he came into East Third, and it used up approximately two minutes to walk as far as the eleven hundred block.

He said to Hep when he located him, "You didn't need to turn a marshall onto me, I made it a half hour this side of the curfew."

Hep was seated at one of the long tables with a mess of papers spread out in front of him. It looked like some kind of a report. His heavy black hair hung limply and his eyes were bloodshot and tired. As Matt came in he slowly raised his head, crushing out his cigarette.

"You can sleep inside if you want, tonight," he said, "there's more room since the boys left at midday. You can sleep any place you want, it's only for one night."

Matt's body stiffened. He asked quickly, "What happened? Why is it only for one night?"

Hep tipped back his chair, pushing out his long legs and easing his bottom. He said, "The division sails for Cutlake tomorrow."

"Cutlake!"

"Sure, Cutlake. Don't tell me you didn't pick that name up yet. Cutlake, McBain, Andersville, Gath. Costs too much to ship direct, besides it would be bad strategy an' that's something you can't ever accuse Laban of. The trip should take five days to a week, depending."

"Depending on what?"

Hep's deep-set eyes gleamed quizzically. His face took on an expression of complete innocence. "How should I know? Oh, say, how'd you make out with Hazel?"

Matt avoided his eyes. "Okay," he said evenly, "I made out okay."

"Hazel's one swell girl," Hep said, observing him shrewdly. "I've known Hazel a long time." Matt did not open up to that lead at all. He said, "I'll sleep outside, there's more air outside." He started to head for the washroom then came back. "Oh, say, Hep, can I take an hour off tomorrow morning to drop in at Lincoln's and say goodbye to Hazel? I'd like to drop in on Harry, too." He stopped directly below the white drop light.

Hep regarded him steadily for a moment, "You look all pooped out," he said.

"That swim," Matt said, "I'm not used to sea water. The salt water takes it out of you."

"Yeah?" Hep said. "Well, don't swim in any more salt water. Just keep out of it. Just keep out of it," Hep said, giving Matt a wise look. "The boys don't go in salt water and that's the reason. They can't afford to go around looking all pooped out!"

Matt unchecked his blanket roll, went out onto the lot, stepping among the little scattered encampments. Some men were already asleep, breathing thickly, muttering, stirring, others sat around in groups or lay on their elbows talking. From uptown came the night-muted roar of the traffic. A train howled over on the tracks. The street was very quiet.

In one corner of the lot a boy was reading by flashlight. Matt distinguished his features, picked his way over and eased down beside him. "'lo Charlie," he said.

Charlie glanced up, shut the book and moved over. "'lo, Matt. Have a good swim?"

"Sure," Matt said, "I left your trunks inside to dry off. Hot!" Matt said, "it's hot enough in there to kipper a herring. Thanks for the loan of the shirt."

"You're welcome," Charlie said. He lay back, clasped his hands behind his head and gazed up at the sky. "There's lots of stars out tonight."

Matt raised his head. "I never noticed," he said.

"There's a thing I'd like to know something about," Charlie mused, dragging his blanket up over him.

"What?"

"Stars."

"What for?"

"I don't know," Charlie said, "when I was a kid I got taken once to an observatory and I guess it made an impression. I'd just like to, that's all."

Matt felt in his shirt and pulled out a pack of cigarettes. "What kind of a life did you have when you were a kid?"

A man's head came up, a voice asked softly and painfully, "Look, will you two kids pipe down so I can get some sleep? I got a bad ear. I think it's a abscess coming up."

CHAPTER EIGHT

The two men pushed their way through the heavy swing doors of Lincoln's department store, past a store detective who eyed them suspiciously and with whom Matt turned to exchange a look of open dislike. As they went down the aisles the basement smells hit them like a wave. Coffee, bacon, dried fruits; meat, fish and butter rancid with the heat. Men and women stopping, pricing, hesitating, waging fiercely the age-long battle of income versus expenditure. Women dumping cash-and-carry stuff into heavy wire baskets slung on their arms. Women hugging the counters, elbowing one another, peering distrustfully at the displayed food. Children darting and crying and waiting in rows on seats drooling all-day suckers. The shrill of cash registers, buzz of talk, big white-globed drop lights that glared from the ceiling. Clicking of elevators, smack of feet on stone floors.

Eddy stopped and stared about him bewildered. "What are we goin' in this place for, Matt?"

Matt was eyeing round the basement. He answered absently, "I gotta say goodbye to a friend."

"Harry?"

"Harry! What d'you think, Eddy? Harry don't work in a department store." He headed on through Smoked Meats to where the line-up of young butchers stood behind the fresh cuts, their starched white coats clean up above and bloody around the waistline. Hazel and four other girls were wrapping meat on the far side, parcelling clumsy cheap cuts and hamburger, hearts and liver and tripe that dripped like wet India rubber. They went through the same motions every time, slapping the paper round, jerking off gumstrip, sliding the heavy packages along to the conveyor.

Matt watched Hazel for a moment before he spoke. He wondered what in hell she was thinking about.

"Hazel," he said softly so as not to attract the attention of the other girls working on the line. She looked up and smiled, not changing colour, not looking surprised in any way. Then her eyes slid over to a man in a business suit and hatless who was walking towards them through Smoked Meats.

Matt said, "I dropped in to say goodbye. We leave for Cutlake midday." A paper of meat was slapped down in front of Hazel and she began to work on it. She talked without looking up, without any slowing down of her hands.

"Oh God, Matt, I hope you get something out of all this in the end, I know how much it means to you."

He leaned down, speaking fast and earnestly, "It means just that much more than it did this time yesterday." She looked up then and smiled and he wanted to ask her was she feeling okay this morning and he did not like to. Suddenly her face altered and she hissed, "Act like you came here to pick up a parcel."

He straightened up. "What for?"

"There's a man behind you. Don't look now but there's a man behind you."

Automatically his head went round. He saw the man who had walked through Smoked Meats. He was strolling through the department as though he were looking for someone. He wore eyeglasses and his lensed eyes moved covertly from side to side as though he expected the man he was looking for to come at him from any part of the store.

Matt jerked his head at the man's back. "Who is that bird anyway?"

"Him?" Hazel said, "that's Shields, the head of the department. I tell you they don't let you stand around and talk here. That Shields has tried to lay every girl on this floor."

Matt's face narrowed. "And has he?"

"Not yet."

"Say, I'd like to push his face in!"

"Sure, you do that. That would work out swell for me."

A woman dragging a bagful of groceries heaved to a stop in front of Hazel. Lean and sallow with untidy black hair. She panted tiredly, "I hope they don't take long wrapping my parcel."

Hazel's voice went flat and courteous. "You'll get your package at the other end, madam."

When the woman had gone she said, "Let me know how you make out, Matt. Drop me a postcard."

"What d'you think," he said quickly, "what d'you think, honey?" A paper of sliced liver was dumped in front of her. As she wrapped it the blood leaked out and she had to drag off a fresh length of paper. He stood there hesitating, trying to get something said. "Look," he began finally, "do you have to go out with that Art again?"

She raised her eyes and gave him a level stare. Slowly, "Not if you don't want me to."

"I got no right to tell you what you do an' what you don't do." He leant forward frowning, speaking hurriedly, "If I was to tell you what a swell kid you are, Hazel, it would be nothing new. It would only be what you'd heard a million times."

Her face closed, she hissed fiercely, "Get going, will you? That Shields, that sonofabitch, has got his eye on me now."

"Okay then, honey, so long. Don't let your aunt get you down."

She smiled at him. "Don't worry," she said softly, "that aunt of mine can't get me now. Nothing can get me now."

The brunette wrapping alongside of her eyed Matt as he went away. She asked, "Where'd you pick up Tarzan?"

"Out of a box car," Hazel said.

"No kidding," the girl said, "where did you pick him up?"

"What do you think of him?" Hazel asked.

The girl giggled, "I didn't have time to find out yet. What do you think of him?"

"I think he's swell," Hazel said. Her eyes went soft and dreamy.

The girl giggled again. "You've found out plenty in a short time, honey."

Hazel looked at her reproachfully. "Your mind," she said, "your dirty, dirty mind!"

* * *

Harry welcomed them with a grin of pleasure. He was at his old game of swatting bluebottles and the ketchup bottle looked like a war memorial. "Well gents, what'll it be?"

"We didn't come to eat," Matt said, "we just dropped in to say goodbye. We're off to Cutlake by the afternoon boat."

Harry laid aside the swatter and scratched at his stump. "It don't seem right to see you boys come in an' not take anything," he said. "What say you have a cuppercoffy anyway? I wish I had something hard to offer you but you know how our hon'rable city is, I got to consider my license."

Matt felt that sharp, warm thrill of pleasure that Harry's company afforded him. Two, three times in the last twenty-four hours he'd met Harry and it felt like a lifetime. The only friendship in twenty-two years that had ever meant anything. "If it won't take above five minutes, then," he said.

"Five minutes it is!" Harry cried briskly. "I know all you boys is runnin' on a schedule." He tied himself into an apron and turned on the heat. As he moved about he talked. "I'm glad you boys come in," he said, "because maybe you can clear up a headache I got from readin' this morning's paper. Nowadays a person don't know what to believe. One moment the papers say this whole mess is a stalemate, next moment they say there's some big million dollar works plan all set to come off. Next moment again they backtrack an' say the works program is all a bunch of hooey. I read that an' then I read it again an' then all I end up with is one beautiful headache."

"You ain't the only one in town the newspapers give a headache to," Matt said. He picked a lump of sugar out of the bowl and ground it noisily between his teeth. "I seen something in a paper yesterday an' I been mad pretty well ever since."

The friendly smell of perking coffee filled the lunchroom. Harry poured two cups and pushed the milk across. He paused with the pot in his hand and his voice rumbled suddenly with exasperation. "They can talk all they want about doin' this an' that an' then not doin' it but the thing don't make sense. S'pose you was to come to me an' say, 'Gimme fifteen cents for a flop, Harry,' an' I says, 'Don't you come bummin' around for money you ain't got no right to.' Then next day back you come an' you say, 'Fer Petesake, Harry, gimme fifteen cents for a flop,' an' I get kinda fed-up an' I say, 'Okay then, come around tomorrow an' I'll make it a quarter.' Then you come around tomorrow an' instead of the quarter I says to you, 'Get th' hell outa here, you bum, I never seen you before in my life!' That kind of thing," Harry cried, the pot trembling in his hand, "it ain't good enough. It don't make sense any more."

Matt's head came up sharply. He cried out, "Eddy!" Eddy's face was like a mask, empty and staring. Matt smacked him between the shoulders. "Eddy! Fer the luvva Pete snap out of it."

Harry leaned over alarmed. "What's the matter with him?" Matt's mouth was dry. "I don't know. Nothing maybe ..."

Eddy rose. He pointed to the cropped place on his head where the hair had been shaved to dress the wound, his lips worked without sound.

Suddenly he shouted, "I seen him comin' before he seen me. I seen that big face on him an' I tried to beat it but I couldn't, I couldn't run quick enough, my shoes wasn't right!"

Matt laid a hand on Eddy's shoulder to try to force him down. Matt's hand was shaking and his spine felt cold. He said soothingly, "Pipe down now, Eddy, all that's a long time ago."

Eddy shook him off angrily. Little trickles of saliva ran down the corners of his mouth. He backed awkwardly away. He stared back at Matt blindly, shouting, "He says to me, 'Get th' hell out of here or I'll knock your goddam head off!'"

A man passing the door stopped. A second man peered over his shoulder. Men paused, nosing, elbowing.

Matt put his two hands on Eddy's shoulders and tried to force him down and Eddy armed him off and sent him crashing backwards, striking his head against a counter stool.

Harry stepped round and pulled him up. "Lemme alone," Matt panted, "I got to get those people away from that door." He stepped to the door. "Nothing serious, jus' a poor guy affected by the heat."

"A friend of yours?" a man asked suspiciously.

"Sure, he's a friend."

"Swell friend. Smacks you down an' he's a friend. If you ask me the guy's nuts."

"I tell you the heat got him, he don't know what he's doin'."

"Maybe the cops'll tell him." From the back of the little knot of men a voice shouted, "Look! He's going to do it again!"

Matt spun round. Eddy was straining back against the counter. He cried out hoarsely, "He says to me, 'I'll knock your goddam head off!'" Suddenly he saw the people there and his face changed. The anger snuffed out of his eyes, his mouth dropped and began to tremble. He put his hand up and touched his head whimperingly. "An' he did," Eddy whispered, "he knocked it right off!"

The people laughed. They thought that was very funny. Matt had to hold himself in from socking blindly at the ringed faces. Stupid crowd faces pressing in, obscene eyes, empty mouths sensation-ravenous. He went up to Eddy, forced him gently down and turned him so he could not see the door. Then he went and spoke to the people, reasoned with them, explained to them, broke them eventually, all the time holding his savage crowd-hate in.

A cop from across the street saw the people drift away and came over. He was green and nervous, one of those called in for the emergency. The most he had ever done was pound a suburban beat and pull in kids on Hallowe'en. Matt saw him coming. He used the old technique. He said respectfully, all the time hating the cop's guts, "Sorry, sergeant, I guess we must have had the radio on too loud. We got listenin' to one of those mystery dramas an' we didn't realize anyone out in the street could hear. They sure do make 'em realistic."

The cop stepped inside. His disbelief came out all over him like a rash. His eyes moved up and down the wall. "Where is this radio? I don't see any radio."

Harry's little eyes became two mocking pits. "You're not askin' me to produce my license, are you?"

The cop was so nervous it was like murder. He said, "I'm not asking you to produce anything, I'm asking where this radio is he's talking about."

Harry gave a coy glance down at his feet. He answered with insulting unction, "I had to take it offa the wall an' fix it down behind the counter here. When it was up on the wall guys was always comin' in an' chisellin' on a news broadcast. Not spendin' a nickel, mind you, just chisellin' ... an' you know how the news has been since Sunday."

The cop knew Harry was lying. He looked from Harry to Eddy's hunched back then to Matt and he shocked up against Matt's eyes. The eyes were hard and dangerous, cold like a steel-spiked wall. "You just want to be careful," he said uncertainly, "just be careful, that's all."

Harry watched him out of the door then he wiped his face with a counter cloth and tossed the cloth into the sink. He looked at Matt admiringly, "You sure handled that well, fella. They must of put the reg'lar day cop on one of the uptown beats. You couldn't of tried that on him, myst'ry drammer or no myst'ry drammer. Does your head hurt where you fell?"

Matt put his hand up. "I never remembered a thing about it till now, I guess I never even felt it at the time." He roused Eddy and brushed him off. Eddy's face was quiet and dazed. He followed Matt obediently out onto the street. Harry took Matt a little aside. "You got something on your hands there," he said.

Matt nodded. He answered soberly, "I know it."

"That's the second time I seen it happen inside of three days," Harry insisted, "is that Eddy safe to have around?"

Matt hesitated, narrowing his eyes against the strong sun. He said at last, "I wish I could make you understand about Eddy, Harry, but I can't, there's too many angles tied in with him. In a week, maybe less, the craziness could pass off."

Harry shook his head skeptically. "But will it?" He caught Matt's eye and added quickly, "Mind you, Matt, I like him. I seen at once the kind of good, harmless guy he is, only good harmless guys like him can cause plenty trouble in any man's revolution."

"Look, Harry, I'll tell you how it is about Eddy. I've sort of got him on probation an' it was me put him there. Either I'm responsible for him for the next week or ..." Matt stopped. He gave Harry a look Harry could not mistake.

"Sweet Jesus!" Harry exclaimed, shocked, "not one of them places?"

Matt shrugged. "I guess so. Where else? First thing you know he'd do some crazy thing an' get himself jugged an' then he'd go right clean off his nut after a half hour in an ordinary jug."

Harry's mind worked deeply over the question. He scratched at his stump, eyeing Eddy anxiously. When he spoke his voice was heavy. "He'd a damnsite better walk right down an' lay his head on the tracks. I had a brother once ... Oh, Jesus," Harry said, his face contracting, "he'd be a damnsite better off stiff than in one of them places. I seen 'em. I know."

Matt held out his hand. He said, "I guess we better be gettin' along. Thanks a lot, Harry. Be seein' you." Harry enclosed his hand in the grip of a live oyster.

"Drop me a line, Matt. 'bye, Eddy. Watch out for the women!" As they turned at the top of the block he shouted after them, "I could give you some dandy addresses in Gath if I thought they'd do you any good." Matt grinned and waved. Harry watched them out of sight then turned back inside wiping sweat beads from his face. Aloud he said, "There go a coupla real nice boys. They got nothin', no jobs, no homes, no place to belong in. What's goin' to become of them in the end?" He glared into the maze of bluebottles and because he was lonely again and sad he shouted angrily, "That's what I want someone should tell me. What's goin' to become of boys like that in the end?"

PART II

·

Transit

CHAPTER NINE

Matt and Charlie stood in the bow of the *Princess Maud*. Behind them the Aschelon skyline fell away above the blue dazzling water. Pier roofs, grain elevators, thick maze of masts close in to the long sweep of the waterfront, strong tapering towers of the big downtown blocks. Tugs and ferries churned up and down the bay and over on the opposite shore a grey, deep-bellied Dutchman was tied up, taking on lumber.

Charlie leaned full into the battering wind. He slapped at his blowing pompadour, a faint colour whipped into his sallow cheeks. "Swell, isn't it, Matt?"

Matt drew in a long salty breath and smiled. "Sure is, Charlie, makes you really feel you're goin' someplace!"

"So we are," Charlie said confidently, "goin' right where we'll get some action."

"You bet, Charlie. That's the way I felt marchin' down to the boat ... people givin' us a big hand, wishin' us lots of luck. I never felt so good in my life before as I do right this minute."

"Same with me," Charlie said, "I guess it's this salt air does somethin' to you!"

"That an' the friendly people," Matt said. "Jese, Charlie, the people out here is a swell bunch." They smoked in a contented silence.

From that day on certain powerful impressions began to register in Matt's mind through the very force of repetition. One was the reaction of the people to the discipline, bearing and air of solid purpose amongst the men. He began to notice it, wait for it, know that sooner or later it must appear. It lent a peculiar colour and dramatic quality to even slight occasions. From city to city there was this same flattery of public attention, this same certainty of playing to crowded houses. Among other things it began subtly to affect the ego. It affected it with a new and heady sense of importance. As in war it brought submerged egos to the surface, nourished weak ones, coloured sickly ones, provided them with a chance to grow and expand.

Matt began to get a kick out of the crowds, out of the people in the streets; he felt the power of mass action, the significance and purpose and weight of numbers. He grew increasingly conscious of the effects of discipline and organization and some instinct within him subscribed to it with less and less revolt, recognizing it as essential to successful mass protest.

On the boat the men kept to themselves, they did not mix with the regular passengers and this sense of group isolation affected Matt in two ways. It heightened his sense of personal reality yet at the same time gave him the feeling that he was only important or necessary insofar as he fulfilled his obligations as a unit to the whole. He did not want to talk much to anyone at the moment. He had certain adjustments to make.

A half hour out from Aschelon they met a freighter, the *Hebe* out of Glasgow. As she churned by, engines pounding, the boys on the little Cutlake boat waved and shouted and the *Hebe's* crew waved and a Scotch voice yelled out, "Give my love to Glasgow!"

After the thump of the *Hebe's* engines had died away Charlie broke the long silence. He was wearing the white shirt and a fake-leather windbreaker. He did not own many clothes but he appeared to have more than most of the boys because of the care he took of them. He kept his socks washed out at nights, too, so they didn't harden with the heat and spoil his feet. He asked, "How come you get such a big kick out of the scenery, Matt? Didn't they have scenery back in Saskatchewan?"

Matt roused himself and laughed with a touch of embarrassment. "I guess they did only I never took time out to notice it."

Charlie looked at him curiously, "What happened about you? You never opened up much. What kind of a life did you have when you was a kid?"

Matt was a little time answering. His fingers drummed on the rail and he watched them carefully. At last he said, "My father was a dirty radical. Sometimes he used to have a half dozen other dirty radicals to our flat in the evenings to talk. I remember lyin' there listenin' to voices. I remember how cold it used to be. My old man was all burned up with ideas but he never made enough to give us any heat in the place and after a while my mother couldn't stand it so she walked out on us. At least I think that was the reason. If there was any others I never knew what they were. She was a big woman but she couldn't stand the cold. I guess she got tired seein' her breath first thing every mornin'."

He was silent for a moment. His brows drew down, uniting with the scar. "One of the first things I can remember is bein' waked by a cop shinin' a flashlight on my face an' shovin' his hand under my mattress to feel for seditious literature. I think that's the first moment I ever hated cops. Funny, I feel jus' the same today!"

Charlie shivered. He zipped his windbreaker up his chest and glanced at Matt uneasily. "I don't know if that's wind," he said, "or listenin' to you talk. What say we take a walk around?"

Matt glanced away quickly. He laughed, "I told you we didn't have enough heat in our place when I was a kid."

Aschelon had sunk to a grey horizon smudge. The boat was passing between small sunbaked islands lazy with peace. Green fields came down flush with the rocks and the rocks, yellow with lichen and shiny with weed entered the water steep and sudden with no incline of beach. The passes were deep and narrow. The boat stayed in close enough to make out people walking on the land.

They stopped to light cigarettes, ducking to dodge the wind. "That's enough about me," Matt said, "what about you? What else do you do except goof at the stars an' hare around doin' committee work?"

Charlie opened up eagerly, "I tell you," he began in that quick, nervous way he had of talking, using his hands while he talked, "when I was a kid I used to like to draw ... always wanted to be some kind of a architect."

"Architect, huh? I guess that takes plenty edjucation."

"Yeah, I know, but every time I see dumps like those places around Luther Street I think what could be done if those old places was torn down an' they did like all th' big cities is doin' nowdays. Y'know what I mean. Put up swell places where the light could get to an' the kids didn't have to dodge the ice wagons. I saw some swell drawin's in a book once ..." He broke off, his hands dropped. "How I talk!" he said. "Ask me something sensible for a change. How I made out peddlin' groceries when my old man went on relief."

Later on they went below with the rest of the boys and had coffee and sandwiches and Charlie saw Eddy asleep in a corner and said maybe they better wake him before the food was all gone. "Leave him be," Matt said. "When he's asleep he can't feel hungry an' I know where he's at."

"Okay, then," Charlie said, "if that's the way you feel."

"That's the way you'd feel, too," Matt said, "if you knew Eddy like I do."

They went back up on the top deck. A man was leaning over the rail. When he saw the boys he edged over and asked for a light. Matt recognized him as the one that spoke to him Sunday on the lot, the man that beefed so hard about the food and the way things were run. He wore a broken-peaked cap dragged down over his eyes to shield them from the sun and a stained and shiny blue suit. The way the wind flapped his pants against his skinny legs it did not look as though he had on any clothes underneath. His coat collar was turned up and he held it clutched across his chest with one hand.

He glanced from one boy to another, gave them that beaten look from under his eyes. "I bin listenin' to you kids talk," he whined, "an' I can tell you somethin' right now."

"Maybe you can," Matt said, "an' maybe we don't want to hear it."

"If I don't tell you, then you're goin' to find it out for yourselves."

Matt eyed him coldly, "I like things better that way."

"What's the matter with you anyway?" Charlie asked, "why are you always beefin' around?"

The man leaned down over the ship's side. With a hand that shook he pointed to the long green swathes of smashing water, tearing off rags of brilliant spray. "See that water throwin' up an' the ship cuttin' through it to beat all hell?" The eyes of the two boys followed.

"So what?" Matt asked, wishing he could keep from giving the man the lead he wanted and not being able to resist.

The man raised his head and spoke against the noise of the wind and the screaming of gulls. "The whole bunch of us is like this ship here, thrashin' and churnin' an' thinkin' we're gettin' someplace. When you look down the side there you'd think this ship wasn't goin' to stop this side of hell, but she'll stop all right." He paused, touched Matt on the arm bringing his face up close, "She'll stop, sonny boy, just as soon as she's told to stop."

Matt felt the irritation creep up over his skin. Nuts, he thought, this stuff is all nuts that this red-eyed little runt is talking. The man seemed to get some kind of compensation out of tormenting the boys. The whining voice pursued remorselessly, "For a week, coupla weeks maybe, us boys'll be pets of the public an' the papers'll play the story up big, an' after that ..." he broke off abruptly. "Tell me," he said to Matt, "you was all through that big Clever trouble. What come out of that?"

Matt frowned. "The most of the boys that was through that mess ended up in th' jug," he admitted after a silence. "I guess nothin' come out of it."

A group of boys drifted up, paused to hang over the rail, hair blowing, eyes slit against the sun. The bantam, Gabby, dark-faced Dick that went around all set for trouble like a time fuse, two faces Matt did not know. The man spoke to Dick, "Hey you, Dick," he said, "don't tell me you didn't do a stretch in college yet."

Dick half raised his head. "What's it to you?" he said. "Sure I done my stretch. I got vagged in Colynos an' spent my nineteenth birthday in jug."

"An' you, Stan! They got you right on the Aschelon blotter."

One of the two strange boys tossed his butt into the sea and laughed. "Sure they got me. They got me twice. Just another local boy makin' good!"

Gabby demanded loudly, "What's the matter with me? I never got jugged yet."

"Nor me," Charlie said, "makes me feel I'd been gypped outa somethin'."

Gabby laughed. "Don't worry," he said, "you will. When we get to Gath we're goin' to tear that old jug apart ... show the town somethin' it never saw before."

Matt felt the man's body trembling beside him in the wind. All shot to pieces, Matt thought, seething, what in hell does a bum like that know? ... all shot to pieces!

The man seemed to sense his thoughts. He turned on him suddenly. "You kids jus' come from a big send-off an' a bunch of flag-wavers! You think I'm nothin' but one goddam bellyache. You think all you have to do when you get to Gath is march around the city seven times an' the walls is goin' to fall down Boom! …" His voice altered, the brief fire died in his eyes. He finished quietly, "But it ain't so. Whatever you young kids think, it ain't so." For a moment his weak bloodshot eyes blinked at the boys, then he went away, disappearing down the companionway with the awkward stumblings of a landsman.

Matt snapped the tension. "He's got no guts himself an' he'd like to take the guts out of everyone else."

"He talks like a pigeon," Stan said with an air of fake importance, "how do we know he's not gettin' his cut?"

"He's no pigeon," Charlie said, "he's just burned out, that's all. Can't take it."

Stan made a quick step forward. "You tryin' to call me a liar?"

"He don't have to try very hard," Gabby said with a wink at Charlie.

Stan swung away from Charlie, "That's what you think," he said, "but I could tell the boys a few things about you they never heard before."

"Go right ahead," Gabby grinned, baiting him. Matt left them in disgust, still wrangling.

He moved about the ship sensing the same tension everywhere. Men huddled into little groups talking, brooding faces silently watching Cutlake grow along the skyline, sleepers with hats tipped over their eyes or faces baking beef-red in the wind and sun.

Hep came by. He stopped when he saw Matt. "How're you making out, Matt?"

"Okay," Matt said, not opening up. Hep removed his hat, easing the pressure of the sweatband. Then he set it carefully back on again. Matt never saw Hep when he didn't wear a hat except to sleep in. He lit a Sweet Cap and passed the pack along. "Sure is good to get out of town for a while," he said. He gazed thoughtfully out to sea. "Stickin' around Luther Street wasn't doin' the boys any good."

"There's a bunch on this boat now scrappin' around like dogs over a bitch," Matt said. "I got fed up so I left them to it."

Hep removed his cigarette and the wind snatched the smoke off his lips. He smiled calmly, "Hell, Matt, there's always a bunch everywhere scrapping that way. When guys get to feeling important that never had the chance to feel that way before you always find that. They get all hopped up and don't know how to take it."

"Hep!"

"Well?"

"What kind of a town is Cutlake?"

"Practically one hundred percent union. We won't run into any trouble in Cutlake."

"Lumber?"

"Coal. They had their own troubles in the bad times so there's bound to be lots of sympathizers. I've known Cutlake on an' off since I was a kid, she's a swell little town."

"There's one guy on this boat," Matt said after a pause, "every time I just look at him he makes me mad. Always bellyachin' over something. The boys call him Beefy. Just when you're feelin' good he comes along an' inside of five minutes he's got you so you might as well go lay your head on the tracks."

Hep smiled pityingly. "Poor little guy, he's got burned up an' kicked around so long everything's gone sour on him. Don't listen to him, Matt, he'll eat your heart out like a rat."

Matt complained, "Why's he got to be around?"

"Why not? Where else has he got to go when he's out of jug?"

Matt reddened. "Sometimes," he muttered, "you make me feel the size of a pea."

Hep smiled. "You're no pea, Matt; all you need is experience."

"*Exper* ...! Say, what th' hell d'you think I've been gettin' all these years?"

Hep laughed. That was one time Matt really heard him laugh. "That wasn't the kind of experience I was meaning," he said and he told Matt to go find Eddy and join the baggage line-up down below.

They took their places in the slow, shuffling queue. The air inside smelt foul and heavy and the regular passengers stared at them curiously as though they were cattle and nervously as though they were dangerous cattle. The boat was filled with cops, too. Lousy with them. Matt was glad to collect his stuff and get on outside again. Cutlake was close in now. Everywhere a feeling of movement had set in among the men. They poured up onto the top deck slinging their baggage, crowding in close to the rail. A black and yellow tug panting ahead of a coal barge passed alongside the ship and the skipper stepped out and waved and the men sent up a cheer. They razzed the skipper and he grinned and shouted words the wind blew away. The wind was strong and fresh and salty and it burned into the faces of the men as they hung packed close along the ship's side.

Back of the landing dock the road was blacked-out with people. A line of parked cars stood on one side of the road, nickel glinting fiercely in the bright evening sun. Matt peered down and gradually he began to pick out individual faces.

Men, lean and shaven and deeply tanned, squat faces, broad in the head like second-generation citizens, mine-workers, men from the mills, high school kids, old, burnt-out men. Women with stout unshaped figures and bare arms wearing cotton housedresses and cheap white hats and a lot that were hatless with untidy sun-bleached hair. Girls with a warm smooth tan, who giggled together as they made the old jokes strictly among themselves. Half-nude kids brown as arbutus, skinny as tikes, running and clambering to get a view. At that time of the day pretty well the whole town was free to turn out.

Across from the wharf a ball game was going on to empty bleachers. Finally the game stopped and the teams came over and joined the crowd. It was that kind of a day. Better than any circus that ever hit town.

Matt felt a return of Sunday's crazed excitement gripping him. His hands tightened on the rail. "Jesus!" he exclaimed, "looks like they expected the militia!"

The boy called Stan was crowded alongside him. He sneered, "D'you think they'd turn out like that for a bunch of yellow rats?"

"Huh?" Matt half turned.

The boy's mouth twisted in the way the heavies' mouths used to twist in the old-time gangster pictures. He said loudly, "What's the army anyway but a bunch of cops with guns? The only way they can put guts into cops an' soldiers is shoot 'em full of liquor an' shove a gun in their hands. Then they're all set to beat hell out of the women an' children!"

A sudden boiling-up came from the men behind. A little gristled man with a depleted body, sunken cheeks and fierce eyebrows elbowed through crying excitedly, "Is that so, squirt? Maybe you wasn't overseas!"

The boy half turned and eyed him with contempt. "You won't catch me takin' part in any sonovabitchin' capitalist war!"

The vet glared at him. His wasted features filled with rage. Finally he exploded the choked and labouring words, "*You ... make ... me ... sick!*"

The boy laughed, pretending to puke. "An' that's the way you make me," he said.

The little man's words rushed out in a passionate spate. "*Talk!*" he cried, "all you young squirts nowadays is good for is talk! Revolution, fire-eatin', what you're goin' to show the town. You squat around on your tails an' what do you do? You talk! If it hadn't bin for a bunch of yellow rats like me, kids like you would have bin born with hare lips an' club feet because of some of the things your mothers would have had to look at beforehand!" He smacked his thin chest, his voice shook proudly, "Damn right I was overseas ... an' you young dime-a-dozen Reds remember that the most you know about defendin' your country is what you read in the funny papers!"

He stopped breathless, wiping his hot face with his sleeve. A man touched him on the shoulder. "Okay, Pop," he said gently, "don't let it get you all steamed up."

The vet swung round, "Steamed up! You'd get steamed up if you'd fought through six wars ... *six wars* ... an' come home rattlin' with a bunch o' ruddy medals an' have to live on three dollars an' twenty-seven cents a month an' have to listen to the way they run things nowadays! Guts! They don't know the meanin' of the word ..." His voice was drowned by a blast from the ship's siren. A burst of cheering rose from the people on the dock. The men surged back onto the rail. Matt glanced over his shoulder. The vet was standing alone, burnt-out, shaken, chest pumping. He looked like something swept up and stranded by a powerful outgoing tide.

Matt glanced away quickly, fighting not a pity but an obscure irritation. No man had a right to look that way, wasted, scrapped, thrown on the dunghill to rot. Matt thrust him from his mind at once. He shoved in close to the rail and joined in the cheering.

CHAPTER TEN

The best way Matt ever felt was when he stepped from the gangplank of the *Princess Maud*. He was part of a movement now that knew where it was headed. He felt that every last one of these people jamming the wharf and piling up behind was for him, for him personally, fighting on his side and that the boys had this whole solid town at their backs.

All this was different to Aschelon, a changed set-up altogether. Small-town, intensely personal, unwearied by the strain of a prolonged sit-down and front page trouble. Even the air was changed. The wind blew in off the water heady with salt and sharp with the tang of burning brush.

At the head of the line marched the committee of welcome, the district organizer and a divisional leader who came over on the *Maud*. Not Laban but a younger man, stocky, red-haired and pallid that Matt did not know the name of. Behind them the men marched two abreast, the young ones ahead, the older, ex-white collar workers behind.

There was one main street in Cutlake and no street car lines. It had most big-town features but on a small-town scale. Neons up over the stores, a new, stucco-fronted movie house with stills of an old Robert Taylor picture, downstairs beauty parlors and upstairs dentists, corner drugstores and one big hardware filled with loggers and miners' supplies and fishing tackle and a set of bank-nite chinaware, rubber boots, shotgun shells, red hunting hats and trash. Woolworths and drygoods, pool halls and barber shops, chiropractors and real estate and the new red and white gas station with the California tiling. Good-looking shiny automobiles angled into the curb and plenty that could remember back to pre-nineteen thirty.

On one corner there was a restaurant that had EAT WITH GUS in broken white lettering across the front. It was a far more high-class place than Harry's but Matt did not care a damn about Gus, squat and swarthy, the type that needs a second shave round five o'clock in the afternoon, standing in the doorway in a soiled white apron, eyeing the parade. He did not begin to compare with Harry in any way. When the tail of the division cleared the dock the crowd broke and swarmed, boys with push bikes and kids running and one big woman striding along pushing a baby buggy. All the way uptown as far as the CSOB hall where the boys were quartered the people followed them.

In the big clattering room where the boys had supper, Matt and Hughes and Gabby and Dick and Charlie sat together. The air smelt of sweat and greens and coffee and gas fumes that drifted in off the street. When Hughes finished his pie he pushed the plate away and cleared a small space to write on. He knew he would not have a place to write later with the meeting scheduled in half an hour and he wanted to record his present impressions as well as the ones he got coming up from the boat while the whole thing was fresh in his mind.

Gabby winked across at Charlie. He asked innocently, "What you got there, Kenny?"

Charlie's voice was gently sarcastic, "He's writin' a book all about the dignity of labour an' the lousy capitalists. Boy, is he goin' to burn 'em up!"

Hughes said earnestly, "Some day this book may be important, who knows?"

"Not me," Gabby said, "I only read westerns." He gave a loud burp.

Hughes sighed, sorting his closely written pages. "Books have been known to move mountains," he said.

Gabby patted his middle. "I got one right here," he said, "a mountain right on my middle. They sure put up a swell supper, all I wish is greens didn't make me so gassy. Hold tight boys! Here she comes again!" He gave a second loud burp and after a moment got up hastily.

Dick glanced round. "An' don't come back," he said. He moved along the bench, giving himself more room.

"What's eatin' you today?" Matt asked. Dick glowered. "Nothin' you'd know about."

Gabby called back, "His pants is blisterin' his seat."

"Balls to you!" Dick growled.

"Aw, shut up," Charlie interposed peaceably, "can't any of you boys be together nowadays without startin' to scrap? Trouble is we've all been together too long."

"Trouble is," Dick said, giving Charlie a sour look, "there's too many guys around here don't know enough to mind their own business."

Matt stirred impatiently. He said in disgust, "Cut it out, can't you?"

Dick dropped his spoon and flared right up. "Who are you anyway? You only come in a coupla days ago. Me, I've lived with that Gabby in camp all winter, then three weeks on a sit-down. God, I hate his face!"

Matt smiled. "Okay," he admitted, "I guess I did talk out of turn. That coupla days seems like a lot longer." He saw Hughes writing rapidly, "What th' heck are you writin' down now, Kenny?"

Hughes did not look up. He went on writing very fast. When he finished he looked up with a proud, shy smile. "I didn't want to lose a word of it," he said, "I think I got it all."

Baird is capturing the idiom

Matt gaped. "Fer the luvva pete, Kenny, got what?"

Hughes blushed. "Naturalistic dialogue."

"What's that?" *using dialogue that captured the way people talked*

"What a book has to have to sell nowadays."

"No kiddin'?"

Hughes gave a faint sigh, "I'm afraid so," he said.

Matt went on staring at him then he touched his head. "Nuts," he said gently, "honest, Kenny, I think you're nuts!" It was that moment Hughes first got the idea of using him in the book.

After supper Matt caught up with Eddy and drew him aside. "What's got into you tonight?" he asked, eyeing Eddy with a mixture of suspicion and concern, "you never said a word all through supper. What brand of dynamite have you got churnin' around now all ready to bust off somebody's head?"

Eddy did not answer at once. His eyes slid to Matt's face then slid quickly away. "I was just thinkin' ..." he began.

"Thinkin' what?"

"That they got a swell secondhand store back there on main street, Matt. Bunches of shoes hangin' up over the window jus' like that one in Aschelon."

Matt's eyes narrowed. "I might of known," he said, "every time I don't hear you around I should start to get suspicious. Where is this store at?"

"I don't remember the exact place, Matt, I never was in Cutlake before."

"Hell, we all know that! Quit stallin', Eddy. Where is this store at?"

Eddy's hands twisted together, he avoided Matt's drilling gaze. If he lied then his mind had to work over the lie a long time so he could end up by believing it himself. At last he mumbled sulkily, "It's between that big hardware an' the barber shop, the one with the red an' white pole that goes round all the time ... Fred's barber shop."

Matt's voice was sarcastic, "So it was Fred's barber shop? The one with the red an' white pole that goes round all th' time." He stopped and his voice altered so suddenly that Eddy retreated a pace in fear. "You sneaked out before supper, didn't you, Eddy? *Didn't you, Eddy?* You went back up there when Hep an' me thought you was with the rest of the boys. You couldn't of remembered all that just seein' it once."

Eddy still retreated. His face wore a mixture of stubbornness and fright. He pleaded, "I jus' wanted to take a look. You promised when we got over here ..."

Matt broke in nervously, "I never promised anything when we got over here."

"You promised when we got to Gath ..." Eddy's voice trailed off but the stubbornness settled and hung, darkening his face like a cloud. Matt gazed at him for a long moment, his mind struggling to penetrate the brain that lay back of those childlike and sinister eyes. Suddenly he shivered.

"Know sumpin', Eddy?"

Eddy shook his head.

"Right this minute I got the same feelin' I had that first day when you was trailin' me through the streets of Aschelon ... scared stiff an' Christ knows what it is I'm scared of!"

* * *

They held the meeting out in the ball grounds with the big floodlights like they used when a game was on. Most of Sunday's props were there; the sound truck, the mike, the rough flag-draped platform, the packed bleachers, the crowd streaming in at the gates and massing like insects underneath the lights. Back of the grounds were the roofs of the freight-sheds and beyond the sheds the sea, smooth and darkening like tarnished silver.

The first speaker was a Cutlake man and after him came the boy with the pale face and red hair. He did not have Laban's stagecraft or control, all he had was anger and a cause. By God, Matt thought, I'll bet he's taken some beatings! He put his hand up and fingered the scar place. He thought, suddenly fired, "there's something I'd like to do!" He strained forward to catch every word, eyes riveted on the platform glare.

"It has been charged," the metallic voice blared, "that there are paid agitators at work among these boys. That is a cover-up charge to hide smug indifference on the one hand and failure to formulate a policy on the other. Any plan whereby these boys may be taken off the streets and put to work at steady jobs with a human standard of living!"

A voice shouted, "You talk like a Red! Who organized the boys in the beginning? Tell us that!"

A second voice angrily, "Shut up an' go home to Mussolini!" Matt glimpsed the two men lunging at one another through the crowd, arms flailing. Finally they were run out by a couple of cops.

The red-haired boy plunged right at the heart of the disturbance. "Sure, these boys are organized! What about the doctors and lawyers and politicians?" Burst of catcalls, men shoving their fingers in their mouths to whistle derisively, brief pandemonium heating the temper of the crowd.

"Just so long as they stayed scattered over the country like dogs, they couldn't stir up trouble, but let them get together into a disciplined, organized body of men that know where they're headed for and what happens? They become public enemy number one and the whole country is headed for red revolution!"

"Swell, wasn't it?" Charlie said afterwards as they chewed over the meeting up at the hall, "the madder he got the better he made it sound. I wish I could get mad like that."

Matt said, "I don't know. Guys that get mad easy has to watch out."

Charlie looked sideways at him. "What d'ya mean? What do they have to watch out for?"

"Nothing. All I wish is I could get up an' talk like that guy, get up in front of a whole crowd of people."

"Golly, I'd be scared!"

"No, you wouldn't," Matt said, "not if you believed the things you was sayin'."

A small middle-aged man appeared at the side door carrying a portable radio. When he got inside he stopped and seemed confused at finding himself in so large a roomful of men. Matt was beside the door. He got up and asked, "You want to put that thing down, mister?"

The radio man was looking around for someplace to plug in. He explained nervously, "I brought a double socket along, I don't suppose there's many outlets in a place like this." As Matt set the radio down he ran his finger along the top lovingly. "She doesn't look much but she's a dandy little machine, came in last week as part trade on a cabinet model. I thought maybe you boys would like the use of her while you're in town."

The men crowded round eagerly. *"Would we!"* *"I'll say!"* The radio man clicked on the pilot light and grunts and squeals began to come from the little machine. He fiddled around with the dial trying to cut out the static.

A blond boy with a lean face and intelligent grey eyes remarked, "Used to be when you'd hear noises like that it was tearing the tubes all to pieces."

"That was in the days before they built machines the way they build them today," the man said. Then he looked at the boy and asked, "You know anything about radio?"

The boy nodded, "I did once."

"Where'd you learn about radio?"

"I used to work as one of the 'lectricians for Manning's over in Aschelon." The radio man opened his mouth to speak, caught the boy's eye and changed his mind. He went hurriedly back to dialing the machine. As the static ceased part of the nine-thirty news broadcast from Aschelon was coming over the air. The voice of the announcer was saying,

"In Aschelon today fifty-three more tin-canners were arrested on charges of obstructing police." The buzzing murmur of talk stopped. Chins rose, slack bodies stiffened, eyes gleamed angrily or darkened with a brooding attention. "According to police the men had been warned that any further soliciting would result in arrests, but they persisted in the face of warnings. It is learned that the citizens of Gath are becoming seriously alarmed by the growing army of unemployed said to be converging on the city. It was announced in Aschelon this afternoon that a further contingent would sail for Cutlake later in the week as soon as sufficient funds had been raised. According to a statement issued late this afternoon the attitude of the authorities remains unchanged and up to the present all attempts at negotiation have resulted in a continuation of the present deadlock.

"On the European front ..."

The announcer's voice was drowned by a furious outbreak of catcalls. Savage razzing broke out in all parts of the hall. A voice shouted, "We'll show 'em deadlock!" "Wait till we get to Gath!" From one corner a loud parody broke out, raw and personal and very, very funny. It bristled with names and local allusions. One of the boys wrote it when the long sit-down was on. Matt caught Gabby's eye over on the other side of the room and Gabby grinned and made an obscene gesture which was his opinion of the man whose name occurred most often in the song.

The little radio man had gone pasty and sick-looking. Through the noise his lips shaped the words, "Maybe I shouldn't have brought the machine along!" Matt stepped up close to him, shaking his head to show he hadn't heard. The man repeated in a frightened shout, "Maybe I shouldn't have brought her along!"

Matt grinned, shrugged, shook his head. When the razzing had died down he asked quietly, "Did you ever see a mob in action, mister? I mean a *mob*."

The little man's head wobbled a negative. "That is, not outside of a baseball game," he added.

"The row goin' on then didn't scare you any?"

"I never thought of it that way."

"S'pose instead of shoutin' all those people had suddenly gone dead quiet. How'd you have felt then?"

The man eyed him uncertainly, "That something was wrong, I guess."

"Okay then," Matt said, "you can figger out pretty near any mob the same way. When it makes a noise then you know there's a way to handle it, but when it comes at you quiet an' dreamy-lookin' then, brother, watch out!"

The man pulled out a handkerchief and wiped his pale face. "You boys had me scared there for a moment," he confessed with a touch of sheepishness. His business card fell out and he picked it up with a laugh of embarrassment. "I don't suppose any of you'll be wanting to buy your own machines for quite a while yet."

Gabby had sauntered over. He said cockily, "Don't be too sure of that, mister."

The radio man didn't know how to take that so he left it alone. He wiped the top of the little machine carefully, "Just keep her covered, will you?" he said to Matt. "A sheet of newspaper, anything, just so the veneer doesn't scratch up. I do quite a business in these little used machines." He nodded quickly and beetled off.

Matt called after him, "Don't you want to see anybody about this, get some kind of receipt?"

"Receipt?"

"Sure. Everything that comes in here has to be checked at the office."

Gabby laughed, "I wish they put me in the office," he said.

The little man shook his head. "That's okay," he said hurriedly, "I'll drop around tomorrow some time and see how she's making out." He gave the boys a frightened look and hightailed out the side door, almost falling down the steps into the arms of a pair of city cops.

Matt stuck a cigarette in his mouth and cracked a match on the seat of his pants. "There goes one little scared guy all right!"

Gabby took a light and exhaled a fast blue jet of smoke. His eyelid drooped. "I wonder what in hell he was scared of," he said.

"Mice, I guess," Matt said. Both boys laughed.

CHAPTER ELEVEN

That was Tuesday night when the boys reached Cutlake and Thursday morning before they moved on to McBain. McBain was a little ex-ghost town pulling back onto its feet. Thirty years ago it used to be more important than Cutlake, before the time when Cutlake really began to come ahead. McBain was less than half-way between Cutlake and Andersville where the first divisions were to mass and wait over the week-end till the next two divisions joined them. Then at the beginning of the week the whole four divisions were to trek to Gath. That was the strategy as planned and the way it ultimately worked out. The men moved on from place to place with the timing and discipline of an army.

Wednesday night Matt and Eddy and Dick and a man named Boyce got passes for the game between Cutlake and the coloured Sons of the Desert. They played it out at the ball grounds. The Sons of the Desert wore little chin beards and they kept the crowd laughing, razzing each other in high-pitched Negro voices. The yelling of the crowd went on all the time and the voices of the kids yelling candy and peanuts and ice cream and the voice of the ref. and the dry, hard smack of driven balls. The crowd had a time razzing the referee, so much so that at last he was taken off and another man put on. Beneath the fierce top lighting the two teams slugged and raced and slid and churned up spurts of dust. The people roared happily and mechanically. The sound hit in waves, coming in strong, slackening, then rushing in strong again. Behind the bleachers in the wide blacked-out expanse, a tiny point of light revolved from a lighthouse among the islands. The moon was red like hot copper.

The four boys drifted in and stood against the fence in General Admission.

Matt said after a while, "Seems funny bein' here again tonight. Cutlake's a smart little town. I like the people an' I like the way they treated us."

Dick half turned his dark kid's face. "Maybe you never stepped off Main Street."

"So what?" Matt said, "why must you always be tryin' to start something?"

Big Boyce interposed, "This thing may be okay by you, fella, but how long have you been doin' it?"

"Doin' what?" Matt asked.

"Doin' nothing," Boyce said and he yelled a name at the referee.

"All my life," Matt said when the crowd had quieted down.

"All your life what?"

"Doin' nothing," Matt said and laughed.

He was picking up this mood easier all the time now, "I only came into town Sunday to join up with the big sit-down."

Boyce spoke morosely. He spoke like a man with some deep discontent day and night gnawing at him. "Yeah? Well, most of us boys has been out since the camps closed down in April an' we're fed up on bein' part of a goddam nickel circus. We go on a sit-down. Okay. For a couple weeks the public comes an' pokes peanuts through the bars. What are we anyway? A bunch of men or the Dionne quintuplets?"

Matt laughed. Boyce rounded on him touchily. "You can laugh all you want," he said. He held up a pair of once-powerful hands, "See those hands? Show 'em the smell of an axe handle an' they'd fold up like putty!"

One of the Cutlake boys smacked out a terrific homer that sailed over the fence and out into darkness. The bleachers rose and howled. Matt joined in. When the row had dropped back to normal he glanced behind. "Did either of you boys see Eddy around anywhere?" he asked quickly.

"Eddy who?" Boyce said, not taking his eyes from the game.

"Eddy!" Matt cried, "you know Eddy!"

Boyce dragged his eyes away for an instant. "Oh, Eddy," he said, "sure, I saw him around a while ago. Why?"

"I gotta find him," Matt said, "that's why."

"What's the fuss? Don't Eddy know how to take care of himself by now?"

"The only thing he knows, an' he knows it perfec'ly, is how to get himself in trouble."

Boyce smiled, his eyes back on the game. "What's eatin' you so about Eddy? He could of gone away, you know. He could of had his reasons."

"No foolin'," Matt said, "this is serious." He stood there with the crowd yelling all round him. Suddenly his face changed. He turned and slipped through the boys by the main gate. He heard Boyce shout something after him.

Outside the gate he paused to get his bearings, then he turned north up Belsize, cut through an alley and came out on the eleven hundred block on Frank Street, right opposite Gus' restaurant. At that hour it was filled with kids eating sundaes and drinking sodas and Gus and a couple of blonde waitresses were moving up and down behind the counter. The sound of Gus' radio came right out onto the street. There were cars parked thick along the curb both sides belonging to people in the movie farther down the block.

Matt stopped again and he muttered, "Between the big hardware an' the barber pole," and his eyes ranged up and down and he tried to remember the position of the second-hand store from having seen it when he came up from the boat. He looked everywhere without seeing Eddy. Finally he asked a man passing and the man told him to walk a block farther up and the store was on the right-hand side. "Look," he said, pointing, "I guess you can make it out from here by the barber pole."

Matt thanked him and he mouched on watchfully, looking for Eddy. There was a light burning in back of the second-hand store but no one moving about. He hung around the window then he stepped in the doorway and tried the door in case there was anyone inside the store could say whether Eddy had been hanging around. A voice behind asked suddenly if he was looking for someone.

He knew enough not to turn quickly as though he were caught trying to bust in the store, he knew enough not to give any sign a cop could pick on. He turned slowly and naturally. "I was looking for a man," he said, "but the man isn't here."

"No?" said the cop, tight-lipped.

"No," said Matt coldly. He walked back onto the street white with rage and he heard the cop's steps move slowly away. He walked on fuming. He could have told that noseying sonovabitch plenty! Anything in uniform made him feel that way now. Uniforms were another bit of class oppression the same way that wars were cooked up by a bunch of pot-bellied financiers.

He walked up and down the other side of the street and waited around outside Gus's but Eddy never showed up, so he thought after all it was him getting to be jumpy and not Eddy's fault at all, and that Eddy had felt sick at the game and gone back to the hall without saying anything. It made him uneasy suddenly the way he got up in the air over the smallest thing. Maybe he was picking up the general atmosphere. He raised his hand and stared at it to see was it quite steady and the hand was steady like rock. He stopped and peered at his own image through Fred's window in the long mirror at the back of the shop and something about the stiff, scarred features jarred him. He looked older than those kids sitting in there at Gus' soda fountain, older than anyone he ever saw of his own age. "Nuts!" he thought exasperated, "What I need is a drinka beer!"

At the end of Frank he crossed over and turned off into Bryant, a dingy side street of wooden buildings with ROOM signs painted on white globes above the doorways and steep flights of stairs with broken rubber treads leading up off the street and windows with Chinese laundry signs, and old, run-down houses, their lights gleaming dirtily through the split blinds and cloudy panes.

Off in the distance he made out a woman walking and a man on the outside of her. He recognized the man by the way the shoulders moved. "Eddy!" he breathed. Automatically his body reacted to danger, grew taut and wary all over. He did not hurry to catch up with them at once. He came up slowly, thinking. By the time he drew level his mind had rehearsed pretty well everything that could develop out of a situation like this.

At the sound of his step behind Eddy turned quickly. His mouth dropped, his eyes darkened with fear. His tongue came out and wavered on his lower lip but he did not try to say anything.

Matt took a sharp look at the woman's rear elevation, then he eased alongside. He did not speak to her at first. He addressed Eddy casually, "Where're you goin', Eddy?" The woman turned. Through the bad light she looked between thirty-five and forty. Her eyes were heavily mascara'd, she wore a doll-hat tipped forward on a mass of bleached, untidily curled hair. Her face was thin, her mouth pinched and hard, and streaked with lipstick, and her eyes had an animal hardness. Matt saw at once what she had. He knew plenty kids that had picked up their dose that way. He knew one kid of sixteen picked it up off a waitress in a coffee shop across from the depot in Clever.

She gave Matt the same kind of look he had given her from behind, then she flashed him a professional smile. "Are you a friend of Eddy's here?" Her voice was a little hoarse. She stopped in front of one of the places that had a Rooms card in the downstairs front window. "Like to come on up with Eddy?"

Matt said, "Eddy isn't goin' up."

He saw the woman's eyes narrow, turn hard and angry like cat's eyes. Then she slipped her hand through his arm and smiled. "Don't be like that," she said in her soft, hoarse voice.

Matt shook free in disgust. "You let me alone," he said, "an' you let Eddy alone, too, or you know damn well what we can do. C'mon, Eddy!"

Eddy hesitated. His glance darted confusedly from Matt to the woman and back to Matt again.

"C'mon, Eddy," she said. Her body pressed close up to him. For a moment he gazed down at her uncertainly. Through the film of his bewildered mind she looked young and pretty and kind. She took a step towards Matt. "You can scram, see?" she said harshly, "Eddy an' me don't want you round, do we, Eddy?"

Eddy felt himself being pulled and he tried to back away. Suddenly he began to be afraid.

Matt stepped round quickly, blocking the path. He said to the woman, "You lay off Eddy right now. He's got no money."

She glared at him. "Will you mind your own goddam business?"

"Eddy is my business."

She looked from one to the other and smiled wisely. "So that's the way it is."

Matt turned white with rage. "Sure," he said, "that's the way it is."

The woman smiled again. "I heard there was plenty of that kind of thing down there among you boys."

Matt took a quick step forward, then he controlled himself. "*Will you lay off of Eddy?*"

"No," she said, "I won't lay off of Eddy, why should I? You know what I can do?"

Matt's body was so stiff that the tension began to hurt. He said coldly, "I don't know anything."

The woman laughed. "You know plenty," she said. Her face narrowed with spite. "Listen," she said, "maybe I don't want Eddy so bad after all, but anything, anything at all that I can do to get *you* in trouble, I'll do. An' all I have to do is just let out one little yell ..."

"If you was to yell that," Matt cut in, "you should of started yellin' twenty years ago." He turned to Eddy, "Are you comin' along, Eddy, or do I have to knock you down first?"

Eddy whispered, "Sure, Matt, I'm comin'!" He jerked suddenly free. The woman spun round and struck him viciously between the eyes. She was wearing a cheap, ornate ring and the coarse setting caught him and slit the flesh over the cheekbone. He put his hand up to shield his face and she struck at him again.

Matt felt the old rage-blindness rush over him. He took a smack at the woman and caught her off balance and she stumbled and fell. Across the street a white light burned in the window of the Chinese laundry. A shrivelled old Chinaman trotted to the open door and stood there watching. He looked like death watching. Then as the woman fell he made a high gabbling sound and a second Chink came out from behind and they stood together in the doorway watching.

Matt seized Eddy. "C'mon, Eddy, *scram!*"

The woman scrambled up, her doll hat had slipped back and dangled foolishly on one frowsy curl. She flew at Matt clawing and yelling. He shoved her away and she sat down backwards. As she tried to rise he kicked her in the tail and she stayed down. He bent over her, made sure she was not out cold. Her face was a mess of powder and smeared blood. She opened her eyes, glared at him and called him a name. Eddy was staring helplessly, his face stupid with horror.

Matt shook him up savagely. "Run!" he hissed. They turned and pounded up the block. From the other side of the street the two Chinks watched them disappear. They did not go across and pick the woman up. They went back inside the laundry, locked the door and turned off the light.

The two men pounded on, Matt ahead. Within the space of a few blocks the town dropped away. The street lamps grew far apart, the rows of shambling houses changed to a few scattered lights set back off the road with stubbled masses of darkness lying between. The air smelt of damp growth and sea wrack. In the distance a dog was barking.

Matt pulled up, choking, half crying. He heard the heavy slap-slap of Eddy's feet behind, then the heaving of his breath. He dropped down on the edge of the boardwalk. His chest was full of a tight pain and he had a stitch with running. Then he caught sight of his bloody hand and reached out and dragged up a bunch of grass and wiped it quickly. He spat on it, tore up more grass, wiped it again. For a long time the two men's hunched forms sat there sobbing for breath.

At last Eddy spoke timidly. "That was terrible," he whispered, "that was the worst thing I ever seen anybody do."

Matt's face was rigid. "Don't talk to me," he said hoarsely, "what you have to do, you have to do. I done a lot worse things than that in my time." He sat staring ahead, then a long shudder shook him. He looked at Eddy with loathing. "Don't talk to me," he said, "don't you ever talk to me again."

Eddy remained silent. His hands began to pick at one another. He scratched himself noisily beneath both arms. Then he sighed. His head was filled with whirling images, jangling and exploding with dizzy sparks of confusion and fear. He held his head to steady the explosions and the sparks grew brighter and angrier till they were a solid ball of flame, blinding him, shrivelling him up.

At last, "You!" Matt cried, "you ..." he choked, "do you know what you may of done?"

Eddy's voice was dead and singsong like a child repeating an old lesson, "Got us in trouble," he recited dully, "I may of got all the boys in trouble."

"An' got me canned for the third time," Matt added bitterly. "I don't know anything else you could of done. I think you did the whole thing complete this time." He stared at his right hand. "I done plenty of the goddamdest things in my time but it takes you to make me hit a woman. 'Sit-downer Slugs Woman.' How's that goin' to look spread all over tomorrow's papers?"

Eddy cringed miserably. "Maybe she won't tell the cops, Matt."

"That's what you think," Matt said. "I could think of two reasons why she wouldn't, an' a half dozen why she might." His voice grew suddenly tired. Mechanically his hand reached into his side pocket for a smoke. "Go on," he said, "what happened? I might as well know."

A car came towards them, bumping over the uneven ground. For an instant the head lights threw a blinding glare. As the car passed a man's arm reached out and tossed down an empty Scotch bottle into the grass. Matt reached for it, held it up, shook it, then threw it away in disgust. "Go on," he said, "what happened?"

Eddy's voice spoke out of the darkness. "I got tired watchin' the ball game," he began, "so I got thinkin' about those shoes I seen in that secon'-han' store an' I thought I could slip away an' maybe find out what size they was an' be back before the game finishes. So I went back an' looked in the window an' there was a light there in back of the store an' presently this lady comes along an' looks, too, an' she ses to me ..."

"*She says to you?*"

"Oh, sure, I never said anythin' to her till she speaks to me first."

"Go on, go on, then what happens?"

"So this lady comes an' looks in the window," Eddy repeated vaguely, frowning, "an' after a time she asks me was I lookin' for somethin' special an' I tell her sure I'm lookin' for somethin' special an' she laughs an' says, 'What's so special?' ..."

Matt broke in fiercely, "Hell, say it in a half-dozen words, not like it was a serial!"

Eddy glanced sideways, then he gabbled on hurriedly, "So she says to come on home with her an' she'll give me a real good pair of shoes for nothin'. She says her husband has a coupla real good pairs of shoes he don't use ..."

"Yeah, I'll bet! I'll bet he has a dozen pair he don't even know about. I'll bet he don't even know he's her husband."

"That lady tol' me ..."

"Christ, Eddy, that one wasn't no lady! She was so mean she wasn't fit to wipe up after an honest-to-goodness, out-an'-out whore."

Eddy dropped his head in shame. He muttered miserably, "Why can't I never do anythin' that's right, Matt? I wanted for you to have one of those pairs of shoes, I didn't want to keep 'em both for myself. Why can't I never do anythin' that's right?"

"I don't know. You was just born that way, I guess." Another silence fell heavily.

Then Eddy's eyes strayed to a clump of bushes on the opposite side of the road. His voice grew dreamy, "I was born in a field, I think, out there all alone in a field. That's where I was born."

"You mean you was born in the nut house!"

"You mean I was born crazy?"

"Hell, how do I know? What's the diff?"

"Because if I was born crazy they could shut me up," Eddy cried, his voice rising in alarm. "I wasn't born crazy, I was born in a hospital with a lotta lights like you see from the outside. I wasn't born in no field, I was born in a hospital like everybody else."

Matt heeled out his cigarette butt. "So what?" he retorted wearily.

Eddy's mind clung to its single idea with a terrible tenacity. "If I was crazy," he insisted, "then I'd want to kill someone an' I never wanted to kill anyone, I never wanted to hurt anyone, an' if I never did any of those things then I'm not crazy, an' they can't shut me up."

Matt stood up and he shivered suddenly. The voice of Eddy gabbled from a long way off. He felt his face stiff and a soreness all over his body like screws tightened on the inside. He put his hand up and felt his face and tried to ease the stiffness out of his jaw. He felt a hundred years old.

Eddy was holding him by the arm, talking, trying to explain something. "Look," Eddy was insisting, "I gotta tell you again what happened so you know I'm not crazy ..."

"Never mind," Matt answered mechanically, "forget it. The best thing you can do is forget the whole thing."

"But I gotta tell you to make you understand," Eddy cried, rushing the words so he could not be interrupted. "There was this big sonovabitching cop dressed up in a grey fedora that comes at me an' says, 'Now you get outa here, move on,' and I ses, 'Where to?' an' he ses, 'How the hell should I know?' an' I ses, 'Just tell me someplace to go an' I'll go.' 'Okay,' he ses, 'I'll tell you someplace,' an' he runs me aroun' into the alley an' then ... an' then ..." Eddy said, breaking off uncertainly, "you come along. There was somethin' else happened in between but I forgot what it was."

"Okay," Matt said, "you got it all straightened out now. Just don't think about it, that's all."

They picked their way among the maze of darkened streets, following the night glow in the sky that hung over Main Street. Eddy spoke once and his words sank like pebbles in the silence. He stumbled on tiredly, the loose gravel working through his shoes. They stopped under a light standard to pick up the name of a street.

"Here," Matt said suddenly, "lemme take a look at that eye. Did the second smack land?"

Eddy put his hand up. "I dunno," he said, "I don' remember. Why?"

"If it did then you could pick up a lovely case of blood poisonin'. Hold still while I take a look."

Eddy raised his face obediently while Matt examined the cut. "I guess it's O.K." he said, "it's formed a clot. Just don't pick at it, that's all. They'll fix it when you get back." They walked on and the silence closed again and hung, dense and heavy.

Outside the rear door of the hall they ran foul of pickets walking up and down the empty street. They showed their cards and went inside. One of the boys picketing called out after them, "What happened to you?" Matt did not stop.

"Who does he think he is?" the picket said.

"They all get that way," the other picket said. He was a little man in glasses and a squashed-looking hat.

"Who does he think he is?" the first picket repeated, fiercely, "who in hell do some guys think they are around here anyway?"

The small picket laughed softly. "I forgot who I was a long time ago."

"Huh?"

"Nothing. It doesn't matter."

"That's what you think. It matters a helluva lot any guy thinkin' he can talk that way to me an' get away with it!"

The small picket laughed noiselessly.

* * *

Inside the hall a lot of the boys were already bedded down. The smells of the night made up a thick, odorous pall. Smoke and disinfectant, stale food and coffee and the overpowering stench of massed body sweat. A low murmur of talk persisted among the waking men. A man sat up cutting his corns while his neighbour looked on interestedly making comparisons and offering advice. Over in a corner Gabby was showing Charlie a bunch of postcards he picked up off a man in the street for two bits. He was offering them around for a nickel a look but so far no one paid a nickel. When he saw Matt in the door he said something to Charlie and Charlie slipped them in his pocket but Matt was not looking at Gabby or Charlie. He went ranging around until he located Hep.

When Hep caught sight of the two boys his eyes gleamed dangerously. "Commere," he said, "I want to talk to you. Come on in the office. So you finally got back," he said. They stepped under the light.

Matt moistened his dry lips. "I gotta talk to you," he said, stiff-faced, "*now!*"

Hep peered at him sharply. The unshaded light carved his features into pale, harsh planes, made cruder the scar mark. There were lines sunk on either side of his mouth and his light grey eyes were dull and hard.

Hep glanced quickly from one man to the other. "What happened to Eddy's face?"

Matt said, "Never mind Eddy. I gotta talk to you, Hep, I gotta talk to you *now*."

Hep started to say something, then changed his mind. "Okay, Eddy, you can go along. Now what is it? What is it you wanted to say?"

Matt waited till Eddy was gone, then he began with an effort. "Nothin' I wanted to say. Somethin' I got to tell you about."

CHAPTER TWELVE

"**D**id Charlie get back from the hospital yet?" Matt asked, stopping the restless moving around he had been doing all morning.

"He got back a half hour ago," Hep said. "They didn't have any report of a woman being brought in late last night outside of a couple of maternity cases."

"Thanks for finding, out, Hep."

"Don't thank me. If that woman had hared off to the police, then the whole thing would have to come out an' nothing I could have done would have made a dime's worth of difference. Don't thank me," Hep said, "but why in hell should she have picked on Eddy?"

"God knows," Matt said, "there must be somethin' about him, they all do."

He followed Hep around some more. "What time are we leaving for McBain?"

"Right after dinner." Hep stopped short in exasperation. "For Petesake, quit following me around, an' quit worrying. If you told me everything, then we did all we could do an' we've got to hope for a lucky break." His experienced eyes lingered a moment on Matt's face. "You know what I ought to do in a case like this?"

Matt nodded, looking away from the eyes. "Are you goin' to do it?"

"How much do I know?"

Matt glanced at him quickly. "You know everything," he said at once, "I didn't keep nothing back. Does anyone ever try to keep anything back from you?"

"I don't know," Hep said, "maybe." The eyes lit briefly with a smile. "You better come along an' get a job of work to do. They want more boys on the inside to help clean up the hall."

In the early afternoon the first trucks began to roll. The division left in ten trucks and around twenty automobiles lent for the thirty-mile trip. A further two divisions were expected in next day to take off later by freight car for Andersville direct where the first division was to wait for them. The newspapers stayed friendly and the general impression left on the town was good. There was talk of a big sympathetic walk-out of loggers and mine workers and a march on Gath solid with sympathizers. The air buzzed with rumours, mostly wild, but outwardly the situation remained deadlocked. The brief spurt of newspaper talk about a million dollar works program to become immediately effective went back into smoke.

Round two o'clock the transportation line-up began to form out in front of the hall. It stretched all up Quarter Street and round the corner. It looked like some old car had died and all its buddies were going on a funeral. Fords, Pontiacs, Studebakers, Chevys and a couple of ancient Dodges still fighting-full of guts. All makes and vintages snailing down behind the big trucks. The men piled in by squads and as each truck drove off the people on the sidewalk gave a cheer and the boys waved back and shouted goodbye. The baggage left by a separate truck with two men checking the stuff and handing out identification stubs. Police moved quietly on the out-skirts of the small crowd but there was no disturbance of any kind.

In the back of one of the pick-up trucks, Hughes sat wedged between an ex-sticker in an Aschelon slaughter house and a man that once kept a lunchroom in the thirteen hundred block on Shroeder. Hughes was having a time with his notes and the heat, sitting up there, waiting for the truck to start. The heat when sitting still was terrific. Every now and then he pulled his glasses off and wiped them and he had to wipe his pencil, too. Hughes was not mechanical. He did not know one make of car from another, apart from having driven them, and nothing at all about trucks except their passing him on the road, and he felt very strongly that the only way to insure a later accuracy was to make notes from life as he went along.

On one side of him the sun had made the restaurant man drowsy and he kept falling against Hughes and making it difficult to write. On the other side the sticker was reading out hot bits from a sex-crime monthly, every now and then breaking off to tell Hughes the kind of things a book ought to have. He said action first, then plenty of sex. He said Hughes ought to read more. Hughes interrupted him to ask could he see for certain whether the name on that big, red truck was Reo and the sticker said, "Why in hell waste time christenin' trucks? What did a truck ever do for anybody?" The sticker was quite a card but Hughes was having a time with him all right.

When the truck finally started the restaurant man fell up against Hughes with a jerk and Hughes' notes were shot onto the floor. He got quite dizzy scrambling for them and getting his head pushed around by the bumping of the truck. There were a lot of little things like that kept happening all the time, like Gabby showing his cards to Saul and then trying to collect a nickel. Things no outsider could know about or get interested in because they were not important from an outside point of view.

Hep was checking his squad when a narrow-faced man, pale with the heat, came by and slung his roll into the baggage truck. He wiped his face with a bare arm, grumbling, "We make camp an' we break camp. Today it's Cutlake, tomorrow it's someplace else."

"O.K., what of it?" Matt said, coming up. Behind him tailed Gabby and Charlie and a crowd of boys waiting to be assigned transportation.

The man glared at Matt. "But where are we gettin', that's what I want to know?"

Hep turned round, took in the scene and at once said loudly, "You know damn well where we're getting. If you don't like the way things are run around here then get up some morning and tell the membership. That's what we have meetings for."

The man pocketed his baggage check. He spoke with a lot of private bitterness, "Trouble is there's too many meetings around here. This past month I went to close on fifty different meetin's an' here we are still paradin' round the country like a bunch of trained seals." He turned away.

Hep called after him sharply, "If you don't like things the way they are," he said, "then you know what you can do."

"Oh yeah? Jus' try an' break away from the organization an' see how easy it is."

Hep's eyes grew suddenly masked and watchful. "If you've got a grievance try going up in front of the grievance committee," he said evenly.

The man shrugged, "Maybe that committee'll find they have to handle the whole bunch of us before long," he said and moved away.

There was a moment's silence, then Hep broke it abruptly. He pointed to an Erskine re-paint job nosing into the curb with an old Buick touring model just behind calling out, "Here you are, boys, here comes our jalopies!" Instantly the tension passed and the boys began piling into the two old cars. Matt, Charlie and Eddy piled into the Erskine while Gabby, Dick and two young kids that joined up overnight climbed into the back of the broad-beamed old Buick and Saul sat with the driver. Hep stood with his arm on the Erskine's door. He looked the car over admiringly, "Nice little paint job you got here," he remarked with a smile.

The owner grinned in appreciation. He ran his hand over the wheel in a pleased gesture. "Believe it or not," he said, "she's got a dandy engine. I guess '28 must have been a good year." As Hep climbed in beside him he felt in his pocket and offered Hep a flattened-out pack of Sweet Caps.

Charlie settled back on the burping springs. "Well," he remarked, "I guess that sees the last of Cutlake."

"Not till we get outside the city limits," Matt muttered. His face was strained. He kept glancing back through the rear window.

Charlie said, curiously, "You sound like you was glad to be gettin' out of town."

Matt just looked at him. "You'll never know!"

The car swung out onto the main highway. A hoarse roar came from the Buick behind. The Erskine's owner thumped on his horn and stepped up the gas. The Buick hauled closer. She gave two angry bellows, and as she rolled by her passengers let out a chorus of derisive yells and the boys in the Erskine howled back.

"Some old crate that!" Matt said with a grin, sitting forward.

The driver picked up the words with touchy owner-pride. He was a solidly-built, elderly man with heavy, clean-shaven features and bright blue eyes. His thick light hair was streaked with grey, the backs of his hands glistened hairily and he had freckles both on the backs of his hands and on his neck behind. He wore a darned blue work shirt and khaki overalls and his sleeves were rolled above the elbows.

"Say, this bus of mine could beat the guts out of that Buick any day if I really opened her up," he said, half turning in his seat, "but it's not worth it. I'm not gonna knock hell out of a good engine!"

A faint grin spread over Hep's face as he stared out through the cracked windshield. He leant towards the driver confidentially. "If all the guys that's got no right to own cars was chased off the roads," he said, "there'd be fewer stuffed shirts behind the wheels an' more drivers that knew where they was headed for."

The man's face turned quickly. He brought his hand down on the wheel with a gesture of pent-up exasperation. He cried, "By Christ, but you said something there!"

Hep answered and in his voice there was a flattering shade of deference, "I could tell from the first that you were the kind of man thinks things out for yourself."

The driver began to open up eagerly. "Mind you," he said, "I'm not one to make trouble an' I never did hold with a lot of pumped-up newspaper talk but things can't go on the way they are now. What th' hell are we payin' taxes for? To keep a bunch of stuffed shirts in power three thousand miles away that don't even know yet we stopped livin' with the Indians?"

Hep chuckled, "That's a good one," he said, "only don't let anyone but us hear you say it." He passed the man a light. "Sounds as though you was interested in politics."

The man nodded soberly. "As I see it," he said, "every man nowadays is in politics whether he knows it or not."

The voice of Hep probed at him delicately. "What I meant was, it sounded like you had a personal interest in this thing."

The man's blue eyes narrowed. He gazed off into the distance, and his silence lengthened and hung in the air like the seething of insects. At last he spoke and his voice was not hot but thoughtful and troubled.

"Well, mister, I tell you," he began, easing back in his seat, "I got two kids, one seventeen an' the other nineteen up in the Sleeve valley right this moment tryin' to land a job, berrypickin'. 'Tryin',' I say. If I hadn't got the odd coupla dollars to grubstake 'em I guess they'd be right back here ridin' down to McBain with the rest of you boys." He pushed one hand through his wiry hair with a quick, baffled gesture. "That's one reason," he said, half turning and speaking into the back of the car, "that I'm givin' you boys the use of the car an' my own time drivin'. I think to myself, well, suppose I ever get laid off or sick or something, there's my own two kids goin' to be in the same place all you others is in right now ... no place at all!" He broke off with a half-ashamed grin. "I never talked so much as this in a long time," he said. "I guess something you said must of got me goin'."

Hep let the subject drop and picked up the new trail. He asked casually, "How are things up in the Sleeve?"

The driver chuckled. "Say, they got a reg'lar witch hunt going on up there now."

"What d'you mean, 'witch-hunt'?" Matt asked from behind.

"I mean they're scared the Reds'll get in an' organize."

Hep whistled softly, "Scared of that, are they?"

"Scared as the dickens. My kids bummed a ride along with two that has some kind of an old crate an' believe it or not, mister, those kids was stopped an' the car searched closer'n a pig-shave."

Hep nodded, "Makes you think, don't it?"

The man's face grew dark and troubled. "I never had no use for Reds," he said, "nor for Red talk, but a man gets to look at things different when they hit him where he lives." His voice rose suddenly in anger, "Lookit!" he cried, "look at the bunch of you boys here ... no job, no place to go, no future, runnin' around the country like a pack of dogs. Give me another coupla years of this kind of thing an' goddammit, I'll be headin' a parade myself!"

"Times are tough all right."

"*Tough!* Times aren't tough. It's the way things is run by a ... Jesus Christ, don't get me talkin' this way, it makes me sweat all over!" He wiped his face and round by the back of his freckled neck. "Just don't get me talking about it, that's all," he said.

On either side of the highway the quiet open country slid by, green and wooded but yellowing from the long drought. Cattle crowded up under the trees for shade and as the miles passed, a gleam of sea shone in the distance like a knife blade lying along the base of the mountains.

In back of the car Eddy's body sagged in heat-drugged sleep. Charlie and Matt smoked. A steady stream of summer traffic sped by, knifing the air with clean, streamlined strokes. A silence fell on the five men, a lassitude made heavy by heat and the monotony of the bumping car. Insects drove against the windshield and from under the rear seat came the faint continuous jangle of loose tools. Less than a mile outside McBain the pace slackened. The long transportation line drew up and from the cars ahead men began to pile out.

The three boys in the back roused themselves.

"What's the idea?" Matt said, getting out stiffly and looking round. There was no sign of a town, no sign of houses, only bare fields, the steaming highway, the hot, unflecked sky.

Hep climbed out, stretching his cramped legs. "What d'you think is the idea?" he said pleasantly. "D'you want this caravan should block the one main street?"

"D'you think they got no traffic regulations around here?" Charlie asked importantly because he was native-born and had been in McBain once before.

Matt tried to shake off a nameless depression, something he never had since he first hit Aschelon. "Looks like they didn't have much of anything around here."

The man behind the wheel raised his hand in a gesture of goodbye. "S'long, boys," he called out, "I sure hope you have luck!" They turned and waved. The Erskine's wheels clutched at the gravel, slewed round and straightened up. The man's hand came out again then the old crate picked up speed and rolled away.

As the squads began to march Matt noticed Eddy limping. He looked down and saw him still wearing the same shot-up scows. He asked, "Didn't they give you a new pair this mornin', Eddy? I asked Hep about it last night an' he said it would be okay."

Eddy's eyes dropped to his feet sadly, "They didn't have none big enough."

"Hell, Eddy, you're not the biggest man in this whole outfit."

"Maybe not, Matt, but I got the biggest feet."

Matt narrowed his eyes against the sun. "Where is this town anyway?" he asked Charlie.

Charlie spoke back over his shoulder, "Right over on the other side of that little hill there," he said. "You can't see anything of it till you come to it."

"I'll say you can't."

"It's a nice little town," Charlie said, "a nice frien'ly little town, nice frien'ly people."

Matt took Eddy's small roll of baggage and slung it up with his own. "If that limp gets bad," he advised, "you better fall out, Eddy, an' I'll wait with you. Maybe they'll send out a truck or something."

Eddy stared into Matt's face. His own lit with a shy unbelieving happiness. He stammered, "You'd do that, Matt ... after all the trouble I nearly got you into?"

"What d'ya mean 'nearly'?" Matt began fiercely, then he grinned resignedly. "Sure I'd do that for you, Eddy. What kind of a sonovabitch do you think I am?"

They watched the cars of the returning convoy, all but the baggage truck, shoot by. The drivers waved and shouted goodbye and good luck. The driver of the old Buick slowed down to call out, "Take care an' don't bust up the town!"

"Okay," Matt called back, "we'll be careful!" The men fell in and marched the two miles into town singing. The people stood stewing in the heat and watching them as they swung by. The porches of the Carioca Hotel and the old Ten Gallon House with the hitching posts still outside were filled with people; farmers and drummers and storekeepers and Chinks and women and the odd breed and lots of kids. They gave the boys a swell hand just as the boys had expected they would.

Right after the public meeting in the ball park the two kids that came in overnight at Cutlake and rode down in the Buick strolled up to Matt at the hall and tried to draw him into conversation. They looked like brothers because they had the same pale, bleached-out colouring and the same air of indefiniteness about their faces, half-baked, not anchored onto anything. When Matt asked if they were brothers they said no, they only came from the same place. From the way they talked it must have been someplace practically out in the bush. They were dressed in washed-up khaki overalls which added to their general impression of being all one flat colour.

They stuck around Matt like flies till he asked one of them, Jim, the oldest, whether they ever worked at any kind of a job before.

"Hell, no!" Jim laughed as though he thought that very funny, "all we ever did was chores around our own homes."

"But we're through with all that now," Ted said and he laughed, too.

Matt eyed them severely. "Maybe you was lucky to have your own homes," he said.

They stared at him as though he had insulted them. "Where'd that ever get anyone," Ted said, "stickin' around their own homes?"

Jim pressed in eagerly as though they were all three members of the same secret society. "Was it true what they said about the cops over in Aschelon usin' vomit gas an' not tear gas when they evicted the boys?"

At that Matt closed right up. "Ask Charlie over there," he said, "he was all through it." They went haring off to pester Charlie and he sicced them on to Hughes. He said Hughes was the thin one in glasses over there and he was writing a book and knew everything, so they went over and settled on Hughes who was having a time bringing his literary schedule up to date. Finally Gabby strolled by and scenting an audience, started in to tell the kids a long fairy tale, practically not one detail of which was correct.

After the kids had gone Hughes asked Gabby whether he wasn't ashamed of himself, stuffing green kids that way. "That was a damn good story," Gabby said, offended, "Where's the harm jus' so long as you can get it believed?"

That was a new angle on Kenny and brought him up short. He said with a touch of envy, "I believe you should be writing this book and not me."

"Aw, sure," Gabby said softening. "Jus' tell me how to spell the words an' I will. See, here, Kenny, here's somethin' swell I picked up off a guy in the street in Cutlake ..." and out came the cards. Gabby was a mystery to Hughes. He could never understand how life bounced right off Gabby while every little thing that happened to Hughes left a dent. He would have liked to put him in the book, too, but he was a bit nervous over trying to reproduce some of the things Gabby was in the habit of saying.

Finally the two boys drifted back to Matt and stuck with him all through supper. They seemed to slide right into the routine. Jim said he never saw so much free tobacco anywhere. He told Matt that Ted never smoked before and that he had not done much of it himself because there was never anything but a little shag round his own home that belonged to the old man. After supper they stood out on the steps trying to drag easily and letting the butts droop from the corners of their mouths. Matt watched them, then he stepped over and spoke to Jim quietly. "You want to be careful at first," he said.

The boy's face turned beet red. "Oh yeah? Maybe you think we can't take beech leaves," he said.

Matt swallowed a grin. "If you can take beech leaves," he said gently, "then you ought to be able to take anything."

"I'll say we can! Jus' because we come from the country, don't think we're hicks." The boy talked out of the corner of his mouth and without removing the cigarette. Matt eyed him for a moment then he flicked the butt from between his lips and stamped it out.

The kid took a step forward, his arms came up then they dropped again. "Hey, what th' hell ..." he began uncertainly. Matt smiled and touched him on the shoulder. "Just because you can take beech leaves," he said, "that don't mean you have to go around lookin' like Dillinger." He saw what effect even in this short time excitement and a little temporary publicity were having on these kids. He saw the thing because he recognized it and knew how the shot-in-the-arm worked. Suddenly he found himself looking back on it like something felt a long time ago while he was still very young. The vague feeling of let-down and mistrust came back over him and remained.

He went inside and Boyce lent him a copy of *Peep* that came in with a pile of donated stuff, but the inside did not come up to the outside, so he swapped it for a western monthly that held him for a time till he found that what he had got interested in was a serial. Finally he borrowed writing materials off Hughes and sat down to write to Hazel, steadying the pad on his knees. At first he chewed on the pencil for a long time wondering how to begin but once he got started then it came quite easily. He wrote:

"McBain.   Thursday.

"Dear Hazel:

"I guess you will be wondering what happened to me unless you read in the papers about our arriving. Well, we finally fetched up at McBain this afternoon and got a great welcome. I am writing this round nine thirty. We move on to Andersville tomorrow by freight car so we will have had plenty variety by the time we get to Gath, boat, car and train. Believe me, Hazel, things work out to schedule around here. I never saw a bunch of boys disciplined the way these boys is. Everyone has a job and it has to be done on time and if he argues or tries to cut up, out he goes.

"This is one damn fine body of men. Of course there are a few heels but you get that anywhere. Living with them gives you something you never can get all the years of lonewolfing and I speak from plenty experience. I talked to one of the older men about this once and he said they got this same feeling in the war they had back in nineteen fourteen I think it was. There is a little burnt-up guy here we call Pop. Well, to hear him drag out the remains and chew over them it seems like that war was the only happy thing he ever did. He has not done anything since except collect medals and relief.

"I don't know what has got into me tonight, something I ate maybe though the food they give us here and in Cutlake has been swell and lots of it. No, it is like something eating up from underneath. The best way I ever felt except that time you and me had together was stepping off the boat at Cutlake with the whole town turned out to give us a hand. It seemed like everything we did then was bound to be right.

"Hazel, one thing I want to ask. Will you cut out going with that Art. I have no right to tell you what you do and what you don't do but I would like it very much if you would stop going with him. He is a heel even if he does wear a tux. Believe me I am not running around with any cuties over here. I wish you could hear the squad leaders roasting the pants off any kid that has ideas.

"I must close now. This heat gets you and not much place to move around. You had better not write till you hear again as I don't know any address or what day we get to Gath. Some time round the beginning of the week I think it should be. I will drop you a line just as soon as I know anything for sure. About all we hear apart from what goes out at the meetings is scares and rumours.

"How is the old lady's religion? Don't let it get you down. I can't give you anything but love, Baby. There is a boy with an accordion been playing that thing all evening till someone told him to shut up. It is not a tune any of us likes at the moment, too personal. I will write again soon.

"Yrs. with love, MATT."

After he sealed the letter and gave the rest of the paper back to Hughes he went outside for air. His eyes felt hard and burning and something at the back of his head was thumping like a trip hammer. He had the feeling that he badly wanted to talk to someone without knowing what it was he wanted to say. Presently Hep came out of the shadows and sat down beside him. Hep removed his hat, ran his hands through his thick black hair and shook his head sharply to clear it. "Chroust!" he muttered tiredly, "has this been a day!" He set his hat back on carefully.

Matt passed him a pack of Caps and after the first few drags Hep's face began to relax. They sat there for some time without talking. Then Matt asked, "Why did you try to sell that driver this afternoon?"

Hep smiled, looking down at his feet. "I never try to sell any man anything ... that doesn't want to buy."

"You know what I mean, Hep."

Hep flicked off a small red bead of ash. His voice altered, "I tell you, Matt," he said, "you never know when a good man may come in useful. Take this chap today. He's not strong for any particular party but he's spent a lot of time thinking and he realizes things can't go on the way they are. There's a man had to think because his kids have tied him right in with the situation. Jesus, you don't have to sell a man like that, all you have to do is just give him a gentle push in the right direction."

As Hep talked Matt felt some obscure issue beginning to come clear in his head. He was a little time making up his mind to speak of it. Then,

"Hep!"

"What is it?"

Matt felt himself reddening foolishly. "Why don't you get a better job with the organization? You could be damn near anything you wanted by this time. You can handle a bunch of men better than half these guys that spend their time harin' around doin' committee work."

Hep raised his head. He looked at Matt across the shadows with a gleam of amusement. "Why don't I?" he echoed gravely and stopped. "I don't know," he added after a pause, "maybe it's because I like working among the boys from the ground up, watching 'em come in green, like you for instance. I like to watch how they shape up, then if they're any damn good at all maybe I recommend them for special work. I'm no good at making speeches, can't think good on my feet. Actually though I do a lot more than just herd a bunch of kids around." He stopped. "Does that handle the question?"

Matt's face was still, his voice grew suddenly strained. He asked, "Would you ever recommend me, Hep?"

"Would I? I don't know. Later on maybe, at present I think you lose your temper too easy." He heard Matt stir, guessed at his disappointment. "When you first come in," he said with half a smile, "you didn't like the discipline much, didn't like getting pushed around. That's right, isn't it?"

"That's right," Matt admitted. For a moment he was silent. "That all seems such a damn long time ago now, seems like a million years." His eyes looked off into the darkness. The stream of men passing in through the gates had thinned now. Up the street the last cars were pulling out from the beer parlour in the rear of the Carioca. Here and there in a window across the street a light flicked on or went out below to reappear on the upper floor. From inside the hall the murmur of voices increased as the men passed inside, checking in for the night.

"Hep!"

"What now?"

"Suppose when we get to Gath an' this stalemate still keeps up, how are they goin' to hold this bunch together so they don't bust out an' fight the cops an' try to tear up the town? What I mean is, how long's this sit-down good for?" Matt asked.

Hep turned, regarding him with a mixture of curiosity and suspicion. "What's suddenly put all this in your head tonight?"

Matt rubbed a hand over his face. "I don't know," he answered uncertainly, "I felt kind of unsettled all evening. I wanted to talk to someone, ask a lot of questions, an' I don't know what in hell I wanted to ask. Maybe this is what I wanted to ask."

Hep nodded. "Sounds like you lost your focus, Matt. Jesus, don't we all do it at times!" Then his hands came up and as he talked the tough sensitive fingers wove and interwove as though he were working on a model, creating a picture tangibly for Matt to see.

"Now here's what you got to remember, Matt," he began slowly, "the thing that's going on underneath a lot of detail and petty snarling and newspaper talk."

"This fight isn't new, it wasn't new five years ago, but here's what makes it hard. It isn't the kind where a guy can go out an' smash something with his hands an' get himself all tuckered out an' bloody that he feels he's accomplished a helluva lot even if he don't exactly know what it is. We can't go out and throw rocks at a bunch of scabs or stand in a picket line, an' we can't walk out for more pay. We can't do any of those things, an' that's what makes it different from straight labour trouble. Can you see that far?"

talking about the fight

"I get it," Matt said, "at least I think I do. Seems like we didn't have much left to fight with though."

Hep chuckled. "Don't worry," he said. "We got a damn high nuisance value, that is, since the days of organization. We can raise plenty hell in our way only, whatever happens, we got to keep the sympathy of the public an' that means every swat we take we have to take with one hand tied behind our backs. There's nothing the public gets fed-up on so quick as trouble. As for the boys busting loose an' starting to tear up the town," he broke off with a lift of the shoulders, "there's not going to be any real danger of that just so long as they go on remembering that the only real discipline they have to depend on is the way they look at this thing in their own minds. By Christ, I think they had that hammered into 'em till they can see it in their sleep!"

Matt got up. He kicked at the coarse grass by the steps, dug his heel into it. Hep saw there was still something he wanted to get rid of. He asked sharply, "What's eatin' you, for Petesake? All this time I don't believe you ever told me the real thing that's eatin' you."

Matt raised his head slowly. He answered, "All I want to know is, what's comin' out of this mess in the end?"

"All *you* want to know! Isn't that all anybody wants to know?"

Matt looked off into the darkness, the scar place between his eyes deepened. "I guess that sounds kind of dumb, a question like that, but it's not so dumb when you come to think about it."

Hep rose and brushed off the seat of his pants. For a moment Matt felt a return of the feeling he got at times when he was alone with Hep, a sense of almost complete isolation. His mind shocked up against some vast impersonal force at once magnetic, implacable and pitilessly single eyed. Hep regarded him in silence. Then, "I don't think," he returned with sudden irritability, "I just go on from day to day. No man's safe that lets himself go around thinking, it gets him jittery an' you can't rely on him any more. What do I know? Maybe this fight'll go over big an' accomplish something ... maybe at the last minute it'll flop."

They went up the steps. "I remember that time in Clever ..." Matt was beginning when Hep turned and cut him short.

"You can't afford to go on anything that's happened before, Matt. Just when you think everything's all set that's the time some damn crazy thing can happen an' shoot the whole carload haywire. Playing wet-nurse to a load of dynamite you can't ever tell."

Matt followed him inside, speaking softly to avoid waking those men already asleep. "What's Andersville like, Hep?"

"Andersville? I can't tell you exactly but they've got a phrase to describe Gath. They call it more English than England. Well, Andersville's something up the same alley."

Matt's voice was vaguely distrustful. "Say, what kind of people are the English?"

Hep shrugged. "The English? They're okay, I guess. After a time you get so you don't notice them."

CHAPTER THIRTEEN

The wayside station of Andersville dozed in the windless sunshine of mid-afternoon. Heat glinted on the telegraph wires, flashed from the curved steel threads of the right-of-way, rose shimmering from the yellow dust of the roadbed. The heat was thick and languid. Dark firs dead-still against a flat sky, hot buzzing of insects, uncool shade, bright light dizzy with heat.

Three men lounged in the shadows of the freight shed. Below them a row of skinny tow-haired kids in bathing trunks squatted like crows along the fence, faces angled expectantly upline. The howl of a train sounded in the distance, then a rumbling on the tracks. The boys' bodies stiffened. When the sound increased and a burst of steam broke above the trees they slid down off the fence and hared off upline to where the freight was settling into the siding.

A man rattling by with a truckload of milk empties slowed down, pulled into the siding. As he drove on past the shed he leaned out shouting, "They've come!"

The three figures moved languidly out into the sun. A big black-haired man in faded khaki overalls smelling of feed shaded his eyes with his hand. His head moved in slow confirmation. "That's right, the boys finally got here." The three watchers gazed silently upline. Through the trees the legs of the men were visible standing in the doorways of the freight cars and back of them still more men. They began to drop to the ground, shouting, laughing, tossing down their baggage. Soon the whole siding seethed with men.

The faces of two of the watchers grew sharp with apprehension. In the small bloodshot eyes of the third sparkled a bright sardonic gleam—Old Man Morgan, libertine of the gay nineties and without visible means of support since the century turned. Tom Hitchcock, worry-eyed, work-scored, pushed his hat back and scratched anxiously amongst his grey and thinning hair. "I tell you," he said, "there's too many men there for this town to feed. A bunch like that could bust the place up, we haven't got the police to handle them."

The black-haired man's ham-like hands hitched at his suspenders. "I guess they shipped the most of the cops on to Gath to act as welcomin' committee," he said nervously.

Old Man Morgan thrust out his spittled chin and spat. "Those cops won't need t'import any gas for their bombs in Gath. They're billetted right alongside of the Legislatur'!" The other two eyed him with disfavour.

"Maybe you think that funny," worry-eyed Tom observed, "but it ain't so funny. A bunch of kids like that makes you think. Don't matter who you are, a bunch of kids travellin' the country like some kind of goddam circus makes you think." Silence met his words. By a single instinct the three men turned and stepped in out of the sun.

Black-hair, heavy and troubled, propped himself against the doorpost, thumbs hooked in his suspenders. He remarked broodingly, "I heard they got the Reds workin' among those boys. Feller told me Reds was at the bottom of this whole trouble."

Old Man Morgan thrust in a fresh wad of tobacco. "Boogy, boogy," he mocked, "someone bin tellin' you bedtime stories, George. S'pose the Reds is at the bottom of the trouble. You can't let a swamp lay around year after year an' not expect to breed mosquitoes."

"I heard that Red story, too," Tom said, "I heard it more places than one."

Old Man Morgan's chin wagged in challenge. "So what? The Reds didn't start nothin', they just come in an' took advantage of the set-up. The whole damn system is at the bottom of the trouble."

The other two heads rose in suspicion. "You turnin' P.P.P.?"

"No sirree, I heard too much of that bunch over the air."

George straightened up suddenly, adjusting his suspenders. He said in a voice laboriously casual, "Well, I guess I better be gettin' along. Got things to do." He moved away.

Tom called out after him. "Where're you goin' so sudden?"

George reddened. "Not goin' anywhere sudden," he retorted touchily, "but I just remembered I got a sack of potatoes in back of the car. I'm goin' to check 'em in at the supply depot they opened up in town to feed the boys." His glance strayed uneasily upline.

Old Man Morgan's eyes snapped with malice. "Buyin' pertection already, huh?"

George gave him a look of dislike. He exploded, "I'm not buyin' a damn thing. I just don't want no trouble out at my place, that's all."

Tom watched the ponderous figure cross the tracks. He said, "Now there's an angle I never would have thought of. Maybe I better see about gettin a case of eggs down there myself."

Old Man Morgan rose and scratched in his armpits. "Balls!" he remarked scathingly. "Scared of a bunch of kids! Balls to both of you!"

"Don't you make any mistake, this is no bunch of kids."

"What is it then? A bunch of Nazis? We could use a few Nazis around here. Balls!" Old Man Morgan repeated and once more he spat contempt down onto the right-of-way.

The columns formed, marched up Main Street heading for the Agricultural hall where temporary quarters had been assigned. Matt was marching abreast of Gabby. He looked about him. The details were familiar, gas station, lunch counter, barber shop, poolroom, corner drugstore, movie house, line-up of cars angled into the curb; but the atmosphere was strange. "So this is Andersville!"

Gabby grinned; he called out, "Join the jobless an' see the world!" The men laughed appreciatively. The words got caught up and passed like a slogan down the lines.

A man behind Gabby growled, "I had enough an' plenty of these public parades ... Aschelon, Cutlake, McBain. Makes us look like a bunch of goddam Shirley Temples!"

An elderly man in shabby tweeds with a frigid English nose and a pointer bitch on a leash paused on the sidewalk to stare. His amazed eyes followed the columns as they swung by. He exclaimed in his choked, cultivated voice, "By Jove though, I'd no idea!"

A grease-stained mechanic standing alongside looked round, recognized him. He asked with a faint smile, "You'd no idea of what, General?"

The general's head reared back in faint distrust. He waved vaguely, "All this," he said with a curious helplessness, "I'd simply no idea at all!"

The mechanic broke into a half smile. He said softly, "I got a kid brother in that outfit somewhere."

A spark of expression gleamed for a moment in the blank British eyes. "By Jove," the general muttered, "is that so? Is that really so?" He twitched at the bitch and stamped off, making little troubled stabs at the sidewalk with the point of his walking stick.

*   *   *

Next day the second and third division boys pulled into town by flat car and the first division went down to meet them and hand them the freedom of the city. Marching back up Main Street it looked like an army had moved into town. The people liked this less than they had liked yesterday. It was unique, it could be dangerous, vaguely it bore the hallmarks of revolution. All those that did not turn out for the big open-air meeting Saturday night chose to remain indoors.

Those that came were round a thousand strong, so many it looked like the district had started giving up its dead. They stood close-ranked in the hot summer darkness, faces quiet with rural dignity, eyes troubled and angry, minds struggling to grasp the truth of a grotesque situation. On one side of the platform massed the seven hundred men and the faces of the people were divided between them and between Laban as he stepped up to the mike on the small, flag-draped platform. Back of him lay the unlighted road, the dense blackness of country night; below him gaunt tiers of raised heads harsh in the white light.

He spoke as he had spoken Sunday, acrid, impassioned, spitting his words in a sort of cold white fury and the people attended almost silently, without excitement, still and brooding and deeply troubled. Then at the last his manner altered, became simple and earnest and compelling, stirring his audience where each man lived.

" ... You good people of Andersville who have welcomed the boys so warmly," he pleaded, "you have had them in your midst long enough to judge for yourselves whether they are organized trouble-makers or boys with a fine sense of comradeship and responsibility. There is only one more point that I want to impress upon you. These boys can fight but only you, the people, can decide the outcome!"

A wave of cheering broke suddenly from the silent people. A man shouted, "*Are we downhearted?*" and out of the darkness a roar of voices thundered, "*No!*"

As the crowd began to move, Matt standing by Saul cried out softly, "The way Laban makes it sound we can't lose!"

Saul nodded, black head moving between powerful shoulders. "He's smart all right. If anyone can spread trouble across the front page an' keep it there, Laban can."

Matt said, "You don't like Laban?"

"I don't have to like him, do I? A weasel's smart but I don't have to like it."

"What do you mean by that?" Matt was beginning, when from the slow-moving mass of people the figure of Hep detached itself and came quickly towards them.

"Hey, you," he said, touching Matt on the arm and drawing him a little aside, "last night you wanted a job of work to do. Okay, here it is. Remember those two kids that came in at Cutlake?"

Matt's body stiffened to attention. "Sure do. They was followin' me around all yesterday like a coupla dogs. What about them?"

"Did you see either of them since the meeting began?"

"Not since Laban started talkin'."

The crowd was breaking now, surging over the uneven ground towards the mass of cars parked below the trees. Hep pulled at his long top lip, eyes peering keenly through the darkness. His manner was hard and concentrated. "Saul and me'll take a look around town and I'll send a couple of boys to check on the beer parlor. We got to find those kids before they have time to get in any trouble."

Matt nodded quickly. "That could have happened. They were a brash pair of kids all right, brashest pair of kids I ever talked to."

A figure stepped out of the darkness. "Can I go along, Hep?"

Hep jumped, uttering a short cry, showing how tight he was strung below the surface. Then he caught himself and laughed. "Jese, Eddy, you gave me a scare, I must be gettin' jittery. Sure go along if you think you can do any good. I'll see you're both checked okay when you come in." He hurried away. Matt ran a few steps after him, started to speak and then stopped, overcome with sudden shyness.

"Well, what now?"

"Nothing," Matt said; then, "I just wanted you to know that I appreciate the chance to do something, I mean something on my own responsibility."

Hep's features creased in a smile. For an instant he looked at Matt with a gleam of affection in his lonely eyes. "Good boy! I wouldn't have given you the job if I didn't think you could handle it. If you have to go into town remember you want to watch your step." He went out the gate disappearing instantly, swallowed by the dark.

Matt looked about. The last cars were dragging and bumping over the rough ground, headlights swerving out onto the road. A figure on a horse jolted heavily by, clop-clop. Black trees thrust against a near-black sky, stars faint like tinsel, smell of bush-burnings, gas fumes still hanging in the air, a hoarse-throated train thundering at a far-off crossing. Then a high, angry shout that came from the thickness of the trees. Matt's head jerked up, listening. In a moment the shout came again. He swore softly, beckoning Eddy on. "C'mon, Eddy, that was too high for a man's voice!"

They headed for the trees, Matt's body moving swiftly, his senses so taut it was almost pain and with the pain the keen, exquisite pleasure of action and decision that were at last his own. Two figures struggled drunkenly among the trees. As the men came up they broke apart, one sat down backwards, the other teetered waving a dark object shaped like a bottle. Matt sprang at him, snatched the bottle and caught him by the shoulder, peering into his face. Eddy panted, "Who is it, Matt?"

Matt shook the bottle and threw it down in disgust. "Who d'you think it is? Those two young sonsovbitches we come out after!"

The boy let fly a wild poke at Matt's face. Matt stood him off with one hand. "Listen, you, Ted," he hissed, "where'd you get that bottle?"

The boy blinked foolishly. His face was dirty and sweaty. He stared at Matt with empty, drink-clouded eyes. Back of them a feeble anger struggled. A sound came from behind. The second boy had staggered up onto his feet. He stood there puking, then he sat down again heavily. He kept getting back on his feet and puking and sitting down again. Matt left him to it in disgust. He caught hold of Ted and pulled him back on his feet and held him. "Now," he said, "tell me where you got the stuff. Did you bust in the liquor store?"

The boy stared at him sullenly, his lip trembling. He would not say anything. Matt let go of him suddenly and as the white face flopped forward he smacked it on both cheeks viciously, jolting the neck up and back. He dragged the boy on his feet and struck him again. *"Did you bust in that liquor store?"*

The boy's head wagged helplessly, the clotted tongue struggled for words. He began to cry. Through his tears he choked out, "That was what he told us to do ... but we didn't do it."

"Who told you?"

"I dunno. He jus' comes up to us an' says ... why in hell don't you kids go out an' take what belongs to you?" He broke off. "Oh," he said, beginning to cry again, "my face hurts."

Matt shook him roughly. "If you didn't get the stuff in the liquor store were did you get it?"

The boy's head came up. After a moment he stopped snivelling and grinned foolishly. He mumbled, "We took it out of a car while the meetin' was on ... half-breed's car. He was layin' all over the steerin' wheel. Hell, we could've taken the whole car ..." he broke off, his face turned green and he puked. Matt let go of him and he sat down backwards. He stayed down a moment, then staggered up, weaving and swaying. He pointed to the boy on the ground and laughed, "He couldn't take it." He said it over several times, trying to laugh, then he began to hiccough.

The headlights of a car fanned out from the cross-roads. When the car drew level with the trees it stopped and a man got out and went round to the back, flashing a light on one of the rear tires. Matt saw the outlines of the man's hat and every part of his body contracted and grew tight. "Chroust!" he whispered. *"Cops!"*

The boy broke into a high laugh. He cried out, "They didn't get me. I could've taken the whole car." He stood there swaying. "Damn half-breed!" he called out, "damn half-breed sonovabitching cops!" He began to laugh and hiccough.

The man with the flashlight was climbing back in the car. He paused, stepped back on the road, stood there listening. Then he said something to the driver and began to come over flashing the light ahead.

Matt glimpsed the boy's mouth opening again and he closed it with a hard jab close in, dropping the boy like a log. Matt dropped with him, spreadeagling on the ground. He hissed to Eddy, "*Down!*" and he felt the thud of Eddy's body behind. He lay there sweating, listening to the snuffle of Eddy's adenoidal breathing and the thudding of his own heart. The grass smelt damp and rank with the odour of vomit. They lay there while the flashlight explored the ditch and advanced part way into the field. It paused, seemed to listen then turned and moved away and the man's long black shape moved behind it. Matt heard the car door click and the bite of wheels on gravel; raising his head he saw the sliding lights grow small and disappear.

He got up stiffly. His mind was ice-cold. He said to Eddy, speaking fast and with great distinctness, "Now here's something you gotta do, Eddy. Listen carefully. Something you gotta *do!*"

Painfully Eddy swung his mind into focus. "I'm listenin', Matt."

Matt peered closely at him through the darkness. "Now this is what you gotta do. Go on back to the hall an' send out a marshall to help me to take these kids in. After that you find Hep an' tell him what happened an' that I'll be checkin' in just as soon as I get this mess cleaned up. Got all that?"

"Say it over, Matt, so I don't make mistakes."

Matt snapped, "By God, you better not!" He repeated his instructions.

"Okay," Eddy whispered. His eyes strayed frightenedly towards the blacked-out road and the dense trees and little beads of fear came out and shone on his hairline.

"Okay," Matt said briskly, "go on, get goin'. Just remember that after you did all that you don't open your trap to anyone, not t' *anyone*, see? You jus' check in for the night an' if any of the boys asks you where you went to you tell 'em you lost your way comin' home from the meetin'. Tell 'em you fell in a ditch an' broke your neck, tell 'em any damn thing you want except what happened. Now beat it!"

Eddy started off then he came back. "S'pose those cops come snoopin' around again," he whispered anxiously. "I wouldn't want for you to get in any trouble, Matt."

"Hell, I won't get in any trouble, Eddy. I could take care of a whole barrel of cops. Oh, an' tell the boy that comes out to bring along a bottle of antiseptic an' some plaster an' rags, I'm afraid I smashed that kid's nose pretty bad." He gave Eddy a push to hurry him and watched the short, heavy figure stumble quickly off and lose itself among the trees.

The younger boy, Ted, had sat up. He put his hand to his bloody face, stared at it and began to whimper. He was crying now with pain and nausea and concentrated misery. His head felt terrible. Jim had sat up, too. His clothes were unbuttoned and dirt and grass spears stuck to his face. Matt let him alone and started in to work on the hurt one. He found a soiled handkerchief in his pocket and worked gently, feeling up the bridge of the nose to find out whether the cartilage had snapped. When he touched it the boy let out a scream of pain. After that he did not try to do more than wipe the blood out of the eyes and stanch the bleeding. He took off his coat and wrapped it round the boy's shoulders to stop him shivering. "Listen, Ted," he said, "I want you to know that I had to do this."

The boy nodded weakly. His lips were swelling up.

"I had to do it to keep you quiet," Matt explained. "When you yelled that first time there I thought we was all gone."

Jim crawled over. He wiped his face with the sleeve of his shirt. "What are they goin' to do with us when we get back?" he whispered. He began to shiver, too. Both kids had lost plenty of their insides this past hour.

Matt did not even look at him. He said disgustedly, "What do you think they do with drunken bums around here?"

The boy snivelled with misery, "I never thought."

Matt said coldly, "Damn right you never thought! Maybe you'll think easier when you end up in the jug."

The boy's face froze. "Th' jug?"

"Sure the jug. Where else do you think they put guys for stealin'?"

"Me steal? I never stole nuthin'. I wasn't the one took the bottle, it was him took the bottle. I just waited around at the back of the car."

Matt's eyes narrowed. "You just waited around! Th' hell you did! You wasn't scrappin' over that bottle like a coupla dogs over a bitch!"

The boy began to weep hysterically. "I never stole nuthin', honest, I never stole that bottle." He pointed at Ted, groggy and fuddled, sitting off by himself holding his face and clutching Matt's coat round him. "He stole the bottle. It was him took the bottle ..." Matt bent over suddenly and yanked the boy roughly to his feet.

"Listen you," he said, "suppose that drunken breed had waked up an' you an' Ted there had got in a fight with him an' killed him, then you'd of been a party to a murder. Okay then, you was with Ted when he took the bottle an' that makes you party to a theft!"

The boy tried to back away but Matt held him. His face was sick with terror, "I can't be party to no theft, my father'ud kill me. He didn't want me leavin' home in the first place. You don't know my father. When he gets mad he damn near kills us all."

A sudden fury blinded Matt. He shouted, "Why, you miserable little rat, you! All you care about is your own lousy hide! Don't you know how they could work up any small thing like this till it makes the whole outfit stink? Don't you know there's seven hundred men in this town tonight dependent on your good behaviour?" His hand dropped, he spat in disgust, "*Beach leaves!* You that was so tough you hadda go around lookin' like Dillinger!"

A man came towards them over the fields. He was bareheaded and as he walked a flashlight bobbed up and down on the grass. When he came up Matt said, "There's a couple of kids here, one with a hurt face." They pulled the boy up onto his feet and the first-aid man went to work on him.

"What happened?" the man asked.

Matt looked at him. "He just walked into a tree," he said.

The man eyed him wisely. "That's what I thought," he said. He looked down at the shivering Jim. "That one there didn't get hurt."

"Not yet he didn't," Matt said.

The first-aid man finished off his job. "What happened?" he asked again. He tossed his bloody rags down onto the grass.

"Better bury those," Matt said, "you never know who comes by here in the morning."

The man pushed the cloth under a tuft and his hand struck the bottle. He picked it up, peered at the label, shook it. "Now I know what happened," he grunted. "Where'd they get the stuff?"

"Stole it out of a breed's car. The breed was too drunk to notice."

The man threw the bottle down in disgust. "I wish they left a drink in it," he said.

"*You* wish it!" Matt said. The small procession started drearily off across the fields.

CHAPTER FOURTEEN

Matt watched the two boys coming down the street towards him in the early afternoon of Sunday. Ted had his nose strapped with plaster, both faces were pale, with heavy, ringed eyes. There was no expression in the eyes. The boys tramped along silently, their small packs slung over their shoulders. Then Ted saw Matt, reddened, and looked away. Jim did not see him till Matt got up and came forward. He fell in beside them. "Jese," he said, "I hate to see you two kids go this way."

Jim jumped at the sound of his voice. "That's all right," he said stiffly, "I guess we just couldn't take it. We weren't so tough after all."

"Aw, forget it," Matt said quickly, "I didn't mean anything when I picked on you yesterday afternoon." He turned to Ted, "I had to give you that sock, Ted, I want you to know I had to do it. If I hadn't, then maybe you would have waked up in the jug. Where are you goin' to now?"

The eyes of both boys challenged him suspiciously. "Goin' to bum a ride back to Cutlake with a man that's leavin' in fifteen minutes," Jim said, "he told us to meet him outside of the drugstore." Neither put forth any invitation to walk with them. Jim's manner was nervous and ashamed. About Ted there was a silent air of bitter hostility.

Matt made a second attempt to break through the boy's hard, angry shell. He asked with a conversational air, "How long will it take you to get home after this guy drops you off at Cutlake?"

The boy did not look up, "I'm not goin' home," he said.

"He's crazy," Jim said.

Matt asked, "If you don't go home then what'll you do?"

"What do you care?"

"I tell you he's full of crazy ideas," Jim repeated nervously, "he's been talking crazy ever since we got kicked out this morning."

The boy's lips set in a tight line. "I know what I'm goin' to do," he said. They turned into Main Street and a man sitting in a car outside the drugstore leaned out and honked.

Jim paused uncertainly. Matt held out his hand. "No hard feelings, Jim, I hope we meet again some time." The boy looked at him then looked away. He shook hands without a word and started off up the street at a run. As the younger one tried to pass Matt grabbed on to him. "Commere, Ted," he said, "I want to talk to you."

The boy writhed in his grip and would not say anything.

"Listen," Matt said, "you're sore an' you got nothing to feel sore about that you didn't bring on yourself. You said just now that you knew what you were goin' to do. Okay, what are you goin' to do?"

"Wouldn't you like to know?"

Matt held onto himself with an effort he could never have put forth in the days before he met up with Eddy. He spoke reasonably, "I didn't ask just out of curiosity."

"What did you ask out of then?"

"Because I've seen this same thing happen a lot of times before, kids gettin' themselves in jams they couldn't pull out of. Don't think I did two stretches in college for nothing, I know what I'm talking about."

The boy laughed. "Don't worry," he said, "I'm smart, I've got a nice little racket all picked out. A man wanted me to come in with him a year ago an' I wish I had now."

Matt's hand dropped, his face altered. "How old are you?"

"Eighteen! What th' hell is it to you?"

Matt considered him for a long moment. "Tough, huh?"

The boy's mouth twitched. For an instant fear showed in his eyes, then he came back quickly, "Tough as hell!"

The man shouted from the car again. The boy turned and ran.

"Okay," Matt called after him, "go to it!" He watched the boy duck in back of the car and a cloud of dust rise as it swerved round the corner at the top of the street.

He turned on his heel and walked slowly back to the hall. As he showed his card at the gate he passed Gabby without seeing him and Gabby gave him a light smack on the shoulder and asked why he was going around looking as though he lost two bits and found a quarter. Gabby fell in beside Matt and asked him how would he like a free look at the post cards. Matt told him to go show them around the nursery.

"Nursery nothing," Gabby said, "lemme tell you I paid two bits for these cards back in Cutlake. Maybe you never saw how a lady an' genelman in Paris, France, conduc's themselves on a honeymoon."

Matt said morosely, "I seen better than those in a penny arcade."

"Okay then," Gabby rejoined loftily, "if that's the way you feel."

"Did you try showing 'em to Hep yet?"

"Jese, no!" Gabby cried, deeply shocked, "What do you think I am?"

"Like a mosquito," Matt said, "always buzzin' around. Why don't you try showin' 'em to some of the boys that got in yesterday, there's five hundred new customers."

"Thanks, brother, maybe I will." Gabby beetled off across the grounds whistling busily.

All round the hall men were resting in the heat of early afternoon, lying asleep in the shade, talking together in little groups. A pick-up team was getting warmed up to go and meet a team of local ball players. Under one of the big trees a boy had dragged out a table and chair and sat pecking away on an old typewriter writing his memoirs. There was no wind here, no smell of salt in the air, just a resinous, inland stillness. A dog that strayed in from the road lay at one side of the steps, tongue hanging out, sides heaving. A man lay close by with his knees drawn up. Every now and then he spoke to the dog and it flapped its tail in an easy, lazy motion.

Matt moved about restlessly, oppressed by the utter lack of vitality in the air, the fatal, swamp-like, smothering peace. This place, Andersville, was hard to take. It lacked the virility of Cutlake, the will-to-survive of McBain, blooming in the calm and sluggish shelter of English tradition, insulated against the struggle, the thrills and the brutality of the living world. The people were kind but they spoke a foreign language. He felt if he did not get free of this drugging, purifying atmosphere soon he would go nuts.

He walked around till he found Eddy mending a pair of Hughes' socks.

"What happened?" Eddy asked. "I seen you three walking up the street. What happened?"

"They was kicked out," Matt said shortly. He sat down and smoked a cigarette, then he got up again. "Look," he said, "I can't stick around doing nothing. Put away that stuff and come for a walk."

"In this heat?" Eddy asked, wiping his face with the tail of Charlie's shirt he was sewing a button on.

"Sure, why not?" Matt picked up the shirt and examined it. "What happened to Charlie?"

"He went for a swim, him an' Kenny an' a bunch of them," Eddy explained, "that's how I got their clothes to do." He folded a pile of mending neatly and took it inside.

"I could use a swim myself only I got no trunks," Matt said as they walked along, "which way is this river?"

"Down past the church," Eddy said, "I watched them go by."

They walked past the little Protestant church with the white picket fence and the piled-up grave flowers wilting in the sun. Beyond the church a heavy grove of maples fringed the road on both sides leading to a wooden bridge. They stopped on the bridge, looking down at the small water flowing over the stones, the bed stripped right down by the drought. Dragonflies skimmed above the whispering current and a few birds rustled secretly among the leaves. The little sound of water was drowsy and cool.

After a while Eddy murmured dreamily, "Betcha there's fish in that water." His face was quiet, profoundly absorbed. Even his voice was changed.

Matt glanced at him quickly. "You like it here, don't you, Eddy? I noticed how you seemed different ever since we came."

Eddy nodded. He answered simply, "I'd like to live in a place like this all the time, Matt, nothin' to get scared of, nothin' to make me do dumb things like I do when I get scared."

"I know it, Eddy," Matt's voice was vaguely troubled, "I seen it even last night. You took that message an' handled yourself so well all through that an' never let out a word after. I seen what you can do, all right."

Eddy took the praise with a peculiar dignity. He said, "I done it because you told me. I don't get scared when you tell me things, Matt."

Matt felt in his pockets and drew out the little sack, and the book of papers. "Funny," he muttered uneasily, "this place takes me all the other way. I feel if I don't get out quick they'll soon be diggin' me under like they done those others we passed in the graveyard just now."

Eddy was silent but the short-lived tranquility had passed from his face. "You wouldn't like to live in a place like this?"

"Hell no, I'd go dead in a week!" Matt passed Eddy a cigarette. For some moments he stared thoughtfully down at the shallow current. "Listen, Eddy," he began suddenly, "what you said just now gave me an idea. Maybe you could stay here an' work around one of the farms."

Eddy's eyes brightened then he shook his head. "I couldn't do that, Matt."

"Why not? They must have one job open in this whole district."

"I couldn't do it, Matt, not unless you come along too."

Matt looked at him quickly then he shook his head. "Not in this place, Eddy, I'd go nuts in a week!"

"I know it," Eddy said hopelessly. He sighed, watching a kingfisher skim the water. "Maybe this isn't such a hot place after all."

A shout rose from farther down the river. Matt's head came up and his face cleared. "There's the boys now," he cried. He raised his hand and a figure waved back from the stream. "Hi, Dick! C'mon, Eddy. I didn't see them down there, they must have been behind those rocks."

He started off quickly round the end of the ramp and along the bank of the river. Eddy followed, stumbling a little to keep up. They came on a dozen of the boys bathing in a sheltered pool cut off from the highway by a thicket of alders. They were climbing on a high rock and diving down into a deep pool lying tranquilly outside the main depleted current. Charlie was sitting with his back to a log sketching a pair of little Siwash kids. He saw them wading in the stream and called them over. They stood self-consciously close together, heavy black hair falling over their faces, squat-featured, sad-eyed, spawn of a ravaged race. The boy wore a torn red sweater and the girl a dirty plaid dress with a green cotton handkerchief tied round her neck.

"I wish I had paints," Charlie said. He laid down his pencil and felt in his pockets. "Any of you boys got any candies on you?" A man dug up a handful and Charlie called the kids over. "Okay you," he said with a smile, "take it and scram!" They hesitated shyly, then the boy snatched the candy, and the pair beetled off into the bush like scared rabbits.

Eddy was taking off his shoes. "Don't you want a swim?" Charlie asked.

"I just want to dip my feet in the water," Eddy said. He wiggled his toes in the cold stream water with a deep sigh of content.

"Corns?" the candy-giver inquired sympathetically.

"No, just kind of bad all over."

"I guess it's the hot weather makes 'em go that way. It's arches with me. Seems pretty near everybody I know has some kind of trouble with his feet."

Hughes was sitting off by himself under a tree working over his notes. He was always going off like that and someone was always coming and sitting by him, Gabby or Saul or Dick or one of the boys from another squad. The thing that embarrassed Kenny most was people asking him how far he was on now. This quality of embarrassment was a symptom of the unrest perpetually at work in him nowadays, a haunting obsession of days and weeks and months going past, and his never getting anywhere. He kept at his MS. in a sort of fever so as to try to fool himself that he was not losing out and slowing down and rusting mentally through lack of normal teaching routine. Kenny was all the wrong temperament for joblessness. Until he stopped kicking against facts and accepted them, he was in a continual state of fighting himself and holding himself responsible. Whenever he saw any of the boys coming over to kibitz casually, his sensitive instinct was to scramble his papers and hide them away. He had to fight this, too, in case he was thought queer. It was dangerous to be thought queer, especially in any large company of men. The only one he felt a sense of security with was Hep. Hep never asked to see what he was writing.

From a distance he watched Matt climb to the rock and take his dive. It was a bad dive but just the same Hughes envied the way he did it. He envied a lot of things about Matt, his spare, hard flesh, his impression of taciturnity and poise. All that he could do to get close to Matt, he did. He lent him writing paper and salts and shaving kit but he knew in his heart that these things were superficial, the same way as physical proximity, eating, sleeping, travelling round together never gave him the one thing he needed if he was to graft Matt unforgettably into a book.

He watched him come up out of the water now, dripping like a wet Airedale. "Did you do much swimming when you were a kid?" he asked.

"Fresh water," Matt said, throwing himself face downwards in the sun and forgetting Hughes instantly. Hughes went on watching him, trying to penetrate by intuition what he could never hope to arrive at by experience. He tried to sense what went on inside of Matt, made him tick over.

"The thing I feel about you," he ventured finally, "is that you can take it." No answer. "I wish I could," Hughes said, this time more loudly.

Matt raised his head an inch, "Could what?"

"Could take it like you do."

The legs of Hep passed in front of Matt's narrow vision range. He sprang up. "Hey, Hep!" he called out.

Hep turned, "What do you want?"

"I want to talk to you," Matt said, "I didn't know you were down here."

"Where's your clothes?"

"Over on a log."

"Scram into them then. What d'you think this is—a nudist camp? Don't forget we have to protect the fair womanhood of Andersville."

Matt flashed him a grin. "What I saw up to now wouldn't start a revolution!"

"S'fact, though. Believe it or not, that's one of the things these towns we go through is scaredest of."

Matt looked at Hep to see if he were fooling. Then, "Holy Jesus!" he said disgusted, "what kind of sonsovbitches do they think we are?"

"When you want me," Hep said, "I'll be over there."

"Goin' for a swim?"

"Makin' up my report."

"Don't they give you a rest one day in the week?"

Hep shrugged. "You boys has to eat an' sleep an' move around the same Sunday as any other day."

"Okay," Matt said, "I'll be right over."

"Here's a towel if you need one," Hughes said, holding it out.

Matt thanked him, towelled himself hard all over and threw it down. He climbed into his jeans, pulled his shirt over his head, buttoned his jeans and stepped back into his shoes.

"You certainly did that quick," Hughes said. He held out a pack of Consols. Matt took one, cracked a match on the seat of his pants and gave Kenny first light.

"There's something I wanted to ask you, Matt," Hughes began nervously after a couple of drags. "This book I'm trying to write ... I wanted to put you in it. Would you mind? Fiction of course. No actual names."

Matt stared at him. "Why would I mind?"

"I don't know. I just thought I'd better ask you, that's all."

"I don't know what it is you're talkin' about," Matt said. He started to go off. "Hey, Eddy!" he called out, "don't sit too long with your feet in that cold water, you want to watch out for your kidneys." Hughes gazed after him wistfully. Hughes lent him stuff and did him favours and tried to draw him out sympathetically but he never got an inch nearer to the essential quality, the only part of Matt that would have done him any good.

Hep was writing with his back to a log. "Sidown," he said without looking up, "I don't like people moving around while they talk."

Matt lowered himself onto the ground.

He watched a boy dive off the rock. The boy's body cut the water like a tossed-down knife, clean and straight and beautiful. He said, "That kid could make an Olympic team if he was taken in hand. He must be one of the bunch that come in yesterday, I never saw him before."

Hep glanced up, his eyebrows rose. "What was it you wanted to talk to me about? Making up an Olympic team?"

"No fooling," Matt said, "I wanted to talk to you about those two kids that got kicked out this morning. I think they got a raw deal. Why wasn't the sonovabitch found that sicced them on to stealing the bottle?" He gave Hep a look filled with meaning. "You know damn well how that could have happened."

Hep made little stabbing marks with his pencil. He countered sharply, "That's one of the things we can't ever prove."

"I still think they got a raw deal."

"They might have but just the same we can't afford to risk getting the whole shooting match balled up on account of a couple of brash kids; there's too many people would be glad to see this trip bust up in a riot. We can't afford to take chances."

Matt scooped up a handful of dirt and let it run through his fingers. "You took a chance on Eddy an' me," he said, "you took one helluva chance."

"I know it," Hep said, "don't ever make me mistrust my judgment."

Matt stood up. He cracked a fallen branch sharply between his two hands. "Just the same I hate to think of those kids." He told Hep the whole incident and what the younger one had said. "There's one kid headed for trouble so quick a cop couldn't pick up his license number."

"So what?" Hep cried, his irritation masking a sense of his own powerlessness. He shuffled his papers together and rose. "There's so damn much of it, Matt, there's so damn much of that sort of thing that you can't afford to let it get you. You've got to keep looking at this as a whole, not as a lot of little individual units."

Matt frowned, "You told me that before someplace," he muttered.

Hep's voice rose, "Sure I told you it before an' I'll keep on telling you. Goddammit, if those kids hadn't got in trouble here, then they might of got in trouble in Gath where we could least have afforded the stink. You can't go beating yourself up against pinpoints of justice an' injustice, you've got to see this picture as a whole. Those kids had their chance and they just couldn't take it."

Matt gave a short laugh. "Funny!"

"What's funny?"

"That's what that Jim kid said at the last, 'I guess we just couldn't take it.'"

"Forget it," Hep said, "it's over an' done so forget it. You'll have so damn much to think about these next few days you'll have plenty to do to keep yourself an' that Eddy out of trouble."

He turned and cupped his hands round his mouth and shouted to the boys still in the water. In a moment they began to collect under the trees, drying themselves hurriedly and climbing back into their clothes. They rose up from all parts of the small wooded-off space. Matt asked, "What time do we get into Gath tomorrow?"

Hep shrugged, "What time does any freight get anywhere?"

* * *

As the last cars pulled out the following afternoon the handful of watchers up by the tracks shouted and waved and the boys on the flat cars waved back and a ragged cheer went up for Andersville. The men on the last car waved till the station was out of sight.

Outside the freight shed Tom and George and Old Man Morgan watched the end. As the last car finally disappeared Old Man Morgan moved in out of the sun. "Well," he remarked dryly, "I guess that sees the last of 'em. So far as I know the virtue of our women is still intact an' the same goes for our plate glass winders."

Tom eyed him distrustfully. "What I want to know is, what happens when they get to Gath? Mark my words, there's goin' to be bloodshed there the same as there was in Aschelon."

George's heavy jaw described a circular movement, then he spat out a mouthful of wood chips. He answered broodingly, "Make what happened in Aschelon look like a picnic! Were you at the meetin', Saturday night?"

"I would of," Tom said, "but at the last the wife got sick an' I couldn't make it. I heard they had a big turn-out."

"Biggest turn-out since Armistice. Say, if that Laban ain't a Red then I got Siwash blood!"

"Red, huh?"

"Reddern a cocker bitch." George's eyes were dark with a smouldering grievance. Tom remarked it and his curiosity was aroused. He tried to draw George out farther by enlarging the subject.

"Tell you what," he observed darkly, "the authorities made their big mistake when they let the Reds in at the beginning. They let 'em in an' now they can't get 'em out again."

Old Man Morgan stirred impatiently. He said, "Maybe the Reds give 'em something the authorities forgot. Maybe they give those boys discipline an' the feel of workin' together. Made 'em feel important, like they amounted to something. Kind of a unity ..."

The words lanced the boil of George's festering resentment. He horned in heatedly, "Unity, hell! Say, three of 'em came by my place

Sunday when I was out in the orchard, an' I ses, 'Maybe you boys would like some fruit?' An' one young squirt comes back, 'Do we have to pick it ourselves?' I ask you! *'Do we have to pick it ourselves?'*"

Tom clucked in sympathy, putting out further bait. "An' what did you say?"

The colour rose and spread over George's face; a deep outraged flush. "I sez, *'Why you lazy, good-for-nothin' young sonovabitch! ...'* I sez. By Christ, I was so mad I couldn't think of nothin' else to say!"

Tom's eyes strayed uneasily down the empty tracks. He hitched at his suspenders. "Bunch of Reds," he muttered, "a bunch of goddam Reds!"

Old Man Morgan squatted on a bale of feed. He rummaged in his clothes and pulled out a charred pipe and a handful of loose shag. He glanced from one man to the other and his little bloodshot eyes snapped with malice. He mouthed fiercely, "Bunch of balls! Did either of you sissies have a match?"

PART III

·

Gath

CHAPTER FIFTEEN

Above the pounding of the wheels Matt shouted, "What time do we get into Gath?"

Hep's head half turned as he shrugged, and his mouth shaped words that looked like, "What difference does it make?" Then he leaned over, "Don't sit there an' get sick."

Matt broke into a grin and raised his voice, "I rode more miles this way than the most of these boys put together." His hands gripped the sides of the car, his eyes avoided the flicking ties and looked off over a countryside still new to him.

The car was filled with men and the car in front and the one behind. Above the drumming of steel he heard their voices and the noise of their feet. He heard all these things going on behind him but they were only sounds from a long way off, they lacked the edge of urgency or novelty and for the moment they were unimportant in every way. The thunder of wheels and the sliding past of the flat, green countryside, the monotonous rhythm, the spaced telegraph poles, the hot glitter of sun on wire, these things filled his eyes and his mind like a familiar drug, that, and the burning wind on his face.

The train kicked up a swirl of hot yellow dust that dulled the bushes along the right-of-way and the wild blue and purple lupins straggling down the embankment. The trees in the orchards drooped with fruit. From time to time a flash of white among the green showed where hens were picking in the front yards of small, neat properties set back off the road.

A seed farm slid by, streaking the earth with brilliant strips of yellow and purple and pink, with clear blue and dazzling orange. After a time the country grew less inland, an arm of the sea ran in at full tide covering the long green flats, the salty freshness came back into the air.

After a time Matt felt the old box-car drowsiness creeping over him, his eyes began to ache, his head felt heavy. He edged back, pulled in his legs and drew into a corner, and a man with a knotted handkerchief tied over his head moved over and made a space. Beside him a boy was snoring, head limp, body shaking with the motion of the car. It was hot inside and the dopey feeling grew stronger and the steady murmur of voices grew less and less distinct. Presently Matt's head sagged and he slept, dreaming that he was falling down a crevasse that had no bottom. He never touched bottom, he simply fell and fell with the wind roaring past his head. Then a boulder broke loose and struck him heavily on the shoulder and he opened his eyes to find Eddy shaking him awake. He stared at Eddy a moment stupidly, trying to focus him.

"Wake up!" Eddy's voice shouted excitedly, "we got there!"

Matt got up stiffly, rubbing his aching behind. He took a minute to connect. He felt half-slugged, hungry for air. All round him men were dropping off the cars, tossing down their baggage. Squad leaders were haring up and down the right-of-way going through the familiar ritual of collecting up their squads. The original detachment that came over direct from Aschelon on the Sunday were lined up at one side of the tracks as welcoming committee. Men shouted to one another in recognition, others stood up and waved their packs.

Matt dropped down and fell in with the line of men that formed along the tracks. As they began to march, the engineer leaned out of the cab, waved a gloved hand and shouted good luck. A man shouted back, "Thanks for the buggy ride!" and a second man called out, "That got here two hours late!" There was a brief outbreak of good-natured ribbing as the columns marched clear of the little depot and out onto the streets. Apart from the noise of the train and the stir of the men themselves, the quiet at the depot was complete. The important transportation of Gath was not handled by rail but by sea.

As usual the younger men marched in front. On all sides Matt glimpsed boys of eighteen and upwards, beardless faces sweating, a strange set look in their eyes. They sang as they marched. There was no break in the singing today, no wisecracking with the people on the sidewalks, no ribbing among the men themselves. That was what marked the arrival as different to Cutlake or Andersville or McBain, that and the absence of any crowd. The columns came on and came on. They moved through town disciplined and detached as an army.

Two impressions got over to the people most strongly, amazement and the physical threat of numbers. Amazement at the youth and bearing of the men, profound disquiet at the realization that they had reached the final leg of their journey and were pledged not to move out without a showdown. The impression of unity and purpose added to the threat of numbers. All these things the people of Gath had read about, the rioting in Aschelon, the shouting headlines of the past six weeks, the long trek down. They had read of them yet without a sense of reality, protected as they were by a unique insularity of mind.

Everywhere police reinforcements moved quietly about the streets. The police did not appear openly to observe the men but the men eyed them grimly and the effect penetrated to the people themselves and sent them home shaken and vaguely stirred to shame.

In few other towns could the contact with reality have struck so deep or proved so alarming. Only in a city free from the strife and virility of big-scale organized labour, bred in the mannered British tradition and preserving it with the stranglehold of a fierce gentility. Only in such a place could the minds of the people have been so stirred and their seeing so unbelieving. They went to their homes that day shocked and a little punch-drunk.

On the corner of Flower Street and Pastoral Avenue the column halted and broke three ways. One division marched up Flower, the second held on a block and turned into Lavender, and the third went the whole length of Pastoral as far as the intersection, and halted outside the Angel Arms.

Opposite the Angel was a junk dealer and along from that an auto-wrecking yard and next to the yard the windowless shell of an empty bottling works. The auto-wrecking yard had a sign outside, VISIT GATH, YE OLDE ENGLISH CITY. Another sign below read, GEORGE LAZURUS AUTO WRECKING, HIGHEST CASH PRICES IN CITY. COME INSIDE AND LOOK AROUND.

Across from the junk dealer stood a row of abandoned wooden buildings that used to be two-bit flop-houses in the days of Diamond Jim Brady. The Angel Arms came alongside of them on the corner of the block. An ex-whorehouse, the Angel flourished in the genial era when Pastoral Avenue used to be a great place for drunks. Today even drunks did not come there any more. Beyond Pastoral lay the streets of Chinatown and beyond Chinatown lay Gath again, Ye Olde English City.

The other two buildings, the Orsino Hotel on Flower Street and the Quanta House on Lavender owned the same professional past. Architecturally the details varied, but intrinsically they were the same. City sores like these were not referred to publicly the same as syphilis is not referred to publicly, and for the same reason, because it is well known that the body civic is above contracting social disease. Therefore the Angel, the Orsino and the Quanta House stood there waiting for Time to get them, but the jobless stepped in ahead of the gong before Time had had time to finish off the job.

Through the glass-paned doors and up the steep flight of stairs that led directly off the street the feet of the second division boys trooped in noisily. The glass was caked solid and no light got in except what came in from up above. On the right of the stairs where the front office used to be, the fixtures had been torn out, leaving the floor heaped with dirt and rubble. Strips of discoloured paper drooped from the walls and a couple of faded circus posters and advance publicity of a five-year-old religious revival were pasted against the front window.

From the first floor, looking up through the well of the stairs the building rose to two upper landings and on each of the three floors only the inside rooms had windows. Traces of the days when the Angel enjoyed a good steady turnover, mixed white and Oriental, still hung around. The fancy paper on the walls and the white china doorknobs gave the correct touch of Edwardian gentility to this blend of ex-vice and current squalor.

Matt felt Charlie nudging him. "Chroust!" Charlie muttered in disgust, "*what a dump!*"

Matt smiled grimly, "You're tellin' me!"

At the head of the stairs the inflow of men dammed up. They hung around waiting to be assigned to quarters. The voice of Gabby was heard complaining loudly that the city failed to provide service with the rooms. He said they could cut off light and water if he got serviced the other way. In the middle of a sentence he shut up suddenly. It sounded like someone had stepped on his face.

On each of the three floors squad leaders hared around billeting men and marking out stations. Several minor fights broke out and one boy had his cheek cut open. He said he wasn't going to sleep in any goddam sweat-box, city or no city. Finally the boys on the second floor got fed up and staged a raiding party. They dragged him out and dumped him against a wall and left him to come around when he was feeling more appreciative.

Hep had the two end rooms at the foot of the passage on the first floor, one each side. The front room was a single and the one across on the inside with the skylight was a double. He gave Matt, Eddy, Hughes, Gabby and Charlie the double, and took the single himself with Dick, Pop and Saul. Boyce and Beefy that made up the remainder of the squad now the two Cutlake boys were gone, were billeted in with three from another squad farther down the passage. The way Hep figured it was that Dick had a habit of yelling in his sleep, or if he didn't yell then he talked a lot and that as Pop was deaf it wouldn't affect him and as for Saul and himself, they were veterans and they could take it. He thought Dick might start trouble boxed in with the younger boys. Hep did not feel the heat like a less rangy type of man but there were little trickles of perspiration running down his face, and every word he said he bit at as though he resented the sound of it. Matt never saw Hep really rattled before but he saw him rattled now.

Matt went on and dumped his stuff, then he stepped across the passage to Hep's room. Below the window there was a small expanse of roof space. He legged over the sill, walked to the edge and looked down. Another man came out after him. They stood together silently looking down into the canyon below. Then the man pushed out his chin and spat. "Yeah," Matt said, "that's what I was thinkin', too!"

Below them a sinister shambles of roofs and rotting shacks ran like a gulch between the backs of the tenement houses. Off to one side a garbage dump was piled with empty cans, dead tires and rusting auto guts. Beside the dump stewed a small pool with refuse floating and above the pool a flock of gulls fought noisily over the ageing garbage.

"An' this is the town," Matt said, "where I heard you had to practical-ly own a license to breathe the air!" He picked up a half brick and tossed it down. The gulls rose in an angry cloud. Behind him more men were legging over the low sill. In a little while the air grew charged with their muttering and their discontent. A small commotion broke out at the back.

The man, Beefy, broke angrily through. His eyes lighted on Matt. He seized Matt's arm. "You!" he cried shrilly, "Remember what I told you that day in Aschelon?"

Matt's face grew closed and cautious. He said, "I don't remember anything you told me in Aschelon, it's too far back."

The man's hand dropped in disgust. "He knows damn well what I told him. I told him then they was foolin' us, leadin' us into a trap." A sudden tenseness gripped the men. Their feet stirred uneasily, the anger seething in their faces grew confused and brooding as though the mind of each turned inwards seeking confirmation or denial.

In the lane below the head and shoulders of a policeman appeared, moving unhurriedly. Beefy pointed down, voice shrilling to a frenzy. "Look! They sicced the cops onto us already! I tell you they got spies an' pigeons all over town!"

A boy spoke from behind, voice loud with nervousness, "I heard they cancelled all leaves at police barracks. One of the boys that was here ahead of us told me that when we were comin' through town." A mutter rose, swelling angrily from man to man. A boy shoved his fingers in his mouth and whistled, outbreak of catcalls and derisive cheers. The boy grabbed a broken end of piping shouting, "I'll show that nosey bastard down there something!"

Suddenly from behind an arm shot out, seizing his wrist, twisting it savagely so that the pipe clattered down. Hep shoved through, face livid, eyes gleaming dangerously. He shouted angrily, "What in hell d'ya wanta do? Start a riot?" He lunged at the pipe with his foot and sent it hurtling into the gulch below.

For a moment the men froze, uncertain, seething, half ashamed, avoiding one another's eyes. Hep glanced sharply from face to face. "What's the matter around here? What's got into you all of a sudden?"

Whistler stood flexing his wrist. He answered sullenly, "Where are we goin' from here? That's what we wanta know."

"What do you mean?" Hep said loudly. "Isn't this good enough for you? Tomorrow we clean up these dumps an' meantime the city's fixed up light an' plumbing. What in hell do you expect? Hotel reservation?"

The nervous boy asked, "What do we sleep on?"

"What did we sleep on up to now?"

A voice broke in nastily, "We slept on a bunch of lousy noospapers."

Over Matt's shoulder Eddy shouted, "I slept on the funnies. All through the sit-down I slept on Little Orphan Annie!"

A short burst of nervous laughter. A voice, "How'd she get in?"

A second voice, "She was the hot one tried to crash the gates."

"But she didn't get no further than the boys that signed the passes. When Annie come along they signed their own passes an' got out!" The laughter came again then died at once. Unsatisfied, the men pressed inwards, eyes narrowed by suspicion, mouths hard with tension, faces sweaty in the hot sun. The charged air hung, waiting.

Hep's hands twitched slightly. His voice was quietly sarcastic, "Maybe you'd like us to send down to the Majestic Hotel for blankets an' a spring mattress."

The nervous boy stepped forward. He was less nervous now. "Damn right I would. I'd rather sleep out on the streets than in a dump like this."

"They don't let you sleep on th' streets, the streets is city property."

"Ain't this city property?"

"Sure it is but we might pollute the streets."

"So they give us a dump that hogs wouldn't make no difference to." The loud anger broke from man to man. It increased like a rising wave.

Hep glanced round quickly, his eyes wary. Suddenly his whole manner changed, grew conciliatory. "Okay, okay, boys," he said with a smile, "you can bring all that up at the meeting." He began to break the men, edging them back towards the open window.

They moved grudgingly. Whistler asked with suspicion, "What meetin'? I never heard nothin' about no meetin'."

"Nor me."

"First I heard of any meetin'."

Hep said, "Sure there's to be a meetin'. One in fifteen minutes. After that we eat."

"Why didn't you tell us that before?"

"Sure, why didn't you?"

Hep's face relaxed. He slapped the last speaker lightly between the shoulders and laughed. "Goddammit!" he cried, "you never give me time!"

He stood aside to let the men pass in. As Matt went by he motioned to him to stay behind. Then he pulled out a handkerchief and passed it quickly over his face, round the back of his neck, over his chest and throat. When he was hot or angry he did not show it like a fleshy man, instead he went pale. In his lean throat a pulse was beating. "Well?" he said, softly and dangerously, when they were alone.

Matt stared at him. "Well, what?"

Points of angry light gleamed in Hep's eyes. "What was the idea of starting that row just now?"

Matt's mouth came open. "You're crazy, Hep, I never started anything."

"Oh no? How come that bunch was out here razzin' that cop? Maybe you didn't call them out to come over an' take a look-see?"

Matt went white. He answered stiffly, "S'pose they did come? I never asked them. Anyway if we got to live above the city garbage dump why shouldn't we find out where the stink's coming from?"

Hep blazed up. "Garbage dump nothing! Don't tell me you never lived in worse places than this. They don't build two-bit flop-houses in the high rent district." Then as he looked at Matt his face changed slowly, "Goddammit, Matt, sometimes I can't make you out at all. Back there in Andersville you kept a couple of drunken kids from gettin' the whole bunch of us in dutch, now you go tryin' to start trouble of your own."

"I tell you I never meant to start anything! Hell, Hep, I felt so damned good when we was marching through town, everything seemed O.K."

"An' everything's O.K. still."

"You call this O.K.?" Matt pointed to the crawling tenements, the piles of refuse stewing in the heat. "At least the places where they put us before was clean. But this dump! Listen an' you can hear the rats runnin' in the walls!"

"Take care that's the only place I can hear them running!"

Matt struck at him. Hep ducked aside and his hand came up and caught at Matt's arm with the sinewy strength and quickness of a lean man. For an instant they stood there glaring at one another. Then Hep's arm dropped. He asked tiredly, "What in hell did you want to do a fool thing like that for?"

Matt's voice was brittle with rage. "What in hell did you say a thing like that for?" A moment longer they remained eyes locked in the blazing sun. Then Hep turned away with a shrug.

"I thought I told you some of the things that could go wrong with an outfit like this that night in McBain," he said. "I thought I gave you the whole picture then. Maybe I didn't at that."

Matt kicked at the hot zinc under his feet. He was silent a moment. Then, "The trouble with you these days," he complained, "is that you got this damned organization under your skin. A guy makes the smallest criticism an' you blow right up. This is a dirty dump, it's a helluva dirty dump, if I don't say so someone else will."

Hep stopped and came back. "You think I don't know that?" You think things is going to be easy from now on? Maybe this time next week you'll be taking free transportation back east an' damned glad of it."

A change came over Matt's face. It settled and hardened. The jumpiness and shame and hair-trigger anger drained from it, leaving it cold, almost expressionless: the same look as he wore the first time he walked into Harry's.

"If I could of got anything to do back there I wouldn't be here now," he said, "I told you that in the beginning."

Hep nodded. "I remember."

Matt's voice grew monotonous. His eyes moved past Hep and in them there was an outer blindness, and a clear, harsh inner sight. "I told you then I was through with jungles an' flop-houses an' gettin' thrown off freight cars ..."

Hep was observing him with sudden intentness. He broke up the sing-song voice. "Hey, Matt! What th' hell's got into you all of a sudden? I got other things to do than stand around an' listen to that kind of talk!"

The blind eyes turned slowly and fastened on his face. The monotonous voice went on. "I'm just tellin' you," it said. "If we don't get nothin' out of this trip to Gath then I'm not waitin' around any more, I'm takin' mine the quick way."

Hep shook himself sharply then his hand came out and he gripped Matt's shoulder, anything to break the cold dreaming of the eyes. He cried, "Hey, snap out of it. What's got into you?"

Matt blinked. He touched his head. "The sun, I think," he said in an altered voice, "I must have got a touch of it coming down on the train. For a moment there I felt funny ... but I knew all the time what I was sayin'."

"The hell you did!" Hep cried. He stared at Matt nervously, "If that's what the sun does to you then from now on you better go around in a hat!"

CHAPTER SIXTEEN

A line of boys sat on the sidewalk outside the Quanta House on the fifth day of the occupation. They had been sitting there most of the afternoon, knees up, arms hanging, cigarettes drooping from their mouths, idly eyeing the passers-by. The heat made them listless. Every now and then their eyes were raised, their brows went up, deepening the horizontal lines marking their foreheads but their heads rarely turned. Only if they caught sight of something that momentarily touched their wandering fancy the heads joined in a slow, half-turning movement, then the long peace fell again. They were Gabby, Charlie, Dick and George (Fat) Denning.

A little blonde came down the street, breasts bobbing, hair rolled into sleek curls. She walked right by the boys and did not look at them. The four heads turned to stare after her. Charlie said wistfully, "I'll bet there goes a hot one."

Dick scowled and Gabby tossed his cigarette down in the gutter. He said, "I'll bet she's not as hot as my pants are right this minute." He kept the blonde's thinly covered buttocks in sight till they turned the corner.

Dick spat in disgust. "Wouldn't look at us. Who does she think she is anyway? Who does any girl think she is?"

"Aw shut it," Charlie said uneasily. They lapsed back into silence.

The sound of shunting came from the railroad yards, the heavy dong-dong of the engine bell, the jar of couplings, the blasting of steam. Traffic snailed up and down the narrow street, produce trucks, ice wagons sweating water, heavy duty trucks loaded with sand and gravel. They turned at the end of the block, rumbling out across the bridge. From the other side of the inlet came the shrill whine of a shingle mill.

Dick was chewing on a match, working it round and round at one corner of his mouth. Finally he broke the silence. "I thought we was goin' to send a delegation to see the legislatur."

The eyes of the other three boys were fixed earnestly on a cockroach making the ascent of Charlie's right shoe and crossing to come down the other side. When the cockroach had accomplished the trip in safety a little sigh of relief broke from them. Charlie raised his head languidly, "What was that you said?"

"I thought soon's we got here we was goin' to send a delegation over to talk to Gus."

Charlie slapped at his drooping pompadour, "So we are," he said. "Didn't you hear what Laban said at the big meetin' Wednesday night?"

"I wasn't at the meetin'."

Gabby and George leant forward, their faces suddenly betrayed an absorbing interest. "What happened to you?" George asked.

Dick took out a pocket knife and began to scrape dirt from under his nails. "Pills," he said. "Damn things half blew the guts outa me, I had to stick around the Angel pretty near all day long."

The chorus clucked with sympathy. "I know them horse balls," Charlie said. "Gripe you somethin' terrible but they sure do the work."

"What happened at the meetin'?"

"Well, they had a dandy bunch of speakers and Laban said soon's another two hundred or so of the boys gets here we're goin' to appoint a delegation. He said we figger to have around fifteen hundred boys in Gath before we're through."

Gabby inquired politely, "Since when did they put you on the executive?"

Charlie reddened. "You know what I mean," he said, "and anyway why shouldn't I say 'we'? It's all of us."

Dick raised smouldering eyes sullen with suspicion. "That kind of talk may be okay at meetin's," he said, "but it's goin' to take time an' money to get that many men concentrated. I don't mean to sit around forever growin' corns on my tail."

Gabby winked at George. "The pills didn't fix him after all, he's still grouchy."

George eased his fat rump a shade to drag a flattened pack of Consols from his side pocket. He said, "This life suits me, brother, I never ate so reg'lar in a long while. Those boys they have in there is dandy cooks."

Dick gnawed on his fingernail. "So what? We've been sittin' around here for five days now without the smell of work, I can't see we're a yard further on."

Charlie leaned across George. "No kiddin', Dick," he asked seriously, "if they come along an' offered you a job, what could you do?"

"Who? Me?" Dick said, suddenly nonplussed.

Gabby nudged George and nodded at a girl across the street. "I could do with a nice bit of tail," he said and laughed. They all laughed except Dick. He sat there brooding, chewing on his nails. Finally he got up and moved away. The others gazed after him.

Gabby said softly, "Why don't he go get himself a nice job?"

The faces of the other three grew derisive. "Yeah, why don't he? I'll bet he never thought of it." A boy stepped out from the office with a pile of donated magazines. Mechanically the hands of Charlie, Gabby and George reached out. In a little while the line lengthened. Hunched forms, idle hands, empty faces, rumps squatting languidly in the hot sun.

Inside the Quanta House Hughes was seated at one of the long tables sweating over his notes. Gaffney, the ex-sticker, was sitting opposite to him picking his teeth over a sex-crime monthly and helping Hughes write the book. Even Gaffney saw he was going through some kind of hell.

"What's stickin' you now, Kenny?"

"Nothing," Hughes lied miserably.

"Sure there is! I seen you stop off an' hold your head over and over this past half hour. Somethin's gummin' up the works."

Hughes saw it was no use trying to stall so he relieved himself with a burst of truth. "This is going to be a hard book to write, far harder than I figgered on," he said. "Quite apart from the actual writing and the entire absence of plot, there are a lot of technical difficulties. One is keeping it clear of anything that might border on libel."

Gaffney's face showed interest but no light.

"What th' hell's libel, Kenny?"

Hughes said grimly, "Something the publishers' lawyers watch out for."

[handwritten annotation:] cannot write about anyone metafiction b/c Baird going through this while writing this novel.

Gaffney made a gesture like brushing flies. "If they don't like the book then let 'em read something else. Why go around with birds like that in your hair?" He tapped the magazine with a hairy forefinger, "Now take this here, Kenny, or one of them westerns, that's the kind of stuff you oughta study up on. Plot, plot all th' way, keeps you bang up on your toes!"

Hughes sighed, "I can't seem to write that sort of stuff."

"Another thing you gotta have is lotsa sex," Gaffney went on, warming to the work, "you gotta be full of sex as an egg."

Hughes pulled off his glasses and rubbed his straining eyes. He said earnestly, "I don't think you quite get what it is I'm trying to do. This book of mine is to be more than just another book, it's to be a ... a kind of a social document, a book that will bring before the nation this whole problem of unemployment that is festering on its body like a bloody sore ..." He stopped and his mouth dropped open. His face grew entranced and visionary. Gaffney stared at him, putting it down to heat. "Bloody Sore!" Hughes murmured, "I've lain awake nights trying to think of that. BLOODY SORE, by Kenneth Hughes!" He leant over, touched Gaffney on the arm. "What do you think of it?" he asked, his voice shaking a little.

Gaffney threw his weight back, put his head on one side and pushed up his full under lip. He took so long to answer that Hughes began to watch him nervously. Then he shook his head.

"No?"

"No!"

"But what's the matter with it?" Hughes was almost crying.

Gaffney screwed his finger in his ear. "Sounds kinda profane to me."

"*Profane?*"

"Yup! I tell ya' Kenny, if I was a fella that bought books an' that kind of truck I wouldn't buy a book with a name like that."

"But why not? What's the matter with it?"

Gaffney eyed Hughes a moment in silence then he said impressively, "A person buyin' a book with a name like that don't know just what he's gettin'. Maybe it ain't quite nice to have around the house."

Hughes groaned. He stared at the ex-sticker like a sick dog. Gaffney pushed the magazine over to him. He pointed to the cut of a half nude sexslayer finished in sepia. "Here's what I mean," he said with a touch of severity. "A guy sees a picture like that, snappy, sexy, lotsa pep. Now that guy knows what he's payin' for, knows what t'expect from the start. But with a name like yours ... well, maybe he's goin' to get some kind of a shock an' he's not goin' to like it. Get what I mean? Take the magazine, Kenny, take it an' have a lend of it. Maybe it'll give ya some good ideas!"

The sunlight in the doorway darkened suddenly. Both men looked up. Hazel came in off the street. She asked, "Is there anyone by the name of Striker around here? Matt Striker."

Hughes got up quickly and came forward. "Hello, Hazel!"

She looked at him again. "Kenny! I didn't see who it was at first coming in out of the sun. Is Matt anywhere around?"

"He may be down at the Angel," Hughes said, "I'll go in the office and find out."

"If you tell me where this Angel is," Hazel said, "I could go on down there myself and save you a trip."

Hughes hesitated. He looked over at Gaffney. "She better wait up here, hadn't she?" he said.

"Oh sure," Gaffney said, getting up and coming forward to be introduced.

Hazel glanced from one man to the other. She asked, "What's funny about the Angel?"

Gaffney eyed her with polite disapproval. He said with dignity, "Nothin's the matter with the Angel, they just don't like ladies around. You know how it is, a bunch of boys together. I'll go on down an' tell Matt you're waitin'. Kenny here can do the honours."

"He didn't like me much," Hazel said with a smile when Gaffney had gone.

"He's always like that," Hughes said apologetically. "He's one of the night marshals down at the Angel and he gets suspicious over every little thing."

"I guess he has to be on his toes at that," Hazel said, "I guess all the marshals have." She sat down across from Hughes and asked him how things were coming along. She remembered about the book and asked how that was coming along, too. After his first shyness passed Hughes found her easy to talk to. He realized afterwards what a long time it was since he really talked to a woman and told her about himself. That brief contact with Hazel did something to Hughes, it drew him out of himself, made him feel warm and happy and clever. Later on when the reaction came it left him more unsettled and unsure of himself than ever. Kenny was the type who needed a woman badly.

"Hello!" Hazel said when Matt came in off the street.

"Hello!" he said, "when did you get over?"

"I came over on the day trip. They give us an hour on shore."

"Have a good crossing?"

"Oh sure, I had a dandy crossing. There were a lot on the boat."

"Oh sure," Matt said, "a fine day like this there would be."

They stood there awkwardly. Slowly the colour spread up Hazel's cheeks, her fingers snapped and unsnapped her white handbag. She said, speaking fast and brightly, "I thought if you had an hour to spare we might go out and take a walk around."

Matt made an effort to shake free of the paralysis that gripped him. Seeing her again suddenly brought home to him why the rule about women had to be rigid and rigidly enforced. Their presence made war, intruded the natural into the disciplined unnatural, brought with it forces at once savage and dividing. He was glad to see her and because he was glad he wished to hell she had not come over. Later on maybe when things cleared and began to shape up but not now. Through his first pleasure he felt a return of the old angered frustration and he stood there showing it. "Wait a minute," he said with an effort, "I'll go in the office and see if it's okay for me to get out now."

Hazel pulled out her lipstick and began doing her lips. She said casually, "If it's not then never mind. I know how it is around a place like this." She worked on her lips, shaping the colour, concentrating.

Matt dived into the small boarded-off cubbyhole that served as an office. Inside a boy sat with his feet up reading an old *Liberty* and a second man was pecking at an ancient office-model typewriter with a mess of sheets and carbon paper lying beside him. A bunch of the boys stood around jawing and smoking. A man in a cotton cap and blue suspenders was sitting at a roughly built table making out his report. Matt asked him if it would be okay his going out for an hour and the man made a note of his name and the time and told him to check in as soon as he got back. When he came out again Hughes made a sign he wanted to speak to him privately. Hughes pulled out half a dollar. "I thought you might want to take her somewhere," he said.

Matt said stiffly, "Thanks, Kenny, that's damn decent of you."

Hughes' face glowed even at that small praise. "It's nothing," he said, "I just thought you might be out, that's all."

"Out!" Matt said, "I never was in! How'd you like it if every time you wanted to feed a girl someone else had to pay for it?"

Hughes glanced quickly at him. "I don't think I ever had it happen to me."

"No? Well, I had it happen to me. Last time I took her out she hadda pay her own cheque. Maybe I shouldn't let a little thing like that worry me by this time. I just don't like it, that's all."

"I didn't mean to offend you, Matt."

"Hell, Kenny, you didn't offend me! I got no right to be offended anyway. Don't think I'm not damn thankful to feel that much change in my pocket." He went outside to Hazel. As they walked up Flower Street the heads along the sidewalk turned to gaze critically.

Gabby yawned. "What say I go knock that guy's block off?"

The chorus spoke languidly, "What say we all do?"

* * *

"Where are we going?" Hazel asked. She looked at her watch, "I've only got three-quarters of an hour left now."

"I know a little place called the Blind Spot where we can get tea," Matt said, "we've got plenty time." They walked along.

"You're looking thinner," she said, "I noticed it when you first came in, kind of changed-looking."

"Shouldn't be, we get plenty t' eat around here." He made an effort to tear loose from the constraint that still held them. "How's things in the meat department? Still punching a time clock?"

A fine line appeared between her eyes, she looked straight ahead. "I don't have to punch a clock any more now."

He stopped. "You mean you lost your job?" She nodded.

"How come?" he asked quickly.

"Remember that floor manager I pointed out? Well, one afternoon round five o'clock I blew right up and told him what I thought he was and he had me fired. I was all ready to blow up the day you came in and I finally blew."

He laughed, "Good girl!" Then his face grew serious. "What'll you do now?" They began to walk on slowly.

She shrugged. "Art said he could get me a job as cashier at that dance place. He said the one they got there now don't bring in the customers like a young one would, he told me she was all shot to hell. You could see that the night we passed, couldn't you? All shot up and finished-looking. I feel kind of sorry for her, getting thrown out on her ear."

He pushed his hands down into his jeans. "Art," he muttered savagely, "that pimp."

"Maybe, but he's got the job in his pocket and I can't afford to be out. I wish you knew the line-up of girls waiting for the job an' some of the things they'd do to get it. I wish you knew all that," she said.

"How long have you been out?"

"Since Monday."

"What does your aunt think?"

"She thinks for me to get another job quick."

"Even if it's through Art?"

"Sure, why not? Art's not so bad." No answer. They walked along like that, talking in slot-machine tempo, stopping at the intersections, waiting for the lights to change. Hazel said the things in the stores over there looked a lot dearer than they did over in Aschelon, Matt said that must be because they didn't handle the same volume of trade. Hazel said every time she saw a window dressed up nicely it made her think of all the things she wanted, and Matt said he guessed that was the way with everyone.

Hazel stopped outside the show windows of a big furniture store that had mid-summer sale notices plastered across the glass. One of the windows had a cream and buff painted bedroom suite with a bright pink bedspread and a pink silk bed-light and a long, hard cylinder with a gold tassel dribbling from the shirred ends, placed where the pillows should have been.

She pointed to it and laughed. "I'll bet that thing must have come out of Hollywood back in the days of Mary Pickford," she said. "How would anyone ever lay their heads on a thing like that?"

Matt stopped, too. "I don't remember that far back."

"Nor me," Hazel said, "but I've heard people talk about it." They drifted a block further on towards the Neon above the Blind Spot. "Gee," Hazel said, "it must be swell to win a sweep or something. All that money coming in for just doing nothing."

"I wouldn't be fussy about the sweep," Matt said, "all I'd want would be enough coming in steady to meet the monthly payments." They laughed and the constraint broke between them. Then Hazel's hand came up and squeezed his arm, he felt like something had snapped inside his head and he could move around. "Gee," she said, "I was glad to get your letter!"

"What day did you get it?"

"Last Friday afternoon. I think it got me feelin' too good, that's why I told that old So-and-So off on Monday."

Matt grinned. "What did you tell him?"

Hazel's face grew dreamy with recollection, she spoke softly, "I told him, 'Why you old sonovabitch, you! You think you've got every girl in this department in your pocket!' He has too. I wish you could have seen his face!"

Matt laughed in admiration. "I'll bet it was something!"

"Yeah," Hazel said, "it was something all right." There was a short, significant pause. Then, "Okay at the time, but not so good after. Like waking up from a good party with a hangover. It's not so hot for anyone being out these days."

"You're tellin' me!" Matt said. They did not stop at any more windows or go on kidding after that.

The Blind Spot was a little place with a candy counter and booths and a tinny radio playing from the back alongside of the handprinted notice that said Ladies Rest Room. A woman with short brown hair and a bad case of B.O. came up and took their order. Hazel asked her to make it snappy on account of catching the boat. "You shouldn't do this," she said, after the woman had gone.

"Do what?"

"This," Hazel said, "bringing me in here, I didn't need the tea."

She recognized the look that came over his face from seeing it that night outside Cal's in Aschelon. She quickly switched the subject.

A cat leapt up onto one of the tables and sat there washing itself. The twangling of the radio changed to the voice of the announcer, "And now, folks, one of your real, old-time favourites. How many of you can put a name to it?" The gramophone needle began to scrape, then came, "I Can't Give You Anything But Love, Baby."

The woman appeared from the back with the tea. She remained, hovering. "Anything more you'd like?"

Matt asked, "D'you mind turning off that radio?"

The woman eyed him with a faint mistrust. "Well really ..." she began. Then she caught Matt's eye and went round to the back and a moment later the music snapped off. In the sudden silence they looked at one another. Hazel set the tea-pot down, let it stand beside the empty cups.

"Matt!"

"What?"

"You know what I came over for?"

He shifted his eyes, avoiding hers. "The trip, I guess." His fingers snapped at the edge of the menu card.

For a moment she looked at him, her lip quivering, then her face slowly hardened. "For Chrissake," she said with dignity, "don't be like you were when I first saw you this afternoon, you had a face on you then like a piece of rock. I nearly walked right out on the street again."

He frowned, snapping at the card, not looking at her. He asked, "What did you come over for?"

"What I didn't come over for," she cried with passion, "was two bucks worth of fresh air. Listen," she said, setting the pot down and facing him squarely, "I didn't come chasing you, I know damn well what the rules are about girls around here an' why they have to have them. I came because ... oh hell," she said breaking off, exasperated, "a girl doesn't need love around you, she needs a rock drill!"

Matt's head came up. For a moment they stared at one another help-lessly, their eyes burning. "That's what you think," he said bitterly, "that's what you think!"

"I'm sorry," she said, "I shouldn't have said it."

"That's okay," he said, "how were you to know?"

The cat rose and leapt down onto the floor softly, stalking past their table, eyeing them with a satiric yellow gleam. The woman came round from the front, pushing at her frizzed brown hair, repeating the routine question, "Anything more you'd like?"

"Plenty," Matt said.

"He's only kidding," Hazel said.

"That'll be fifty cents then," the woman said. She stood there waiting while Matt dredged up the money, Hughes' money. As they went she gave Matt a look of dislike.

They walked down to the boat by Fontaine Avenue, avoiding the main streets. Fontaine was prettily laid out with poplars planted along both sides. When the wind blew the leaves fluttered like price tags. The air smelt of low tide and warm tar macadam. They came in sight of the masts of the harbour.

"You never told me yet why you came over," Matt said.

She glanced up at him with quick suspicion, then her eyes changed. She answered quietly, "I came over so's I could get one day's rest from job-hunting and think over this offer of Art's."

He shook his head. "That's not all you came over for."

She answered him after a silence. "I wanted to find out how things were going with you boys because I know how much to believe of the newspapers." She smiled, "I guess I came to check up on the Boy Rod-Rider. Remember?"

He stopped and for the first time gentleness came into his voice, "Sure, I remember," he said, "I remember a lot of other things as well." His eyes went past hers, in them struggled a mixture of brooding frustra-tion and stubborn purpose. "Maybe you think I'm pretty cruel," he said, "or just plain dumb, but I've got a lot working inside of me since I left Aschelon, more than you'll ever know. I didn't even have time to sort it out myself yet, all I know is that a lot's got to happen around here an' happen quick an' that we've got to look at this thing big, not just a little local fuss. We've got to think of the situation as a whole, not just ourselves all the time."

She glanced at him quickly. "That's how Hep used to talk. I used to hear him talk that way when the first sit-down was on, always at the boys to see this fight as bigger than themselves. Sometimes I used to think that he didn't care what happened to Hep just so long as the organization was going along okay."

Matt smiled, "Not quite human, huh?"

"It's like I used to feel about the store sometimes ... me underneath and something at the top that's not quite human."

"Know what that something is? That's invested capital. That's what's got to be swept away."

"Couldn't someone else sweep it away? Must it be us?"

"We've got to push, too, everyone pushing a little, that's what starts it rolling."

She began to walk on quickly. He's got the bug, she thought hopelessly, he's got the Red bug right in his hair. Next thing you know he'll be heading a May Day parade.

People swarmed about the pier gates carrying bags weighted down with food. A flock of gulls sailed above the boat, white wings shining against the blue. The sunlight struck sparks in the bay and there was one big private yacht moored. There were extra police today mixing with the crowd. The faces of the people shone with sweat and were creased with the exasperation of hurry.

Matt and Hazel stopped at the pier gates and women with bags and men shouldering children pushed on past them. The boat blew the five minutes hurry-up blast.

"Well," Hazel said, "I'd better be getting along, I'll bet the most of the good seats are gone by now. Tell Hep I was asking for him. Wake up," she said, giving him a little push, "I'm on my way!"

He did not answer at once. He did not seem to hear that last thing she said at all. He began to speak slowly, still with the same deliberate, riveted look, "Listen, Hazel," he said, "I guess I must of seemed like pretty bad company today ..."

"I didn't think of it that way, Matt, I guess I shouldn't have said some of the things I did, too. I just wanted to know how you were making out over here, that's all ... I mean while I still had the time."

He caught her suddenly by the arm and began to speak fast and a man passing by glanced back over his shoulder uneasily. He seemed to think it might be some kind of an assault. "Here's the thing I wanted to say all along, Hazel. How about you an' me getting married, honey? Maybe that sounds crazy to you now because I got nothing, but believe me, I won't stay that way. If I can't get mine one way I'll take it another. How about it? I'll bet your aunt would be tickled to death to get you settled down. Didn't we have fun together that first time, didn't we? That's how it's going to be all the time ..."

She stared at him, gasping, "Matt, you're crazy!"

He cried with a sort of triumph, "Sure, honey, you got me that way!"

"I mean I never thought you had it in you."

"I never thought so myself."

"But it's crazy, we're crazy. Between us we haven't even got a job."

He laughed, whistled a few bars of "I Can't Give You Anything But Love, Baby." For a moment she struggled in his hard grip. "Matt," she cried, "you're losing your mind. I tell you between us we've got nothing."

"We've got ourselves. That means we got everything."

Slowly her face changed. She shook her head, "Oh for Chrissake, for Chrissake," she said quietly, "you know where that gets you."

"Where?"

"On relief ... with extra allowance for each child."

He winced as she had made him wince once back in Aschelon. "Scared?"

She looked past him. "I guess so, I guess I am scared, I know too much."

His hands dropped. "Scared of gettin' beaten up by a washboard?"

"I ought to be shot," she said. They moved aside to let the final stragglers pass. A woman was dragging a child by the hand and the man with her stooped and hoisted a younger one, whimpering, up onto his shoulder. The man, the woman and the walking child broke into a tired, heavy-footed running. Hazel watched them out of sight. "I ought to be shot," she said again, "I used to think that whatever I was I was a gutty girl. I don't know what happened."

He looked at her, doubting and puzzled. "What are you scared of, honey? I thought you told me you wanted your own home."

"Sure I want my own home an' I don't mind working for it. All I'm scared of is our insides ... getting eaten away. I've seen so much of it. I don't want us breaking just one more trail to the relief office."

Behind them the policeman was closing the gates.

"Give us a kiss anyway," Matt said.

"Oh, sure, hon," she said. They kissed. Behind them the policeman was looking their way. They kissed again.

"There's two Art don't get," Matt said. "Listen," he added jealously, "don't take that job he offered you. I know Art's kind. He's a bum even if he does wear a tux, like I said in my letter."

She clung to him. "Oh God, Matt! I love you!" They kissed again fiercely. Her eyes slid past his shoulder and she jerked free. "Look! He's shutting the gates!"

He gave her one more quick one and watched her dodge by the cop at the gate. In a little while she reappeared among the heads crowding the ship's rail. She waved and called down words that were drowned by a blast of the siren. There was the grumble of the gangplank being withdrawn, the slap of cables, the heavy slop of churning water, the slow outward turning of the boat. The gulls rose in a screeching cloud, the heads and the waving hands grew small. In a little while they were cut off suddenly by the roofs of the sheds.

Matt turned and walked slowly back uptown. He walked on past the line of taxis dozing in the sun, the big white yacht, the bright blue sparkle of the bay. A bunch of boys from the Orsino waved to him from the other side of the street but he did not go over and join them. He did not feel like joining up with anyone then, like hanging around and chewing the old rag. He felt like some new part of his life had begun, some hitherto dead area been quickened and there was pain in it and anger and confusion and he did not know how to handle it. He pushed his hands down into his jeans and his feet drove against the hot concrete and in his eyes there was the slow hardening of resolution but back of the resolution there was the mind fighting and groping at a dead end. When he got as far as Dale Street where the wholesale district began he so far forgot himself and the prime necessity of keeping the organization intact as to call into every place in turn and ask if they had any work, any kind of a job at all. He worked methodically, making as many calls as there was time for before the places closed up for the day.

Most of the places they turned him down quick and cold and the others he could tell were plain scared of him ... that is they were scared of the eight hundred boys in town like him. One office he went into a man pulled out a dollar bill and said he didn't want any trouble.

Matt held himself under control. "I'm not out to cause you any trouble, mister, all I want is a job, any kind of a job at all. I can drive a truck or wrestle baggage or clean windows or do night watchman, pretty near any damn thing you want. Just give me the chance to prove it."

The man slipped the bill back into his pocket now he saw Matt had not come in to stick up the place. He said in a placating voice, "I haven't anything right now, maybe if you were to come around next week ..." Matt knew that line by heart and he did not have to come west to learn it. When he left the man got up and watched at the window till he turned the corner of the block. He knew he was being watched and it started the rage boiling up in him. He thought, "What in hell does he think? That I'll double back and stick up his measley little office?" That set his mind working another way, turned it towards the thing that the man had been so evidently scared of. Matt knew there were a bunch of the younger boys, kids around eighteen like Dick for instance, had been talking that way among themselves. All they needed was an experienced leader, one old enough to use his head, not too old to take chances ...

By the time he got back to the Angel he was hot under the collar and soreheaded and ready to resent every detail of his surroundings. The noise and the rawness of the stories and their age, the sweat smells and the lack of privacy and the comfortable acceptance of bum status that had settled in among certain of the older men. He was sore and every place he went he showed he was sore. He did not make any effort to make it less or to hide it.

After supper Hep came up to him casually and drew him outside for a smoke. Hep had a barometric mind and the senses of a stoat. He removed his hat and placed it carefully on his knees. As he rolled himself a cigarette he remarked quietly, "I heard Hazel came over today."

"Yeah," Matt said, "Hazel came over." He refused to be drawn. He felt like a heel but he was still hot. He gave no lead and invited no confidence, just sat there staring sullenly ahead not admiring himself. Through the open windows of the Angel the up-and-down drone of men's voices drifted out. A boy sat silhouetted on the upper floor, knees drawn up in the window space, laboriously darning a pair of socks. The windows made harsh squares of light in the noisome old building. There was the sound of an accordion, the soft, lazy, jogging rhythm floated clear out onto the sidewalk. A swollen copper moon eased slowly up over the freight sheds and from far away came the lonely hooting of a train. As the moon cleared the sheds the mess of empty barrels and junk on the opposite sidewalk showed up like sores.

Hep spoke out of the shadows. Not curiously or hurriedly, just that calm relentless probing. He asked, "Where'd you go after the boat left, Matt?" He passed Matt a made cigarette.

"Where d'you think I went?"

"That's what I'm asking you."

Matt eyed him by the flare of the match. He answered deliberately, "First of all I went an' deposited my paycheque at the bank, then I dropped in an' had a coupla beers, then I went around to Sandy's an' shot pool for an hour."

"Okay, okay," Hep said, "no need to get sore. I only asked you a question."

Matt dragged irritably and exhaled fast. "If you really wanta know," he said, "I spent the last coupla hours walkin' around town tryin' to scare up a job," and he added meanly, "I don't know why you asked me that. You know damn well what all nine of us does twenty-four hours a day."

Hep ignored the jibe. He spoke reasonably, "Don't think I don't appreciate how you feel, Matt, but you've got to remember that what happened to you today has happened to damn near every man in this whole outfit ... has been happening for years. If it hadn't then none of us would be here now."

Matt did not answer because he could not think of anything he wanted to say. Besides it was unanswerable. Yet he could not rid himself of this sense that Hep was out to sell him something and that the thing he was selling was more important in Hep's mind than whether the customer wanted it or not. Once again he felt in the presence of that force inflexible, impersonal, untainted by pity, larger than any single man. Or maybe, he thought, it's because I'm so damn soreheaded tonight that I'd be suspicious of anything anyone said to me.

"The thing I'm trying to make you see, Matt," Hep went on, patiently, "is that what happened to you today is the one reason we got organized in the first place. Any guy that's floated around as long as you have should be the first to appreciate that."

Matt's right foot began to tap. "Yeah, I know," he admitted. "You don't have to sell me that idea, I got that far on my own."

"Then you got the very reason back of the organization." Hep turned and for a moment he eyed Matt steadily. "Now suppose all the boys was to do like you did, start drifting around town singly asking for jobs. Where'd they end up?"

Matt looked down at his feet. "They'd end up right where I did, I guess … no place at all."

Hep's voice altered suddenly and grew brisk. "Okay then," he said, "what's the answer? I'll tell you what's the answer! Organization's the answer! Either you starve singly or you stick by the things that's trying to help you. If all the boys went back to bumming around trying to pick up casual summer labour, what's to become of the organization?"

Matt got up restlessly. For a moment he was silent, gazing off down the empty tracks. The moonlight made them gleam dully, more than pewter, less than silver, long twists of coldly glistening steel. His foot hacked at the sidewalk, "I don't know what's got into me tonight," he said at last, "I know all the stuff you said was true but it still don't make any difference to the way I feel."

Hep rose. For a moment the two men stood side by side. Suddenly Hep spoke, sounding irritable and tired. "I know damn well what's got into you, Matt, an' don't think you're the only one."

A laugh sounded from the inside and two men came and stood in the open window. They leant out, arms propped on the sill. The man who laughed said, "That was a hot one! I sure wish I could remember 'em the way you do."

The second man grunted with discontent, "That ain't the only thing that's hot around here tonight but what's it get you? All a guy can use around this lousy dump is a goddam icebag!"

Hep's mouth tightened in the darkness. "You see?" he muttered with a jerk of the head, "that's the way they'll all start to bellyachin' if something isn't done pretty quick." He eyed the risen moon with disgust. "What we need around here tonight is a damn good shower of rain!"

CHAPTER SEVENTEEN

Monday morning, after the regular meeting, Matt sat on the sidewalk outside the Quanta House listening detachedly to an argument going on behind him between a bunch of the boys, and two official job-offerers, sent over by the authorities to let loose four farm jobs among the eight hundred men. The jobs paid twenty-five per month and board, and the duration was seasonal. The reason Matt felt detached was because he had been among the first to offer and been turned down on the grounds of being a transient. On either side of him sat others of the sidewalk gang, among them Gabby, Dick, Charlie and George (Fat) Denning, also detached for personal reasons.

The air was stuffy and overcharged with too long absence of rain, and the smells hung and did not move away, gas fumes and dust and the odors of stale cooking. More boys lounged around, listening with varying degrees of curiosity or indifference as the dickering went on.

Gabby looked along at Dick. "You was beefin' just the other day that you didn't have a job. Why don't you go after one of them nice jobs the gents back there is handin' around?"

"Whad'dya mean, why don't I?" Dick returned, "I don' want to go work on a farm. Why don' you go after one of 'em yourself if you love a farm so much?"

"Who? Me?" Gabby said, genuinely shocked. "Get up at four in the mornin' to go muck around the cows. Whad'dya think I am? I'd as soon go join the militia!" he turned to Charlie. "Whyn't you go work on a farm, Slappy?"

Charlie looked down at his hands. "I did once," he said, "the job lasted just four weeks, then I was out again. Season closed."

Gabby reached round and struck a match on the sidewalk. "Where'd you go after that, Slappy?"

"I bummed around a couple weeks waitin' for the camps to re-open, then I went back in. Jees, was I sick of that bunch by April!" Lines of doubt, confusion and the effort to fight off apathy deepened in his forehead. He went on, "The young ones was mostly all right but the older ones couldn't see no good in anything. All they could do nights was sit around an' kick hell out of everything from toilet seats down to the gov'ment. After a time that makes you go kinda dead inside, like you didn't care a goddam about anything. I don't think I ever heard one constructive idea in the lot. That camp was where I met Hep first time."

Matt's head came round with quick interest. He spoke across Fat (George). "I heard that was when the boys first cooked up the big sit-down."

"That's right," Charlie said, "gave us something t'occupy our minds."

"Did Hep have a lot to do with that?"

"Oh sure, it was Hep started us talking."

Matt probed keenly, "Kind of like a little secret society between the bunch of you?"

Charlie laughed. "Secret nothin'! Hep didn't try to keep nothin' secret. Believe me th' authorities knew all about this sit-down weeks before we pulled it. Hell, we didn't put on any Ku Klux act. I guess they must of had this same thing going in most of the camps."

"Paid agitation, huh?"

"I don't know about it's being paid," Charlie said, "but the agitation was there all right. I guess if it was paid they didn't pay much or Hep an' fifty or so other guys I could tell you th' names of around here, wouldn't still be runnin' their feet off to keep us boys out of trouble. Why don't you go apply for one of those farm jobs, Matt?"

"He's a transient," Fat horned in, mincing the word; "they don't hand out jobs to transients."

Gabby grinned, taking up the chant. "He lost his domicile. Naughty, naughty, lost his domicile!"

Matt smiled but his eyes were cold. "Shut it," he said to Gabby, "I heard that too often for it to sound funny any more."

Charlie leant forward. "No kiddin', Matt," he said seriously. "What does that mean anyway? I thought you told me you was born back in Saskatchewan."

"Sure, I was, but I beat my way up an' down a half dozen other provinces since and I didn't stay long enough in any one of them to establish residence."

"Haw, haw," Gabby laughed delightedly. "Listen to the fancy words! He must of been studyin' up on the criminal code."

"You mean you don't belong any place at all?" Charlie insisted. "You mean if you was to go into any one of these nine provinces an' try to collect at the relief office, they could say, 'Hell. what're you doin' comin' in here an' tryin' to chisel? You don't belong on our books,' an' you wouldn't belong?"

Matt nodded grimly, "That's right. The only place I could apply an' be sure of gettin' room an' board is the can."

"But you'd have to break the law first."

"Oh sure, I'd have to break the law. That's no trick."

Charlie stared at him. "I guess you wouldn't have to establish domicile in a province before they'd put you in the can? I guess they'd lock you up just as easy whichever of the nine provinces you come from. Kind of like a squirrel cage, ain't it?" Charlie said perplexedly, "round an' round an' never gettin' any place."

Matt got up. He said irritably, "There's too damn much talk around here an' not enough action. Talk, talk, this whole thing is goin' up in one big cloud of talk." He moved away.

"Sometimes when he looks at me I feel like I'd stepped into a frigidaire," Charlie said, his eyes following Matt. "I'm going after him to see he don't get in any kind of trouble. Honestly," Charlie said, coming back for a moment, "can any of you boys figger just where a guy like that does belong?"

Fat made a gesture with his right hand, flicking imaginary sweat off his face. "In this heat?" he mocked lazily. "A day like this I couldn't even figger how many fingers I have on my right hand."

Behind the sidewalk sitters, the argument was drawing to some sort of a compromise. Three of the boys went back in and came out again slinging their dunnage. The fourth man to accept the official offer was Saul and his stuff was down at the Angel.

Gabby eyed them, then he turned back in disgust. He spat in the gutter. "Trial horses! Betcha they'll be back inside of three days!" He said it loudly and with an air of being on the in. He got up and stretched, "I'm goin' inside to get me a coupla *Libertys*."

Hughes was coming out with Saul behind him. When Gabby saw Hughes he cried, "Hello, teacher! Didn't they get you on the farm yet?"

Hughes had this trick of blushing he could not control, whenever he found himself the focus of attention. He stammered, "Me? What good would I be on a farm?"

"How about it, boys? Wouldn't you like to see Kenny downing warm hog's blood to keep his strength up?"

Saul's voice broke through the snicker of laughter. He eyed the hunched bodies of the sidewalk gang with disfavour. "You think that is funny, huh?" he demanded. "Look at these hands! Skilled hands! They don't want a job pushing cow dung around but still I am taking it because it is work." He mispronounced the word thereby giving it a dignity and solidarity denied by the English language. His accusing eyes moved from face to face so that the eyes of many of the men slid uncertainly away. "You think this is funny because your bellies are still full, but wait two days, t'ree days ... By that time the people of Gath are tired filling your idle bellies and then either you must starve or go out on the streets and fight so you can get back in the can to eat." His voice deepened with exasperation, "I tell you this sitting around is not funny any more. It has been going on too long a time."

He moved heavily away behind the three other men and none of those left had the presence of mind to answer him. For some moments the silence remained brittle and charged. Then Gabby spoke irritably, "There's one guy learns his from a script!"

Dick stuck a match in his mouth and clamped down hard on it. He said, "Hell, why don't he call a meetin' an' really listen to himself talk!"

"Yeah, why don't he?" came from a boy farther down the line, but it was an echo without conviction. The heat and the flies and the stillness came again; that and the crawling stream of traffic up and down Lavender. From time to time there was the whine of saws when a gust of hot wind carried the sound across. Freight cars crashed noisily in the yards and black, full-bellied switch engines steamed back and forth.

Matt and Charlie went up to the Orsino and stirred up a couple of teams of softball and played a game in the park and lay around afterwards in the shade, gassing and swapping stories. After dinner a gang from the Angel went swimming and by night-time Matt was so sore with one more day of hanging around that he was all ready to blow up.

Hep called him into the office. He said, "Go on down an' put this letter on the boat, I missed the last delivery. Take Eddy along. Maybe tomorrow night I can rustle up passes for the movie."

Matt stirred impatiently. "How many tomorrows do we have to keep hangin' around? We've been here a week already. I thought when we got to Gath we was really goin' to show the town something."

Hep glanced up sharply. "These things take time."

"Yeah? Laban didn't even get to see Gus yet an' those two love each other like rat poison!"

Hep went pale. His lips drew back and through his bared teeth he hissed like an angry snake, "Sometimes I wonder why I waste my time on a bunch of thankless young bums that don't know yet when the best's being done for them. Here we are, bustin' heaven an' earth an' our own guts besides, to keep this thing alive so you kids can get something you never had before, an' here you are ... " He stopped, turned away in disgust. "Go on," he said, "go on down and mail that letter before I do something I could be sorry for!"

"He flew up, didn't he?" Eddy said when they were walking down Lavender.

"Sure did," Matt answered morosely, "slightest little thing nowadays an' we all do."

"He never used to fly up like that in Aschelon, Matt. I remember all through that sit-down ..."

"Skip it, Eddy. Can't you forget you ever was in Aschelon?"

"Most times," Eddy said, "but sometimes I remember." He peered off into the shadows nervously. When they turned down into Pastoral and along by the abandoned buildings he pulled his old trick of keeping close to Matt all the way.

After they gave the letter to one of the stewards that was a friend of Hep's and promised to mail it first thing in the morning, they waited round to watch the boat pull out. They leant on the rail and looked out over the harbour, watching the lights winking on the water and the swirling shadows of the piles. The lights made small shimmering pools of colour and the water looked like oil, a full, smooth sheen with scraps of driftwood floating in it. Beyond the end of the breakwater gleamed a red-eyed buoy.

A Chink cook dressed in white was moving about the galley of a freighter tied up at the next pier. A cat, tail high, stalked frigidly across the deserted foredeck. The lights made her look like a ghost-ship.

Eddy's face had lost its confusion. He sighed with content. "Peaceful, ain't it, Matt? Kind of like Andersville, nothin' to get you scared."

Matt brought his palm down sharply on the rail. "I don't know," he said, "it looks too peaceful to me. We don't want a lot of peace around here, we want action." Presently he voiced his growing fear, "I tell you, Eddy, this whole thing looks like it was goin' to end up in a mess of talk. Talk, talk, never gettin' any place."

He felt himself tapped on the shoulder. Second only to getting smacked about the head, he hated most for anyone to come pussy-footing up behind and plant a hand suddenly on his shoulder. He turned and saw a middle-aged man with full pink cheeks, a clipped moustache and wet lips that pouted as he talked. "Tell me," he began, "why don't young men like you join the navy?"

Matt did not understand him at all the first time. He spoke in the high-pitched educated voice that used to sound so funny when the better talkies first came in. "I said why don't boys like you join the navy?" he waved vaguely at the freighter, "ships, you know." He did not mean that kind of ship of course.

Matt stared at him coolly, not liking, not disliking, not thinking of him either way. There was some quality about the English made him feel not enmity, but hard-boiled and detached, part of another life and world and generation, not even talking the same language. "I see it's a ship," he said.

The well-cut voice complained, "Why don't boys like you join one of the Services instead of sitting round day after day, waiting for the world to hand you a living? Gad, sir, when I was your age young men weren't afraid of work! You can't tell me there isn't plenty of work for those that really want it."

Matt smiled. "Trouble with us is we don't want it."

The Englishman gave a short outraged gasp. He took a moment to re-connect. "You mean to admit that you boys don't *want* to work?"

Matt drawled insultingly, "That's what you just told us, mister. Maybe you could find us something to do?"

The man's face changed. It moved from embarrassment to anger, then anger with a touch of plaintiveness as though he had been handed a low punch. "Who? Me?"

"Why not, mister? You seem to know a lot about the general situation."

The eyes popped with incredulity. The high voice choked. "Gad, sir, I don't own a damned employment agency!"

Matt smiled down at the water. Then his head came up so suddenly that the man backed away. Matt took a step forward. "You ought to go in the business," he breathed softly and savagely, "there's plenty openings right now. You ought to go in the business."

The man gave him a startled look, then reared round hurriedly and walked away. He looked back once to make sure he was not being fol-lowed.

Eddy gazed at Matt in admiration. "You certain'y know how to make guys mad jus' lookin' at 'em," Eddy said, "you don't need to do nothin', just look."

Matt pried loose from the rail. "Maybe I shouldn't've said that," he replied, walking slowly away, "I guess I didn't have any right to bite him off at the neck. I don't know ... every damn thing I say nowadays seems to bite somebody off at the neck."

They walked up past the harbour, approaching Pastoral by the low road that ran parallel to the railroad tracks. The squalid streets were quiet and steeped in shadow, the high canyons running between the blocks were blacked out except where the moonlight fell in patches, sharpening angles and creating crude planes of light and darkness. These streets that appeared merely dreary and damned by day took on a sinister air by night. The lighting, bleak and widely spaced, added to the macabre effect. When a cat darted out of an alley and scudded across in front of the two men, Eddy's eyes popped with fright. He let out a short, startled scream.

Matt jerked round. "Whatsa matter, Eddy? Whatsa matter?"

Eddy stood there shaking. His face was white. For a moment he could not say anything. Matt went up and shook him. "Snap out of it, Eddy! What d'you mean by throwin' a scare into me like that?"

"I don't like cats," Eddy excused himself, ashamed, "I didn't see that cat till it came right in front of me," his eyes strayed frightenedly around. "I don't like Gath," he whispered, "I wish we could move out of this town quick."

Matt observed him closely. He choked down his irritation and spoke patiently. "S'matter, Eddy? You was okay a minute ago when we was down watchin' the boats. You told me then what a swell town this was."

Eddy's was the primitive, unreasoning terror of a once-scared child. "That was quiet down there," he insisted, "but the streets ain't like that. Every place I go people stare an' the store people give me dirty looks like I was hangin' around to pull a stick-up or somethin'. There's too many cops around ... there's cops everywhere." He broke off, grabbed Matt's arm and pointed. "Look! Goin' by the end of the lane there! Every place I go I see cops!" He added darkly, "I was once beat up by a cop."

Matt's body stiffened. He hissed, "Pipe down, you crazy bastard, d'you want to get beat up again?" He dragged himself free and caught Eddy by the arm to get him moving along. But Eddy shook him off. The mixture of fear and anger that before came and went unsteadily, had settled on his face. He glared at Matt. "If any cop ever tries to beat me up again, you know what I'll do?" His arms came out suddenly, hands stabbed at Matt's throat and fastened there.

"Hey!" Matt shouted but the words died in a gurgle. Eddy's fingers sank farther into his throat. He struggled wildly like a cat on a spit. He felt his eyes beginning to pop, they felt ready to burst blood. Eddy's face swam through the darkness till it and the darkness became one. Feebly he clawed at Eddy's wrists.

All at once the red mist cleared from before Eddy's eyes. His hands dropped. For a moment he stared at Matt then slowly his face froze into recognition. He put his arm up dazedly and wiped his face. Matt stood there choking and panting. His knees were shaking. He began to massage his mangled throat. When he could speak he whispered hoarsely, "You crazy bastard, you! What did you want to do? Murder me?" He stared at Eddy in horror. His hands went back to his throat, rubbing it tenderly, easing his head around to get the normal blood flow re-established.

Eddy whimpered, "I didn't see it was you, Matt. I thought for a moment there you was that cop again ..."

Matt sprang at him and smashed him brutally across the face. "Now you know it wasn't!" he cried. "Now you know it was me!" The blow rocked Eddy to his knees. Matt smashed at him again and Eddy sprawled on the sidewalk, his nose spurting blood. After a moment he got up painfully, cowed and confused.

Matt's face was white, his eyes blazed angrily. His knees still shook. "An' you was the one I ses to myself, 'Now Eddy's begun to get more sense an' settle down so maybe they won't have to shut him in the nut house after all.' You was the one I was thinkin' all those things about. Chroust!" he choked in disgust, "I should of had my head examined!"

He turned and began to walk quickly up the street and Eddy trailed miserably behind him. His hands hung loose at his sides, his mashed features wore an expression of fixed and patient misery. Every now and then he put his arm up and wiped his bloody nose with the sleeve of his coat. After a time he edged up closer.

"Matt!" Matt did not turn. "Are you still mad with me, Matt?"

Matt answered bitterly, "You damn near killed me, what d'you expect ... that I'm goin' to stand up an' read the Thanksgivin' Service over you?"

"I didn't know it was you, Matt. Everything jus' went black on me. You know I'd lay right down an' let you walk on me if you wanted."

"What good would that do if you'd of choked me to death first?"

Eddy's head dropped in shame, "I never done anything like that before."

"The hell you didn't! What about that time in Harry's?"

"What time?" Eddy's voice grew afraid. Matt glanced back sharply.

"Forget it," he said, "never mind." He began to walk on again fast.

They trailed along Indian file as far as the corner of Pastoral. On both sides of the street the windows of the old, deserted buildings blinked dully in the moonlight like eyeless sockets. Farther along a light was dimly visible through a side window of the junk shop. Opposite to it squares of light lay on the sidewalk, from the upper floors of the Angel. The boy with the harmonica must have been right out on the sidewalk tonight. The rest of the street was empty and very quiet.

Matt stopped and waited for Eddy to come up. Eddy's eye was beginning to swell and there was a dark smear of drying blood below his nose. Matt told him to stand still while he felt around the eye. When he touched it Eddy let out a sharp yelp of pain. He went through the old routine of cleaning Eddy's face to remove the battle scars.

"Every time you get in trouble somebody socks you, an' I have to do the clean-up job," he muttered; "at least this time I had the satisfaction of sockin' you myself." He examined Eddy's bloated and darkening face with a twinge of remorse. "Maybe I shouldn't have socked you so hard but, God, you asked for it! For about a minute there you had me more scared than I ever was in my life."

Eddy pulled his smashed-in pan into a faint smile. He answered patiently, "I didn't mind what you did to me, Matt." He put his hand up to feel the swelling and drew it back with a little jerk of pain.

"Now listen here, Eddy," Matt began, "an' listen good because I'm sayin' it for the last time. Ever since that scrap over in Aschelon you an' me have kind of strung along together, haven't we?"

Eddy's head swung up and down. He began to shuffle with his feet.

"Now when you first found me an' I first found you, you was liable to do crazy things for no reason at all."

An expression of stubbornness closed over Eddy's face. "I was beat up by a cop," he recited dully, "I was beat up by that cop." His eyes strayed, his feet continued to shuffle.

Matt made a gesture of impatience. "Okay then, go on in the alley if you want, then you can keep still an' listen good ... because, by Jesus, there isn't goin' to be no next time from now on!"

Eddy scuttled heavily off into the shadows like a giant rabbit. When he returned his large, swooping shadow fell in beside Matt's rangy one as they walked on side by side.

Matt rubbed his face perplexedly. "Goddammit, Eddy," he began, "you make things so hard. Every time I think I got a little ground under my feet you kick it out."

Eddy's hands closed and unclosed. "I don't mean it that way," he said.

"Sure you don't mean it that way, just the same as lightenin' don't mean any harm, but just the same it can tear into a house an' damn near rip it apart."

Eddy was silent. After a moment he said timidly, "I done better since I came over here, I didn't do no dumb things since I got to Gath."

Matt said, "That's what makes you such a heck of a problem, Eddy. You behaved so quiet an' sensible all this last week you got to be pretty near the best worker in the squad. Then when I begin to feel proud at the way you can behave, you go an' pull some damn silly trick like you done tonight." Matt put his hand up and felt his neck tenderly.

"I got to hit you," he cried helplessly, "I got to get mad with you an' knock you around just to teach you! Jesus, sometimes it seems as though I got to damn near kill you to knock sense into you ... that is, if you don't kill me first!"

Eddy stared ahead up the squalid street. He said quietly, "You can do it, Matt. You can kill me if you ever got to do it."

Matt looked round at him startled. He really means that, Matt thought. Me, a bum that's newly smashed his face in! He said abruptly, "Well, Eddy, I hope it don't ever come to it, that's all." I got to start watching him all over again, he thought; maybe I didn't pay enough attention to him since we came to Gath, too busy feeling sore on my own account. I got to start watching Eddy all over again.

CHAPTER EIGHTEEN

Matt stood in the doorway of the Angel silently sizing up the boy that came over from the Orsino to take Saul's place. He looked between twenty and twenty-five, with hair that lay back in deep kinks pompadour style, a sharply-pointed nose and eyes that shifted constantly while he talked. He wore a dirty pink shirt and soiled blue serge pants and there was about him an air at once brash and furtive. He was talking loudly in fast, ex-gangster time. In one hand he waved a two dollar bill.

"So I sez to her, 'Lady,' I sez, 'I was born in the province of Ontario, but my folks is dead and for the past five years I've bin so many places lookin' for work that by now I don't belong in any of 'em.' 'Why don't you go join up with the sit-down boys?' she sez. For a moment I hadda think about that one, then, 'Lady,' I sez, 'I've had enough sittin' around to last me, I wanta get out an' work.' 'That's the spirit,' she sez, 'I only wish all the boys felt the same,' an' she opens up her bag an' pulls out this two dollar bill." He broke off to laugh. "Boy, did I hand her a line!"

The laugh, deepened by a slight current of uneasiness echoed from the boys standing around the door. Matt pried himself leisurely off the doorjamb. When the boy caught sight of him he stuffed the bill in his pocket.

Matt eyed him steadily. "Better keep that money out of sight," he advised, "there's people here in Angel that wouldn't like to see that kind of money floatin' around."

The boy eyed him insolently. "Yeah? Who, for instance?"

Matt's face went expressionless. "I didn't see you around before. What's your name?"

"My name's Ralph but you can jus' call me Kinky." He smoothed his hair and grinned complacently. "I wish I had a dollar for every girl that said she wished she had my heada hair."

Matt drawled, "What did she want to use it for?" A snigger came from the boys around the door.

Hep stepped out from the inside. "Hey, Matt," he called, "can you drive a light truck?"

Matt's deadpan manner dropped from him instantly. "Sure thing. I drove for a transfer outfit once for six months till the outfit went bust."

"Good boy!"

"I guess they got the dope on most of the things I did back in the office."

Hep smiled. "What in hell are you worrying about?" he said, "I believe you." His hand scooped down into his back pocket and drew out a badly crushed envelope. "I don't know where this went before it came here but it certainly looks as though it went around town." He studied the address with a grin of amusement.

Matt took the envelope. It was addressed, "Mr. Matt Striker, c/o The Sidowners, Gath." Across the upper left hand corner was scrawled "Personal."

"Who's your buddy?" Hep asked.

Matt slit the envelope with one finger and turned the page to find out the signature. His face relaxed with pleasure and surprise, "Well, by Jesus, Harry!"

"Is that the one-armed guy over in Aschelon?" asked Hep.

Matt nodded. "That's right. They don't come no better than Harry."

Something in the way Matt said it seemed to afford Hep satisfaction. He smiled, "Okay, boy, you got five minutes to find out what Harry has to say. Stick around here so I don't lose track of you." He popped back indoors.

Matt spread out Harry's letter, holding it out of the sun. There was a greasy thumb mark in the margin and a small brown coffee stain in the middle of the page where Harry must have been interrupted by the entrance of a customer. The writing was large and it spread over both sides of two pages, finishing with an elaborate signature and a vertical postcript.

"Dear Matt," Harry wrote,

"How are you makin' out? I read in the papers where you boys do not seem to be doin' so good. I guess Gath is getting jittery all right the same way Aschelon done when the big sidown was on. You wasn't in town then but cops, this whole town was crawlin' with 'em.

"I hope the papers is all wet as always when they say you boys is not doin' so good but I picked up the same news over the radio so I guess the radio is not all wet too. Anyway I sure hope things work out O.K. I see in the papers where they sent another fifteen of the boys to college yesterday for tin-cannin' on the streets of our hon'rable city here. That jug must be so full now they must be hangin' 'em from the roof."

Matt turned a page, picking up the trail with some difficulty owing to Harry's system of numbering.

"Say Matt talkin' of cops they was a scrap inside of my place Satday nite, a couple of drunks got thrown out when the beer parlour round the block closed up at eleven-thirty. Well these two gay birds come in an try to start a fight so what do I do? I smacks the pair of 'em down and just then a cop comes by an' makes it a dragout. Those birds was so plastered they was a pleasure to handle and anyway I got a lot more pep in this one arm than most has in two. Say do you know who that cop was? The same sonov-abitch that comes snoopin' around when your pal Eddy cuts up that day.

"How is Eddy? How's yourself? I hope all you sidown boys gets jobs before you grow corns on your tails. Drop in again first day you get back to town. I must close. All the best,

"Yrs. faithfuly,Harry.

"P.S. Say listen to this one Matt. What help can you boys expect from the big shots back east when everything west of the Rockies is still a god-dam Indian encampment? I thought that one up myself and I think it sounds good but try and get a paper to print it. Yrs.Harry."

The voice of Hep shouted from down the block, "Hey, Matt, get a move on there!" Matt stowed the letter, and hurried down to where Hep was standing by the door of a Ford delivery wagon. His right hand was tightly bandaged.

"What happened to your hand?" Matt said, as he pushed his foot down on the starter and the crate pulled out from the curb. Hep grinned faintly. "I twisted it last night," he said. Matt turned and looked at him. His face grew serious. "How many tried to make the break?" he asked.

"Half a dozen fool kids from the Orsino gone sour on sitting around,"

Hep answered. "When I met them they were all set to stick up a couple of drugstores and a gas station. They was so scared it was funny."

Matt whistled, snaking the truck cautiously amongst the congested traffic on Lavender. "Did they have guns?"

"No, lead piping an' a bit of wood carved to look like a gun."

"Where'd they get the piping around here?"

"They must of dug it out of the junk yard across the street."

"Yeah," Matt agreed, frowning, "I guess they could of at that. What would have happened if they'd stuck up one of those places?"

Hep said dryly, "Same as happens when you pull the pin out of a Mills bomb, I guess." He broke off and signalled Matt to slow down, "Round to the left and straight out from there."

They drove through town and passed squads of boys from the Orsino marching towards the park. There were police, too, moving round in pairs. The town was very quiet and orderly with the public, the sit-downers and the police all maintaining the same nervous, cagey tension.

They drove out by the Brecon Road, that paved highway that within the first two miles touched the fringe of the country. The same thing went on mile after mile, small white houses and weathered barns with the lichen growing on the shakes. On one side the country stretched away into acres of oak-studded green, rising and falling superbly like parkland. Sheep cropped at the rich grass and cattle lay out in the fields. The sky was a hot, clear blue with nothing except the resting cattle to foretell the later coming of rain.

Matt held the truck down to an even thirty-five and eased back in his seat. "Pretty country around here," he said.

"Some of the prettiest country you could see anywhere," Hep said. He stuck a made cigarette between his lips. "Slip me a match will you? I forgot to bring any."

They lit up. Matt's face puckered with a drift of smoke. He tossed the match out the side. "Different from the city," he said, "in the city it's dog eat dog all the time, an' the only ones that don't get eaten is the ones that is too tough to digest. Where are we goin' anyway?"

Hep said, "There's an old man named Chandler lives out here somewhere. His kid, Tom, was in my squad all through the sit-down. When he went to hospital on the Sunday you dropped into his place."

Matt nodded. "I remember Charlie tellin' me. He showed me the pictures in the paper."

"When I went to see him in hospital he told me his father had this little place off the Brecon road, fruit an' vegetables an' some stock. After what happened to Tom the old man ought to be ready to give his all for the Cause."

"That why you brought the truck along?"

"Sure. Red over at the garage gave me the loan of her for the afternoon. I thought maybe we could pick up a sack of spuds or anything the old man happened to have layin' around. It's too far out for the boys to canvass."

Matt was silent for a time, taking quick drags on the cigarette, a frown creased between his eyes. He seemed to take a deep breath before he spoke.

"Hep!"

Hep opened his eyes. The heat had made him drowsy. "What is it?"

Matt spoke with constraint. "Hep, one of the boys round the Quanta yesterday was talkin' about you."

"Yeh?"

Matt's voice was stiff with effort, "He said you went from camp to camp stirrin' up trouble. He said you'd been in sixteen camps altogether."

Hep smiled slightly as though he enjoyed a certain inward pleasure. "Whoever that guy was, he was wrong."

The strain eased from Matt's voice, "That's what I told him."

"He should have said eighteen camps," Hep corrected gently. "So far I've been in eighteen camps and every camp I went I stirred up trouble."

Matt kept his eyes on the road, carefully skirting a pothole. "What kind of trouble?"

"The same kind all over. Every place I went I preached that a man had a right to own his own job and his own stake in the community, but that they've got to get together to prove it because they couldn't prove anything singly. Most of 'em knew that already, but what they had to learn was to fight an' make it stick. But I never did start anything, Matt, all I did was to try to get the boys to light their fires all in the same place, not just a lot of little flare-ups that couldn't amount to anything."

Matt chuckled. "You must've stirred up plenty trouble all right."

"I stirred up so much trouble," Hep replied measuredly, "that the camp bosses was always findin' some excuse to pass me on to the next camp. I never knew but one camp boss that didn't hate my guts and that guy's on relief himself now." He broke off, allowing himself one of his infrequent laughs. His eyes snapped with malice. "Then along comes the sit-down an' believe me, the day the first sit-down was called something came to town."

"Yeah, I guess so," Matt said, "when was that anyway?"

"Way back in '35," Hep said reminiscently, "though actually they was pulling off sit-downs in France somewhere in the fourteen hundreds, but the sit-down that happened in '35 wasn't called, it just went ahead and happened of itself, and after that they began to wake up to what they'd got. Up until the trick gets pulled too often and the public goes fed-up on it, there's more horse-power to a sit-down than all the riots and skull-splitting parties ever staged."

Unconsciously Matt was slowing down the truck, letting her cruise along. He was listening eagerly, conscious of the old spell, feeling once more that power in Hep that drew him even while at times its harshness repelled him. "What d'you mean 'horse-power'?" he asked. "Where's the horse-power in a bunch of guys squattin' on their tails?"

Hep spoke carefully, choosing his words, making his thought explicit. "Look," he said, "when a guy squats down on his tail an' stays there, he's actin' quiet an' peaceful, he doesn't commit any act of violence or sabotage an' in most cases he maintains his own discipline, the same way we've done here. So what happens?"

"Clubs an' tear gas an' the riot squad ... that's the way it worked out in Aschelon," Matt said doubtfully.

Hep smiled. He flexed his bound right hand gently with the fingers of his left. "So they call out the riot squad an' what happens?" he went on. "The boys get so damn mad at being beaten up when they never done anything, that they swing right over to the union or the party or whatever the opposition is, they swing right over and sign up."

"Like me," Matt broke in softly, "I got beat up in '35 an' I've been mad ever since." He put his hand up, fingered the old scar, "I don't know yet why I didn't lose an eye."

"You got to remember something else as well," Hep went on seriously, "public sympathy can swing over big too ... that is, if the thing don't drag on too long. But at the beginning the authorities don't stand a chance, everything they do is bound to be wrong and nine times out of ten they're so dumb they act against their own interests. Hell, they handed us that build-up in Aschelon on a plate! The newspapers played it up big. Maybe you saw some of those cuts of the clubbing of unarmed men?"

"Yeah," Matt said grimly, "I saw them. I didn't need no cuts, though, I saw Eddy."

"An' I saw a dozen Eddys," Hep said quickly. His lips twitched with a return of malice. "I tell you, boy, the sit-down's got something. You got to use strategy to handle it right, dramatize it. It stinks to hell to the employers an' the authorities, but about all they can do is to get mad an' take it. Another thing, the sit-down's sociable. Guys get to know one another pretty well if it turns into a stay-in, an' they recognize they got to behave because it's their own strike an' not some tailor-made stunt put on by a strike leader that's liable to sell 'em out and skip at the end of it. See what I mean, Matt? Maybe a lot of people think of the sit-down as guys just sittin' around on their fannies an' not doin' much else, but, by Christ, if it's handled right the sit-down can be dynamite!"

Matt's eyes had grown hard and bright. His hands tightened on the wheel.

He said in a steady voice, "I told you in McBain I wanted to get in and become part of the movement ... the whole movement back of this little fuss," he added, using the word "movement" with a certain shyness.

Hep's eyes glinted for a moment. He remarked softly, "Paid agitator, huh? Sew red buttons on your underwear?"

"I'm not foolin', Hep. When I first come into this thing I come in with nothin' to lose but my pants, an' I didn't care a goddam what happened to them just as long as I could take a hard enough sock at someone or something." The excitement had died from Matt's face, leaving the eyes clear and cold.

"So what? That was the way most of the boys come in."

"Yeah, but these last weeks things has been different," Matt went on, speaking fast. "I got a feelin' of importance, like I really amounted to somethin'. For the first time in my life it mattered what I did an' if I forgot to do it. I got a feelin', too, gangin' around with the rest of the boys. By Jesus, Hep, I'll do any damn thing in the world before I'll go back to how I was before ... an' you know it."

Hep's mouth tightened. "That's what I'm afraid of!"

Matt's head came round sharply, "You're scared of somethin' an' you won't say what it is."

Hep said irritably, "Damned right I'm scared, I'm scared of a lot of things." He thrust his head out, and held up his hand. "Better slow down under that sign an' let's see where we got to."

They drew up under a signpost where four roads forked. Hep read the names. "I think it's a couple of miles that way," he said, pointing down a dirt road cut deep by wagon tracks. "I remember Tom told me to turn left where the sign read, 'Malloy Cross Roads'."

Matt pulled the truck round and took her down a rough, sun-baked side road. Sleek cattle grazed in the fields and stout lambs shook their dangling tails, stampeding wildly toward their ewes as the truck crashed by. A tall white barn and a prim two-storied frame house showed through the trees.

Matt slowed and Hep sat up and flung away his cigarette. He read out the name on the mailbox, "'Thos. Chandler'. I guess this must be the place all right." He got out and unfastened the wire gate and Matt swung the truck in between the white-washed posts and up the short, curved driveway. Large whitened rocks were set at intervals along the edge of the neatly clipped grass and in the middle of the plot stood a small concrete bird bath. Screening one side of the porch, the branches of the old-fashioned rose bush had been trained against a network of garden twine. There was a meticulous, almost doll-like air about the place. As the truck drew up a collie pup bounded out from the side of the house, its amber body fawning and writhing with delight.

Hep let his hand rest for a moment on the dog's ruffed neck. He looked at Matt significantly. "Maybe this is a good omen," he remarked. "I hope we get the same welcome from the old man. I wonder whether there's a chance he'll be in." He rapped on the framework of the screen door and waited. Inside the hall was a well of darkness. A faint smell of floor polish and cedar shavings mixed with manure rose in the nostrils of the two men. No sound came from the house. The dog sniffed at their heels for a moment longer, then bounded off down the steps. "Wish he'd of stayed," Hep said, "a dog or a kid around gives you a handle to work with."

Matt turned and looked back down the garden. "The old man sure has a pretty place out here, wonder why Tom didn't stay and work on it. How is Tom, by the way?"

"Last report that came over he wasn't doing so good," Hep said, "they think he may still lose the sight of that eye. Kind of makes it difficult to approach the old man in one way, yet in another ... Oh, what th' hell," he said breaking off with a shrug, "you never can tell how a person will react in a case like this. Maybe the old man will feel he wants to give his all for the Cause, maybe he'll kick hell out of us." They stood there waiting. Hep knocked again. Matt shivered suddenly. Then Hep touched his arm and the bodies of both men stiffened. Hep said, "There's the old man now!"

Matt whispered, "What are you scared of?"

Hep snapped back irritably, "What d'ya mean 'scared'? I'm not scared of a damn thing."

A door at the far end of the passage opened and a flood of sunlight streaked into the dim hall. The short, brisk footfalls of a low-statured man came towards them down the passage. The light at the back made him invisible until he pulled open the screen door.

Matt's throat contracted so sharply that he coughed. A peculiar rigidity tightened his jaw. He heard the quick intake of Hep's breath as the old man stepped out into the sun. The whole left side of his face was gone. Over the crater-like shell of what had once been a cheek and an eye socket he wore a dark green shade. The shade cut off the face at the left nostril, extending below the jawbone up to the line of the hair. In the half face that remained burned a bright, sea-blue eye, the piercing eye of a young-old man. His hair rose in a thick white crest and his toughened skin was burnt tan-red. He wore a faded work shirt and overalls and at the base of his throat glistened a small cup of sweat and a few wiry hairs. Every detail of his person was scrupulously neat and he moved with an air of resentful energy. For a moment some quality in him subjugated both men so that they stood before him tongue-tied.

He looked them up and down and from the twisted mouth issued a single word, "Well?"

Hep stared back into the bright blue eye. "Mr. Chandler?"

The eye focused sharply. "I'm Chandler. What do you want of me?" He peered past them suspiciously, seeking a car in the driveway, "Drummers?"

Hep smiled a disarming smile. His voice was friendly. "No, Mr. Chandler, we haven't come to sell you anything."

"Damned right you haven't, but you might have tried."

"My name is Hepburn," Hep began, "this is Matt Striker."

Chandler glanced from one man to the other, "That doesn't tell me a thing. What I want to know is what did you come here for?"

Hep said, "Your son, Tom, was in my squad, Mr. Chandler. I went to visit him in hospital the day before we left Aschelon ..."

The old man's head came up suddenly and his face changed. It grew harsh and sunken. "Ah!" he cried, "now I place you! Well, you could have saved yourself the trouble. I don't know anyone called Tom, I never heard of anyone by that name at all."

Matt felt Hep grow rigid at his side. Unaccountably his own hands began to sweat. Hep said quietly, "I think we came to the wrong house, Mr. Chandler, we're sorry to have troubled you."

Terrier-like the twisted lips fastened on the word and echoed it. "We? Who's the 'We'? The old man turned on Matt, his eye bright and challenging, "Who the hell are you? What part have you got in all this?"

Matt's tongue came out and moistened his stiff lips. He said, "I came along to drive the truck, Mr. Chandler. I took your son's place in the squad."

The old man eyed him stonily. He repeated with a frozen dignity, "I told you before, I have no son."

Hep interposed quickly, "Goodbye, Mr. Chandler, we're sorry to have brought you to the door for nothing." He turned to go down the steps.

The old man thrust out a muscular hand and seized him by the arm. Some depth of fire generating from inside him seemed about to find vent. "Wait," he cried, "you didn't drive out all this way just to talk about Tom. What in hell did you come for?" His pitiless eye darted from face to face then the corded muscles of his neck and his small temple muscles tightened. His whole body seemed to spring to arms. "I know who you are now! You're a pair of those goddamned Reds that were the ruin of Tom in the beginning. You came to see if there was anything left you could take from me."

Again Hep interposed soothingly, "Listen, Mr. Chandler ..."

The old man's voice swept him passionately aside, "Tom would have been working on this place today if it hadn't been for meeting up with men like you and getting his head filled with lies. Reds, that's what you are, a bunch of goddamned Reds!" He glared at Hep, his mouth twisted after words. "You don't work yourselves and by Christ, you prevent other men from working. Wherever you go you stir up trouble and teach boys to lie around and rot in idleness rather than accept honest labour." He raised his arm and pointed it shaking, over the fields. "You teach boys the land isn't good enough for them any more, teach them that the army and the navy and the police is made up of a bunch of dirty yellow rats. Do you want to see something? Something that no man but me has seen in twenty years? I'll show you!" Without warning his hands went up fumbling with a knot behind his head. He pulled off the shade, baring the left side of his face. "Look at that! I got that fighting, so the country could breed swamps and the swamps could breed vermin!"

The two men stared in horror. Matt was white, he felt weak and gut-sick. His eyes could not look away. The sunlight beat on the shattered flesh, the sightless, hairless cave that had once been an eye, the distorted shape without jawbone or cheek-bone, the twisted mouth, all seamed together in one grotesque, unspeakable design.

The old man's voice thrashed on, fighting for words. "You say you're out to find work for the unemployed. Right now this town is seething with unemployed, yet when I want a boy to work on my place I have to hire a Jap!" He broke off, leaving an unfilled silence. "When I think of what men like you did to my boy ..." His voice shook thinly. The rage died from his face, leaving it bitter and tired and old. The left side did not change at all, the horror kept on staring without expression. Suddenly Matt felt a desire to laugh. He wanted to laugh and laugh and shout with laughter. He had to hold himself in.

The old man's hand dropped. He said woodenly, "I told you once I had no son." Then as they still seemed to hesitate, "What are you waiting for? You've done everything you can. What in hell are you waiting for?"

* * *

They were out once more driving along the still, sunbaked roads. The truck rattled over the potholes, the tools danced crazily behind. A milk wagon slewed by, jangling with empties.

At last Hep broke the silence. "Well," he said "do you still feel like one of the noble saviours of the down-trodden masses?"

Matt was a long time answering. "I don't know how I feel," he said finally, "I feel kind of numb. But I know the things he said about us weren't true, I know that."

Hep began to unbind his tightly wound hand. He tossed the bandage out on the roadside and sat flexing his fingers. "Maybe they were, some of them," he said. "I wouldn't know." His voice was heavy and lifeless.

"Even if they were," Matt persisted, "the idea back of them wouldn't change."

"Idea back of what?"

Matt spoke with an effort. "What I mean is that if all of us in this little dump here was to get kicked to hell tomorrow, the thing we're fightin' for would still go on an' a lot of other guys would still go on fightin' for it."

Hep laughed shortly. "Kick this thing to hell tomorrow an' the boys'll all make up a nice little party an' go along with it. Don't make any mistake about that. You heard what the old man said ... they weren't trained under gunfire."

Matt's eyes strained off into the distance. Once more he saw the old man's hand clawing at Hep's arm, the horror of the distorted features. For a moment he felt sick. He said bitterly, "God, Hep, there was something terrible about that old man. There was something pitiful, too ... he had everything laid out so neat."

Hep turned on him with a snarl, "So what? Just because he hoes his turnips in a straight line that makes us sonsabitches!"

Matt stiffened. "That wasn't what I meant," he said, "an' you know it."

Hep cut in harshly, "What you meant was turn left at the end of the road there. We got one more call to make while we're out here."

Matt turned left without a word. He felt hurt and hostile. The old anger rose in him like a red flame. He had a time hanging onto himself.

At last Hep felt in his pocket, drew out a half-smoked pack of Consols and passed it across. Matt took one in silence. Hep struck a match. He said quietly, "No need to stay sore all day."

Matt did not turn his head. He answered stiffly, "I'm not sore. I just don't like gettin' jumped on that way."

"*You* don't like gettin' jumped on! Lemme tell you something! I picked you today because you been bothering me for some kind of special work. I picked you out so I could watch how you handled yourself, an' first off what do you do? You start in usin' two dollar words like 'pitiful', an' 'terrible' an' havin' the gall to tell me you didn't like gettin' your damn little tail jumped on!" Hep was breathing hard. His eyes had grown bright with anger.

Matt was staring fiercely ahead. His face was stubborn. "Neither I did," he said, "no guy likes gettin' jumped on that way. Why the hell should he?"

"How do you think I liked it, standin' up there in front of the old man an' havin' to take it? D'you think I liked that whole job of work any better than you did?"

"I don't know, I never thought ..."

Hep's voice lashed him remorselessly, "Damned right you never thought! Didn't I talk to the old man civilly? What right had he to stand there an' call us a bunch of dirty names? Did I slug Tom over the head? Let him get after the bastards that done the work!"

They drove on in a hostile silence. At last Matt forced himself to say, "I guess I just couldn't take it, I didn't have the experience." He got rid of the words grudgingly, looking straight ahead.

Hep allowed the silence to come back and remain. After a time he said more quietly, "Every once in a while a guy runs into some part of the work that he doesn't like, but he can't afford to let it affect him. He does it an' forgets about it. There's plenty things a man has to do that he don't even like to think about after, but he has to do them just the same. Get what I mean, Matt?"

Matt was cooler now. He was cooler and ashamed. Also he began to have the feel of a new kind of experience. He was beginning, "I'm sorry I blew up ..." when Hep leaned out and signalled for the truck to pull up.

"Hey, slow down a minute," he called out, "I think we went too far."

A boy was coming down the road, herding a solitary Jersey. Hep hailed him to ask for the Bannerman farm. The boy raised his switch and pointed to a group of buildings a quarter mile down the road. "That's the place," he said, "I just come from there."

Matt pulled the truck in under a big walnut tree by the gate. "Widow lives here named Bannerman," Hep explained, "maybe she's good for a touch. She ought to be, her old man left her nicely." He looked at Matt and grinned, "The old lady's a queer mixture, sex an' religion in about equal parts."

Matt grinned back. "Sounds like she got sugar in her gas tank."

Hep chuckled. "The religious ones has an amazing natural capacity. Anyone that's worked around 'em much knows that."

"Kind of bedroom evangelism."

"Seems like the most of 'em can't get their tanks filled any other way. Seriously though, Matt, women have a big drag in this game ... the mother angle."

They went in the gate. A boy wearing a torn straw hat and overalls was digging in a flower bed close by the house.

Hep asked, "Is Mrs. Bannerman inside?"

The boy left off digging and eyed him dourly. "You better go knock on the door," he said.

"Wonder what he's so mad about?" Matt asked as they climbed the steps.

"Maybe he's sore because he has to work all day. Did you ever notice there are some guys like that?"

Hep rapped on the old-fashioned, glass-panelled door. A grey-green cat leapt up onto the porch and rubbed suavely against his legs. The spatter of a motor-cycle sounded coming down the road. Hep's body stiffened. The motor-cycle rounded the bend, slowed up noisily, and pulled in behind the truck. Hep's lips drew back in a sound half snarl, half exclamation of surprise. "*Speed cop!*"

Matt asked quickly, "What can he do to us? We weren't speeding."

"He can ask us did we have a driver's license, I never thought of it till right this minute. By Christ, you got to be on your toes every damn minute of the day!"

Behind them the door opened and a woman looked out. She was fleshy and middle-aged, with hard dabs of rouge on each cheek and jet-black hair rolled into untidy curls. She wore a pink cotton housedress and cheap oriental earrings dangled coquettishly from her ears. Where the parting came in her hair the dye had begun to grow out, leaving a quarter inch of dead and brittle-looking grey. About the whole effect there was a mixture of wistfulness, homeliness and faded lechery.

Hep removed his hat. "Good afternoon, Mrs. Bannerman. We were out this way so we thought we'd drop by."

The woman held out a soft, heat-damp hand. She smiled at Hep coyly. "It's been a long time, Mr. Hepburn," she said, "how are things going with the boys?"

Hep's tone was confidential, "Well, I tell you, Mrs. Bannerman, things aren't too good."

"But I thought they had everything they needed. The papers said donations was still comin' in good."

Hep's voice was suave. "Up to now, Mrs. Bannerman, but you know how the public is ... all pepped up one minute and losing interest the next, but just the same the boys has to go on bein' fed. I thought maybe you'd like to send a little something back to headquarters."

The woman eyed him hungrily and beneath the dabs of rouge a sluggish colour rose. Matt wanted to smile till he remembered he was learning still another new technique.

"If you could call back tomorrow, Mr. Hepburn," the woman said, "maybe around supper time so we could have a bite together?" she hesitated coyly, "I could have a lamb ready for you. Carl down there can do the slaughtering ..." Her voice died in a choke, her mouth stayed open. "Oh my gracious !" she cried with a hiccough of surprise, "what does a policeman want in here?"

The speed cop was coming up the path. He was a handsome cop. The sun glittered on his polished gaiters and metal trim. His eyes moved between the woman and the two men. He asked, "Did these men come soliciting?"

Hep stepped in quickly. "I have a signed permit," he said, producing it. The cop glanced at it, handed it back. "That thing's no good out here."

"Why not?"

The cop said, "You're a half mile outside the municipality of Brigford. Before you can solicit here you'll have to have a permit signed by the reeve."

Hep's face narrowed. He folded the paper and slipped it back in his pocket. "Is that so?" he murmured, his voice soft with malice. He turned to the woman with a smile. "Too bad, Mrs. Bannerman, I guess we're out of luck. Thanks just the same."

She began to protest uncertainly, "But these gentlemen are friends of mine, officer. Even if they can't have anything maybe they'd like to take a look around the place."

The cop hooked his thumbs in his belt. Standing that way he looked handsomer than ever. He answered courteously, "Sorry, madam, but I have to see these men clear of the municipality."

As they went down the steps the woman made a little choking sound of anger. "That lamb ..." she began, then she saw it was hopeless. She watched the small procession go through the gate, the two men ahead, the cop moving behind.

The cat stole up to her skirts, fawning. She stooped and picked it up and for a moment her fingers dug into its thick neck fur so that it writhed and sprang free angrily. Then with a little sigh she turned indoors. The cat, poised watchfully, made a sudden rush and flew past her legs into the hall.

★ ★ ★

Matt jammed his foot down on the starter and as the engine coughed noisily back to life he glanced behind to where the cop was straddling his machine. He muttered viciously, "Those bastards do ask for it!"

Hep settled back calmly. "What d'you want to do? Fight the army? Don't tell me you don't know enough yet not to get fresh with cops."

"I know it," Matt said, "but I don't like doin' it. I hate their guts too much. Me an' them has been on opposite sides too long."

Hep said quietly, "Just the same that's no excuse. I don't like 'em any better myself, the sonsovbitches, but that don't prevent there being plenty decent cops, an' about a million or so that's just too dumb to do you any harm if you're smart enough to spell three-letter words. Same's there's decent guys and dumb guys on the other side in a war, only you can't afford to admit it."

Matt shook his head stubbornly, "I still hate their guts. I got pushed round too long an' too hard."

"You'd of got pushed around some more if you'd tried to get fresh with that cop back there. First thing you know he'd of asked to see your driver's license."

"Say, that's right! Why didn't he? He must of known we didn't have one."

Hep shrugged. He pulled out the little crushed sack of tobacco. "That's one of the things we'll never know. Just once in a while for no reason at all you get a break like that; it's got to happen sometimes."

Matt pulled the truck round and half a mile farther back they passed a white sign by the roadside, Municipality of Brigford. He twisted in his seat and looked behind. The powerful red machine had slowed. It waited a moment then turned off down a side road. He let out a short breath of relief. "Well," he said, "there goes our guard of honour."

He turned and looked at Hep curiously. "Why did you want to be so polite to the old woman back there at the last? You must have known by then she wasn't good for a touch?"

Hep blew a thin smoke stream down his nostrils. His face wore a half-puzzled look. After a moment, "I don't know," he admitted, "except that she was a human being an' maybe she got some kind of a kick out of thinking she made an impression. It don't cost a nickel to be human. You can write that down on your cuff as being one of the things I brought you out to learn."

Matt chuckled, "I guess at that she don't have much fun on the home reservation. Carl there didn't look like a case of hot pants."

Mile after mile the sultry wind blew by. The engine began to boil. They crawled the last half mile into town with steam and rusty water spurting out from the radiator.

"You felt pretty sore at me this afternoon, didn't you?" Hep said.

Matt reddened. He answered with a half-ashamed grin, "You got me so damn mad once back there I pretty near saw red. Seem's like somebody's gettin' mad all th' time. If something don't happen quick around here we'll soon all be tearin' each other apart."

Hep pulled at his long top lip. "It'll happen all right."

"When?"

"If I knew the answer to that maybe you an' me wouldn't be sitting here so quiet now."

PART IV

·

Transit

Chapter Nineteen

With Thursday came talk of still more men being shipped over from Aschelon, and from Aschelon itself a minor outburst against monkey-minded Reds stirring fake emotionalism and holding the forces of law and order up to public ridicule. In both cities harassed authorities writhed beneath the same spotlight of publicity, and a lot of persons not ordinarily supposed to look ridiculous were made to appear so.

The people themselves were angry, nervous and bewildered. Staled by sit-down talk and jittery with rumours of sit-downs still to come, what exasperated them most was that out of the mess of buck-passing, mud-slinging and stalemate no concrete solution had emerged. They talked on street corners, gathered in uneasy crowds below the windows of the Gath Settler, chattered vaguely of Marxism and revolution. The crisis hardening around them made news from Europe sound like the far-off echo of pop-guns. That was one of the better, more comic aspects. The prosperity of the hardware men was another. They were sold dry of locks, bolts, chains, bars and all forms of trick window fastenings.

That same night, Thursday, Matt wrote a letter to Hazel. As usual he borrowed all but the stamp off Hughes. Kenny was going through his notes on the floor, readying the MS. for the big bust when it broke and try-ing not to notice the row going on round him. Eddy was reading the Settler funnies. He had on a pair of cotton underdrawers too small for him, and his feet were bare. The toes were red and puffy and agonizingly calloused. From time to time his eyes would rest broodingly on his swollen toes.

Gabby and Charlie were somewhere about the building catching up on the grapevine. Gabby had given up trying the cards commercially. His total take to date was a couple of slugs and a wooden nickel. But where a smaller man would have gone around howling that he had been gypped, Gabby turned the cards into a free show and collected in publicity what he failed to collect in cash. He even tried the cards on the cop that pulled him in Friday. Gabby was like that, always making some kind of a grand gesture.

In the room opposite Kinky and Dick were wrangling halfheartedly over a pack of greasy cards while Pop lay on his back on a pile of dirty newspapers, his sunken lips pushing in and out, bellowlike, as he slept. His pants dangled drearily from a nail above his head. Men kept passing and re-passing to go in the toilet next door. Every time the old plumbing burped it sounded like it would tear loose from the walls. Matt wrote with the paper on his knee, steadying it on a four-months-old copy of the *Saturday Evening Post*.

"Hazel dear,

"How are you honey? I think things is about ready to bust open over here now. These last twenty-four hours they have been running around in circles the way I would be now if I did not make myself sit down and write to you, but so far I can't see anything fresh come out of any of it. This whole town is boiling with cops. They try to keep them undercover but we know they are there. They have every big building guarded like they expected the Nazis.

"The city has turned thumbs down on a tag day but the boys has voted to go ahead and hold one anyway tomorrow so I guess you will be reading in Friday's papers where a lot more of us has been sent up to college to finish our education. Believe me Hazel there is getting to be fewer and fewer non-college boys among us if you get what I mean. I told you didn't I, that I got sent up twice back east, once for incite, the other time vagged. But suppose they only send a guy up for ten days for obstructing an officer (tin-canning to you) they got him tabbed and if he gets in any kind of a jam later they can look up his criminal record. Isn't that something? Maybe you can tell me what.

"But the joke is that this jug over here don't hold more than fifty including drunks so they can't afford to pick up too many of the boys or somebody is going to look ridiculous. One thing I can tell you for sure and about the only thing is that the boys and the Gath people is both getting pretty damn fed-up on this whole mess. It's going to break soon and if it don't break the right way then it's going to bust right open and make what happened in Aschelon look like a picnic. But what gets me and is getting all of us is what's coming out of it in the end? Where's the big work and wages program that this fuss was first raised about? All I can see at the present if things don't change in the next twenty-four hours is getting shoved right back to the old shuttle game.

"Look, Hazel, try to get this. On Monday I tried for a temporary farm job and it was okay till they found I wasn't a local boy. I guess that is fair enough from their angle but it does not help me. Okay then I am not their baby, where the hell do I belong? Excuse the language but it gets pretty raw living among a bunch of boys like this. I come from Saskatchewan in the beginning like I told you but the authorities there are moaning around with a bigger jobless problem than they can take care of already. They are sending telegrams and shoving heaven and earth around just so they won't get any of us boys dumped back on their hands. Besides I have floated around the nine provinces so long now I don't belong in any of them. That's a fact. It would take too long to explain why here but it's a fact. I don't belong in the country unless they have a war and want to shove a gun in my hand. Well Hazel maybe if that's all they have to offer I won't wait for a war. I'm not dead but I ought to be. They got no place to put me alive.

"Look, I sound kind of bitter and fed-up and different to the last time you saw me but what I am trying to say is this. You can stick around waiting for me for the next twenty years till they shake up the whole economic system around 1960 or so but maybe you would not care to wait that long. It is no use telling you it in any other way, you are reading the papers same as everybody else. A bunch of kids got sore Tuesday night and tried to bust out and take theirs but nothing come of it. What I think is there will be a big row suddenly and maybe I will not try too hard to keep out of it. Anything's better than this damn waiting around.

"There is a lot of guff talked about the responsibility for this mess and the usual buck-passing. But the most of us boys don't want to be anyone's responsibility, all we want is the chance to be responsible for ourselves.

"I must close now or I shall go on spieling all night. A school teacher named Hughes gave me the paper to write on and loaned me his pen. He is writing a book about this sit-down, as if anyone wanted to read about it, they are even fed-up by now on what they buy in the newspapers. Hughes is nuts all right but he is a good guy, fancy, a school teacher. We have all sorts here. I wish I had better news to tell you and I didn't even ask yet if you had landed a job of your own. This sitting around gets you kind of wall-eyed, you can't see or think of anything else but what is going on around you. Anyway I love you honey though at the moment it don't do you much good. I can't give you anything but love baby. Remember that tune in the Blind Spot? I don't like it any better now than I did then. That day seems like a long time ago now. So does the first one in Aschelon. So does the evening. I don't want to start talking about all that or it will get me savage.

"Just as soon as things are more sorted out this end I will write again.

"Yrs with love,

MATT.

"*Later*: Have just heard we quit these dumps Saturday. The city only loaned them to us for twelve days. Nobody seems to know what is going to happen after that. Laban is running around town like a wet hen, he and two or three others I don't even know the names of or whether they are connected with us or only outsiders trying to dicker over some kind of a settlement. There is too damn much horse-trading going on around here, too much talk as well.

"I think a lot of the boys would have skipped before this only they didn't have the price. There is a good deal of growling going on but mostly just fed-up. Most of the boys is just laying around not saying much. I think we all feel the end's in the air. The city medical officer that comes every morning to inspect these dumps says the way the boys keep them is a big credit to the organization. I wish you could of seen them when we first moved in. They are not much better now but at least the bugs has stopped running up the walls. I should of taken you up-stairs when you were over, you would not of believed the upstairs unless you had seen it.

"If you write back, address c/o Red Carson's Service Stn. corner of Grant and Dudley as after Saturday we shall not be here. Maybe at that you will have to address c/o the City Jail if I get picked up this morning. I am on the eleven o'clock trick, the first boys go out at nine.

"Keep your chin up honey, you got a dandy chin to keep up as well as everything else. Don't forget the change of address.

Love,

MATT."

He mailed the letter Friday morning before going on the eleven o'clock can-shaking trick on the corner of Conklin and Shard. It was a good spot where two main streets branched and he could watch the boys on three other corners. By the time the eleven o'clock shift came to go on, forty-five of the boys had been picked up and their cans confiscated and forty-five more had snapped right in and taken their places. The heaviest pick-up of the day was five at one time around nine-thirty in the morning before any-one was out on the streets. There was no disorder and all arrests were made by experienced cops, disappointing some of the boys who hoped to make fools of the green men the same way they did over in Aschelon. Hotels and department stores closed off their main doors and sprinklers worked overtime on the clipped lawns outside all official buildings. By mid-morning news had come out that the men intended to stand by their agreement to vacate the ex-brothels at noon, Saturday, according to schedule. There was a wind blowing this morning, a hot, smoky wind and the approaching change in the weather grew more pronounced. The thought of rain made the citizens more nervous, that is, if anything could have made them more nervous.

Matt was waiting around outside the Quanta at ten forty-five with Gabby and Charlie and some of the Quanta boys when a man hared down the alley that led through from the Orsino and shouted to them to come up and get their cans. He shoved his fingers into his mouth and whistled. All along the sidewalk men began to rise, loose, hunched forms tightened into a moving unit.

Gabby turned and called back to a man inside the office, "So long, Stan. Betcha dime I eat dinner on the city."

"Oh, yeah," Charlie said, overhearing, "where are you goin' to get the dime?"

Gabby smacked Charlie between the shoulders. "Whatsamatter, what-samatter, Slappy? What are you scared of?"

Charlie's eyes wavered and he grew red. "I'm not scared of a thing, I just don't want to get jugged, that's all. I stayed out this long an' I don't want to get shoved in for collecting nickels on the street."

Gabby let out a hoot of brash delight. "You got all the wrong idea, Slappy. He's got the wrong idea, hasn't he, Matt? This jug here has an old English atmosphere we shouldn't miss."

Matt eyed Gabby with a wise smile. "You ever been jugged before, Gabby?"

"Who? Me? Not yet, but am I goin' to raise hell when I get there!"

Matt's eyelids drooped, "Yeah, I'll bet," he said. He ran ahead to catch up with Charlie.

When Charlie heard the slap-slap of Matt's feet he turned quickly. His face was twitching and colour still burned in his sallow cheeks. "Commere," he said, catching Matt by the arm, "I want to talk to you." His manner was nervous and mixed with the twitching round his eyes there was a strange rigidity about his cheeks and jawline.

"What's the matter?" Matt asked, eyeing him curiously. "Are you sick or something?"

"Listen, Matt ..." Charlie stopped.

"Go ahead, I'm listening."

Charlie stole a look at him then dropped his eyes. He gulped, hesitated, then began to speak very fast. "My old man's had a lot of bad luck, Matt. I told you about him, coming over on the boat from Cutlake that day, remember?"

"Yeah, I remember."

"Well, this may sound kind of dumb to you but I just don't want him to get stuck with any more on account of me. If I get jugged an' he hears of it, it'll just about break him up. See what I mean?"

Matt pondered the question briefly. "Hell, that's nothing to be scared of," he said, "just don't give your right name. I'll bet that's what half the boys in this outfit has had to do one time or another. I had a half dozen aliases myself, I'll bet I can't even remember the name I started with."

"Yeah, I guess I could do that ..."

Matt looked at Charlie more closely, then his manner changed. "Hey, Slappy," he said gently, "your old man isn't the real reason. What's the real reason you don't want to get canned?"

Charlie kicked at the sidewalk. Suddenly he looked up and his eyes were panicky. He choked, "If you wanta know, Matt, I'm scared. Makes me go all sick here," he pressed his diaphragm, "I guess I just can't take it. I'm not like Gabby an' the rest of the boys, I got no guts, that's all."

A man running into the alley shouted to Matt to get a move on. "Okay," Matt called out, "I'm comin'." His mind worked fast. "Listen," he told Charlie, "you go back down to the Angel and find Eddy an' see he don't get in any kind of trouble while I'm gone. I'll make it okay and ask them to send out another of the boys to take your place."

Charlie's face cleared gratefully. Half crying he began to pour out his thanks. Matt cut him short, "Hell, that's nothing. You beat it down to the Angel an' keep Eddy out of trouble. If that isn't a full-time job then I don't know what is." He watched Charlie move quickly down the street. His face was perplexed. "Can you beat it?" he exclaimed softly. "That's something I never saw happen before."

He turned round and hared off up the alley that led through to the side entrance of the Orsino. As he climbed the stairs he looked about curiously to see how it compared with the Quanta and the Angel, he was never in this place before.

The main entrance on Flower Street looked out on abandoned lower premises, a second-hand clothes dealer and the Sun Ray Mission Undenominational All Faiths Welcome. The mission had passed right out all but the faded lettering and the dark paint drearily obscuring the lower half of the window. Matt saw these details at a glance as he turned in the door. The side door was the same as the front entrance, that is, both bore the same rusted padlock scars. Generally speaking it looked like the maggots had foreclosed on the building fifty years too late.

Matt took his place in the line-up on the stairs as the men moved slowly up to the room on the second floor where the cans were given out and the squads dispatched. He heard the dispatcher calling out names. One by one the boys ahead took their turn, receiving cans and the blue chest bands lettered JOBS NOT JAIL, the same as they wore in Aschelon. The whole atmosphere hummed with organization and once a man had a job assigned he lost his slack, directionless air and moved out with snap and decision. There was a checkers' table where the early shift turned in their cans and another table where a man was pasting labels on fresh cans. Men hurried in and out, their feet rumbling on the wooden stairs. The place inside was the same as the Angel. The walls and the ceiling looked like they had broken out into body sores.

He moved over to the window till his name was called, trying to pick up a breath of fresh air. The smell of the place was terrible—old male sweat and fumes that rose from the well that ran down the side of the building and closed off air and daylight. The men's feet smelt and their stale clothes and a lot of them sat around in shirtsleeves with damp yellow sweat patches under their arms.

Hughes was up there, too, moling around till his name was shouted, picking up detail he would need later when it would not be there. Kenny was conscientious. He wanted to record the stink as fact. But he was also sensitive, more sensitive than the majority of men round him, so while they came right out and called these places dirty dumps and then forgot them, Kenny worried over them in detail, looking for some angle of approach that would really handle the subject. If he had ripped right into them and the book had ever been published, these dumps might have made Hughes famous.

Whenever he saw Matt he came over. He was still trying to study Matt, to penetrate him as a type, and Matt was always avoiding him because Hughes made him feel uncomfortable. He spoke to him now because, hell! Kenny was always so decent about lending stuff. Matt guessed it must be something in himself and not in Hughes at all that made Kenny so hard to take.

"'lo, Kenny!" he said, "don't tell me you're goin' out on the streets rattlin' a can with a ribbon pinned across your chest." He stood with his back to the window, hands thrust down into his jeans, eyes moving restlessly about the room.

Hughes considered him handsome in a rugged, unfinished sort of a way. He can take it, Hughes thought, how I envy anyone like him that can take it. "I want the experience," he said with that touch of wistfulness that prevented his ever really being popular.

"Scared?"

"What of?"

"Maybe they'll pick you up an' shove you in the jug."

"Oh, but I need the experience there, too."

Matt started to laugh then he stopped and looked at Hughes. "God, Kenny," he said, "I believe you got guts after all."

Hughes blushed with pleasure. "Oh, no," he said earnestly, "I have no guts at all, practically anything scares me."

Matt put a hand on his shoulder. "Just the same, Kenny, I think you got guts an' lots of 'em. Goin' to college don't scare you at all."

For a moment Hughes hesitated. Then, "It would if it wasn't for the book, Matt."

"Kind of a litery martyr."

Hughes smiled quickly, "I hope so," he said.

Matt heard his own name called. He shouldered through the crowd and up to the table to get his can and then on to the table where the chest bands were handed out. He took the band, turned it right way up and smiled, "First time I ever wore one of these things," he said to the boy distributing.

The boy glanced at him, "Is that so? Weren't you over in Aschelon?"

"Sure I was but they didn't give me a decoration. Guess I was too new to the business." The boy's eyes moved past him. He took up another band. "Okay, brother," he said, "there's a line-up waiting behind you."

As Matt hurried downstairs he heard Hughes' name called and Gabby's. Hep was waiting below. He fell the squad in and they marched uptown, dividing at their beats. Matt was one of the first to drop out. Gabby turned and shouted after him, "Be seein' you in college!"

Matt waved at him, "Sure, Gabby, be seein' you !" He smiled at Hughes. "S'long, Kenny, don't let the cops get rough with you!" Three other boys dropped off at the same place and took up their stand, one on each corner of the intersection.

They did not solicit, they stood there rattling their cans. All over town there was this sound of rattling cans. After a time it had an eerie effect, like skeletons rattling round. The result made the total take heavy. Subconsciously everyone that dropped in a dime felt they had laid their part in the skeleton flat that way. The hard, dry sound of the coins struck on the ear as something personal and haunting. The people that dropped in money fooled themselves that they did not hear the rattling so sharply once they paid their dues.

The town was filled with tourist cars and the boys attracted plenty of attention, more than they could hope to have done at any other time of year. The blue chest bands fluttering in the bright sun and hot, gusty wind were an effective touch. One of those details of shrewd showmanship heightening the whole effect, that and the hollow rattling of the cans. It brought to Matt's mind something he had once heard Hep say about the art of dramatizing trouble. The look in the eyes of the tourists was different to the look in the eyes of the natives. The visiting eyes were curious, friendly, amazed or skeptical according as this bizarre foreign spectacle affected them. Above all they were unhaunted or nearly so.

Matt had some funny things happen to him. One big, expensively-dressed woman with stag legs and an overweight torso stopped and after feeling around in her bag as though she were chasing a fifty dollar bill dredged up a nickel. She gushed, "Do tell me because I'm so, *so* interested, what do you do with your spare time?"

Matt just looked at her. "Madam," he said, "all my time is spare."

The she-alligator reacted as though she had been stung in the fanny by a bee. She ankled off down the street hell-for-leather, her tail and the tail of her silver fox neckpiece swaying in unison.

The most of the people that dropped their dimes in the kitty were decent and friendly and scared. Practically everyone asked the same question. Where were the boys going after they vacated the dives next day? Matt told them he did not know, which was true. That answer only made them more uneasy and sent them off muttering. After a time he began to pick up the same look in all the eyes. The thing they were scared of was wordless but the fear was there just the same. It was a mixture, very obscure, of conscience and evaded responsibility over a long period, together with consternation that this jobless scourge had come right out on their own streets after having rattled round vaguely in the political cupboard for the past eight years.

The one fear that was not vague, was the terror of personal violence or damage to property if the dam of discipline among the men ever broke suddenly. Matt saw that fear without any equivocation at all in every pair of eyes he looked into. Damn right he saw it. After a time it began to make him mad. He thought, What th' hell kind of sonsovbitches do they think we are!

Hep came by shortly after twelve, checking on the squad. When Matt saw him he patted his pocket. He said after he collected half a dollar or so he emptied the money out so the can would go on sounding hollow. Hep grinned and said, "I see you've been out collectin' before."

Matt said, "I've been out doin' everything before."

"What the hell, you old snapping turtle," Hep laughed, "what's got you sore, now?"

"I'm not sore," Matt said, "I just get tired of bein' goofed at like I was some kind of a wild beast." He pointed to the boys on the opposite corners. "Why didn't they bring the wagon around this way yet?"

"Guess they didn't want any trouble in the business section," Hep said. "Oh say, Matt," he added, "Dick got picked up on the nine o'clock trick an' Gabby got his an hour ago. I heard they picked up round fourteen other boys on the late shift."

"Maybe that's why they slowed up now," Matt said, "they got no more place to put us. Wonder how Gabby makes out, he was all set to tear up the jug."

"Not the last time I saw him," Hep said.

A duck-faced little man in eye-glasses fussed by and dropped in a quarter. His eyes moved uneasily from man to man and he hesitated as though he would have liked to say something. Then he changed his mind and went on quickly. Matt gazed after his neat trotting back. "I tell you, Hep, this whole town's jittery as hell."

"You're tellin' me! I could have told you that a week ago. Don't think they're the only ones. If Laban or someone doesn't pull some kind of a settlement out of this within the next twenty-four hours, we can't guarantee anything." Hep started to go away, then he turned and came back, "By the way, what happened to Charlie?"

"He felt sick, sick at his stomach."

"Did he go back inside an' get it taken care of?"

"He wasn't that sick. I sent him back down to take care of Eddy."

"The hell you did! Whose orders?"

"My orders," Matt said, "he wasn't sick at all, he was just plain scared of goin' to the jug. I never saw a case like that before. I promised I'd make it okay with you an' I forgot."

Hep pondered the oddity. "Funny," he mused, "I heard of that but I never actually saw it happen before, not on any little two-for-a-nickel charge like obstruction. Thanks, Matt, I'll see Charlie when I go down there."

Matt watched him leg across the road with his long, half-loping stride. He stayed a moment talking to each of the boys on the other corners. An old woman came up and stopped. She rummaged around in a shabby brown bag and brought out a dime. Her hand in its black cotton glove shook a little. She murmured in delicate apology, "T'isnt much, son, but it'll maybe buy one of you boys a packet of cigarettes."

Matt smiled at her. "Thanks, ma'am," he said.

She raised her hand in a quick gesture of denial. "Don't thank me," she said. "Seeing you boys standing around idle is a disgrace on all of us. It's us should thank you for conducting yourselves like gentlemen." She bobbed by, clutching the bag to her body, anxiously peering out for traffic as, half-running, she started to cross the street.

At exactly twelve forty-five he had an odd thing happen to him. He knew the time because he had begun to be hungry and watch the clock. The clock was the Neon-faced one where Conklin turns into Dudley outside the cigar store. A man came towards him along the sidewalk and whenever Matt saw him he hoped he would stop. He was a man around fifty, tall, spare, with squared-off military shoulders and a clipped moustache. He had authority and he didn't need band wagon tactics to advertise it. His presence gave off an impression of discipline and integration, of having got himself under so that he knew where he was going.

Matt watched him come up close, fascinated. Jesus, he thought, I'll bet there's a dandy boss to work for! The man stopped, eyed the band across his chest then said with a dry smile, "'JOBS NOT JAIL.' Curious alternative! Almost as curious as Butter or Guns." His eyes came up, measured Matt dispassionately then he moved on without dropping anything in the box.

Matt looked after the powerful, squared-off shoulders with a quick sense of disappointment. Maybe the man had a prejudice or something and never gave to canvassers. Just the same he would have liked to have had the chance to talk to a man like that, really talk to him. He would have liked to go after him, touch him on the shoulder, make some excuse to speak to him. It was a crazy notion and he let it go at once. But he thought about the man for a long time after. It was the first time he had ever seen a man of that class to admire and with a wish to serve. It was a screwy notion, echo of some old slave complex. The man had probably been born to easy money, a good education and a soft job. Nuts! Matt thought, jerking himself up, the guy never even troubled to put his hand in his pocket and pull out a nickel!

But something about the brief contact left him unsettled and he finished his last ten minutes with thoughts thrashing around in his mind like whale fish. What Hep just said, Saul and the squirrel cage, snatches of Laban's speech on the Aschelon Ball grounds, Hazel, Harry, the kids that broke out at Andersville, Tom's old man, Eddy ... He stopped at Eddy. Eddy was tied in with everything that happened since that first Sunday. Eddy was the one thread running clear through. First thing he did when his time was up was to go down to the Angel and find out how Charlie made out.

He met the division from the Angel marching up to the Quanta for dinner. He fell in beside Charlie. "Did Eddy give you any trouble?"

Charlie met his eyes with a touch of embarrassment. "Hell, no," he said, "he just kept movin' around all mornin' like a bear on a chain. Every now and then he'd stop an' say 'Maybe he's got picked up, Slappy', and I'd say, 'Don't worry, Eddy, they won't pick him up', Then he'd walk around some more and stop suddenly and begin all over again, 'Maybe he's got picked up now, Slappy. Why don't we go out and see?' He was so scared about you he couldn't rest."

For a moment Matt did not answer, then he said softly, to himself, not to Charlie, "Funny thing about Eddy, I never seem to have done anything for him but roast the ass off him. I never gave anyone hell like I gave Eddy."

Charlie went on eagerly, anxious to show himself an able guardian, "Every now and then he'd start talkin' about his feet, how they was givin' him gyp all the time and he never had a good pair of shoes yet. Honest, Matt, I think that Eddy's crazy."

Matt answered slowly, "I don't know, Slappy, I wish I did ..." He raised his head abruptly, "Talked about his feet, did he?"

"Talked about 'em on an' off all the time."

"You ever seen Eddy's feet?"

"Not to notice 'em. Why?"

"Nothing," Matt said frowning. He was silent a moment. "All I was wondering was how badly Eddy wanted those shoes. Once back in Aschelon he wanted a coupla chocolate bars so he tossed an empty gas bomb through a plate glass window to get 'em."

Charlie turned. His eyes bulged. "No kiddin'?"

"No kiddin'."

Charlie touched his forehead with a knowing grin. "Crazy," he remarked, "just soft up here."

Something in Charlie's complacency touched Matt to rage. He cried, "Holy Goddam! How'd you like it if you got smacked in the face by a billy?"

Charlie gaped. "Was that what happened to Eddy?"

"I thought everyone in the world knew about it by this time. Sure, that's what happened to Eddy!"

CHAPTER TWENTY

At a meeting held that same evening, the day's take was announced, twelve hundred three dollars, sixty-four cents. Even if a good part was a nervous city's tribute money, the amount was good and proved a certain solidarity among the sympathizers. After the meeting the squads fell in outside the Quanta and marched back to quarters. Discipline was screwed down tight tonight and no passes issued for leave or the movies. Hep did not come up to the Angel until later in the evening. He stayed down to talk at a meeting of squad leaders. Since sundown the wind had risen. Dust and waste paper swirled on the street corners, the sky raced with drifting rack. The acrid smell of burning brush grew stronger with the heightened wind.

Back at the Angel Matt sat in on a game of rummy for half an hour, then he got up and gave his seat to another of the boys. It was odd without Gabby and Dick around. When they were there they scrapped together all the time, nothing mean, just good-natured cat-'n-dog stuff, but now they were not here he missed them. He missed Gabby's swagger and the way Dick's belly-aching could make him mad. He heard the same thing on all sides. Wherever a boy had been picked up and jugged he left a gap in his gang or some other boy minus a buddy. That was how it always went after weeks of living together, eating, sleeping, scrapping, toeing the same mark.

Finally a man lent him a copy of *We the Workers*, a labour weekly published over in Aschelon. "An' brother if you don't quit stalkin' around like a blinkin' tiger," he warned, "it's goin' to be just too bad for you. We got enough spooks up here tonight. Take it an' read it an' fer Chrissake keep still!"

Matt gave the man an ashamed grin, "I'm sorry," he apologised, "I didn't notice I was movin' around so." He took the paper and sat on an up-ended fruit crate in Hep's room by the window to read up on the printed end of the general situation as seen by the editor and the rest of the *Worker* boys. For the past two months the paper had been running scare headlines on the sit-down, keeping every angle pumped full of gas. Matt started out to read the paper right through, sports and everything, but he began to lose interest after page one because the stuff stopped convincing him. The gist of it was to paste the opposition as a bunch of sadists and yellow-bellies and the after-effect was as impressive as pre-election speeches. Or maybe the atmosphere was not right to appreciate good reading. He laid the paper aside and legged out over the low sill to get a breath of fresh air.

He walked to the edge and peered down. Below him the ground dropped to a pit of darkness. Across the gulch a few grisly lights picked out the sprawling backs of the tenement houses. Somewhere down there among the shadows a pair of cats lusted raucously. God, he thought, it's ugly! It brought back kid-nights in Clever when he and the gang used to shin out the back windows. Gang of alley rats they'd been, gang of goddam alley rats. Just the same he had stayed clear of cops and the detention home. He had stayed clear of trouble the other way, too, because he learned early how to take care of himself. A guy had to learn that before he was out of short pants. He used to listen to kids tell how they flopped girls behind billboards and down by the sheds in the yards but he had appraised them coldly as phonies; show-offs eager to impress. The first time he ever laid a girl it had not come up to expectations but he guessed that was always the way. A guy heard it talked about so, he got to expecting too much.

Deeper flashes out of the past came back to him. His father's face the night his mother went away, the eyes that watched silently, fearfully, greedily from the doorways down the hall, the dank chill of the unheated building, the final slamming of the outer door. His father he remembered more vividly than his mother because he had lived with his father longer. He was a man with nervous, burning eyes, fighting bitterly an injustice too vague and terrible to defeat. His mother's eyes were different; slow and cold and without colour, like rock.

He thought of Hazel, too, and of the letter he wrote her, wondered whether he had made things seem too pointless and drifting. Maybe something would shape up out of this mess yet. Tomorrow would come the real showdown. These past three weeks felt like a hundred years. He remembered suddenly that tomorrow was his twenty-third birthday.

He stayed outside chain-smoking and presently the buzz of talk from inside grew loud. A half-dozen of the boys had drifted into Hep's room. In their midst stood a red-headed, dour-faced Scot, McVey, that came over with the last division. He had blue and red tatoo markings, a ship on his chest and a dancer and a pair of hearts on the inside of his right arm. His chest and forearms had a coarse growth of red hair, lighter than the rest.

"Here's what I say," he was proclaiming in his sour Low-land tones, "we came over to Gath to sit till we got a works program. So far we never got one. Okay then, let's go on sitting. If they want these dumps tomorrow let them come and turn us out!"

A voice, "Like they done in Aschelon? No, sir, no more gas for me!" There was a quick murmur of assent.

McVey smiled dourly. "Don't worry, they won't try anything like that over here. They don't want us puking in the gutters of Gath."

Kinky headed in through the group round the door. "Want to bet on that?"

"Sure, I'll bet on it. They had trouble enough in Aschelon. Don't think us boys was the only ones to take a bad smell!" There was a short burst of laughter that died self-consciously away.

Kinky pushed his hands in his pants pockets, rocked back on his heels eyeing his audience cockily. In his fast, machine-gun style he demanded, "Whatsmatter round here these days? Why are we sittin' on our asses like a bunch of sick old women? Why don't we go out an' take what belongs to us?"

There was a tense pause then a half dozen voices rushed in.

"Yeah, that's what I say!"

"Don't we have to end up in th' jug whatever we do?"

"Sure we do! What say we march out of here tomorrow an' dictate our own terms?"

"Oh yeah? Dictate terms to the army an' the navy an' the merchant marine!" The chorus of voices boiled excitedly.

McVey quieted it with a gesture. "Save that idea for the committee o' the League o' Nations."

"Sure, why not?" Kinky jeered, "one more committee's not goin' to be noticed. 'Take it to the committee, take it to the committee', that's all we hear around here. We can't push a spoon in our mouths without the okay of some goddam committee."

There was a commotion round the door. The short, gristled figure of Pop steamed in dressed only in pants and a pair of burst canvas shoes. His shrunken torso pumped against his bare ribs, his eyes snapped belligerently. "What you young squirts want to do?" he cried, "run a menagerie? Maybe you don't know there's people tryin' to sleep upstairs."

"Sleep?" McVey said, "who's gettin' any sleep around here tonight?"

"Maybe you're not but there's a kid with a abscessed tooth upstairs tryin' to hold on to himself an' all this racket don't help him. I just came down from givin' him my pillow."

A boy grinned, sheepishly. "Okay, Pop, don't let it get you all steamed up. We didn't know about the kid but we know now."

The veteran glared at him. He pronounced darkly, "You don't know nuthin' but what you read in the noospapers, an' you don't read the noospapers. You kids make a good man sick. Wait till you live in one of them totalizer countries where they tap your telephone wires."

Kinky laughed. He eyed the little man with contempt. "They can go right ahead an' tap mine."

The veteran spun round excitedly. "There you go! There you go!" he cried. "Don't you young squirts never appreciate anything? You go around kickin' hell out of the committees because they're tryin' to help you. What was the most of you anyway but a bunch of jungle rats, gettin' smacked off freight cars an' sleepin' in ditches? I got no patience with you kids nowadays ... maybe you didn't come near to gettin' your guts blown out in a real war."

The boy shouted angrily, "Who are you callin' a jungle rat?"

McVey interposed, "That's enough, cut out the fighting."

"Why should I? We had this war shoved down our throats like it was the only thing that ever happened."

"So it was ... the only thing that ever happened to a lot of men."

"He called me a rat!"

The little man steamed back into the argument fiercely, "So you are, a no-good jungle rat. It's cocky young squirts like you start all the trouble around here." He beat on his chest, his voice filled with pride and mixed with the pride there was a burning scorn. "Think you're pretty goddam tough, don't you, Squirt? Tellin' all the rest of the boys what to do, gettin' fightin' mad on a mouthful of hot air! Trouble with you is you can't take it. Look at me, six wars an' ten years on relief an' I can still tell you where to get off." He stepped up closer, "Who th' hell are you anyway? I don't seem to remember your face. For all I know you may be a pigeon ..."

Kinky stepped in without warning and took a vicious poke that failed to connect. All around the room men fell back instinctively, clearing a space. Bodies tensed with surprise. More faces appeared at the door and those in front were shoved forward from behind. For a moment they milled in a confused wave.

The veteran skipped aside. His dukes came up. He stood there dancing jerkily, calling for Kinky to come in and take it. Matt legged in over the sill and dragged the window down behind to keep the noise off the street. He shouted delightedly, "Go in an' take him, Pop!"

Kinky turned angrily. "What is this? A cock fight?"

The dried-up, prancing figure ducked in and ducked away. "You come in an' see whether it's a cock fight or not."

Kinky hesitated, eyes narrowing. All about him men watched with half-nervous grins. "Okay then," he said loudly. "You asked for it!" He got set to haul off when the vet lowered his head suddenly and charged like a goat. A shout of laughter went up, not nervous now but loud with enjoyment. From all sides came cries of, "Stay with it, Pop!" "Let 'um have it!"

The boy's sallow face grew pink with anger. He stepped in fighting and from the onlookers came a sharp, dry gasp as they realized that this thing had ceased to be comedy. The vet dodged aside and for a moment his thin chest seemed to swell with rage. He charged unsteadily, landing a light blow to the side of the head. Then he ducked back and began to weave jerkily and the men by the door pressed back to give him room.

After that the boy stopped fooling. He came in and smashed, rocking the vet back into the arms of the crowd. Blood spurted from his nose, spattering his bare chest. McVey stepped in to stop the fight. He grabbed the boy and as he did so the vet charged, game as an angry bantam and caught Kinky a beauty on the left cheek that raised a shiner next day. The boy tore loose and the two men went down in a clinch, hammering one another wildly. The boy had age and weight but the vet was tough and he had once been fast and he used to be fair in the army. They rolled together like apes and as the men at the door gave ground and fell apart Matt stepped out and booted Kinky in the tail. The men were laughing like children now, yelling at the vet to stay with it. He was snuffling blood and swallowing it and choking it up. The shape of his face had changed oddly, the front part had caved right in. His jaws worked shakily as though they were chewing on a mouthful of marbles.

They rolled out into the passage, clawing and pounding. The top of Kinky's head came against the door of the toilet, forcing it open. He struggled to get free and climb back on his feet. The vet still came at him, bloody and game, his chest spattered with blood, blood on his pants. He took one wild, jerky poke at the boy's face, caught him off balance, and sent him crashing back over the toilet bowl.

There was a wild yell of glee. The crowd pressed forward, craning, shoving from behind. McVey broke them apart. He grabbed the two men, one in each hand and dragged them back on their feet. "Okay," he said without the slightest change of expression, "that's enough now."

The boy's eyes gleamed angrily. He shouted, "Goddam you, you little rat!" He leant forward and drove a savage poke across McVey's body and the vet crumpled suddenly like paper. A gasp of horror came from the onlookers. For an instant McVey eyed the boy, a gleam of pleasure coming over his dour features. "Ye would, would ye?" he murmured, then his huge fist smashed out and the boy went down. McVey turned abruptly. "Take him away!" The men hesitated. They stared fascinated at the boy's bloody head. "Take him away!" McVey shouted, "Godsteeth, is there no one around here understands King's English?"

Two men came forward silently and lifted the boy away. As they went through the door others craned forward and watched without speaking. The excitement had cooled from the faces now, leaving them tense and uneasy. For a moment longer they hung there uncertainly. Then, by ones and twos they began to melt off down the passage and back to their own rooms.

Matt and another of the boys were working over the vet trying to pull the bridgework back out of his throat. They worked over him till two of the Red Cross boys came and took him away. He let himself be helped without protest. He was limping and he could not straighten up. He kept pointing to his mouth and clucking. Then as the boys helped him to his feet he turned back to Matt, hissing fiercely, "Shunovabish smashed my p'ate ..."

"God, that's tough," Matt said. The vet held up the pieces in his hand. He was almost crying. "Damn shunovabish," he whispered, "wai'll I ge' i' fixhed!"

"There goes one little game guy," Matt said, looking after him with a smile. "Maybe he rides that warhorse of his too much, but he sure is game."

McVey put his arm up, wiped his hot face and caught sight of the closed window. "Who in hell shut the window?" He dragged it full up. Then he spat casually on his blood-splashed hand and wiped it across the seat of his pants. He said briefly, "Better clean up this room before Hep gets back."

"You're telling me," Matt said. He and the boy that helped with the vet worked over the room for a half an hour cleaning the mess off the floor. After that he went across to his own room and started taking his clothes off. Charlie was there already and two boys from upstairs. Eddy was bedded down in his corner on a mattress made up of newspapers. When Matt came in Charlie asked what time it was.

Matt said, "A man out there told me it was just past midnight."

Charlie's face went worried, "I wonder," he said, "should we take our clothes off?"

"What d'you mean?" Matt said, stepping out of his pants. "Nothing more's goin' to happen around here, tonight."

"Oh no," one of the boys said, "that's what you think. You wasn't there the last time."

Matt looked from one to the other. "Whatever it is," he said, "I don't get it."

The second boy's face took on a look of importance, "Eviction rumours," he said, "they've been flyin' around all evening."

Matt burst out laughing. "Let 'em fly. Hell, they aren't goin' to evict us, we aren't trespassing. You heard what Mac said in there." He hung his pants on a nail. "The way some of you kids talk you're like a bunch of overweight veterans gettin' together over the last war. You go about wearin' that Aschelon business around your necks like it was a medal or something."

"Oh yeah," first boy said huffily, "I don't like critics that never was in a fight tellin' how the fight went."

"Maybe you'd talk better if you'd been on the spot," his buddy added with a superior smile.

Matt looked them over a moment in silence, then he sailed into them like a grandfather. "Listen, you two," he said, "you didn't get your heads beaten off in Aschelon or any place else," he touched his nose. "Fights," he said, "what do either of you know about fights? I was in fights before ever you stopped wettin' your diapers." They shut up after that and went off. They could not argue away his scarred face.

Presently Hughes came in very quietly, carrying his shoes. He whispered to Matt that he had been trying to talk to Kinky and the old man about the scrap while their impressions were still fresh. He said he hadn't had much success. Kinky was just beginning to come around and though the vet would have been proud as hell to have talked, his bridgework had got too broken up. Kenny said it was too bad about his bridgework and he thought in the morning they ought to take up some kind of a collection among the boys. He sat there rattling on, talking because he could not sleep and finally Matt left him to it. Matt was so tired he turned over, dragged up his blanket and slept like a dog.

He had a dream and in this dream he was fighting a war as part of an infantry division, harried by its own artillery. He could hear the thud of the horses' hooves and the heavy artillery rolling up. There was shouting as well. The whole war was a mess. He was tired and wanted to sleep and the war would not let him. The noise of the fighting went on and went on, and grew louder.

Suddenly he woke and sat up. Hughes was sitting up, too, knuckling sweat out of his eyes. Matt watched him fumbling for his glasses and he thought how funny Hughes looked, sitting up there with nothing on but his glasses. He thought he should always remember how Kenny looked at that moment. Charlie was heaving around sleepily. It had just begun to dawn on him that something somewhere was wrong.

There was a row going on overhead, scraps of plaster falling. Matt got up and turned on the lights. Men were dragging themselves sleepily outside to find what the row was about. A few still had their clothes on, others were hurriedly buttoning themselves into their pants.

A noise of scuffling came from overhead. The men herded together nervously, gazing up the narrow well of the stairs. Suddenly a door burst open and a man's body came flying out.

A gasp came from the watchers below. Matt felt sweat come out on his hands and tickle in his armpits. The man above grabbed for the stair-head. He came stumbling down the first flight. The look on his face was blind and frozen, his lips were drawn back stiffly, his eyes wide with terror. Two other men shot from the room behind, trying to grab him.

Matt saw him dive for the second stair-head. For an instant the plunging figure seemed to hesitate, hung teetering wildly, then crashed down, thumping from tread to tread. Half-way down it disappeared from view.

Matt heard the body slithering and bumping, then the final thud. Men ran to the rail and peered over. Somewhere up on the third floor a man started to laugh hysterically. Matt did not wait to see what went on after that. He heard the man being brought up later, the clumsy, halting steps of the bearers. He went back inside the room. He knew if he stayed out there in the passage he would be the next to laugh.

Eddy was still sleeping. Charlie crawled back into his blanket looking sick and not saying anything. A moment after Hughes came in, his teeth clacking. Matt grabbed hold of him and shook him. "Aw shut up," he hissed, "stop those damn teeth of yours. D'you want to wake Eddy an' stir up one more hornet's nest?"

Hughes peered at him strangely. Matt looked away. "What'sthe matter?" he asked harshly.

"You're scared," Hughes whispered, staring. "I never saw you look that way before. I believe you're scared, Matt."

Matt laughed derisively, "Me scared? What has anyone got to be scared of around here?" He turned and went back to bed, "Only of goin' nuts," he muttered, "that's all anyone has to be scared of around here."

Hep's head appeared in the doorway. He looked around the room then he came right in. "Okay, boys," he said in his soft unexcited voice, "you can go right back to sleep now, everything's under control."

"What happened?" Matt asked, forcing himself to sound easy.

Hep got down on his haunches and the three men drew closer. "This guy upstairs," he explained softly, "is a very nervous guy an' subject to dreams. Earlier in the evening a bunch of the young kids got razzin' him, told him the cops was comin' to pull an eviction round five o'clock an' it must of got preying on his mind. So he has this crazy dream about it all happening like that an' wakes suddenly an' doesn't know where he's at." Hep stopped. For a moment no one spoke.

"What happened when he fell?" Hughes asked nervously. "It sounded from up here as though he broke every bone in his body."

"It sounded that way but his weight falling up against the stairs made it sound a lot worse than it was. He didn't break anything. A couple of the boys is working on him now," Hep said, "he'll be okay by morning." He stood up. "Lay down and get some sleep, you can't tell where you'll be tomorrow." He nodded and went out. They heard him stop in at every room. Gradually the first excited noise of talk died down, and the house settled back to familiar night sounds, snores, coughs, the crackle of newspapers, mutter of sleep-talkers, the occasional smack of bare feet as some man hurried down the passage to the can. Hughes tucked his coat under his head and lay down. A moment later his head half rose. "Did it ever occur to you, Matt, that there was something cold-blooded about Hep?"

Matt stretched his tired body out flat, feeling the temporary sense of let-up that came from contact with the hard floor. He did not even bother to answer Hughes the first time. When the question came again he muttered briefly, "What th' hell? Hep's bigger than the rest of us, that's all."

Hughes lay there on his back staring up at the ceiling. "I don't quite know how to explain it," Hughes whispered after a pause, "but I think cold-blooded is the word. Hep's an interesting study." He sighed with a touch of wistfulness. Hep was another one he wanted for the book.

Matt heaved around on his side. Through the darkness his eyes gleamed and his lips drew back in a snarl. "Listen, you," he hissed, "if you wake Eddy now I'll rip you apart!" Hughes jerked round in surprise. He took one look at Matt's face and shut up. Soon Matt heard his regular breathing as it blended with Charlie's snores and Eddy's adenoidal snufflings.

Suddenly the rhythm broke. Eddy reared up. He stared ahead with sleep-blind eyes. His lips moved, muttering thickly, "Shoes … he promise … shoes …"

"Oh God," Matt breathed wearily, "do we have to go into all that again?" He laid Eddy gently back with the flat of his hand. The heavy body did not resist. It slid down, rolled over on its side and the rhythm of breathing re-established at once. Eddy had not wakened at all.

Matt did not lie down again. He sat up there staring at the dirty wall. Through the shadows the old dark stain showed where some liquid must have been thrown years before. He tried to connect some kind of pattern among the dim, discoloured scrolls. Suddenly he knew he wanted a drag, then remembered that he could not smoke in a room with no windows and three men sleeping. Then he thought maybe he would borrow Charlie's flash and write a letter to Harry but he did not have any equipment and Hughes was asleep. He looked at Hughes sleeping and he thought, Kenny's a damn sight tougher than he thinks he is. Finally he stepped into his pants, took down his coat and shoes and crept out of the room and downstairs. He told the two boys on duty that he had to have a smoke and they let him stay. He went outside on the street in front of the door and smoked a cigarette.

There was no light except the one wavering drearily on the corner of the block. From out at sea came the sound of wind drumming. He watched a policeman walk slowly by on the opposite side of the street, trying padlocks. Presently the dawn began to show, wasted and windy, a wet sky swimming with cloud. He stayed where the boys picketing the door could keep him in sight. Now and then he talked to them. When daylight came he went round to the back and took a cold shower and sloshed water over his head to take the stiffness out of his eyes.

Chapter Twenty-One

"Hey, Hep," Matt called out as Hep hurried past the room door shortly before eleven the same morning, "do we have to go all through town on the end of this thing?"

Hep called back without stopping, "Sure you do. Stop beefing and get it down on the street ... you and Eddy an' Charlie an' Kenny. When you get it set up, another couple of the boys'll give you a hand."

The four boys picked up the parts of the old brass bedstead and trooped clumsily down the steep dark stairs. "Does this make us look dopes!" Matt exclaimed in disgust. "Watch out, Eddy, you're trailin' that thing on my heels."

They moved awkwardly out onto the street and began assembling the antique on the sidewalk. Hoots of delight went up from the boys already out there and the remainder of the Angel boys as they clattered down behind, slinging their baggage. They crowded round laughing and joking and razzing the exasperated burden bearers. One of the boys fetched out socks and a pair of underdrawers and slung them between the posts of the bed on a length of twine. There were shouts of approval and a lot of further suggestions. As the division marched off one of the men looked back and waved at the noisesome old building. "Good-bye, you little love nest!"

and a voice further down the line shouted, "What happened to the love?"

Charlie nodded at the Angel, then at the piled-up junk on the opposite sidewalk. "We cleaned up these dumps," he said, "why don't they set us to clean up the town?"

"Maybe we'd clean it up too good," Matt said. From his doorway Morris "Junkie" Adler watched the division march away and turn up onto Lavender. His face did not have any expression at all.

The Orsino boys were swarming out from the alley, merging with the Quanta divisions outside headquarters. They were packing their stuff slung over their shoulders or under their arms, bedrolls, cartons, a few battered grips and a further sprinkling of antiques to add to the parade. One man carried an old-fashioned wooden-backed mirror, two others supported the ends of a broken-down plush couch. When they caught sight of the bedstead heading up the street they broke into yells of delight.

The bed-carriers set down their burden while the rest of the squads formed. "Where'd they get all this junk anyway?" Matt asked Hep, "what's the idea of makin' us pack it around?"

Hep grinned. A faint pleased malice gleamed in his eyes. "All I know is we got orders to make this parade look as ridic'lous as possible," he said.

"No foolin'?" The boys began to swarm round excitedly, firing questions.

"What's the big idea?"

"Where are we goin' anyway?"

"What are we supposed to be? A bunch of refugees from the Spanish war?"

Hep held up his hand. He said in that soft voice that somehow contained the maximum authority, "All you boys has to do is march when you're told to and keep right on campin' on the tail of the man in front." He went off to headquarters. The huddle remained, still gassing excitedly.

Eddy remained a little apart. His face wore a mixture of concentration and guilt. He glanced over towards Matt, pulled a torn scrap of newspaper from his pocket, gazed at it a moment, then thrust it quickly back. Now and then his hand strayed to his pocket but he did not pull the paper out again.

A shout sounded from up in front. The fooling stopped abruptly and the men fell in. Matt became aware of Eddy behind him. He glanced at him for a moment, unobserved, and his face grew uneasy.

"Eddy!"

Eddy's head came up. He started round guiltily. "I wasn't doin' nothin'," he said.

Matt eyed him with suspicion. "That's just your trouble, Eddy. You're the only guy I ever run into that could do nothin' an' still get himself in a jam. Snap out of it!" The men ahead began to move. Matt stooped and grasped his bed leg, "Here, Eddy, heave her up!" Eddy heaved obediently. Charlie and Kenny raised their end, and the lumbering object got under way. The boys fell in step, the socks and under-drawers began to flap in the wind and a delighted cheer arose from the small crowd gathered on the sidewalk.

A girl standing close by gave Matt the eye and he winked at her. He called back to Charlie, "Looks like we're goin' to steal the show after all."

Charlie shifted his grip. "I wish I knew how far we have to pack this thing," he complained.

A man in front grinned back over his shoulder. "Better go ask the strategy committee!"

As the columns marched through town rumours flew ahead of them. When the men passed by the big pile of official buildings, the lawn sprinklers started up suddenly, in a manner to suggest a state of jitters in the highest quarters. As the water went on the men broke into a gust of laughter. They left off singing to laugh.

The crowd got a certain human kick out of the parade, but the affair had bad political significance. It was bad for the city and thanks to shrewd timing and smart strategy, it held the authorities up to the maximum public ridicule.

At the main gate of Lennox Park the van of the army slowed and wheeled in. All down the line excited comments ran, "So this is where!" "Why didn't we think of it!" "Jese, will this place be cold at night!" As the last squads moved in the columns halted and broke, scattering among the trees. Squad leaders hurried about marking off stations, jockeying for best positions. The men followed, dumping their packs.

There was a small lagoon in the park with trees all around and under the trees and close by the water was number one position. Hep and two others marked out stations close by the water.

The six boys anchored the brass wreck under a tree and the man whose underwear had been flying at the masthead came over and claimed it hurriedly before it could be claimed for him. Matt borrowed Hughes' shaving kit and the old-fashioned, brown-backed mirror and set the mirror against a bush and shaved, wetting his brush in the lagoon. He combed his hair, returned Kenny's stuff and took an hour's sleep and after that he felt less as though he had been dragged up from the dead. He left Eddy washing out a pile of socks. Each pair he washed the owners paid him with a stick of gum. He hung over the lagoon grinding like a contented cow. A lot of the boys had taken off their sweaty socks and sat with their feet in the water.

A few passers-by wandered self-consciously about the park eyeing the strange encampment nervously. Motor-cycle police cruised up and down the walks and a few foot police were on duty but the presence of the police was not in any way marked. The boys stuck around their own stations, gassing, reading, tossing a softball. One boy had a uke. He sat under a tree strumming oldtime songs, while the little man in glasses that was gate picket in Cutlake sat next to him mulling over a chewed-up copy of Plutarch's *Lives*.

When Matt woke he wolfed around trying to pick up news. One man told him he just heard Laban had skipped town and the organization was getting shot to blazes. Another, an elderly, emaciated-looking man with stiff, frightened hair, said he heard the whole bunch was to be shipped off to the old military jug on Lotus Island.

"Nuts!" Matt said, "whoever started a kids' tale like that goin' around?"

The man answered in a stubborn whine, "I don't remember where I heard it first but a lot of the boys is sayin' it's true."

"Then a lot of the boys is nuts!"

The man gave him a distrustful look. "There's plenty of 'em believin' it jus' the same." He beetled off to spread the rumour some more.

Eddy came up, wiping his wet hands on the seat of his pants. "Matt!"

"What is it, Eddy?"

"Where we goin' to sleep tonight?"

"Christ, how should I know?"

They walked out beyond the dark fringe of firs and onto the cliffs. The sea was grey, the sky dull with low-hanging cloud. The high tide swept in, pounding hell out of the driftwood. Gulls screamed, tossing and wheeling inland against the wind.

"Matt!"

"What now?" Matt's manner was nervous and morose.

"It's goin' to be cold in that park tonight."

"So what?"

"I was only thinkin' that you could use that coat they give me. Cold don't make no difference to a heavy sort of guy like me."

"Oh sure! Cold don't make no difference t'anyone!" Then he put his hand up, touched Eddy quickly on the shoulder, "I'm sorry, Eddy, I didn't mean to jump on you that way."

Eddy said slowly, "You didn't mean to maybe but you done it just the same."

"Huh?"

"Things kinda pop outa you, Matt. Every time you get mad you want to take a poke at everything." Eddy's face was distressed.

Matt was silent. After a moment he said perplexed, "Point about you, Eddy, a guy never knows what's goin' on inside of you. One moment you're so dumb then the next moment ..." he broke off, frowning. Then his manner changed abruptly, "Hell, what's the use? Come on back to camp. Maybe it's time we went for dinner." As he turned a fleck of wet whipped his face. He glanced up at the sky. "*Holy Jesus!*" he cried out sharply, "*rain!*"

Back among the trees men were hurriedly drawing away from the open, dragging their stuff into shelter. The wet did not penetrate the thick fir boughs. There was no moisture coming through yet, only a lowering sky and squalls of fine blowing rain.

A boy struggling with an awkward pack threw Matt a hard grin. He muttered, "I wish I had a machine to tell me how many miles I walked in the past three weeks. If I had that machine now, d'ya know what I'd do with it?"

A man with bandaged ankles laying out a solitaire hand in the shelter of heavy trees looked up. "What'd you do, sonny boy?"

The boy looked round, his eyes burned resentfully. "I'd smash it right against that tree you're sittin' under!" He slung his pack up over his shoulder and stumbled on.

Solitaire gazed after him. He rubbed a hand across his stubbled chin. "Trouble with you young kids," he said, "you want everything t'happen at once. Now take me. I floated aroun' so long I don't expect nothin' t'happen any more an' I don't hafta worry." He smiled at Matt, showing a blackened row of broken stubs, "I just ate dinner so what th'hell?"

"Okay for you," Matt said, "you can take it."

The man's thickened fingers fumbled with the cards. He said, "I like patience. You c'n play it anywhere, you don't hafta rustle up anyone to play with an' you get so you don't notice the time."

"Patience! What else does anyone play around here?"

Solitaire talked to himself hoarsely, gently, "Kinda like dope I always think, only dope costs money an' this needn't cost ya a nickel." Hep's voice sounded suddenly, cracking out an order down the line. Matt snapped back to life and ran.

The second division marched uptown, ate a hot dinner and immediately after the squads re-formed. Everything moved smartly today, the air crackled with rumour. There was no hanging around, no gabbing. The sidewalk glistened dully in the rain.

Matt looked all round for Eddy, then he went back inside to see if he were still eating and after that he began to be worried and ask among the boys. One man said he saw Eddy go outside after he was through eating, but he never saw him after that. Hughes came out hugging a bunch of papers, looking chilly and worried. He caught sight of Hep and burst out excitedly, "D'you know what's happening in town today?"

Hep eyed him steadily. "Does anyone know what's happening in town today?" Matt looked at him and he was sure that Hep knew a lot more than he said.

"What's eatin' you now, Kenny?" Matt asked.

Hughes said, "I heard they just passed a by-law making meetings and parades and all public gatherings illegal without a permit. In any part of the city that is," Hughes said, "I wrote it down, I have it here." He began to read from quotes.

Hep took the paper out of his hand, tore it slowly into pieces.

"But I wanted it," Hughes cried, "I need it for my book, I needed the exact wording!" He dived for the pieces and flattened them out carefully.

Hep watched him, wall-eyed. "Don't worry," Hep said, "there isn't going to be any book."

"Not going to be any book? After all the work I put in collecting material?" Kenny's face was funny all right if there had been anyone there to laugh.

"I mean you got nothing to make a book out of," Hep said, "no plot, nothing." His voice sounded tired and fed-up. Matt wondered what he was really thinking.

Just then big Gaffney came out wiping his mouth with the back of his hand. He stopped to join in the huddle.

"Well, if it ain't the litery society in session! How's the book of the month comin' along, Kenny?"

Poor Hughes reddened. He said in a choked voice, "Hep just told me there isn't going to be any book."

Gaffney's attention had wandered. He was eyeing a snappy little tart ankling down the other side of the street. He answered absently, "Say, that's tough! Don't Hep think there's goin' to be any revolution?" The tart turned the corner. Gaffney's attention veered regretfully back. He saw the scraps of torn paper in Hughes' hand. "What you got there, Kenny?"

Hughes read from them as best he could. Gaffney listened, sucking his teeth. He stopped kidding at once. "The way things look now," he said when Hughes finished, "if this deadlock don't break by night those boys out in the park is goin' to stage their own revolution."

Hep gave a cold wolf-grin. His mouth was the only part of him that smiled. He said softly, "Whoever heard of rain an' revolution? Jus' try an' start a riot among a bunch of guys that can't keep their asses dry." There was a moment's uneasy silence.

Matt broke it abruptly. "All this isn't helpin' me to find Eddy."

"Eddy? What happened to him?" Hep asked.

"I didn't see him since dinner. What you think, Hep? Maybe I better stay back an' look for him. You know Eddy."

Hep frowned. He thought a moment. Then, "Maybe you better had, Matt. Come right out to the park when you find him. Maybe he left something down at the Angel an' went back to look for it."

Matt started away and Gaffney called after him, "Try the lost horse trick on Eddy." Matt shrugged to show he did not get it. "If you was a lost horse," the sticker shouted, "where'd you go?"

God, Matt thought, are all the guys connected with this thing goin' nuts or is it only me? Hep's right. There's no plot to it and no sense. Just a mess of talk and a bunch of boys sitting around on their tails and not getting any place.

As he turned into Pastoral he gazed round at the squalid old buildings in disgust. He felt a sharp wave of disappointment and disillusionment at the high pressure of the past three weeks, reaction against the whole freak circus. When he got down to the Angel the place was closed up. There was no one around on the block except "Junkie" Adler, the kike, standing in the doorway across the road.

"You vant something?" he called out when he saw Matt try the door.

Matt went over. "I'm lookin' for a boy named Eddy, maybe you know who I mean."

The kike shrugged. "So many boys," he said.

"Yeah, but not many like Eddy." Matt used his hands, "Big shoulders an' not very tall. Kinda lost-lookin'. Did you see him around?"

The kike shook his head. "I never seen anyone around since you boys left this morning," he said, and he went back indoors.

Matt turned into Flower and moved slowly past the Orsino. He peered down the alley and shoved his head into the office of the Blue and Tan Taxi and asked Nick, the dispatcher, had he seen Eddy around at all. Nick shook his head. "Never seen him around all day." The phone rang. "Sorry," Nick said, "I'd like to of helped you. Blue and Tan Taxi! ..."

Matt hung around outside then he turned back down the alley, crossed over to the Quanta and inquired at the office, thinking maybe Eddy had come in in the meantime. The office was noisy and crowded, the typewriter banging, men haring in and out. No one had time to dish out information, they were all too busy trying to collect it. Finally he dropped into a lunch counter on the corner of Lavender and asked Phil, the counter-man, if he saw Eddy come by at all.

Phil was a short man with wiry red hair, freckles and white skin like a woman's. Even the backs of his hands underneath the fuzz were white. He followed wrestling both in Gath and over in Aschelon and he knew a lot of the angles and the dirt from the ground up. He knew where they fixed the matches and how much the boys got paid. Matt and Eddy used to drop in often. Matt liked listening to him talk.

He was leaning on the counter with the paper spread out.

"Hi, Phil!"

Phil glanced up. "Hi, Matt! I was just readin' up the latest on the sit-down. What I want to know ..."

Matt cut in. "That's what we all want to know but I can't stop to talk now. Did you see Eddy around anywhere?"

"Eddy? How about callin' up the Children's Aid?"

"No kiddin', Phil, this is serious. I gotta find Eddy."

Phil glanced at his wet head and shoulders. "How about takin' time out for a java? Maybe it'll help you think."

Matt hesitated, then he slid up onto a counter stool. "I oughtn't to," he said. "Make it a quick one."

"I wish I could," Phil said. He threw back his head and gave a quick chin lift to show what he meant. "If you wantta drink beer in this town, brother, you gotta go out in the sticks to get it."

Matt grinned wryly, "Don't even talk about it," he said.

Phil slid him over coffee and a stale doughnut and they got down to cases. He asked, "Did Eddy have anything partic'lar on his mind? Anything he talked about lately that could of got workin' in his mind an' gettin' him down?"

Matt thought that over then he set his mug down suddenly and stared at Phil. His face was shocked. "Holy Jesus no! Eddy never had anything like that in his mind. What d'ya want to go thinkin' of a screwy thing like that for?"

Phil saw Matt took it like it was a thing that really might have happened and he was sorry he brought it up. He said quickly, "Now maybe he never had anything like that in his mind at all. All I meant was we gotta consider all the angles."

Matt wiped his face. "There's one we can leave alone right now." He stared at Phil askance. "No use thinkin' of a silly thing like that."

The counterman explored a new trail. He was disturbed over Eddy in a way that only a person that really knew Eddy could have been. He asked thoughtfully, "Now was there anything special he might of wanted to do if he could of got away to do it ... anything he might of wanted for himself?"

Matt pushed away his empty mug and rose. Suddenly his body stiffened. He cried softly, "There *was* something Eddy wanted! An' I went around town all afternoon an' never thought of it. Am I a dope!"

"Never thought of what, Matt?"

Matt began to talk fast, "Lissen, Phil, if you was Eddy ... you know, kinda like Eddy is, an' you wanted a pair of shoes bad where'd you go? Flash type of shoes, fancy-lookin'. What store'd you go to?" He pieced together parts of the story of Eddy and the shoes, enough for Phil to be some use but leaving out the important details.

Phil pushed a pale hand through his fiery hair. "Now lemme think," he began.

Matt cut in, "Sure you think ... an' think fast!" His eye fell on the paper under the counterman's hand. It carried a full-page spread, advertising a one cent sale at a place called Richmond's Style Shoes in the eleven hundred block on Cleat Street. The banner ad ran, COME AROUND SATURDAY AND GET A PAIR OF SHOES FOR ONE CENT! For a moment Matt stared at it dumbly. It hit him like a blow between the eyes. Then, "Look!" he cried, "I'll bet that's where Eddy went to!" His voice shook.

Phil stared at him, not getting anything like the full force. "Hey, wait a minute," he began, "how would Eddy of known to go there?"

"How would he? Couldn't he of seen that ad. in last night's paper. Why, last night he sat up an' *talked* about shoes! Holy Jesus! He could of got himself in th' jug by this time. You don't know Eddy like I do!" He started for the door.

Phil came round, calling after him, "Did he have any money?"

"Hell, Eddy don't need money! All he needs is an idea an' something hard to toss through a plate glass window." He hared off up Lavender, head down against the rain. The town looked wet and dreary. There was an unreal air about the torn sky and grey streets after the weeks of brilliant sun.

The usual crowd, only more today, was gathered under the windows of the Settler reading up late flashes on the jobless crisis. The eyes of the people followed Matt nervously, identifying him with the movement and wondering was he a spy or did he have information about some new form of sit-down. One man tried to stop him to ask for news. Matt brushed by him, not noticing him or the crowds from the rest of the scenery.

He stopped on the corner of Dudley and Cleat, and looked up both sides of Cleat Street. Half-way up on the right hand side there was a double window with big banner notices of a one cent sale. The window was filled with shoes. They looked like they had been swept there by a typhoon. All white, black and white, white and tan, sport shoes, snappy dress Oxfords, canvas running shoes. Just cheap, effective-looking stuff built for quick, seasonal turnover. On one side, the store was next to an alley, with a walk-up tailor on the other side. The street itself ran parallel to Lavender, four blocks over from the Quanta. He could have saved himself a walk around town if he had realized that in the beginning.

As he approached the open door he saw a small crowd just inside, blocking the entrance and his heart went right down and hit the sidewalk. From the street the crowd looked like an ordinary sale mob but he knew better. He did not see Eddy, did not hear his voice. He just knew by instinct that Eddy was there.

He headed in cautiously, staying on the outer ring of the crowd. He heard a man's angry voice, then the voice of Eddy, stubborn and protesting. He felt the little side muscles of his face snap tight and the tautness spread and pick up every muscle in his body.

He said quietly, "Lemme through here, please," then as the crowd did not break at once, "lemme through, will you!" There was a half-turning of heads, then a man moved grudgingly aside. The place smelt like a tannery. There was a row of cheap, oilcloth-covered fitting chairs and footrests, empty boxes, scattered shoes, tiers of more boxes rising flush with the walls, a showcase facing the door. A man in an imitation Palm Beach suit and a wilting Panama hat sat in his stocking soles. His own shoes, bulged and trodden, had wet soles.

Eddy stood holding onto a pair of tan and white scows, holding them high as though he were scared they would be snatched away. When he saw Matt he looked so relieved it was funny. "Hey, Matt," he shouted, almost crying, "I paid my cent an' now the man says I can't have the shoes!"

Matt took in the scene with desperate, experienced eyes. The bag-bellied, youngish shoeman with the pale cheeks and the hair greased back, pompadour style, his acne-faced assistant in the fake shepherd check hovering nervously in the background. Matt settled right down to a steady tension, he did not show any emotion at all. He asked quietly, "What's the trouble, Eddy?"

The shoeman stepped forward. He glanced suspiciously from one man to the other. "What is this?" he asked.

Matt noticed he had little beads of moisture on his white forehead and in a way Matt felt sorry for him. At first Matt felt sorry for him because he knew Eddy. He said, "You got a one cent sale advertised for today, haven't you, mister?"

"I most certainly have."

"My friend here read your ad wrong. He thought you was advertisin' the shoes at one cent a pair, not one cent for the second pair if the customer buys one at the reg'lar price. That's all, mister. C'mon, Eddy, we got to be gettin' back to the park!" There was a noticeable, prick-eared reaction from the onlookers. Maybe I shouldn't have said that, Matt thought, now they got us tabbed. He repeated loudly, "C'mon, Eddy, we got to get goin'!"

Eddy hung back. He held onto the shoes and his face grew stubborn. He said, "I paid my cent. I got a right to these shoes." His eyes slid away rebelliously and would not be held.

Matt gripped onto himself, keeping the desperation out of his voice so it would not sound weakened. "Listen, Eddy," he said, "you read that ad wrong. Can't you see what you're doin' cuttin' up this way?" He glanced nervously towards the door expecting to see the head and shoulders of a cop.

Eddy's free hand fumbled in his pants' pocket. He pulled out the crumpled ad from last night's Gath *Settler.* "See, Matt? I didn't read that ad wrong. See what it says in big letters right across the top, COME AROUND SATURDAY AND GET A PAIR OF SHOES FOR ONE CENT."

The shoeman broke in angrily, speaking directly to Matt. He did not try to work on Eddy any more. "You know very well what that ad means and how these one cent sales work."

Matt looked at him coldly, hating his fat, youngish face. "I know, mister, but my friend here don't seem to. Maybe next time you'll word your ad clearer. I never did care for these come-on ads myself." He turned to Eddy, appealing, menacing, "For Chrissake, Eddy, drop those shoes an' come!"

Eddy did not drop the shoes. He did not move. In an angry singsong he repeated, "I paid my cent, I gotta right to these shoes."

The shoeman made a sudden choking sound. He took a step forward and Eddy backed cagily away. He stepped round the end of the showcase so the showcase was between them. A woman goofing on the ring of the crowd began to giggle. Matt pulled out his handkerchief and wiped his face. The shoeman turned and passed a signal to Acne-face. Matt caught the signal and his arm shot out and he grabbed Acne and held onto him. Matt's eyes were dangerous. "Better not try to run us out, mister, you don't want to start anything you may be sorry for." Acne-face squirmed. He did not make any real effort to break away.

A man laughed and said, "Stay with it, Eddy!"

"Don't let him gyp you, Eddy!"

"Good old Eddy!" The people pressed in happily. They were enjoying this. They felt included in the game.

The shoeman gave one furious look around. He saw Eddy freezing onto the shoes, the people crowding in off the street. He did not try to hang onto himself any more, he did not care if his store was full of people. He called out in a loud, high voice, "I know who you two are! You're two of those lazy, no-good bums that have been ruining my summer trade. Damn no-good unemployed! You wouldn't work if you were paid!"

For an instant a little silence fell. The crowd strove forward, breathing softly. The eyes moved one way. They watched Eddy with a frozen, fascinated look. His face slowly darkened. He moved forward and his body stiffened and took on a menacing, glacial calm. He whispered, "You wantta take away my shoes. *You wantta take away my shoes!*" Matt watched him, powerless. This was the first time Eddy ever got away from him.

The shoeman stepped back hurriedly. His white-skinned forehead shone with fear. Eddy kept moving towards him, shoulders dropped, eyes small and red like an angry bull. The man made a false step and sprawled backwards over a fitting stool and a pile of loose boxes jarred down on top of him. Matt sprang forward and grabbed Eddy. He lied desperately and fast, shouting in his ear, "*Cops, Eddy! Scram!*" The look on Eddy's face changed instantly. His mouth dropped open, his eyes grew blank with fear. Matt struck the shoes out of his hand and he did not try to hold onto them. As they dived for the door the shoeman scrambled up onto his feet shouting something about threat of bodily harm. The crowd opened for the men to pass through then closed again solid. A man's voice called out gleefully, "Don't let him get out after them, the cheap little squirt!" The people stayed there laughing and kidding. They held the man prisoner in his own store.

Matt turned right down the alley. Half-way down he dodged into a closed doorway, dragging Eddy after him. They stood pressed against the door, chests heaving. Matt's face was damp and grim, on the face of Eddy there was a look of confused annoyance. He held the shoe ad still tightly grasped in his left hand. They waited there, listening for the street noises to change; for the wail of a squad car, the tramp of boots, the excited babble of witnesses. The rain blew mistily across their faces, the sounds in the street did not change. After a time Matt went down the other end, looked out cautiously and beckoned Eddy. "Come on," he snarled. "I guess they didn't turn the cops onto us after all."

They headed for the park by the back roads, the shortest way. Matt did not trust himself to speak at all. He walked fast and blindly, hands jammed down into his jeans, muscles like taut bowstrings.

At last Eddy broke the long silence. He said breathlessly, "You're mad at me again, Matt, but what did I do?"

Matt choked at him half-audibly, "Don't talk about it! Jus' don't talk about it, that's all!" He quickened his stride.

"But look, Matt, read what it says," Eddy thrust the paper at him, "COME ROUND SATURDAY ..." Matt snatched the paper away. Eddy's voice rose to a howl of wrath. "But I didn't do nothin' except what the paper said an' that sonovabitch gyps me outa my pair of shoes. He even has my cent I paid him."

Matt started to shout, then he stopped. He gazed at Eddy in silence. "I don't know," he said hopelessly, "I can't figger out anything from now on, I'm through, licked. You licked me this time, Eddy."

Eddy's mind struggled with the complexities of right and wrong. Like an angry spark the single idea still smouldered. His mouth grew stubborn. "Jus' the same that sonovabitch gypped me ..."

Matt turned on him. Matt's eyes were ugly. *"Will you shut up?"*

They tramped on in silence. Ahead of them loomed the dark and shadowy outlines of the park. Then, "I didn't mean to get us into no trouble, Matt, I only done what the paper said." Once more Eddy recited the ad monotonously, like a prayer.

Matt spoke bitterly. "You always has to do the things you do. Always, ever since I known you, you had to get in some kind of trouble an' every time you got an airtight case. Pair of shoes for one cent! Why you poor, half-wit dope ..." He raised his eyes and broke off abruptly. He pointed ahead. "Hey, Eddy, look! What's goin' on over there?" He broke into a run. "The whole bunch is gettin' on the move!"

Beneath the trees figures were massing together hurriedly in the dusk. Squad leaders shouted orders to their men. The air was filled with the clamour of breaking camp. Men ran by, made awkward by their swinging baggage. Matt hailed one of them as he stumbled past. "Hey, you, what's goin' on here?"

The man panted, "They come to a settlement."

"They what?"

"They come to a settlement."

"What kind of a settlement?"

The man shrugged impatiently. "I was standin' too far away to hear good, but around five-thirty Laban come out and read out a lot of terms an' the boys voted to accept. We're marchin' back to the floozy-houses. That's all I know." He ran on dodging among the trees.

Eddy plucked Matt by the sleeve. His face was anxious. "What's he mean?"

"I don't know," Matt said, "I'm goin' to find out." He grabbed onto a boy, caught him by the shoulder and held him. The boy squirmed. "Hey, what's the big idea?"

Matt said, "Listen, you, I got to get some information around here."

The boy squinted at him with suspicion. "You won't get none out of me."

Matt laughed half-hysterically. "Why, you lug," he cried, "I belong here!"

"Then if you belong here how come you don't know what's been goin' on?"

Matt answered hurriedly, "We just got back from town. What about those terms?"

The boy still eyed him with distrust. "You mean the ones Laban come out an' told us?"

"Sure."

"I didn't hear the whole thing, but Laban come out an' said they'd agreed on some kind of a settlement an' the boys was to vote yes or no. Just vote the way we all were, yes or no." He broke off. "Why in hell do you want to know all this?"

Matt glared at him. His voice shook. "Why, you damn little squirt," he cried, "if I was a pigeon d'you think I'd waste my time on a dope like you?"

The boy blinked at him. "I guess the whole thing's over," he mumbled. He felt Matt's grip slacken suddenly and ducked away.

For a moment Matt stood in the midst of the hurrying camp.

He stared at the dim figures of men running. His face was white and still like a carved face. His eyes were like stones. "Yeah," he said slowly, "I guess the whole thing's over all right."

Ahead through the trees a voice cracked out an order. Men flowed solidly together into a unit. The first of the columns began to march through the dusk, arms swinging, feet thumping. They came on singing. Mechanically Matt stood aside and pulled Eddy with him. They stood alone under the trees watching the men go by. The faces of the marchers were blurred and featureless through the dusk and rain. They did not have separate identity, they were only a part of a whole. Matt stared at them blindly. Eddy's face was bleak and puzzled.

A man ran up and touched Matt on the shoulder. "Which division do you boys belong in?"

"Second."

"Okay, then, get over there by the bridge." Then the man came closer and peered into Matt's face. "What's the matter? You sick or something?"

Matt shook himself to slacken the tenseness of his body. "I'm okay," he said, "for a moment there I felt sick but I don't feel sick any more."

"Then get over there by the bridge," the man said, and hurried off.

They went over and joined up with the rest of the boys. A short distance away a man stood on a bench haranguing a small group of stragglers. Matt recognized him by his voice. He was Sklar, the "Red." Matt once heard him speak at a meeting and never forgot. There were things about Sklar reminded him of his own father, only Sklar was younger.

He was shouting, "Hokay, hokay, we make peace with the dictators, but we are not through! Work, work," he flung out his arms passionately, "look what is crying out to be done! Work crying out to be done everywhere! Roads, houses, empty land! Yet because we want to do it we are subverting the government. Look!" he smote his chest, "when I was working I went to night school to make of myself an educated man, to learn to think, maybe. Hokay, I am a revolutionary, a Red! They drag red herrings across the trail, they scream 'Red', 'Red!' and nothing is done. They pick up a handful of young boys and throw them in the jug for trying to stay alive. They call us trouble-makers ... any little smell to drown the one big stink!"

He broke off glaring at the handful of men remaining. His face worked passionately, "Pushed around! Always pushed around so no one is responsible. I tell you we are not even in the country!" A sudden rain squall blew across his face. The listeners began to drift away. They moved uncertainly, not meeting one another's eyes, not speaking. Only Matt and Eddy remained.

His voice rose again, "Fight! Fight! Stick together! One more day maybe, twenty-four hours longer an' you win. But give in now and what have you?" He stopped suddenly and plunged down off the bench. He gazed round and the look on his face grew dazed. He came up to the two men and peered from face to face, discovering their features.

He put his hand up and let it rest heavily on Matt's shoulder. "Oh, it's you," he said. His voice changed, sounding tired and hoarse, "I didn't know." He nodded bitterly at the departing men. "Sheep! They fight like sheep. One runs, they all scatter!"

Matt laughed harshly, "What d'you expect them to do? Stay out here and catch pneumonia?"

CHAPTER TWENTY-TWO

Later that evening he wrote a letter to Harry. He felt he needed to talk to Harry. He never consciously felt that way before but he felt it now. The way he felt about Harry, he was the only one whose friendship did not make demands. He did not ask anything in return, not obedience like Hep, nor vigilance like Eddy. Harry gave what he had free, the same way he gave the handout that first Sunday in Aschelon.

Tonight all Matt knew was he wanted the chance to ease up onto a counter stool and watch Harry manipulate his small fixings behind, watch him push in a handful of picks and grind on them while his little wise eyes peered out from their sockets of rolling flesh, listen to him talk, and every now and again when something came up he had to mull over, watch him scratch thoughtfully at his twitching stump. Harry had a lot of things other people missed out on. Maybe they gave him that when they took his arm away.

"Dear Harry," he wrote,

"Thanks for yrs. of Wednesday. I sure was glad to get it. You asked how we are makin' out. Well I will try to tell you. You will have to remember all through that there are a lot of inside angles I can't know about and all you will get is a personal slant and maybe in the end plenty of it will add up to be bull because the hardest thing to get hold of among a bunch of boys that has been livin' the way we have is the actual truth about anything. For that I guess you had better read the newspapers.

"God Harry has this been a day. In the end Eddy and me missed the finish because we was not in the park when Laban come out and put the terms up to the boys to vote on. Why? You guessed it. Eddy cut up and I had to hare off uptown and pull him out of a jam. The way he looked at it he still thinks he was in the right.

"Anyways the boys took a vote. I guess they would have voted 'yes' on prohibition at that stage, anything to get out of the wind and rain. God,

Harry, the rain over here can be cold. Maybe it can be just as cold in Aschelon. I never found out. Believe it or not we was all thankful to get in undercover even back to these dumps. They seem like Home, Sweet Home. Last thing I heard they are to begin shipping us over to Aschelon tomorrow at the rate of so many head per day.

"Talking of that I guess you will want to know the terms of the final sign-up. I got them off Hughes who is a school teacher. Nuts, but a good guy. We have all sorts here.

"Here are the terms as Hughes gave them to me. They are likely to be right if they come from him. *One.* Us freight car cowboys have been offered relief at the rate of three bucks, seven cents per week for a month and free transportation back where we come from, if we skip within that time. *Two.* Local boys, that is ones that belong in this province, will be given six bucks, seventy cents every ten days so long as they don't collect twice in the same place and can prove they are honestly looking for work. (Did you ever try to prove you were honestly looking for work, Harry?) They done it this way to keep the boys on the move. I didn't get the names of where they collect outside of Aschelon and anyway they would not mean anything to me as I do not know the country but they are all up in the Sleeve Valley and from what I hear of conditions up there a monkey could not get a job picking fleas off another monkey much less if it spoke the English language. I heard the same story from a man that drove us from Cutlake to McBain. He has a couple of kids up there and he should know. It is all very well to sign a bunch of paper but talking and signing don't create seven or eight hundred jobs overnight.

"Rumours is flying round thick as bats. Some of the boys feel this has been a sell-out at the last and they have been let-down. They are leery because this thing snapped shut so sudden in the end. Others are saying Gus came to terms because he was scared of a big sympathetic walkout. Another guy was spreading it around that Laban had a swell job offered him but he wouldn't take it because he wanted to stick with the boys, so Harry your guess is as good as mine. All we freight car cowboys know for sure is that we are right back where we started. About the only way we know we are alive is that we are liable to get locked up for trying to prove it.

"Listen Harry and try to make sense out of this because I cannot. Where do we go from here? We just don't belong any place. What are we anyway? Just a bunch of bums with the wanderlust? I don't think so, not from what I have seen of these boys by this time. Mind you, there's plenty bums and some it wouldn't be a damn bit of use giving a job to because they couldn't use one but that don't handle the main issue. Not any part of it.

"Extras are out on the streets and the papers is playing this settlement up as a great big triumph for the boys. Balls, Harry, it is a great big triumph for nobody. All it is is just another patch-up. Public patch-up number million and one, three months from now they will be shoving us back in the jug for trying to pick up a meal off the streets.

"Did you ever do a stretch in college Harry? Believe me, it is no YMCA, and it don't take long to graduate with top honours. That is the future kids like these, not just this little bunch here but thousands all over the country has got to look forward to. That or jungles and freight cars and fifteen cent flop houses. Look at me. Twenty-three to-day and I sure can hang up a sweet record. Two stretches in the can and more and better coming up. Why not? What have I got to lose? Vets like me can take it but what about the young kids? I guess if we was some kind of mineral land or had oil gushing out of us the big money interests would take us over and turn us into cash but on the hoof we are not worth a nickel.

"Reading this over it sounds kind of bitter. I guess part of it is reaction from the high pressure of the past three weeks but I am not doing any apologizing because the stuff is true and hell someone is going to say it sooner or later. One reason I am spieling on like this is because I feel jittery, I feel something is going to happen all the time. Nothing can happen. Everything's happened that can happen over here. I just can't settle, that's all. There's plenty others feel the same way to-night. I will ask Hep can he get Eddy and me passes for the movie if I can locate Hep.

"Maybe you did not get so far reading this letter. It sounds like my last will and testament. To make it quite legal I hereby will you all my worldly goods. That's a hot one Harry. All my worldly goods. I guess that means Eddy. Poor dope, he would lay down his life for me to walk on but I got to keep watching him all the time. You know what I mean.

"First day we get shipped over we will drop in. Believe you me Harry I am not going to sit around. If I can't get mine one way I will take it another. I have a reason and I wish you could get a look at her. Well you will. Just the same right at the moment I don't know where I am at so I will close. Eddy sends his regards.

"I must close now Harry. I wanted to talk to you pretty bad tonight. All the best, Matt."

"PS Do not write again here. I would not get it."

Matt borrowed a big envelope off Hughes. He had a job raising the postage but Kenny and a couple of others helped out.

Kenny was very low about the settlement. He was a local boy and the terms seemed to hit him like a bombshell. He asked Matt how he was going to go bumming around the Sleeve trying to snitch a job some Douk or Jap had overlooked. Matt tried to cheer him up by telling him a lot of bull about some school job opening up in the fall but Hughes just looked at him. "You know that's not true," he said.

"Yeah," Matt said after a silence, "I know it's not true, Kenny. They got teachers to burn." He felt ashamed at having strung Kenny along even if he did mean it in the right way.

Charlie came into the room. He said loudly, "Why don't they burn 'em then or plough 'em under?" He sat down on a pile of newspapers. "Lemme tell you something," Charlie said, pulling out a comb and beginning to comb his hair very fast, "those little one-horse towns up in the Valley have got more on their hands than they can take care of already, they can't even find work for their own boys."

He spun round suddenly. His eyes blazed in his sallow face. "They can tell us to go to the Sleeve or they can tell us to go to hell, but I'm not goin' to either. I'm goin' to town, right to town," Charlie said. "See you in Paris!" He went quickly out of the room.

For a moment after he had gone neither man spoke. Then "What's got into him?" Matt asked uneasily. His eyes stayed on the open door.

Hughes said, "I don't know, he was behaving funnily all afternoon. Perhaps you'd better go after him."

Matt shook his head. "I better stay right here where I am. Another two minutes of this and I'll be actin' that way myself." He felt in his pockets and pulled out a flattened half empty pack of Players.

Hughes went to his shabby grip and dragged out a pile of paper. He sat down with his back to the wall and began to paw over the pages. "Whatever happens," he said, "I shan't give up, I shan't desert the ship."

"Ship? What ship? Don't tell me ..." Matt broke off and stared at Hughes. He swallowed. "Don't tell me you're goin' nuts too."

Hughes pulled off his glasses and polished them. "The book," he explained earnestly, "whatever happens I shall still persist. More than ever a book like this will be needed now." He hesitated, eyeing Matt uncertainly.

"I asked you in Andersville if you would mind my putting you in the book, building you up into the sort of central representative character and you said no, you wouldn't mind. Remember?"

Matt started to laugh, then he stopped. He saw that this crazy idea meant something to Hughes. He answered soberly, "Sure, I remember now."

Hughes blushed. "Well, I've been trying to work on that idea ever since but I don't seem to have got very far. I ... I don't feel I know you well enough even yet, not the sort of things I need to know, how you feel ..."

Matt stood up. "I don't know just how I feel myself now, not after what happened today. Maybe some other time, Kenny."

"Tomorrow?" Hughes persisted. "You know, Matt, you've always been awfully decent to me."

"Hell, Kenny, I never done anything but use up your horse balls."

"It's not that ..." Hughes was beginning, when Matt closed on him.

"Whatever it is," he said, "let's not talk about it now." He had to get away. Another minute and he would have pasted poor patient Hughes right on the kisser.

He went upstairs and dropped in on the boys on the second floor. Every place he went groups sat around gassing about the terms of the settlement and about their own futures. A lot of the older ones had gone back to playing cards or checkers. Matt watched them, wondered how they could take it so calmly. Maybe they were not that way inside. He heard plenty of the other kind of talk as well, men sore and resentful, men grim and satiric, men boiling with vague threats, men stoical because, goddam it, they had eaten regularly for the past two months. The bums came out and yelled loudest because they would have to get back on the streets and work at bumming. Talk, talk, smoke. Little private meetings called to talk and talk some more. Enough free gas to float a balloon.

A man concentrating on a checkers board glanced up as Matt went by. He called out irritably, "Sidown, brother, sidown!"

Matt flashed back, "That's all I've bin doin' for the past three weeks."

"Well, do some more of it," the man said. He kicked the door shut as Matt went out.

He went downstairs and met Hep coming in the front entrance. "Hello, Matt," Hep said, "I was just looking for you."

"For me?" Matt said quickly. It was the first time he felt anything near pleasure today.

"Come on back inside," Hep said, "maybe I can take time out for a smoke." They went in the empty cave that used to be the front office. A single old-fashioned drop light hung from the ceiling. Anything outside the direct glare of the light lay in shadow. They sat on a couple of wooden chairs with the backs broken out and Hep fetched the makings from a side pocket.

"By the way," he remarked casually, "you never told me what happened to Eddy."

Matt sat forward, resting his elbows on his knees. He answered guardedly. "He took some crazy notion he wanted to go window shopping. I found him hangin' round a shoe store on Cleat Street. They had a big sale advertised, I guess he saw it in last night's paper."

Hep passed over a cigarette. "Yeh," he said, "so I heard." Matt sat up. "What d'ya mean you heard?"

"Why not? I just have to keep check, that's all."

"Check! You know what's goin' on in every corner of this whole damn organization!" Matt frowned. He took a deep drag to keep himself from flying badly off the handle. "Okay, then, if you knew so much why didn't you roast the pants off the pair of us, Eddy an' me?"

Hep sighed. "Today? What the hell d'you think I am? Today's been the kind of a day when anything could have happened to anybody." He sounded played-out. His face was drawn.

They sat there in silence. Rain smashed against the windows, spattering down from a broken gutter.

"Hep!"

"What?"

"You said just now you were lookin' for me. What for?"

"I just wanted to find out how you were making out."

"Meaning what?"

Hep said gently, "You know damn well what I mean."

Matt stared down at his feet. He was a moment answering, "I took it bad, I guess, "he admitted, "I've been around all evening steppin' on everybody's toes. I guess I just couldn't take it."

"You mean you're sore because you think nothing come out of it today?"

"Seems like nothing come out of any of it in the end, seems like all we took was a beatin'."

Hep's head came round. He eyed Matt gravely. "That's because you don't get what it's all about. You don't see what bringing this little stink here out in the open can do for the big main cause. All you're lookin' at is just one little corner."

"All I'm lookin' at is what I can see. Goddamit, Hep, if Laban had held on just one day longer someone would have had to do something. We just couldn't of stayed out in that park an' starved to death. What did he get out of this quick sign-up?"

Hep's voice sharpened. "You don't like Laban."

Matt's brow creased stubbornly. "I never seen enough of him to find out. Back in Clever he was pushin' out handbills an' I never got to talk to him, at least I think it was Laban. This guy had a different name but he was the dead spittin' image. Since then I only saw him in front of the mike an' at meetin's. He can get you at meetin's so you're damn near holy-rollerin'. I guess he's all right. He's just too clever for me, that's all."

Hep crushed out his cigarette. "Laban's okay," he said. "He's smart as a fox an' smart the way a fox is because that's the way he has to be. What d'you think he's doin' all the time ... drawin' up a settlement with the Ladies' Aid?"

A boy pushed his head in the door. "I got a message for you," he said to Hep, "you're wanted up at headquarters right away."

Hep rose. He removed his hat, carefully smoothed down his thick black hair, then he set the hat back on again. "Okay, Stan," he nodded, "I'll be up there inside of five minutes." The boy dodged out again.

Hep stood there buttoning his coat up close, settling his head into his turned-up collar. As he went out Matt hurried after him. "I wanted to ask you, could you rustle up a couple of passes for the movies for Eddy and me. I can't sit around the Angel anymore ... not after last night."

"I guess so. Come on up to headquarters an' we'll see." They walked up to the Quanta, heads hunched into their coats. The usual Saturday night crowd was drifting around town. The town was dreary. The wet pavements and the wind made it feel like fall instead of summer. On one corner a group of Salvationists were blowing brass instruments to a small crowd.

When they reached the door of the Quanta Matt stopped. "There is something I wanted to ask you," he said. They stood in the doorway out of the rain. He spoke with an effort. "Something I once talked to you about, Hep, that day we drove out to see the old man."

"I've only got a minute, Matt, but go ahead."

Matt said passionately, "I told you then how I wanted to stay part of this fight! I don't care what I do, how you use me, just give me a chance, that's all! I wasn't so hot that first day but I did a job on those kids at Andersville an' I done Christ knows how many jobs on Eddy first to last. Like I told you that day it never mattered before what I did or whether I forgot to do it but these past three weeks it's mattered a helluva lot. It's mattered to me anyway. I told you all that before, I don't need to tell you it all again. I'll do any damn thing you ask me to, Hep. You must know that by this time."

Hep regarded him silently for a moment. When he spoke his voice was heavy and tired. "I know it," he said, "Jesus, I know you mean it, Matt, but what can I do? I've got no power to hand out jobs or make promises."

"You could recommend me to the committee."

"They couldn't use you if they wanted to."

"Why not?"

"Because there's too long a line-up ahead of you. Why, there's …"

Matt's face changed. He broke in harshly, "You don't need to tell me the rest, I heard it before."

A man came out and touched Hep on the shoulder. "They're waiting inside," he said.

"Okay," Hep said, "I'll be right in." For a moment he eyed Matt uncertainly. "I'll do my best," he said, "maybe tomorrow …"

Matt's mouth tightened. "Oh sure," he said, "maybe tomorrow!"

Hep went inside. After a moment a boy stepped out with two passes for the Klahowyah Gymnasium and Athletic Club where they put on the wrestling shows Saturday nights. "Hep told me to tell you he thought you'd maybe like these better than a movie. Step on it if you want to get in for the prelims," the boy added, "show starts at nine-fifteen."

Matt thanked him and headed back down to the Angel to pick up Eddy. On the way he dropped Harry's letter in the mail box on Pastoral in time to catch the last downtown collection. Then he went in, found Eddy and they started back uptown. As they left a boy with a letter in his hand stuck his head out and called after Matt but he did not hear. A shower of wet blew down from a broken gutter and the boy pulled his head in quickly. "I guess it can wait," he said to his buddy, "Red must of brought it over from the garage." They studied the writing and made cracks about it's being in a woman's hand.

"I'll give it to him when he comes in," the boy said, "if he don't come in too late."

"An' if you're still awake," his buddy said. "If I know anything about you before he gets that letter it'll be tomorrow."

The first boy grinned. "Well," he said, "maybe tomorrow!"

CHAPTER TWENTY-THREE

The Klahowyah Gymnasium and Athletic Club was five blocks over and a block beyond Cleat. Matt headed for the short cuts. The Neon-faced clock outside the cigar-store on the corner of Conklin and Dudley showed up nine-thirty. The wind blew the rain in sharp squalls.

As they came up past Sandy's poolroom Matt noticed a man going in.

He called out, "Hi, Slappy," recognizing Charlie. Charlie spun around as though he had been sniped. "Oh, it's you," he said a moment later. He said it with a short out-going breath that showed he had been scared one moment and relieved the next.

Matt eyed him curiously. "Sure it's me," he said, "how come they give you a pass into Sandy's?"

Charlie's eyes darted nervously up and down the street. "They didn't give me a pass," he said, "what d'ya think?" He moved a few steps farther on so it would look as though he were talking in front of the barber shop next door. Matt nodded at the poolroom window. "So that's your way of goin' to town!"

Charlie hesitated then he drew Matt a little aside. "Commere, Matt. You wouldn't go back on me if I told you?"

Matt looked at him steadily. "After all this time? Hell, what d'you think I am?"

"Okay, I knew you wouldn't. Remember those two kids back in Andersville? That Ted one that said he was goin' in with a man?"

"Yeah, I remember them. How did you get to know all about that?"

"Never mind how I knew," Charlie went on hurriedly, "the point is I'm goin' in with this same guy. He's got a nice little racket over in town runnin' all sweet and smooth an' he has to have salesmen, ones that's young and smart an' know their way around."

Matt stuck his hands in his jeans. "Why, the dirty sonovabitch!" Then he laughed. "He certainly picked hot ones when he picked you two kids."

"You can call him names if you want," Charlie said, "but he's the only one come out an' offered me any kind of a job."

Matt's manner changed and grew serious. "Job my foot! Inside of a month you'll be in the jug."

"Oh, yeah? What about you? Where'll you be inside of a month?"

Matt's mouth hardened. He avoided Charlie's eyes. "Anyway," he said, "the idea's crazy. That's the kind of thing you can do a stretch for ... an' I don't mean no thirty days."

Charlie looked down at his feet. He spoke carefully as though he had given the matter plenty of thought. "S'pose I do," he said, "what's so hot about my life before? I never learned anything, all I ever saw was my old man on relief an' beefin' about the times. All my life I've been yellow, never stepped out and took what belonged to me, but I'm through with all that now." He raised his head. "You heard what Kinky said last night? Okay, that's me from now on." He put his hand in his pocket and dived up a crumpled scrap of paper. "Look," he said, "in case you ever want to come in, Matt, here's this guy's address in town. Maybe I could help you get in. You an' me has been swell friends, I wouldn't want to see you stuck."

Matt took the paper. "Thanks," he said, "I'll keep it." He eyed Charlie with pity. "I still think you're crazy, Slappy, you don't know what you're lettin' yourself in for. Why, only the other day you was the one that was scared to shake a can in case they put you in the jug."

Colour rushed into Charlie's sallow cheeks. "That was the other day," he said. "I done some thinkin' since then. I found out what was wrong with me."

Matt stared at him, taking a moment to connect. "I found out what was wrong with me," Charlie repeated. The old nervousness was coming back into his manner. He sounded excited underneath.

Matt said slowly, "You think that'll put guts into you?"

"I know it," Charlie said. "S'long Matt, be seein' you!" He started to go away then he came back quickly. He was out and out jittery now. He caught Matt by the arm and his hand shook. "You wouldn't tell, Matt?"

Matt smiled greyly. "Don't worry," he said, "I won't tell. Hope you have luck." He watched Charlie disappear inside Sandy's.

"Well," he said to Eddy as they walked on, "there goes the last of the gang. Gabby an' Dick in jug an' Slappy headin' there so fast you can't see him for smoke. Seems like you an' me is the only ones stayed out of trouble."

Eddy beamed proudly. "We did that all right," he said. "We stayed out of trouble clear to the end."

Matt was reading the address on the paper, then he slipped it into his pocket. "Funny," he said, "I come into town with just an address on a piece of paper an' I'm goin' out the same way." They walked on down and turned into Cleat Street. "What are you goin' to do now, Eddy?"

Eddy answered promptly, "I'm goin' to do whatever you do. I got no place to go but with you. I don't want no place to go but with you."

Matt turned and gave him a puzzled look. He spoke gently, "Hell, Eddy, I got nothin' to offer you, I got nothin' even to offer myself."

"I don't want nothin' offered me, Matt. I wouldn't know what to do with it if you did."

"Did what?"

"Did what you said ... offered it to me."

Matt frowned and the scar drew down and became like an old deep wound. "I don't know why you want to stick with me, Eddy. Christ knows I roasted the ass off you. Every darned day it seems as though I had to roast the ass off you for something." They walked on a little way in silence. From down at the end of the street came the clash and shunting of the railroad yards, the far-off howl of a train.

Eddy's eyes strayed to the other side of the street. He said reproachfully, "Like today?"

"Like today, what?"

He pointed over at the big sales banners plastered across the store window. "Like today," he said, "you roasted the ass off me for something I never done. I was right, Matt, see what it says across the window there." He began to recite monotonously, "Come around Saturday ..."

Matt glanced up startled. He broke in, "I never noticed that was where we got to."

"I noticed it though," Eddy said, "I noticed it just as soon as we turned round at the bottom of the street." His voice grew suddenly angry, "I know where I've been gypped. I know where that sonovabitch takes my money and gyps me outa my pair of shoes. Why, look Matt! He even put those very shoes back in the window!" Eddy started to cross the road and Matt pulled him back.

"C'mon, Eddy," he said, sharply, "at the rate we're goin' we're not even goin' to get in for the main bout."

Eddy obeyed but he obeyed unwillingly. His mind remained locked to the single idea. "Jus' the same," he mumbled, "that sonovabitch gyps me outa my money an' outa my pair of shoes."

Outside the Klahowyah gym they fell in with the shuffling line-up. The crowd did not bother to come in for the prelims. A man standing along-side of Matt spoke to him. He was stout and friendly, with a bad skin. Matt asked him if he knew what the card was for tonight, and the man said, "It got a big write-up in the sports page if that tells you anything."

"Not a thing," Matt said, "I don't even know the names of the hams that work this circuit."

The man laughed. "Hams is right. I don't know why we pay good money to watch these big hunkies take such good care of one another." Matt showed his passes. "If we had to do that," he said, "we wouldn't be here now."

The man eyed him with interest, then he noticed Eddy. "So you're two of the boys," he said. His face grew serious, "I tell you, brother, there's lots of angles of that settlement today that I'd like to hear you talk about. What say afterwards we go over to my place and have a glass of beer?"

"Thanks," Matt said, "but we got to be in on time. Thanks just the same."

"Discipline, huh?" the man said, looking important. "Well, this town's certainly got to hand it to you boys for the way you behaved up to now, I wouldn't want to be the cause of getting any of you in trouble. What say we sit together, anyway?"

"Sure," Matt said.

"Then I can give you the low-down," the man said. He seemed pleased at finding himself with a couple of national characters and very anxious to do the right thing. There was a big crowd tonight. Some imported Hindu was taking on Sinbad the Sailor in the main bout of the evening and the fans had turned out as well as a lot of the Hindu's compatriots. The gym was low-roofed, with tiers of seats rising on four sides and ringside seats and chairs brought in for an extra big night like tonight. A loudspeaker blared swing music. Matt and Eddy and the stranger picked up three chairs by the door, two in the third row and a single in the row behind. The man let Matt in first and then went in after him and Eddy took the odd seat.

Matt looked round. "You okay, Eddy?"

"Sure," Eddy nodded, "I'm okay." Every time he leant forward Matt could feel him breathing.

They got in in time to watch a two-fall match between a barnyard Romeo and an ex-firehand. The firehand wore purple trunks and Romeo wore green trunks. Both boys had their names lettered in white across the backs of their bathrobes. The man with Matt pointed out the ex-fire pug and said believe it or not he was a local boy that used to work around the city fire-halls but now he was drawing down all kinds of money in the South.

"For this kind of thing?" Matt asked.

The man laughed. "For this kind of thing," he said, "funny, isn't it?" Matt watched the blond gorilla pulling his cheap tricks and getting paid for it and he did not think it so funny. Then the fireman missed with a flying tackle and lunged clean through the ropes and knocked himself out cold and had to be carried off and the man next to Matt grinned and said, "I guess that puts out his fire for the night!"

After that there was a no-fall grind between a Texas cowhand and a Czech and from then on Matt began to get really into the atmosphere. He got up on his feet and yelled with the crowd. Behind the fake pantomime he picked out the flashes of real wrestling and recognized that here was something that could have grace and strength, meaning and timing and speed. These last things he learned in the final bout of the evening. When the Hindu eased through the ropes he recognized that here was the thing he had come to see. The Hindu had the most perfect body Matt had ever seen on a man. He was a mass of muscle, not crude and bunched and ropey but beautifully distributed all over his body. He had bare feet and he moved with the true panther grace. He was the easiest, most graceful mover Matt had ever seen. He wore red trunks and a red turban. His skin had a sort of glow to it. He made Sinbad look like a gorilla.

When the match started the crowd grew perfectly still. The kind of silence fell that Matt knew because he recognized it—like when Laban stepped up to the mike—instinctive mass-homage to a thing masterfully done. The only sounds were Sinbad's groaning and the light shuffling of the Hindu's bare feet and the sharp smack when he sprang free of a hold. Matt watched him, fascinated. He watched him use his body like a spring, tough and supple and quicker than the eye. All without rehearsed grunting or contortions or fake agony, keeping himself unsweaty and unmarked. He got the first fall in three-quarters of a minute. The crowd rose and roared. They expected it was all going to be like this. Outside the glare in the ring the air was blue and twisted with smoke. The faces of the people were excited and hard from yelling. That was something Matt recognized too. It brought back Sunday in Aschelon and the night in Andersville when Laban spoke. These things came back to him out of a dream, he did not think of them consciously. He rose with the crowd and yelled.

When the noise died down he leaned back to speak to Eddy and Eddy was not there. Another man was sitting where he had been.

For a moment Matt felt his insides turn over. He felt weak and gut-sick. He half rose in the smoky light and tried to pick out Eddy among the dim tiers of faces. Behind him there was a muttering and uprising. A woman's voice told him to sit down or get out. The man next to him dragged his eyes from the ring. "What's the matter?" he was beginning, when he saw Matt's face. "Oh, my God!" he exclaimed and stopped. For a moment he could not look back at the ring.

Matt choked, "Heat! I gotta get out of here," and he shoved by the knees of the man on the other side. He asked Louis at the door, speaking very fast, "Did anyone come by here in the last five minutes, a young, heavy-lookin' guy?" He stopped, not knowing how to describe Eddy. Louis stared back with that deadpan of his. "I mean did anyone ask for a pass out?" Matt said, his face white and tight.

"No one went out since the main bout started," Louis said, looking bored. Matt started for the stairs. Louis called after him, "Did you want to come back in again?" Matt did not hear Louis' voice at all.

* * *

When the house lights dimmed for the wind-up round between the Czech and the Texan, Eddy got up quietly and slipped through the crowd round the doors and padded down the stairs. He moved quickly, and silently. His face wore a fixed, smouldering look. When he reached the street he glanced both ways then broke into a jog-trot. He lowered his head against the rain and as he ran he muttered angrily, "Sonovabitch, he tried to gyp me outa my money an' my pair of shoes but he's not goin' to get away with it." He muttered as he ran. He put his arm up and tried to push the rain away.

On the corner he hesitated, then doubled back into the alley that cut through to Cleat Street. He followed the trail like an angry hound. A young cop was walking slowly by the other end. He sighted Eddy's weaving figure. Eddy remembered the doorway and dodged aside. He stood with his body pressed back. He heard the cop's slow feet pause, turn, then come on, slapping heavily through the puddles. He spoke to Eddy. Eddy did not move, he stood there pressed back against the door. The cop did not know where Eddy was, he only knew a man was somewhere not far off.

He came right to where Eddy was standing. Suddenly Eddy's eyes grew mad. He reached out and took a smack at the pale moving smear that was a face. His fist connected with a sharp thud. The cop's hand flashed for his billy and Eddy smacked at him again. He felt the hard cutting edge of the man's teeth and the feel of the teeth made him wild. He sailed in blindly and the cop raised his billy and brought it down over Eddy's right eye, opening up the old place.

Eddy cowered back. The light blow cleared his head and his guts turned to water. The millions of little angry sparks that danced in his mind went out, leaving it terrified and dazed. He put his arms up to defend himself, and as he did so there came the heavy pounding of feet as Matt plunged into the alley. He saw the picture dimly, the cop with his billy raised and Eddy's arm up defending himself. The old rage-blindness rose, choking him. He charged at the cop from behind, bringing him to his knees with a terrific rabbit punch. Eddy stood there, hands coming slowly down, one side of his face dark with blood.

"Oh, Christ!" Matt choked. As the cop tried to rise he smashed at his face. The man's hands came up, trying to shield his face and Matt kicked them aside, driving straight at the head. Elbows bent, body working, he drove again and again. Even when the man's body slumped over limply he still drove at it.

Eddy seized his arm. "Don't do it, Matt! You'll kill him! You don't want to do that!"

Matt thrust him off. "What do you know? All my life I've been waitin' for a chance like this!" His feet smashed at the head and ribs of the fallen man.

Eddy clung to him sobbing, "Don't do it, Matt! They're goin' to kill you, they're goin' to kill you for this!"

The look on Matt's face was rigid and blind. Sweat poured off him, his breath came in thick, angry sobs. His feet worked, he panted hoarsely, "I couldn't take it! I couldn't take it!" The man's face and head were smashed bloody and shapeless. They were not a face and head any more. Eddy rocked up and down distraught, then he turned and began to run. He saw a policeman standing on the corner. He waved at him frantically, shouting, "You gotta come here quick! In there!" He pointed down the mouth of the alley. "You gotta make Matt lay off, or they'll get him and kill him for this!"

The cop blew his whistle, then he ran on ahead. A cruising prowler car happening down Cleat Streat slowed and pulled into the curb. From nowhere a crowd came running. They massed about the mouth of the alley, foaming hungrily round the squad car. They tried to find out from those in front what was going on.

Eddy watched the two men climb from the car, then a look of horror froze his bloody face. He pushed through and caught one of them by the arm. "What are you goin' to do?" The man shook him off and headed quickly into the crowd. Eddy stared at the place where he had gone. His lips moved stiffly and from out their agonized working a little hoarse sound came. "I didn't mean they should get you, Matt, I meant they should keep you from getting yourself killed." He tried to break through the people and they swept him aside. He ran up and down on the fringe of the crowd and the wail of a second squad car sounded coming round the corner.

Eddy wrung his hands. Then he threw his whole weight into the pressing bodies ahead. A man turned and cursed him. He cried, "What d'you think you're tryin' to do?"

Eddy shouted wildly, "I'm tryin' to get through to Matt!"

A woman looked round then she gave a little scream. "He's crazy!"

Eddy glared at her. "I'm not crazy."

A second woman pointed, "He is crazy! Look at his face!"

"Sure he's crazy. Look at his eyes!"

"He's part of it. He's part of the riot in there. Look at his cut face!"

"The jobless are staging a big riot!"

"Sure, they're staging a riot. I always knew it would come to it!"

"RIOT! RIOT!"

The chorus rose and swelled. Eddy glared round helplessly. He saw the old crowd lust, the mass of swimming eyes. Suddenly he turned and ran. He ran on down Cleat. He bunted into a man coming the other way and the man tried to grab him but he tore loose from the man's hand. Behind him in his mind he felt the feet of the mob and he shouted for Matt to save him. "Jus' save me this once, Matt! Jus' this once more!" He ran down onto Pastoral, hesitated, then headed blindly for the yards. There was the howl of an oncoming train, the glare of a great single eye of light, the low grumbling on the tracks. He plunged on over the ties and shouted at the train. "Stop!" Eddy shouted. He stood there waving his arms and the rain beat on his face and the wind swept his voice away. The light came on, growing on the steel, throwing a blinding glare along the right-of-way.

Suddenly he stepped out onto the tracks. His voice broke to an angry sob.

"Stop! You gotta stop! I gotta get away from here!" The sound was caught up by the grinding steel, the black, doll-like arms were thrown full in the sweeping glare. Suddenly his voice stopped. His weaving arms were jerked flat like semaphore blades.

The crashing of steam came on and on.

Explanatory Notes

These explanatory notes clarify and contextualize many of the various historical references and obscure or problematic terms that appear in *Waste Heritage*.
These notes also attempt to identify the British Columbian place names that
Baird has altered and disguised. The remapping of the geography of the novel
has entailed a significant amount of research involving rigorous close reading
and cross-referencing of significant textual passages, archival research in several west coast collections, consultation of historical maps and documents,
comparison of the geography and chronology of Waste Heritage to newspaper
articles of 1938, and hours spent walking and driving the streets of Vancouver,
Victoria, and Nanaimo. It is, of course, not possible (or desirable) to fix all of
the places in this novel in a "real" geography with absolute certainty. Some
places cannot be identified due to a lack of sufficient textual detail or support-
ing documentation. Others places appear to be entirely fictional. These
explanatory notes include all places that can be identified with reasonable
confidence. The rest are omitted.

CHAPTER ONE

3.17 *Trans-Canada*—The Trans-Canada Limited was a luxury passenger train
service that ran between Vancouver and Montreal on the Canadian Pacific
Railway beginning in 1907. The service was cancelled for economic reasons in 1931. In 1938, when Matt arrives by rail in Aschelon, other trains
that followed the same route but lacked the amenities of the original service were commonly referred to as "Trans-Canada" trains.

3.18 *Capper Street*—Cambie Street, Vancouver.

3.20 *Aschelon*—Also spelled "Askelon" and "Ashkelon." Several critics and
reviewers locate the source of Baird's allusive renaming of British
Columbia's two largest cities Vancouver (Aschelon) and Victoria (Gath) in
2 Samuel 1:20: "Tell it not in Gath, publish it not in the streets of Askelon;
lest the daughters of the Philistines rejoice, lest the daughters of the uncir-

cumcised triumph." Aschelon and Gath are Philistine cities that were occupied by the Israelites when they entered the Promised Land. Baird's allusive renaming is ironic: the sit-downers never triumph in their occupations of Vancouver and Victoria and their "promised land" remains elusive and unattainable.

4.25 *East Third*—East Pender Street, Vancouver.

8.13 *Alcazar*—Hastings Street, Vancouver.

8.16 *Snider*—Main Street, Vancouver.

10.36 *Mack Sennett*—Mack Sennett (1880–1960) was a Quebec-born comedian, singer, dancer, actor, clown, director, set designer, and founder of Keystone studios. Sennett is best known for his slapstick, physical, bawdy comedies, which were most popular in the late 1910s and early 1920s. After producing more than a thousand films, Sennett declared bankruptcy in 1933 and retired shortly after. He is well-remembered in film history for creating the bumbling Keystone Cops and for giving Charlie Chaplin his first job in Hollywood.

11.3 *Clever back in '35*—Regina, Saskatchewan. A reference to the historic "On to Ottawa Trek" of 1935. After failing to secure union wages, a group of unemployed single men abandoned British Columbia's work camps and made their way to Vancouver. On 3 June 1935, they left by train for Ottawa where they hoped to bring their case before the federal government. Stops and rallies that generated public support were held in various towns and cities in western Canada: Kamloops, Golden, Calgary, Medicine Hat, Swift Current, and Moose Jaw. On 14 June, the trekkers arrived in Regina. The Conservative government of R.B. Bennett, in an attempt to halt the advance of the protestors, ordered the Canadian Pacific Railway to consider the trekkers trespassers, and concentrated RCMP officers in Regina to disperse them. The group sent several representatives to Ottawa to meet the government, but negotiations broke down. On 1 July Bennett ordered police to disperse a crowd gathered in support of the trekkers. In the riot that ensued, hundreds of people were injured, one person was killed, and downtown Regina sustained heavy damage. The trekkers were disbanded, and Bennett lost the next election.

13.4 *Fourth*—Keefer Street, Vancouver.

CHAPTER TWO

14.11 *mufti*—Plain clothes worn by a person who is entitled to wear a uniform.

14.16 *Luther Hall*—Ukrainian Hall, 805 East Pender Street at Hawks Street in Vancouver.

14.25 *Sweet Caps*—Sweet Caporal cigarettes. A popular brand of the Depression era.

19.33 *Luther*—Hawks Street, Vancouver.

CHAPTER THREE

20.9 *Golden Heart Mission, Undenominational*—Ukrainian Hall (Luther Hall) is around the corner from the Sacred Heart Parish at Campbell and Keefer.

20.11 *Jap*—Derogatory term for a Japanese person.

20.13 *rookeries*—A rookery is a crowded and/or dilapidated tenement.

24.29 *vag. charge*—Vagrancy charge; often used by police to target the unemployed and homeless during the 1930s.

26.7 *January 10th, 1930*—Julius Caesar crossed the Rubicon on 10 January 49 BCE. Roman law forbade any army crossing the river. When Caesar broke this law, armed conflict became inevitable.

27.14 *Woolworth's*—Frank and Charles Woolworth founded this chain of five-and-ten cent stores in 1911. These stores, located in the centre of many North American cities in the 1930s, sold discounted merchandise at lower prices than most local merchants. Woolworth's was also the first chain to put merchandise on display for customers to handle.

CHAPTER FOUR

35.34 *Greta Garbo*—Greta Garbo 1905–1990) was a Swedish-born Hollywood actress. *Conquest*, released 4 November 1937, in which Garbo played Napoleon's mistress, would have been her most recent film at the time Matt was in Aschelon.

36.26 *Aschelon Trust*—The Royal Bank of Canada at 400–404 West Hastings on the southwest corner of West Hastings and Homer Streets (Alcazar and Troy). The Royal Bank Building was known as one of the first of the "temple banks" to be built in downtown Vancouver and, therefore, coincides with Baird's description of the bank's "chased copper doors." Further down West Hastings (Alcazar) and visible from Hastings and Homer is the former Stock Exchange building (the present-day Simon Fraser University downtown campus) along with numerous other financial buildings (built in the style of the Bank of Canada building) that Matt Striker describes seeing as he stands on the corner of Alcazar and Troy.

36.33 *Gath*—Victoria, BC. See above note on Aschelon, Chapter One.

37.9 *the ball grounds*—Oppenheimer Park in Vancouver (delimited by Powell, Dunlevy, East Cordova, and Jackson) was home to numerous protests held throughout the 1930s and where the pivotal rally was held following the events of 19 June 1938.

37.12 *Troy*—Homer Street, Vancouver.

38.31 *"Hold the Fort For We Are Coming!"*—The labour song of the On-to-Ottawa trekkers of 1935:

HOLD THE FORT

Chorus:
Hold the fort, for we are coming
Union men be strong!
Side by side we battle onward,
Victory will come.

We meet today in Freedom's cause
And raise our voices high;
We'll join our hands in union strong
To battle or to die.

Look, my comrades, see the union
Banners flying high;
Reinforcements now appearing
Victory is nigh.

See our numbers still increasing
Hear the bugles blow;
By our union we shall triumph
Over every foe.

Fierce and long the battle rages
But we will not fear,
Help will come whene'er it's needed,
Cheer, my comrades, cheer.

44.15 *half-way round the park there was a bridge linking up the two sides of town. Harry pulled up so Matt could look back down the bay*—Stanley Park, Vancouver.

44.17 *Arabian Nights*—A collection of magical and romantic Arabic tales from the tenth century A.D.

46.10 *kike*—A derogatory term for a Jewish person.

46.25 *Neon clock in the Brand block*—The clock on the top of the Vancouver Block, built in 1910, and located at 736 Granville Street.

CHAPTER FIVE

48.23 *Lincoln's Basement*—Woodward's Department Store, Vancouver.

51.19 *Shroeder*—Granville Street, Vancouver.

54.23 *pigeon*—A person who is easily tricked or misled. A stool pigeon is a police informer.

CHAPTER SIX

62.21 *split Romeos*—A sleek men's shoe resembling a slipper that was first popular in the 1930s.

63.12 *Haywards*—Spencer's Department Store, Vancouver.

65.17 *Vickers*—Cordova Street, Vancouver.

65.18 *Pier F*—The CPR dock at the foot of Granville and Hastings.

65.28 *Crime-Thrills*—Possibly *Thrilling Detective Magazine*, which ran from 1931 to 1953 and published stories similar in tone to those described in the novel.

68.14 *little Eliza an' the bloodhounds*—In *Uncle Tom's Cabin* (1852) by Harriet Beecher Stowe, Eliza, an escaped slave, makes her way across the frozen Ohio River while pursued by dogs.

CHAPTER SEVEN

71.18 *Palace on Shroeder*—The Capitol Theatre, located at 820 Granville Street in Vancouver, opened in 1921 and became one of the main theatres devoted to cinema along the popular line of Granville theatres.

71.19 *the new Bette Davis*—Bette Davis (1908–1989) was an American-born Hollywood actress. *Jezebel*, released 10 March 1938, in which Davis played an antebellum New Orleans belle, a role for which she won an academy award, would have been her most recent film at the time of the Vancouver sit-down strike.

75.5 *Grecian as the Parthenon*—Completed c. 435 BCE, the Parthenon, a temple to the goddess Athena, sits atop the Acropolis of Athens.

77.33 *Swing Bar*—The Yale Hotel at 1300 Granville Street, Vancouver.

78.7 *stacombed*—Stacomb was a men's hair application, popular in the 1930s, designed to make hair "stay combed."

81.13 *Cutlake*—Nanaimo, BC. Baird writes that the men obtained transportation from Cutlake south to McBain by '28 Erskines and a Buick. The *Victoria Daily Times* reports that the men obtained 24 automobiles and one truck for transportation to Victoria, 76 miles south, "with meetings at Ladysmith and Duncan on the way" (22 June 1938).

81.16 *McBain*—Ladysmith, BC (see note on Cutlake, above).

81.16 *Andersville*—Duncan, BC (see note on Cutlake, above). The third contingent from Vancouver reached Nanaimo on 23 June 1938 and spent the night in the United Mine Workers of America Hall. The next morning "they marched to the railway depot and climbed aboard the [Esquimalt and Nanaimo] freight train to Duncan (*Victoria Daily Times*, 24 June 1938). The men arrived in Duncan on 25 June, shortly after 2:00 p.m. The front page of the *Victoria Daily Times* contains a photograph of the men jumping from the empty cars in the freight yard of the E&N Station in Duncan on 25 June 1938. Baird's novel describes the route of the third contingent accurately, although her enumeration of the different divisions varies because she eliminates the first contingent that sailed to Victoria directly: "Two divisions were expected in [Cutlake] the next day to take off later by freight car for Andersville direct where the first division was to wait for them." Baird describes how the men used the Agricultural Hall in Andersville as temporary headquarters. The front-page of the *Victoria Daily Times* contains a photograph of the third contingent of men marching from the E&N station to the Agricultural Hall. The caption reads, "Two hundred men at Ladysmith are on their way to join another 200 at Duncan to proceed to Victoria Monday" (*Victoria Daily Times*, 25 June 1938).

CHAPTER NINE

93.1 *Princess Maud*—SS Princess Elizabeth.

97.35 *You think all you have to do when you get to Gath is march around the city seven times an' the walls in goin' to fall down Boom!* An allusion to Joshua 6:1–27.

100.17 *arbutus*—An evergreen tree with reddish-brown bark.

CHAPTER TEN

102.18 *Robert Taylor picture*—Robert Taylor (1911–1969) was an American-born film actor. His most recent film at the time the novel takes place was *Three Comrades*, released on 2 June 1938. In this film Taylor plays a German veteran of World War I who faces a bleak future in a devastated Germany but finds hope through romance and involvement in left-wing politics. *Three Comrades* was the only film for which F. Scott Fitzgerald received a screen-writing credit.

106.11 *Mussolini*—Benito Mussolini (1883–1945) was fascist dictator of Italy from 1922–1943.

CHAPTER ELEVEN

110.1 *coloured Sons of the Desert*—*Sons of the Desert* is a comic 1933 Laurel and Hardy film in which the actors deceive their wives in order to attend a meeting of their fraternal organization, "The Order of the Sons of the Desert."

111.2 *Dionne quintuplets*—The five Dionne sisters, born in 1934, were taken from their parents by the Ontario government and made wards of the state. They spent the first decade of their lives in a hospital in Callander, Ontario at the centre of a tourist attraction called "Quintland."

111.26 *Belsize*—Skinner Street, Nanaimo.

111.27 *Frank Street*—Commercial Street, Nanaimo.

112.35 *Bryant*—Wharf Street, Nanaimo.

115.6 *chink*—A derogatory term for a Chinese person.

CHAPTER TWELVE

121.18 *Quarter Street*—Bastion Street, Nanaimo.

123.11 *Erskine*—An automobile manufactured by Studebaker from 1927 to 1930.

125.1 *the Sleeve valley*—Possibly the Comox Valley, which is 108 km north of Nanaimo. Baird situates the Sleeve Valley somewhere north of Nanaimo and describes the valley as a place where people earn a living picking berries.

129.24 *Dillinger*—John Dillinger (1903–1934) was a notorious American gangster and bank robber.

CHAPTER FOURTEEN

149.32 *Siwash*—A derogatory term for a Native Canadian person.

CHAPTER FIFTEEN

161.21 *Flower Street*—Store Street, Victoria.

161.21 *Pastoral Avenue*—Johnson Street, Victoria.

161.23 *Lavender*—Yates Street, Victoria.

161.24 *Angel Arms*—The Empire Hotel, 507 Johnson Street, Victoria.

161.33 *Diamond Jim Brady*—James Buchanan Brady (1856–1917) was an American financier and philanthropist of the Gilded Age. His enormous appetite and fondness for jewellery were legendary.

162.3 *Orsino Hotel*—The Occidental Hotel, 1403 Store Street, Victoria.

162.4 *Quanta House*—St. Francis Hotel, 564 Yates Street, Victoria.

CHAPTER SIXTEEN

173.30 *Liberty*—A general-interest, popular American magazine that ran from 1924–1950. It published both work by serious literary authors and celebrity gossip.

176.4 *Mary Pickford*—Mary Pickford (1892–1979) was a Toronto-born film star, producer, and co-founder—with Douglas Fairbanks, D.W. Griffith, and Charlie Chaplin—of United Artists. She was known as "America's Sweetheart" and was the first woman to earn more than $1,000,000 per year in Hollywood. She won an Academy Award in 1929, and retired from acting in the early 1930s. She played in more than forty feature-length, silent films, and was the most important Hollywood actress of her era.

CHAPTER NINETEEN

217.12 *Gath Settler*—*Victoria Colonist*.

218.10 *Saturday Evening Post*—An American, weekly news journal that began publication in 1821, and was widely read in the 1930s.

221.6 *Conklin*—Bastion Street, Victoria.

221.6 *Shard*—Langley Street, Victoria.

228.19 *clock was the Neon-faced one where Conklin turns into Dudley outside the cigar store*—1121 Wharf Street, Victoria.

CHAPTER TWENTY-ONE

243.24 *Lennox Park*—Beacon Hill Park, Victoria.

244.15 *Plutarch's Lives*—The best-known work of Greek historian Plutarch (46–119 CE) is *Parallel Lives*, a series of paired biographies of famous Greek and Roman men.

244.20 *Lotus Island*—James Island.

250.17 *Cleat*—Courtney Street, Victoria.

251.3 *Dudley*—Wharf Street, Victoria.

CHAPTER TWENTY-TWO

261.10 *Douk*—A derogatory term for a Doukhobor person. The Doukhobor are a Christian sect of Russian origin. Many immigrated to Canada in 1899 to escape persecution for their refusal to join the military.

266.9 *Klahowyah Gymnasium and Athletic Club*—The Army and Navy Veteran's Club, Victoria.

Textual Notes

The uncensored 1939 Random House (RH) edition of *Waste Heritage* serves as copy text for this edition. The textual notes that follow comprise alternate versions of several passages that Baird rewrote for the 1939 Macmillan (Mac) edition (see critical introduction for the story behind these changes), and emendations made to the copy text in the current edition. Each entry records the reading of the present text before the square bracket (]) and the reading of the Random House and Macmillan editions after the square bracket. The page and line numbers appearing at the beginning of each entry are keyed to the current edition. To distinguish emendations made to the RH edition from Mac variants, the former are indicated with the notation, *ed.* in the notes that follow. These emendations are of several types.

Spelling, punctuation, and obvious typographical errors have been corrected and noted. Baird's inconsistent spellings have been standardized and made to conform to the *Canadian Oxford Dictionary*, Second Edition; in cases where the *Canadian Oxford Dictionary* does not provide an entry for a word, the *Oxford English Dictionary* has provided the standard. The list below indicates only the first instance of a spelling correction and its variations. For example, the first instance of "discolored" has been emended to "discoloured" and this change has been noted; subsequent occurrences of "discolored," "colored," "coloring," etc. have been silently emended. No attempt has been made to correct or standardize Baird's sometimes inconsistent idioms and colloquialisms such as "sonovabitch" and "sonofabitch." In certain instances, such inconsistencies attempt to reproduce differing accents and inflections and are likely intentional.

In a few cases where sentences in the copy text are very unclear and/or grammatically incorrect, a word has been inserted or deleted; all insertions and deletions have been listed among the emendations below.

Minor spacing problems in the Random House copy text have been silently emended.

In the short period between the publication of the Random House and Macmillan editions in 1939, a small number of the accidentals noted here were corrected. This list indicates changes made in the current edition to the Random House edition and variant readings in the Macmillan edition.

3.26 grey] *ed.*; gray RH, Mac

5.22 an] *ed.*; an' RH

6.10 He scratched his stump and his face grew serious ... "Pretty bitter, ain't you?"] Alternate reading appears in the Macmillan edition:

He scratched his stump and his face grew serious. "Seems like the country's waitin' to get a real scrap on its hands so all you guys can be heroes overnight."

"Yeah? An' where do we wake up the next mornin'? I ask guys that an' they just look at me. Maybe I didn't ask the right guys."

"Pretty bitter, ain't you?"

6.22 discoloured] *ed.*; discolored RH, Mac

7.15 dryly] *ed.*; drily RH, Mac

12.33 "Sure, Eddy, why not? Come on! let's get goin'.] *ed.*; "Sure, Eddy, why not?" "Come on! let's get goin'. RH, Mac

13.30 Eddy frowned] *ed.*; Eddy, frowned RH, Mac

13.30 labouring] *ed.*; laboring RH, Mac

15.1 We got no matches.] *ed.*; We got no matches, RH, Mac

16.27 knew] *ed.*; new RH

17.33 behind] *ed.*; hehind RH, Mac

19.21 hairline] *ed.*; hair-line RH, Mac

20.28 vomiting] *ed.*; vomitting RH, Mac

21.23 fidgeting] *ed.*; fidgetting RH, Mac

22.28 odour] *ed.*; odor RH, Mac

23.8 organization] *ed.*; organisation RH, Mac

23.19 he gave it to me] *ed.*; he gave it me RH, Mac

26.14 dishwashing] *ed.*; dish-washing RH, Mac

32.20 apologize] *ed.*; apologise RH, Mac

34.17 motorcycles] *ed.*; motor cycles RH, Mac

35.31 haring] *ed.*; hareing RH, Mac

39.4 jail] *ed.*; gaol RH, Mac

41.36 Chevy] *ed.*; Chevvy RH, Mac

44.6 "No, I never heard that one," Matt said. Harry went ahead and told it.] *ed.*; "No, I never heard that one," Matt said, Harry went ahead and told it." RH, Mac

45.7 travelogues] *ed.*; travellogs RH, Mac

45.10 neighbourhood] *ed.*; neighborhood RH, Mac

46.8 favour] *ed.*; favor RH, Mac

46.27 realize] *ed.*; realise RH, Mac

47.2 He took us for a drive] *ed.*; He took us a drive RH, Mac

49.6 regulations] *ed.*; regulatioons RH, Mac

50.4 downtown] *ed.*; down-town RH, Mac

52.33 aging] *ed.*; ageing RH, Mac

53.9 cops'] *ed.*; cop's RH, Mac

54.12 Hep's] *ed.*; He's RH

56.35 someplace] *ed.*; someplace RH, Mac

59.24 Lincoln's] *ed.*; Lincolns RH, Mac

60.13 rumours] *ed.*; rumors RH, Mac

61.18 favourites] *ed.*; favorites RH, Mac

67.5 temporize] *ed.*; temporise RH, Mac

67.12 sweatshirt] *ed.*; sweat shirt RH, Mac

72.8 swimsuits] *ed.*; swim suits RH, Mac

72.20 bra] *ed.*; bra. RH, Mac

79.7 cheque] *ed.*; check RH, Mac

79.17 paycheque] *ed.*; pay check RH, Mac

81.9 night.] *ed.*; night? RH, Mac

83.21 India rubber] *ed.*; india rubber RH, Mac

87.27 off!'] *ed.*; off'! RH, Mac

96.18 an'] *ed.*; an RH, Mac

99.10 sympathizers] sympathisers *ed.*; RH, Mac

103.31 peaceably] *ed.*; peacably RH, Mac

104.11 dialogue] *ed.*; dialog RH, Mac

105.27 props] *ed.*; props. RH, Mac

106.3 riveted] *ed.*; rivetted RH, Mac

107.9 "Would we!"] *ed.*; Would we!" RH, Mac

107.20 Manning's] *ed.*; Mannings RH, Mac

111.28 blond] *ed.*; blonde RH, Mac

117.6 'What's so special?' ..."] *ed.*; "What's so special?' ..." RH, Mac

119.4 picketing] *ed.*; picketting RH, Mac

121.16 effective] *ed.*; effective, RH, Mac

122.33 pocketed] *ed.*; pocketted RH, Mac

124.1 a solidly-built] *ed.*; solidly-built RH, Mac

125.16 now.] *ed.*; now? RH, Mac

131.25 You know what I mean, Hep] *ed.*; You know what I mean. Hep RH, Mac

132.26 parlour] *ed.*; parlor RH, *Mac*

136.4 spittled] *ed.*; spitalled RH, *Mac*

137.12 What is it then? ... Old Man Morgan ...] Alternate reading appears in the Macmillan edition:

> What is it then? Mickey Mouse in person? Fine lotta sissies! Scared of a bunch of kids!" Old Man Morgan repeated and once more he spat contempt down onto the right-of-way.

143.18 cartilage] *ed.*; cartilege RH, *Mac*

144.4 "You] 'You RH, *Mac*

144.23 behaviour] *ed.*; behavior RH, *Mac*

148.4 street.] *ed.*; street? RH, *Mac*

148.27 "Betcha] *ed.*; 'Betcha RH, *Mac*

150.12 "the candy-giver"] *ed.*; "The candy-giver" RH, *Mac*

153.15 "You've got to keep"] *ed.*; "You've go to keep" RH, *Mac*

160.20 "formed along the tracks"] *ed.*; "foamed along the tracks" RH, *Mac*

161.35 whorehouse] *ed.*; whore house RH, *Mac*

163.11 billeted] *ed.*; billetted RH, *Mac*

167.35 "Hey, snap out of it."] *ed.*; "Hey, snap out of it?" RH, *Mac*

169.16 "Pills,"] *ed.*; "Pills." RH, *Mac*

172.25 honours] *ed.*; honors RH, *Mac*

174.6 "It's nothing," he said] *ed.*; "It's nothing." he said RH, *Mac*

177.10 I Can't Give You Anything But Love, Baby] *ed.*; I Can't give You Anything But Love, Baby RH, *Mac*

178.19 harbour] *ed.*; harbor RH, *Mac*

188.10 Libertys] *ed.*; Liberty's RH, *Mac*

219.17 I don't belong in the country .... "Look, I sound kind of bitter ..."] Alternate reading appears in the Macmillan edition:

> I don't belong in the country unless there is some kind of a big bust-up overseas in which case I guess the authorities will quit wondering what province we belong in just so long as we can do the work. The way some guys is talking that don't sound far off.
>   "Look, I sound kind of bitter ...

219.33 spieling] *ed.*; speeling RH, *Mac*

226.6 dramatizing] *ed.*; dramatising RH, *Mac*

260.12 all over the country] *ed.*; all over the the country RH, *Mac*

260.28 Maybe] *ed.*; Maye RH, *Mac*

260.35 I have a reason] *ed.*; I have a reason. RH, *Mac*

261.4 "Matt.] *ed.*; Matt. RH, *Mac*

261.24–25 I'm not goin' to either] *ed.*; I'm not goin, to either RH, *Mac*

263.1–2 private meetings called to talk and talk some more] *ed.*; private
   meetings called to talk and and talk some more RH, *Mac*

266.32 Hi, Slappy,] *ed.*; Hi, Slappy. RH, *Mac*

267.6 Charlie's] *ed.*; Charlies RH, *Mac*

269.22 "I noticed it, though, "Eddy said,] *ed.*; "I noticed it though," Eddy said,
   RH, *Mac*

CANADIAN LITERATURE COLLECTION/
LA COLLECTION DE LA LITTÉRATURE CANADIENNE

The Canadian Literature Collection/La collection de la littérature canadienne (CLC) is a series of nineteenth- to mid-twentieth-century literary texts produced in new critical editions. All texts selected for the series were either out of print or previously unpublished. Each text appears in a print edition with a basic apparatus (critical introduction, explan-atory notes, textual notes, and statement of editorial principles) together with an expanded web-based apparatus (which may include alternate versions, previous editions, correspondence, photographs, source materials, and other related texts by the author). Originally planned by Ruth Bradley-St-Cyr in 2004, the CLC has grown to include Dean Irvine of Dalhousie University as collection director and English-language general editor, Colin Hill of the University of Toronto, Glenn Willmott of Queen's University, and Misao Dean of the University of Victoria as advisory editors, and Gregory Betts of Brock University as web editor.

PRINTED AND BOUND IN OCTOBER 2007 BY
TRI-GRAPHIC PRINTING LTD., OTTAWA, ONTARIO
FOR THE UNIVERSITY OF OTTAWA PRESS

EDITED AND PROOFREAD BY RUTH BRADLEY-ST-CYR
COVER AND TEXT DESIGNED BY ROBERT TOMBS
TYPESET IN 9.5/13 FF QUADRAAT
PRINTED ON WILLIAMSBURG
60 LB OFFSET SMOOTH